WHO WOULD YOU SACRIFICE
TO SAVE WHAT YOU LOVE?

ARACHNISS

SHAWN C BUTLER

Arachniss

A TERRIBLY DELICIOUS NOVEL

By Shawn C. Butler

To anyone who feels trapped,
and everyone breaking free...

You are not alone

Petit Fours

"A spider lives inside my head
Who weaves a strange and wondrous web
Of silken threads and silver strings
To catch all sorts of flying things,
Like crumbs of thoughts and bits of smiles
And specks of dried-up tears,
And dust of dreams that catch and cling
For years and years and years..."

- Shel Silverstein -

Captain Peg Pinky

SOMETHING WAS EATING DAVID'S SON.

It was early spring in Boulder, that season when god decides the weather by a roll of the dice—sun or rain, hot or cold, maybe snow, probably sleet, and then another roll. Outside the nursery window, leaf-laden trees fluttered in a cool morning breeze as David Chambers leaned over his son's crib to inhale that smell that only babies provide: the scent of new life, hope and contentment. Jason was eight months old and grabbing at the air with pudgy hands and feet, smiling every time he realized they were *his* hands and *his* feet. He was trying to trap spidery shadows cast by the octopus mobile dangling just out of reach. He had a bright, happy smile, he slept through most nights, and he was missing the tip of his right pinky.

David reached for his son, heart racing, and then froze.

Wait.

Nothing was eating Jason. His son was born without his right pinky fingertip, just like so many other children during the pandemic. Some missed toes or earlobes, eyes or arms, and of course many were missing things they couldn't live without. Over nearly two decades of failed vaccines and quarantines, riots and social media doom-casting, hopeful parents lived in fear of birthing screaming, limbless babies or their gray-skinned remnants. There were millions of stillborn children—shrunken things held by stunned fathers and broken mothers left with nothing but questions no one could answer.

The pandemic never ended; everyone just got used to it. At first, people marked their losses with before-and-after pictures of lost lips and fingertips, noses and toes. Friends offered sympathy and outrage or thoughts and prayers until falling silent and dropping away. Now if you woke up without an eye, you just popped in a prosthetic from the drugstore, winked ironically and told yourself it could have been worse. You were still alive. You could handle this. A platitude a day kept the nightmares away. And there were amazing new prosthetics: sleek, robotic and AI-powered wonders that made losing a limb practically beneficial, or so people told themselves as they hung up their arms before bed and dreamed of phantom limbs.

They called it *the vanishing* or *erasure* and a hundred other things, but the formal name for the disease caused by a still-unidentified virus was SHAS—selective human autosarcophagic syndrome—which was a misnomer or at least misleading; the first victims were dogs and cats, billions of them, leaving the world a sadder, quieter place long before the first human woke up with the first missing limb.

Billions of body parts and millions of lives were lost long before David lost a kidney in college, almost unnoticed, like it had gone out for a drink one night and forgotten the way back. His wife, Alicia, had misplaced a few feet of intestine that allowed her to eat anything without gaining weight, though she couldn't have told you when. Theirs were invisible wounds, meaningless things they were reluctant to mention for shame at how much more others had lost. There was a term for that, too—*untouched*—but you weren't supposed to say it out loud.

Jason had been touched but was still perfect. He was born laughing and was always healthy and happy, so what did it matter if he was missing a little fingertip?

Except.

David squeezed his eyes shut, opened them, and tried to shake the feeling that something was wrong. His stomach turned sour. He just couldn't shake the memory. The day before, he'd come into the nursery and played pattycake with Jason and he could remember his son's tiny hands, hot and sticky, the delighted smile at each light contact, and all ten of his fat little fingers very much *there*. He was sure of it. SHAS took fingers and limbs, but it didn't make you forget what was lost.

"David?" Alicia sidled up next to him, hand on his arm, making goofy faces at Jason, who made goofy faces right back and then either farted or filled his diaper. "You okay?"

He looked at his son, at his wife, and back again. The nausea was gone. The memory was more déjà vu than real, just his imagination or the ghost of a dream. Why else had they given him his nickname? How could he think something was *eating* his child? He was just paranoid, afraid of what the virus had done to their first son, Alex, and that wasn't something he wanted to think about.

"Yeah, sweetie," he said. "I'm great."

Alicia sniffed. David grimaced. More than a fart.

"Rock-paper-scissors?" she asked, meaning, *Dear god, please no, I just showered.*

"No." He reached again for Captain Peg Pinky. "I got this one."

Stranger Danger

BACON SIZZLED AND SNAPPED in the pan, launching drops of blazing grease onto David's bare hand. Each time, he yanked his hand back and licked off the delicious bacon bomb, more concerned about getting the hot bit of flavor than burning his skin. He loved cooking meat, well, he loved cooking and Alicia loved bacon, so a few burns came with the territory. He could partially cover the pan. He could turn down the heat. But where was the fun in that? There was pleasure in the pain, or at least distraction.

Pop! Salt-cured pork belly browned and rippled. *Pop!* Burn. Lick.

He snapped off the gas and transferred wrinkled brown bacon strips to paper towels on the counter. The towels soaked up grease and he thought what he always thought, that this was once part of an animal, fat of the flesh, belly of the pig, hanging heavy between stumpy legs and a twirly tail, now trimmed and sliced and—

He flinched as something touched his arm.

"Yoink." Alicia snagged a piece and did the usual hand-to-hand hot-bacon dance—"Ouch-ouch-ouch!"—until sticking the end in her mouth. She sucked air over her tongue and looked at him with wide, goofy eyes. "Hot-hot-hot."

"Every time," he said, smiling as he remembered the first few years with her and how he loved her quirky openness and the derpy, dorky inner child she shared with no one else. It was rare to see that side of her anymore.

"Thooo good." She took another bite. Sucked air. Swallowed. "Eggs?"

"On the way." Scrambled with a little cheese. Served with freshly squeezed orange juice and two slices of unbuttered wholegrain toast. Sunday fun-day, but no champagne in the OJ because they were heading out right after breakfast.

At the kitchen table, Alicia made herself an egg-bacon sandwich as David poked at his eggs and watched Jason survey his empire. He had such strange focus for a kid, wide-eyed but unblinking, like a chubby emperor watching his minions from his highchair throne as milk dripped from the corner of his mouth. A fat little tongue followed, and David stuck out his tongue in return. Jason giggled and dribbled more.

"Who's a pirate baby?" David asked. Jason waved and slapped his plastic tray.

"Let's walk," Alicia said, meaning, *let's go burn off this bacon so I can have more bacon.*

*

DIAPER CHANGE, BODYSUIT AND SOCKS. Little shoes, pain-in-the-ass coat, puffy green hat with puffy green ears, running stroller with all-terrain tires, pacifier, binky, spare diapers, formula, baby wipes, adorable retro Elton John sunglasses and bacon rolls wrapped in paper towels. David pushed the stroller while Alicia nibbled. The sun blasted off the few remaining patches of ice under bushes and trees, melting so quickly it steamed. David checked to make sure Jason was warm. He glowed with hot red cheeks. Too warm. David pulled off the hat.

They walked past old split-level houses with attic windows, redwood fences, paneled doors in red and green, Subarus and BMWs on the street mixed with 4Runners and the inevitable Teslas parked by haphazard sidewalks. Several blocks later, they were at the Beach Park playground. It was padded in the modern liability-avoidance style, with little swings, a rubberized seesaw and tiny jungle-gym, all fenced off from the grass of the larger park as if danger lurked in the newborn sod. The twin four-year-old Balasubramanian girls wobbled on ambiguous rocking animals near the back and answered the age-old question of how much winter clothing can you fit on a child?

The answer was all of it. It was impossible to tell what they were missing, but David knew they'd lost matching sets of pinky and index fingers on both hands. Their mother, Padme, watched from a nearby bench with a bemused smile that seemed to say, *let's see you get into trouble now, bitches.* She waved a bare one-fingered hand backward, giving them the finger but also not—her usual joke.

Alicia waved and took off toward one of the other couples David didn't remember the names of despite having met them several times. The wife was undeniably attractive and the husband was a tall, square-jawed, scruffy-faced, big-pec, skinny-Jean, tight-ass motherfucker. He was holding his little girl's hand as she kicked at a belligerent patch of snow by a strangely unpadded rock. He nodded in David's direction and David nodded back. He intentionally never learned the man's name, and Alicia intentionally never told him, or so he pretended, but he was often there with his little girl, like a Cool Dad display model who escaped from the storefront and didn't know where else to go. Alicia touched his arm and her hands started moving in some wild pantomime; she probably couldn't speak if you tied her arms to her side. He hoped she got bacon grease all over his trim-fit Patagonia puffy.

David wheeled Jason over to a bench and sat down, waving his fingers for Jason's entertainment. Jason waved back and blew bubbles. Damn, he had a cute little kid.

"Damn, you have a cute little kid," a woman said. David looked up in surprise. It was whatever-her-name-was, Cool Dad's wife, little girl in tow, maybe five years old. Jason smiled hello. The girl smiled back.

"Hi. I'm sorry." He fought the urge to offer his hand, but no one shook hands anymore. It was amazing no one in the playground wore masks. It was years since the last mask mandates, but only because the government had lost control of the situation and no one obeyed anymore. The virus no one could identify was officially endemic, which apparently meant it would go away if they ignored it. "I'm David."

"Don't be sorry. I'm Franzia. We've met before."

"Franzia?" David said carefully. "Like the wine?"

"Like the *boxed* wine. It's a double-wide trailer-trash name with just a hint of inbreeding."

"Your mom liked to drink?" David asked, smiling.

"Mom *loved* to drink. And yes, that's how I was conceived," she said with a slur. He wasn't sure if she was teasing, it was the cold in the shade or she'd actually been drinking. "Want to know my middle name?"

"God, no."

"Wise man. So, David? That's original. You like slaying giants?"

"That's Jack. More of a goliath man myself."

"All sling, no beans?"

"Funny." Was she flirting? He didn't understand infidelity and would never cheat on Alicia but, still, it was nice to be noticed. "What's your daughter's name?"

"Tell the strange man your name, honey."

The little girl opened her mouth and yelled, "Go fuck yourself!"

David choked and then coughed himself into a sweat. Franzia and her foul-mouthed offspring watched him with identical little smiles. They had done this *many* times before. No one else seemed to notice.

"Stranger danger," he wheezed. "I get it. They won't see that coming."

"Honey, this is Mr. Chambers. He lives up the hill with the fancy people. Tell him your real name."

"Charlotte," she said, pouting. Her real name wasn't as fun as parentally approved cursing.

"Nice to meet you, Charlotte. And we're not fancy, just lucky on the timing. This is our son, Jason."

"He's adorable," Franzia said. "Going to have to watch that one. Just the little finger?"

David looked up, surprised again. It was a weirdly direct question. People weren't shy about what they'd lost in the pandemic, which was probably the only good thing about it—everyone lost body parts and found compassion in the process—but still, you didn't just blurt it out.

"Close." David nodded. "Just the pinky. And a little toe."

"Have you noticed?" she asked quietly, as if the trees were listening. "You and Alicia are like me and James?"

"Who?" .

"My husband," she said, smirking. "We're all the same."

He doubted that very much. "What do you mean?"

"We have all our parts. None of us are missing anything. What are the odds?"

"Huh," he said, feeling uncomfortable but not bothering to correct her. She meant nothing *visible*. He assumed Franzia and James were as externally untouched as he and Alicia. The odds against all of them living in the same neighborhood were astronomical. After twenty years of SHAS, people without obvious missing parts were almost freaks. Were they supposed to high five? He looked toward Padme to make sure she hadn't heard his thoughts, then glanced at Charlotte and instantly regretted it. She looked down and hid her hands behind her back.

"Don't be shy, honey," Franzia said. Charlotte frowned and showed her hands, missing all of both pinky fingers, the usual starting point for progressive SHAS. It moved from fingers to the arms, toes to the legs, outside then in, or randomly stopped until it started again. Nobody could count to ten in elementary school anymore. Jason was exceptionally lucky. He could count to 9.67.

David remembered his impression that something was eating Jason, and it came back in a dizzying gray that dimmed the sun. He'd seen Charlotte at the playground the week before. Had she been missing her pinkies then?

"You okay?" Franzia's hand was on his arm. His eyes were on her hand.

"Fine," he said. She dropped her hand, but he'd forgotten all about Charlotte's fingers.

"Well, Jason's lucky," Franzia said, "but my baby girl's one-hundred percent, aren't you wild thing?"

"A hundred-ten on a good day," she said, smiling brightly. "And every day's a good day."

"I like your act," David said. "How often do you practice?"

"What act?" they asked simultaneously, heads cocked to the side, confused. David smiled and nodded, appreciating the shtick. He loved it when families had their own thing. During the early years of the pandemic, people learned to love being stuck inside with their families or bad things happened. Bad things happened anyway, but they were worse if you lost your mind during the hundredth round of Monopoly.

"There's something under your eye," Franzia said.

"Hmm?" He wiped a finger across his right cheek and came away with a beige smear on the tip. *Oh, that.* "I was changing Jason and he kicked me," he said. "Not too good with the makeup, I guess."

"Strong little kid," Franzia said, impressed. "Soccer star in the making."

"Wanna see me pick my nose?" Charlotte asked, fighting back to the center of attention.

"Honey, no." Franzia reached for her daughter but it was too late; she'd already jammed the pinky stubs on both hands up against the base of her nose. It looked like she was burrowing for gold in her brain. David snorted.

Franzia shook her head. "I'd like to blame that on my husband, but…"

"It was your idea?"

"Boxed Wine Bitch all day long," she said, then winced. "You didn't hear that, honey."

*

FRANZIA AND CHARLOTTE WERE BACK with their perfect All-Occasion Husband when Alicia returned, looking for somewhere to wipe her hands. She finally settled on her jeans, but then she always settled on her jeans. If she ever walked in the woods, bears would eat her alive, starting with her pork-scented thighs. She came up and pecked him on the lips, and he tried to accept the PDA without flinching.

"How's Colorado Ken?" he asked.

"Oh, James? Did you see his biceps? He must do pullups in his sleep. But then he's a detective or something."

"James?" The name just wouldn't stick in his head. "He's a cop?"

"I guess." As if she didn't know. Alicia was a Denver city prosecutor. They probably saw each other downtown all the time. "You and Franzia were getting along."

"Well, she is named after a fine liqueur."

"Did they do the 'go fuck yourself' thing?"

He nodded. "I nearly swallowed my tongue."

"I was tasting Jason's formula and spit up on myself." She leaned over Jason's stroller. "We'll need to work on his game. He can't pull off the sweet little girl act, so we'll have to find a different angle. He'd make an adorable Dr. Evil with his missing pinky tip." When she straightened, her smile and eyes had narrowed. "Was she flirting?"

"You wish." But his heart jumped with instinctive guilt. "I've done nothing to justify your betrayal with Bubble Butt McChesty Flex, so keep it in your pants." Though he had to admit, he loved Franzia's no-bullshit personality.

"Then what were you talking about?"

"Her daughter's nose-mining skills."

Alicia looked confused.

"I'm sure she'll show you." He looked up, catching James in revealing profile. "Jesus, does he stuff his pants?"

"Why are you checking out his pants?"

"How am I supposed to answer that?"

"Well, you'll have plenty of time to stare. I invited them over for brisket next Sunday."

Now it was his turn to pause. Why didn't she ever ask? "I guess I better get out the smoker." He glanced at his wife, annoyed, then suddenly more attracted to her than he had been in months. Maybe it was the weather and the promise of spring renewal: that annual hope for better things. Or maybe it was the thought of smoking meat.

"What?" she asked.

"I'm just glad you have low standards."

"Me too. Can you imagine having to look at yourself in the mirror next to that? Nightmare. You can only suck in your stomach for so long."

"Now you tell me." He pushed his gut out. "Buddha Belly, activated."

"God, don't do that in public."

He sucked it back in. "Embarrassed?"

"Are you kidding? Turned on. Let's get out of here."

David turned to walk back. "Don't forget Jason."

"Who?"

*

THE DAY WAS GONE and David couldn't remember what happened to it. Sometimes he lost days like socks and neither ever came back. He lay in bed as Alicia slept and tried to reassemble hours that melted and flowed when he focused on them. In his memory, Jason's finger was a watery blur, sometimes there, sometimes not, and he knew he'd ruined his actual memories; he was seeing what he wanted to see or feared, factually useless, the kind of recovered recollections that drive eye-witnesses insane and police to drink.

What color was her hat? Blue, no, she wasn't wearing a hat, wait, no, it was a man with blue hair. No…

He shook his head and tried to guess what time it was. Alicia hated clocks and there was no way to tell time in the room without looking at his phone, which was in the living room, along with their clothes and two empty wine bottles. He couldn't remember the last time they'd had sex without a preceding argument, and it felt oddly incomplete without the catharsis of anger. Maybe that's why they had trouble finishing.

Captain Peg Pinky, he thought. It was a stupid nickname, sure, but they wouldn't call a baby with all his fingers peg-something. It made no sense. But he couldn't shake the feeling that something was wrong.

Charlotte's fingers were there, gone, there, gone, like mental whack-a-mole.

Damn it. It was time to talk to someone he trusted more than himself.

He got up quietly to shower, check on Jason and find his phone.

Pedro Sees All

"HMM," DAVID MUMBLED. "Not big enough."

He'd sketched *Pedro the Peripatetic Polar Bear* over sixty times over the last few days, and every time his last thought before starting a new page was, *the eyes aren't big enough.* Which was weird, because Pedro was more than ninety percent eyes, like an albino Chihuahua with a thyroid condition.

David scowled and glanced at the baby monitor, hoping for a distraction, but of course it was silent; Jason slept like the dead after his first feeding. Sometimes David thought he was part cat, or Alicia was drugging him, but whatever it was, he was a dream to take care of.

Rain fell in the backyard, lost in impenetrable fog through his window to the backyard. He could only tell it was raining by the soft white noise, like wind in the trees. His stomach grumbled. He thought about getting more coffee for his giant Best Dad Ever mug and looked at the monitor again. Sighed. Rain always reminded him of his father and long walks in the wet woods of the Rockies. Those were their favorite times in the outdoors, when other hikers hid in their tents or RVs and the forest was left to them and the animals.

He closed his eyes and tried to remember what his father looked like, but all he got was a smell: wet metal tools and damp wood with something like cinnamon. He opened his eyes and looked for the only picture he had of his birth family anywhere in the house. It was in a frame on one of his bookshelves between hundreds of science fiction and children's books, turned so he could barely see it from his desk. It showed him with Tommy, his late little brother, and their father in the woods on a log by a fire—bundled up in plaid and coats and warm boots in the middle of a cold day. He had no idea where it was taken or when, but he and Tommy looked healthy, so maybe when he was six and David was eight. Mom was also in the picture, but he'd folded it a few times and bent her back so a phantom hand rested on Dad's leg and the few fingers on David's shoulder looked like a disembodied hand peeking out of his jacket. It always reminded him of advice given to young people with new lovers: if they're in a family photo, make sure they're on the outside, so it's easy to cut them out when things go wrong.

Back to the sketch.

Nope, not quite big enough.

Another blank page appeared. He sharpened his pencil and bent to work, knowing the result would be useless. He just had to go with his giant-eye obsession until he worked through it, and then get back to making Pedro look like an actual bear. He wrote children's books, or tried to, great explosions of surreal colors and impossible places. They usually featured curious groups of animals looking for the source of perfect pearls or what made the sky so blinding-bright and bluey-blue. His editor called him Dr. Seuss, if Dr. Seuss was a naturalist tripping on acid, which he took as a compliment. He wrote under the pseudonym T.C. McSwizzle, where the T was for Tommy, C for Chambers, and the McSwizzle for whimsical anonymity that Alicia violated every chance she got—apparently afraid people would think he was *just* a stay-at-home dad.

He drew an eye the size of the page and colored it all black and no pupil. He supposed he couldn't blame her; the legal world was competitive, and having a successful partner couldn't hurt her image or chances at advancement.

"Hmm," he said again, and then he spent a few seconds wondering how many kids knew what *peripatetic* meant, then a few more on his daily self-criticism for wasting paper instead of going digital, after which he convinced himself a polar bear could be 100% eyeballs, and then the doorbell saved him.

"Olivia!" he called out, trying not to wake Jason. Olivia was their part-time nanny, a precocious ball of teenage energy from an English-Namibian family with an upper-crust British accent that made it hard not to think of her as royalty, but of course she was off on Mondays. He jumped up to reach the door before the bell rang again.

His hand hesitated on the knob. He glanced at his panda slippers. One of the pandas was missing an eyeball, giving it a deranged leer. Who just dropped by at eight in the morning?

He opened the door and it was Kathryn. Of course it was Kathryn. He'd called her Saturday night or Sunday morning and asked her to come by. He was losing his mind. Which he guessed was the point.

"Hey, freak," she said when he opened the door. Kathryn Thorn was his best friend, his longest-term friend, and for many of his younger years, his only friend. They'd come up through the foster-care system together after his parents died, claiming each other as siblings when they could get away with it, and stayed in touch ever since. Now she worked at the Division of Child Welfare, and had since grad school when her running career fizzled out. The *freak* thing was what everyone called the two of them, strange little kids with terrible stories and worse senses of humor, so they'd owned it.

"Hey, Carrots," he said, using one of the many nicknames based on her frothy tangle of red hair: an Irish tempest captured but not contained.

"You going to let me in?" She canted her head and raised her eyes toward the rain and fog

"Oh, sorry." They did the awkward are-we-going-to-hug thing and then hugged, because screw the pandemic or endemic or whatever it was, and then he brought her into the living room where she sat on the couch and he went to get coffee. A few minutes later, they were amped on excess caffeine and each waiting for the other to say something. He found himself doing the usual check; did she have all her parts? She was missing her left pinky and had been since college, but nothing new, at least on the outside. Thank god.

"So," Kathryn said finally. "How's Alicia?"

"Great."

"And Jason?"

Slight hesitation, then: "Amazing."

"And you?"

He knew what she meant. It wasn't a casual question. He hadn't done well in foster care—especially when separated from Karen—never found the right family, aged out of the system and lost his way for a few years. But she meant the dreams, the constant nightmares, asleep and waking, about Tommy and what he remembered about how he died.

"Okay," he said. He hadn't dreamed about Tommy in years, not since college. Maybe he'd drunk it out of himself, or maybe it was meeting Alicia. But not once since then had pasty-white little Tommy rolled his head to the side on the couch and looked over to ask why he let Mommy do it.

"Why didn't you stop her?" he asked again and again, and again, because David had no answer and he just hadn't. Which was enough of a lie to make him feel queasy.

"David?"

"Sorry."

"Stop saying you're sorry."

"Okay. I'm good. How's..." He almost blanked on the name. "...Leslie?" And then he said he was sorry again. Old habits, always apologizing for his existence, as if that would make strangers love him. He knew how he'd looked back in care, like a dog at the pound, hoping every newcomer would take him home with them.

"She's good," Kathryn said. A vintage octagonal broach danced on her necklace, and he wondered if there was a picture inside. She used to have a faded photo of her birth mother somewhere, or at least the woman she thought was her birth mother—some east-coast heiress who seemed far too fantastical for the likes of David and Kathryn. "We're going to adopt. Did I tell you that?"

"That's great." And it was. They'd both wanted children but were left simultaneously infertile by the pandemic, which he supposed was a nice way of saying their ovaries had dissolved at almost the same time. Kathryn called it their SHASterectomy and laughed every time. Sometimes it was funny. "Have you picked a child?"

"Not yet. It's a long process." She put her coffee down. "David, I'm so glad to see you. I really am. But when you called, you sounded…off."

"Freaked out?"

"More than usual. And it was two in the morning."

"Yeah…" He thought about blaming Alicia's clock embargo, but who had clocks anymore?

"So, what's going on?"

"You'll keep this between us? Private, I mean?"

"Until I can't. You know that. Is something wrong with Jason?"

He put his coffee down, grabbed his thighs and tried to clear his head. Jason was fine. He was just…

"David?"

"Come on," he said, standing. "I'll show you."

They went into the nursery with all of its brightly colored walls and the crib mobile with orange and purple and green octopuses that probably looked like psychedelic spider butts from Jason's perspective. He'd have to move that. David sat in Alicia's disused nursing recliner while Kathryn leaned in to look at Jason, lifted his blanket, walked around the crib and looked again. He made sure she saw his truncated pinky. Then she came back and he handed her his journal from on top of the little white dresser. He tracked everything. Jason's weight and activity level, how he slept, his bowel movements, including frequency and consistency. Now that he thought about it, maybe he was the problem. Who did all that? Kathryn flipped through the journal, page after page with some very nice little charts he'd printed from Excel, and then handed the journal back.

"Okay," she said, her voice flat and uninflected, and then he followed her back to the living room.

"So?" He sipped cold coffee, waiting for bad news and condemnation.

"So that's the healthiest baby I've ever seen. I talked to your pediatrician after you called. He sounded a little put-out to be bothered on the weekend, by the way. Something about golf and freedom and the American Way. I even talked to your posh-sounding nanny. Is that accent real? Jason's fine." She cracked a smile. "And he's hella cute. Are you sure he's yours?"

"Screw you." But he couldn't help smiling. She made him relax just be being there. She knew him. She wouldn't judge him. He could just say it out loud.

So? Say it. Out loud.

"David, what am I doing here?"

"I thought something was eating him," he blurted.

She blinked. "What?"

"He's missing his pinky and—"

"And it's been missing from birth. I was at the hospital when he was born, remember? But I still asked for confirmation. They faxed me pictures, which I should have brought along. Perfect baby boy missing one digit on the right pinky and another on the left little toe."

"Little toe?" he asked, alarmed. Wait. Of course. The little toe was so small and pudgy it was hard to tell, but there was no toenail there. How could he forget that?

"David, what's wrong? You're worrying me."

Not scaring, worrying. Careful words.

"I know. I would have sworn he had all his fingers and toes. Sworn it until just the other day. And then I saw this other little girl…" He stopped himself too late.

"Another girl?"

"From the park. She's missing both her pinkies, but I thought…"

"You thought someone was eating her fingers? Going house-to-house and nibbling on baby pinkies, changing medical records and erasing memories?" She waited for denial he couldn't provide. "That's a very sophisticated cannibal conspiracy you've come up with. You haven't changed political parties, have you?"

He exhaled. It sounded ridiculous when she said it out loud. It sounded ridiculous when he thought about it at all.

"You must think I'm insane."

"No, you're the most sane—sanest...?" He nodded. "...sanest person I've ever known. And I *know* you. You look scared. Is this really about Jason and this other girl?"

"Charlotte."

"You know I love you, right? We're family. There's nothing you can't tell me."

He nodded. "I know."

"And you do remember what week this is?"

"This week?" He looked at his hands. Why were they shaking?

Why didn't you stop her?

"Oh, crap," he said. This was the week Tommy and his parents died. No wonder he was on edge.

"Jason's fine, David, but you should talk to Kiaraa. You're seeing her, right?"

He nodded to avoid the question. "I know." And given what week it was, he already had an appointment—the annual check to make sure his brains weren't any more scrambled than the average omelet. He might actually show up this year.

"You remember those old songs we'd sing?" she asked. "That morbid Tom Lehrer stuff?"

"Yes." They were terrible songs, but she was trying to distract him. "No wonder they thought we were freaks.

"I told Leslie about them. Sang her a few verses of Rickety Tickety Tin."

"God, why?"

"I don't know. I just remembered how they made us laugh. She didn't laugh. I think she's reconsidering parts of our relationship."

"Does she know you're tone-deaf? She's probably just glad you never went to karaoke."

"She does now, and true." She faked a shudder. "Are you going to be okay? You know I'm here. Anytime you need to talk, I'm here." Quick smile. "Even at two in the damn morning."

"I know. I feel like an idiot. I'm…" He was going to say *sorry.* "…just glad I got to see you. Maybe we can all get together? I'm grilling again. Come over Sunday. Bring Leslie."

"Grilling meat? I thought you were going back to—"

"Didn't go over well."

Kathryn nodded. Her mouth opened to ask the question she never asked but he thought she always wanted to. He waited, hoping she would, grateful she wouldn't, trying to keep his face neutral. Her mouth closed and she nodded to herself. He felt himself relax, relieved but disappointed. Relippointed? Disrelieved? Either way, he was a little surprised she didn't ask about his marriage again. Was he hiding it that well?

"Well, I've got to get to work," she said. "Let us know what to bring."

"Can you bring your fruit salad? Any time after one."

"That should work. Oh, how's the new book?"

He pulled one of several folded sheets of paper from his pocket and handed it to her. She unfolded a page that was just giant eyes and a vague hint of polar hair. She held it at arm's length and smiled.

"Can I keep this?"

"Please. I have a trashcan full of them. Do you think kids know what peripatetic means?"

"I don't know what it means."

"It means itinerant or wandering. Traveling a lot. I used to think it meant vertiginous, like you'd feel looking down from a high parapet, but no. How's that right?" Kathryn shrugged in bemusement and he sighed in disappointment, an exchange they'd had a thousand times. Pedro needed a new adjective and book title. *Pedro the Preponderance of Pupils* should work.

"You'll figure it out," she said, refolding the drawing. "You always do."

They hugged fiercely at the door. David watched her get into her car from the front step, hand on the door, like someone watching a relative move out. Maybe someday she'd ask. Maybe someday he'd have the courage to tell her. He knew he had to. He just dreaded having it out in the open.

She pulled into the street and waved. He waved back and forced a smile.

Back in the office, he flipped through their digital albums on his laptop, hundreds upon thousands of photos and videos at every stage of Jason's life, from bloody birth to yesterday. Missing fingertip. Missing toe-tip. Clear as day. But then, for some reason he couldn't explain, he printed out a few of the images and put them on his desk. They were unambiguous shots of Jason and all his digits, just to be sure, you know, there wasn't a cannibal conspiracy.

Pedro watched through dozens of giant eyes on the wall, wide with amusement.

He really was losing his mind.

Why didn't you stop her?

Great question, little brother, which he could never answer. Instead, he went online and ordered thirty pounds of meat. Aged, grade-A, prime packed beef from a local ranch for delivery by Friday. He looked over pictures of brisket, fat-back, strip steaks, filets and rib-eyes, beef ribs and pork, slabs of bacon and loin. Added some flank steaks and rib-eye, and then some pork ribs. Might as well use the garage freezer. Maybe he could get some fish for ceviche and sushi after all the heavy meat. His stomach growled in anticipation, and he wondered if this was how Alicia felt when she shopped for shoes.

*

ALICIA'S BLACK GIVENCHY PUMP *THUNKED* into the wall, four-inches of designer Italian heel embedded in the eggshell-finish right next to the master bathroom door. Thank god she'd left the spiked Alexander McQueens in the closet. David wasn't sure what impressed him more, the force of her throw or her terrible aim. She'd missed him by at least a yard. Sometimes he wondered if her anger ruined her depth perception or if she wanted an excuse to repaint the house. Either way, he fought the usual feeling of arousal mixed with fear and the disturbing knowledge that this was exactly

how his mother acted when she let her anger show, which made the
arousal part a little gross.

"Alicia," he said.

"Don't." She stomped over and yanked the shoe out with both
hands. He could probably fill the hole with spackle, but it would take
a while to get the painted finish right.

"I didn't mean—"

"You called Kathryn?" It wasn't a question. "You thought I was
abusing our son and you called your friend from child welfare?"
Because the pediatrician had told her. Of course he had; everyone
was trigger-happy since they lost Alex. Lost him. Like he'd wondered
off. "*Kathryn?*"

"It wasn't like that," he said. And who else was he going to call?
Alicia was like social erosion; she'd worn away at his relationships
one by one, year after year, until only Kathryn remained. One reason
he didn't get to know James, Franzia or even Padme was to avoid the
inevitable jealousy.

She clenched the shoe to her chest and started to shake. He knew
this stage. In a few seconds, she'd drop the heel and cry, a full-body
sob like there was an ocean in her that could only escape in tidal
misery that wracked her entire frame. It was his least favorite part,
complete emotional collapse after violence, because it was so hard to
muster the empathy he was supposed to feel. She didn't mean it. She
didn't want to hurt him. And on and on. Mostly, he felt tired, and
anticipating that tiredness, felt exhausted. It was hard to keep his eyes
open.

Just throw the damn shoe, he thought. Maybe she'd get lucky and hit
him, and he wouldn't have to stay for the next part. But she dropped
the shoe and started to cry and he thought, *fuck*, but then he went
over to hold her as something cracked inside her and a tsunami of
grief looked for a way out. Just like his mom.

It's okay, Mommy.

Fucking gross.

When they'd whispered their apologies and she cried herself to
sleep in his arms, moonlight cast long black shadows across the

sheets and he tried to remember when they'd mounted the clock above the bed. It was hideous. Burnished silver, pewter or something else coldly modern, with eight serpentine arms like a sundial. Black numbers on an iridescent nacre face. It was like one of Pedro's giant eyes watching over them. Why had he let this atrocity in the house, let alone over their bed? It ticked off the seconds, the minutes, the hours, and he hated every one of them. If his arm wasn't trapped under Alicia, he would have thrown it out the window.

"David?" she whispered.

"Yes, baby?" *Baby?* He winced at the clichéd vocabulary of love. Honey, hun, sweetie, babe, lover and love. When was the last time they weren't lies? They were good at lies. He was even better at appeasement. Sometimes when they were out in public, he almost believed the lies himself. It was performance art, like busking for salvation.

"You don't really think I'd hurt Jason, do you?" Her voice was wet with desperation.

"Of course not," he said, not sure if he was lying or not. He hadn't thought his mother would slowly kill Tommy, day after day, month after month, his life ticking away like hands on a shitty silver clock until he couldn't even go to the bathroom on his own anymore. Sometimes David allowed himself to hope, which was dangerous, but that wasn't entirely fair to Alicia. She knew he had trouble trusting women, had always known it, and never held it against him, even when she could see it in his eyes. Maybe she liked it. But no mother wants to be accused of child abuse. He might deserve a shoe-throwing or two.

But the clock had to go.

Yeehaw!

IT WAS PROBABLY THE BEST brisket David had ever made. He set a tray of sliced meat on the table between two lawn chairs and watched James eagerly shovel slices onto his plate. He took a few cuts, waited, took a few more, waited and took a few more, glancing around like a kid at a shrimp buffet who wanted *all of it*. David nodded to put him at ease and then walked back to the grill. He had chicken on the way, and some grilled vegetables only Kathryn and Leslie would eat. The fish never made it out of the freezer, which was probably a good thing; he'd ordered scallops, and Alicia was picky about her mollusks.

Brisket was cut from the cow's lower chest, or breast, around its front legs, producing twenty pounds of cartilaginous connective tissue that was buttery, delicious and tender if properly prepared. And David's brisket was always properly prepared. He bought the best prime whole packer brisket he could justify, trimmed away excess fat and seasoned with a rub of coarse kosher salt, ground pepper and garlic. The resulting brisket was smoked with a combination of hickory and cherry for around eight hours. Then he wrapped the 165-degree meat in peach butcher paper and smoked it for another eight. After it sat in an insulated cooler for at least an hour, he sliced the tender meat against the grain into fatty (point) and lean (flat) sections ready to serve. It was half science, half art, and the other fifty percent was probably love. He certainly loved the smell of hot cooked flesh with bacon and ham accents gifted by the salt, and even the delicious feel of capitulation as he took the first bite.

He chewed and swallowed and felt like he was eating porn, relishing the pleasure while dreading the guilt and nausea that followed. He hated thinking about the animals that had suffered and died for his pleasure. Pleasure and disgust churned in his stomach like oil and water, never mixing, elements eternally at war with each other. Ambivalence, Kathryn might have called it, but she knew him well enough to know it was more than that: the blending of incompatible chemicals to release toxic gas—steam in a pressure cooker, ready to blow him apart. Which was melodramatic. He took a deep breath, inhaled the smell of grilled chicken and the tang of roasted pepper, exhaled one more time, and the pressure released safe and unheard.

Kathryn sat by Leslie on the other side of the backyard patio, close to each other and far from everyone else. Leslie was a tall Black woman topped with an assertive globe of natural hair, making Kathryn's ball of fiery red hair look small by comparison. They kept their eyes down, avoiding Alicia while Alicia pretended they didn't exist. She chatted with James and Franzia while James bopped Charlotte up and down on his knee between massive mouthfuls of meat. Two of Alicia's work friends were there, a whippet-lean lawyer couple who clearly knew James. Their ten-year-old son seemed to find his phone infinitely more interesting than anything else. Both attorneys had gorgeous prosthetic ears, art deco jewelry more than decorations and definitely not their work ears. There was a myth that lawyers were harder hit by the pandemic than others, missing more limbs, dying more often, but at least they had the money to look fabulous doing it. Their son was missing both legs below the knee and sported prosthetics that were practically bionic. David imagined him jumping thirty feet in the air without ever pulling his face out of his phone.

Franzia glanced at David and raised a pointedly non-alcoholic sparkling water (apparently there was a history there) in salute. He nodded, lingering on her smile, and then turned his attention to Padme and her husband Samesh. They sat with their daughters kitty-corner to the attorneys, eating brisket with a ravenous glee that made him wonder what diet rule they were breaking. Padme gave him the bird in the friendliest way and he returned the gesture. Samesh watched the exchange, probably wondering if he should be offended on his wife's behalf, and then resumed his furious mastication. The girls watched their parents eat in clear astonishment, mouths open, like baby birds waiting for theirs but too astonished to ask. Identical twin birds in identical shorts missing identical left hands just like Samesh. The prosthetics were matching and lovely.

David turned his focus back to the grill, stabbing imitation burgers so they bled plant heme, red and metallic as blood. He was thinking about the last time he brought up returning to his vegetarian ways to Alicia. It hadn't gone well. He stabbed them again.

Maybe next year.

He'd been a vegetarian until they were married, and then Alicia made it abundantly clear that wasn't going to work. She liked meat and he didn't feel like cooking two separate meals, or dealing with her snide comments, so gradually he returned to the dark side. The delicious side, he had to admit, but he missed standing for something. Not loudly or obnoxiously like the vegans he'd known in college, just something he did for himself.

Stab, stab, stab.

"I think they're dead," Alicia said from his side, holding an empty serving platter. He started—she always managed to sneak up on him—and put the skewer down before he stabbed something else. She put a hand on his arm, dry synthetic fingers sliding toward his elbow. He willed himself not to flinch. She'd misunderstand and think it was about her prosthetic hand. It was a thing of beauty, far superior to the Balasubramanian models, almost impossible to tell from the real thing and controlled by a chip implanted in her neck that tied directly into her nervous system by a wireless Bluetooth connection. He called it Zombie Hand when she was in a good mood.

When she was playful, she'd pull it off and will it to walk around the table like Thing from *The Addams Family*. It was hysterical and Jason couldn't take his eyes off it. The practical side was that hands sometimes fell off, and instead of having users run around looking for their lost hand, the hand would chase you down and put itself back on. In the morning, Alicia just moved her stump-mount close to the bedside table and the hand jumped up and reattached itself like a codependent limpet.

She pulled her hand back. He loaded vegetables on the platter and exhaled in hidden relief.

"I'm thinking of going vegetarian again," he said, spitting it out. Alicia nearly dropped the platter and then forced a smile. Zombie Hand twitched with confused input. Her face was a marvel of conflicting emotions until it settled on *concerned*. He was just trying to distract her from his reaction to her hand. Maybe he'd gone too far.

"You can't be serious," she said.

Definitely too far. "Not today." He snapped off the grill. "Someday."

"Good. You're the best grill chef on the Front Range. People would riot."

"Well, we can't have that."

Forced smile of tactical retreat given. Forced smile of inevitable victory returned. Alicia walked back to the patio and offered James a vegetable. He looked offended, waving her off with a four-fingered hand. He was missing the same pinky as Jason, but all of it, and like most people didn't bother with a prosthetic. He probably wanted people to know he wasn't untouched. Too much envy and suspicion otherwise.

Strange, David thought, thinking about something someone had asked at the playground last week, but the rest of the thought wandered off on its own and he couldn't call it back.

Franzia zigzagged over with her nearly empty glass in hand, scanning the yard as if checking the perimeter for enemies, studying the bird feeder and a few aggressive hummingbirds that didn't appreciate the attention, squinting at something suspicious on the fence, until she finally arrived next to him at the grill. He nodded. She sipped at her drink and watched her husband suck down a third serving of brisket like a beef Roomba.

"Does he work out?" he asked to break the silence.

She chuckled. "You have no idea. It's exhausting. Instead of a man cave, we've got a basement gym the NFL could train in. I wish he'd watch porn like everyone else."

David smiled and watched Charlotte making faces at Jason in the basinet, and then do the pinky nose-mining trick again. He hoped she didn't give him nightmares.

"So, you're an author," Franzia said.

"Uh-huh." David glanced at his phone by the grill. Alicia made it an hour without telling them. Probably a record.

"T.C. McSwizzle? That's really you?"

He nodded. They were always surprised, like he didn't fit the look. Maybe he needed crazier hair and a bow tie like Benny Beau Beaver from his third book.

"Charlotte loves your books. I think we have all of them. I just read her *Snyder the Eider Spider* last night for the hundredth time. Spiders with wings?" She faked a shudder.

"What?"

"Charlie loves them. Calls them *spooders*." She said the last word with so much love for Charlotte, David could almost taste it in the air. "But they creep me out. Sorry."

"Don't be. Alicia's not too fond either." When he was writing *Snyder*, Alicia wouldn't come in the office for all the spider pictures on every available surface. He might have left them up longer than necessary.

"Fond?" Franzia took a drink. "I'd probably wet myself if I saw a giant flying tarantula."

"Brazilian wandering spider."

"Hmm?"

"Snyder's a Brazilian wandering spider." The first time he'd seen a wandering spider was at the Colorado State University's Bug Zoo with his dad and Tommy. Tommy loved the spiders and insects and phasmids, while David wanted to see snakes, lizards, frogs and all the sticky-crawly things. Tommy tugged him through the spider exhibit with one tiny, cold hand until they were standing in front of a cage that seemed empty until Dad lifted them up to see better. Inside, a spider too big to be real shuddered, cricked and glowered with alien malcontent.

"That's so cool," Tommy said. That was his new word, cool. Everything was cool or super cool or totally cool. And when it wasn't, it was not-cool or so-not-cool or, sometimes, totally cool-less. "What is it?"

"Brazilian wandering spider," Dad said, reading the plaque so David knew he hadn't known beforehand, the first time he realized his dad didn't know everything about the natural world. "The deadliest spider on earth."

"That's so totally cool," Tommy said.

"The coolest," Dad agreed.

The spider had dripped some venom and glared through eight glassy eyes. David didn't think he was cool. He thought he was awesome.

"That's right," Franzia said. "He gave up his vicious venom for whimsical wings."

"I do have a thing for alliteration." His editor called it an obsession.

She held up her free hand and flexed her fingers, a nervous gesture. They were long and thin, like a pianist with dirty fingernails and no polish. Alicia had told him she was an engineer at some secret government facility, and he wondered what she'd been tinkering with. He assumed space lasers, but then he always assumed space lasers.

"Does it ever bother you?"

"What?" He stared at her hand, trying not to think about how it had felt on his arm.

"That we're the only untouched here?"

He thought about telling her about his missing kidney, but that wasn't the point. Everyone was touched in some way, or had lost someone they cared about. What was she getting at?

She sucked in her breath. "What the hell?"

David followed her gaze toward a bedraggled Orange Cheyenne bush by the back fence that was desperately trying to flower. Under the bush at the edge of the grass was a scrawny gray mouse with a banded garden spider on its back, striped black and yellow, with its long front legs clutched around the mouse's neck. The mouse looked at them, sniffed at the air—did mice like grilled meat?—and then ran in a little circle to show off. He half expected the spider to raise a silky Stetson and wave for applause.

"That's awesome," David said. Franzia looked pale.

His father would have known what kind of mouse it was and if being ridden by a spider was normal or not, but that was all pre-SHAS and now normal was a dubious classification. Normal is what happened today, and today, arachnids were riding rodents and that was just fine as fine could be.

He felt in his pockets, looking for his phone. He'd seen something like this online years ago, a squirrel riding a woodpecker, and this was the kind of video that would go just as viral. But just as Franzia snapped out of her shock and reached for her phone, the spider twitched and rode the mouse back under the bush. David fought the urge to call out, Yeehaw! No one else even noticed.

His phone was right by the grill where it had always been. Too late.

"You okay?" he asked Franzia. She'd gone from pale to blanched.

"That," she said, "was not natural. God, I could use a drink."

"But you don't…"

"Oh, don't look so nervous. I had a drinking problem a few years back. Well, I've always had a drinking problem. Did Alicia tell you?"

"She implied there was an issue. I'm so—"

She snorted. "I'm sure it was subtle. Nothing to be sorry about. I haven't had a drink in eons, but that doesn't mean I don't think about having one every minute of every day. And that spider-mouse thing didn't help. You know?"

He nodded and she wondered off in search of something distracting, apparently forgetting the question she'd asked: *Are we the only untouched?* He tried to think of everyone he knew, running through a list of missing body parts, but it was hard to focus and he kept adding people to the list and then taking them off as he remembered what parts they'd lost. He felt uneasy, like he was forgetting something, and kept checking to make sure nothing was burning.

"Spider Cowboy," David said to himself as he closed the grill. "And his mouse, Marvin Moustopheles." His editor was right, he had issues, but there was a book in there somewhere. *Mouselorian,* the Chosen One that could travel in time? The spider could be like Dr. Who with eight little legs and giant eyes.

He couldn't wait until Jason was old enough to tell him about it.

Alexander the Late

YOU DON'T NEED TO GO SHOPPING.

It was a blustery morning and cold outside David's office window, promising a late spring flurry. Inside, it was warm and comfortable and distractingly calm. Olivia was playing with Jason in the nursery, singing in a low, quiet voice that sounded like waves on the baby monitor. There was no reason he couldn't go shopping. It would be great to get out of the house.

You don't need to go shopping. Again. For the third time this week.

Pedro's preposterous pupils watched him from every wall and from sketches on the desk, black holes he could fall into and not come out for hours. He was no closer to drawing a bear. A bear was a real animal with fur and teeth and hunger. What he drew was a more like a metaphor, great eyes watching, following, and expecting something from him. He just didn't know what. He fidgeted and twisted in his chair. His foot tapped madly on the carpeted floor, *tham, tham, tham,* like a metronome.

You don't...

He glanced at a framed picture on the corner of his desk, one of those terrible hospital photos taken by a nurse midwife right after the birth of a child. David was smiling like an idiot in a t-shirt he'd had on for at least forty hours, Alicia looked exhausted, and their son Alex was swaddled in blue like a little Smurf burrito that was just a little too small. You could barely tell he was crying in the photo. He was always crying, and he wasn't the only one. They hadn't been married when Alicia got pregnant with Alex, but one of the great things about SHAS was that oral contraceptives failed. It was like the disease wanted more children to infect, which is why he'd gotten a vasectomy after Jason was born. So they got married and tried to do the right thing, but they never got the chance.

David reached out and touched his first son's already smudged image, wondering for the millionth time if they could have done better. Not that they did anything wrong with Alex; they did nothing other than watch him collapse in on himself like someone sucking the air out of a balloon animal one limb at a time. There was nothing anyone could do. No cure. No treatment. No hope. Doctors didn't even bother coming in the room after his legs were gone. When they took him home, he was already a quad 'amputee' with a tiny torso and head like a baby stub. A *stump, stub* or *gummy bear,* as people called them when no one was listening.

But what Alex was missing in limbs he made up for in lungs. He never stopped crying. They loved him, but it was hard not to hate him too. He screamed. He sucked Alicia dry. He screamed more and louder. David used to think he was angry at the world and everyone in it, and why wouldn't he be? David had whispered to his son that he was wanted, that he was loved, but maybe babies can tell when you're lying. David loved him but Alicia, well, she was tired. And angry. He hadn't known anyone so angry since his mother.

What would Alex have been like as a boy? He'd be almost four now, talking, probably still a pain in the ass—a beautiful pain in the ass—but he was gone and David needed to focus on Jason.

Over the monitor, Jason laughed or burped and Olivia responded with delight.

Alex died three years ago that month. David closed his eyes and tried to remember Alex's face.

Tham.

But all he could see was the tiny coffin they'd buried him in.

Tham.

It was so small it looked like a toy.

Tham.

His eyes snapped open and he held his breath, trying to relax. It didn't work. He checked his phone.

Time to go shopping.

*

DAVID PUSHED AN EMPTY CART down one aisle of Whole Foods after another, his growing anti-materialism fighting the need to put something in the cart so he didn't look like a crazy person or shoplifter. One wheel squeaked and constantly tugged to the right, like a political statement. He jerked to a stop next to a vast array of squeezable baby foods and glared at the apple sauce.

Would Alex have liked you? he asked accusingly. *Are you the apple sauce my dead son would have loved?*

The packaging was intransigent, mocking him with empty promises.

"Hey, David."

David flinched and looked around. Franzia's perfect husband, James, was coming toward him. Form-fitting jeans. Tight shirt with no sign of a distended stomach from beef inhalation. Jaunty topsiders and no socks. More like a social media influencer than a police detective. Did he not get the weather? David glanced self-consciously at his empty cart and snagged three packs of apple sauce squeezables.

"Hey," David said. James was holding a basket full of kid's disposable prosthetic ears, toylike and colorful in shiny blister packs. They fist-bumped and David looked back at the ears.

"For Charlotte," James said.

"But she…" He clamped his mouth shut. Was Charlotte missing an ear? How had he missed that, and who says that to a father? She just had a great prosthetic. He felt like an ass, but hadn't Franzia said she was only missing the fingers? In his memory, Franzia's voice was like adults from a *Charlie Brown* cartoon. *Wa-wa-wa.* Not helpful.

"You didn't know it was missing, right?" James said, un-phased. "Her prosthetic ear's amazing. I can hardly tell it's fake. But she was sad this morning and I thought something fun would cheer her up."

"Really? She doesn't seem…." He trailed off. What was he going to say? Weepy?

"She's not, believe me. She's a happy kid. I cry whenever I see a commercial with puppies. Kidding." He clearly wasn't. "Don't tell anyone. Not a good image for a detective. But Charlotte's a rock. So, when she's sad…well, you know. Char loves being able to change ears like the other kids. You know they trade them? I'm not sure it's hygienic, but she comes home with cool stuff sometimes." He snagged a pack out of the basket. "Look at these elf ears. She'll love these." He looked at me for confirmation. "She'll love these, right?"

"Who wouldn't?"

"Oh, heads up. There's a pedophile in your neighborhood. I'll email you the address."

David blinked. Nice segue. "Near the park?"

"No. They wouldn't allow that." He glanced around and leaned in conspiratorially. "Did you know they're far more likely to get SHAS than the average person?"

David had heard that. Pedophiles, lawyers, politicians and tax collectors, among others, including street cops. David glanced at James' missing pinky. Still no prosthetic. He could do half the nose-mining gag with Charlotte.

"Maybe it's Karma," James said, shrugging. "I hope they all die."

David nodded, agreeing, at least about the pedophiles, but it was strange the virus had such good taste.

"Anyway, I just thought you should know. He has a thing for boys. I mean, older boys, not…" He exhaled. "Well, you know." And this came out in a rush: "You up for a beer later?" He was nervous as a new kid on the playground.

Their eyes met in a weird, accidental guy way and David felt the strongest sense of connection; the way you'd feel when you met a girl you really liked, but in this case nothing sexual, just openness. It was hard to describe. Both men looked away. David felt a jolt of excitement that he might make a male friend. He was astonishingly bad at male relationships despite his history with women, and it wasn't like Alicia allowed him much freedom in friend selection. The only downside was that the connection came with a surge of sadness; he thought James might be the loneliest person he'd ever met. All of that from one casual meeting of the eyes.

James glanced back, waiting for an answer.

"I would," David said. He really would. "But I have an appointment."

James nodded and looked away, embarrassed.

"Rain check?" David blurted, not wanting to hurt his feelings or lose this chance for a connection. "Seriously."

"Yeah, yeah, of course." And then they fist-bumped again and James was gone with his basket of kiddy ears. There was something seriously wrong with Franzia's marriage. Maybe that's why he felt so drawn to her, and now to James. Could he be friends with both of them?

He snorted. Like Alicia would allow that.

A few minutes later, David was at the checkout with a random collection of foods he didn't need. The teenage checker scanned each item off the belt and nodded at David. They saw each other every week, sometimes more. David made sure he always shopped at the same time so he was there. He was a scrawny kid with a big smile, happy green eyes, a trace of acne, and he wanted to be an engineer when he grew up. Or a bass player in a rock band. Or both. Why not both? He had a missing eye and an ever-growing collection of ironic eye patches. It was hard not to make pirate noises and talk about Jason whenever they saw each other.

"How are you today, Mr. Chambers?"

"David," David said for the hundredth time.

"Right," Alex said. "I keep forgetting."

The Unbearable Soul

OATMEAL, SUGAR, FLOWER, BUTTER AND EGGS. Other ingredients in a bowl and then the oven, coming out with the magical smell of fresh cookies. David left a few for Olivia, checked on Jason, and then headed for the garage. A long, distracted and several times off-track drive later, he found himself outside a freshly painted blue door in a hipster strip-mall office complex wondering if James was still up for a beer.

He reached for the knob, pulled back, reached again. This went on until the door opened by itself.

"I'm glad you made it," said Dr. Kiaraa Hoffman, smiling warmly. Six feet tall, vaguely Asian features and dark hair, with small hands that could grip like a vice. They did the usual subtle-yet-obvious check to see if they still had all their limbs. All intact, astonishingly. She was more than ten years older than David but didn't look it. He fought the urge to hug her. She used to love hugs and he could use one, but it had been a while. Now hugs were like first base for the virus, and you could never tell what people felt about them until you did an awkward dance he didn't have the energy for.

"You still have me on the calendar," he said.

"Every year." She held up a dog-eared copy of *The Silence of the Lambs* he was convinced she kept around to freak out her patients. It was usually on a shelf next to a bottle of Chianti and a can of fava beans. "I come prepared."

"Sorry," he said. Sorry he never showed up. Sorry he couldn't explain why. Sorry he—

"Don't be. Come on in."

He handed her a large Ziploc bag of cookies, made with less sugar and a few token raisins to make them seem healthy. The way he knew she liked them.

"You don't have to bring cookies." She popped the bag open and took one out. "But I'm glad you did. What happened to your wrist?"

"What?" His sleeve had pulled up, showing a fading bruise. He couldn't remember when it happened. "Oh, I was moving the desk in my office." Which he hadn't moved in years. He forced a shrug and a smile. Funny how easy the lies came now. "You know how clumsy I am."

"Huh." She nibbled on her cookie. "I don't remember that. Well, come on in, Mr. McSwizzle. It's cold out here."

Inside, David sat on the couch and she sat in her usual old chair, bookshelves behind her, bookshelves to the side, books everywhere and not one of them science fiction, which seemed like a lost opportunity. Maybe he should bring her a book next time, something less morbid than *Lambs*, with space lasers.

The room smelled like a library and her unidentifiable skin cream. Kiaraa was half Korean, half German, and one of those people who were always comfortable in their own skin. She never fidgeted and had no nervous ticks. She could have been a card shark or CIA interrogator, but instead she seemed to look forward to hearing his nonsense.

"It's been, what, four years? I've missed you. How are things?"

He shrugged. "You?"

"Good." And then right to it. "Are the nightmares…?"

"No." At least, not about Tommy. What was the last thing their father had said? *It'll be okay, David. No matter what happens, it'll be okay.* That was the last time he believed those words, but he hadn't been dreaming about Tommy, so he didn't know where to start. His eyes fixed on a strangely familiar clock on the bookshelf to his left. It was octopus shaped, like the one over their bed, and just as ugly.

"Is that new?" he asked

She nodded. "I know, heinous, isn't it? I mean, hideous. Does it bother you?"

"Why would it bother me?" Though it did. It really did.

"It's a test, in a way. We've been having a lot of people with arachnophobia ever since that movie came out. *She Spins.* Have you seen it?"

"No." When was the last time they went out to the movies? He tried to think back, but nothing came to mind. Most non-luxury theaters went under during the pandemic, and Alicia hated drive-ins.

"It's like *Jaws* for spiders," Kiaraa said. "Suddenly everyone's afraid to go back in their garage. Anyway, the eight arms make it just spider-like enough to tell me if it triggers anything."

"So, you scare your patients?"

She shrugged. "I can cover it if it bothers you."

"No, we have one in our bedroom. It's almost identical." Which was odd. Since when did Alicia go for baroque modern décor, let alone clocks? Wasn't there a whole argument about clocks in the bedroom a few years back? And why was it so hard to remember anything? He was decades early on the dementia.

"David?"

"You're still the same age," he said, grasping for distraction. "Sorry. I don't know why I said that."

"Stop saying you're sorry, and thank you." She held her hands up to her face and tilted her head like a doll. "Asian don't raisin." She laughed self-consciously. "You know, I'm half Asian, and I'm still not sure I'm allowed to say that anymore."

"I won't tell anyone."

"So, David." She dropped her hands into her lap and assumed the professional listening position. "What brought you back? I mean, I love the cookies and seeing you, but…"

Direct and to the point. No wasted time. It's one reason he had always enjoyed talking to her; it was like talking to a guy. But today he wouldn't have minded a little small talk. She raised her eyebrows. He sighed and tried to think of how to get started without sounding like he'd lost his mind.

"David, it's okay. Whatever it is, it's all right."

"I know. It's just… I'm having these conflicting memories. Delusions? I'm not sure what you call them. I keep thinking I remember things that didn't happen."

She didn't react, but then she rarely reacted. "When did they start?"

"A few weeks ago. Jason had just turned eight months old."

"And what are you misremembering?"

"That something's eating him."

He could see her trying not to react, which was unusual, but at least she didn't laugh. She knew not to coddle him. He needed to get his shit together his own way, not wallow in it, and she understood that. Then she frowned. That wasn't good.

"What?"

"Well, I'm not sure if this helps—that sounds like a terrible thing to imagine—but it's not uncommon. Parents have enormous guilt about their children's missing body parts. They blame themselves. It manifests differently, but you're not the only one imagining there's something evil behind it. Something monstrous. A real, tangible thing you can fight."

He sat back, relieved. He wasn't crazy, or at least not crazy alone. "Then what do I do?"

"Spend time with your son. He's only missing a fingertip, right?"

"And part of a toe. Good memory."

"Love him. That's all you can do. Love him and forgive yourself."

He almost laughed. As if. "Okay, it's just…"

"What?"

"I called Kathryn to do a private welfare check on Jason. I thought Alicia might be…"

"Ahh. So this is a serious thing."

"Kinda. Alicia didn't understand." Not that he would have either. Part of him wondered if he just did it to set her off. Did he crave the violence now, the only real passion left in their marriage? The answer wasn't as purely negative as he would've hoped. Maybe he *was* the problem.

"Does she feel that same way?" she asked. "That something's happening to Jason, or he's in danger?"

"No. As far as she's concerned, everything's great. Except me, of course."

"So, what you really want to know is how to fix your marriage." She munched on a cookie. "You know I don't do couples' counseling." She didn't even do monogamy. If he remembered, she was pansexually asexual, meaning she was equally uninterested in everyone but really liked hugs, which he loved about her, and they both felt the loss of platonic physical touch like a lost loved one. He really should have hugged her when he came in. "So, I'll tell you what I'd tell anyone in your position."

"What?" He leaned forward eagerly.

"Cunnilingus," she said. "*Hours* of cunnilingus."

It was almost a joke, but by the way she watched him, he could tell she was looking for a reaction. He sat back and tried not to look ill. Had she guessed about Alicia? He tried to think back if he'd ever said anything, but he knew he hadn't. He fought the urge to tug his sleeve down over the bruises.

"I'm kidding, David. Your sex life is none of my business unless you want it to be. Is everything okay between you two? Sometimes marital stress—"

"Yeah, everything's fine." He said that too sharply, frowned. "I mean, there's the usual stuff. But…"

"But?"

What would happen if he told her, if he told someone about Alicia and the beatings? What would she do? No, it was too humiliating. Which was strange, since she knew almost everything. About his mother and father, about Tommy and his nightmares. She knew why he drew children's books and how he got his pen name. But he couldn't stand the thought of her knowing about Alicia, about how weak he was and how he couldn't fight back or leave her and didn't know why. He was a man. He was supposed to be strong, at least physically. It was pathetic. He knew she wouldn't think that way, not given his past, but he did think that way. It was hard not to.

"David?" And then: "Have you remembered anything after your father's death? About what your mother did?"

He flinched, surprised. "No. It's nothing like that. Everything's fine. I'm just worried about Jason."

"Who's perfectly healthy."

"Apparently."

She nodded. "You stopped coming after you and Alicia got serious. I miss our talks. If it's the money, I think your insurance covers it, but…"

"Not, it's not that. I just got busy with work and now Jason."

"Okay, but seriously, come by anytime. You're a friend, not just a patient. We can meet for lunch or take Jason for a walk. I'd like to see him. Whatever works."

"Okay," he said, knowing he wouldn't; he couldn't risk Alicia or someone they knew seeing them talking in public. "I'll pay cash, if that's all right? I can fill out the paperwork next time…"

She just nodded, but there was something on her face. Why insist on paying cash unless you're hiding something?

"Cookies are more than enough," she said. "This one's on the house."

"You're sure?"

"Of course. You know you can tell me anything, right? No matter how crazy it sounds?"

"I know." But he didn't; some things he couldn't say out loud. "Oh, we're having a BBQ on Sunday. You should come by." He made a mental note to make sure Kathryn wasn't coming. It wasn't good to have too many of his remaining friends around Alicia at the same time.

"I'd love to, but I thought you were a vegetarian."

She knew he was, because she was too. It was one of the things they'd talked about when he avoided talking about his childhood during their college counseling sessions.

"Alicia convinced me of the error of my ways," he said. "And it's not like I don't love meat."

Another careful look. He couldn't meet her eyes this time.

"I'll be there. Just tell me when and what to bring."

They finished with a long hug, sincere but platonic, the smell of her hair reminding him of college and strange, hopeful times when the pandemic seemed temporary. Strange that he thought of them as the good old days. At the time, he thought he was miserable.

She started to release him, but he didn't want to let go.

"David?" she asked.

"Sorry," he said, grimacing.

Back to square one.

She Spins

PEDRO WAS A LITTLE BEAR *when the storm came. It was a great and terrible blizzard. The wind screamed. The ice blew. Snow fell up, then down, and tossed around. The sky was white. The ice was white. He couldn't tell up from down and got so dizzy he fell over.*

Lying in the snow, he laughed and played, pretending he was walking on the sky. He never got cold. Well, he did sometimes when he was really small, but not anymore. Not as long as Mom and his sister were around.

Oh, yeah. Pedro stood and squinted into the storm. His eyes watered as he tried to see, but there was just white on white and more white on that.

"Mom?" he called, but the wind was so loud he couldn't hear his own voice.

"Mom!" he yelled, louder, but he couldn't hear that either. Mom and Parisa were out there somewhere, but they couldn't see or hear him. He was all alone.

He turned around and around looking for them, and he started to get cold, or maybe he was just afraid, so he picked a direction and started walking. And kept walking. For hours and then days until he got hungry and thirsty and the storm finally stopped blowing and the sun came out. He was on a great field of ice, like all the Arctic, floating on a sea far below. He'd never seen it so flat or empty before. He shivered. Seeing how alone he was made it worse.

"Mom!" he called. "Parisa!" His voice faded into the air. His stomach grumbled.

So he kept walking. And walking.

He knew if he kept walking, he'd find his mother and sister eventually. Maybe even his father, who he'd seen only once. He was good at walking and there was only so much ice, right? He knew he'd find them soon.

And that's how Pedro became the Peripatetic Polar Bear. Peripatetic is a big word that just meant he liked to travel. And travel he did, across ice and big tossed up blocks of sea ice called seracs. Around pools of water that poured through the ice sometimes and were delicious to drink. He drank and drank and then he walked and walked.

Sometimes he forgot he was looking and enjoyed the beauty of the world.

Sometimes he got hungry and hunted for fish and little things, because he still wasn't very big.

And sometimes he walked because he didn't like to sit still.

He got used to it. Maybe this is life, *he thought.* Maybe this is what it means to be big.

Pedro didn't know what to think about that, so he just walked some more. He walked on and on, day after day, week after week, until he wondered if he was all alone in the great white world. Maybe Mom and Parisa were somewhere else now. Maybe they swam away.

Which was a sad thought. It made him miss his family. So he walked a little faster.

And that's when he ran into a little girl. Nearly stepped right on her.

It was good he didn't because she was small and he would have squished her. Little girls don't like to be squished, he supposed, though he wasn't really sure what a little girl was. He just knew she wasn't a polar bear or a fish and probably didn't want to be stepped on.

"Watch it!" she said. She had big things on her hands and bigger things on her feet, a bright yellow poofy thing on her body and a hat that covered most of her head and face.

"Sorry," he said, looking down at her.

"You should be! Girls don't like to be squished!"

So he was right. He shuffled in the snow. He hadn't talked to anyone in a long time. He wasn't sure he was good at it anymore.

"My name is Shyla," she said. "What's your name?"

"Pedro," he said. "What are you?"

"I'm a human," she said. "Silly bear."

"I'm not silly."

The girl crossed her arms. "Yes, you are. I've seen you before. You walked right by me and didn't even say hello."

"I did?" He didn't remember that.

"Yep. You just kept walking and walking."

"Well, that's what I do."

"Why? Don't you like to sit and play?"

"Do you want to wrestle?" He missed wrestling with Parisa.

"No! Bears can't wrestle with little girls. But we could play tag sometime. Or charades. I love charades!"

Pedro didn't know what that was, but it sounded fun, so he nodded.

"What are you doing out here?" he asked. "I've never seen one of you before."

"I lost my family, or they lost me. I can't remember. But I'm sure they'll show up. They always do."

"Me too!" Pedro said, excited.

"Is that why you keep walking? You're looking for them?"

"Uh-huh." He jumped up and down. "Do you want to walk with me?"

The girl looked around and said, "Sure. For a little while. We can be friends."

"I've never had a friend before," he said. "Is it like walking?"

"It's better than walking. Because it's fun even when you're not doing anything."

That made little sense to Pedro, but a lot of things didn't, and most of them turned out to be fun or even delicious. Not that the girl was delicious. He didn't think bears were allowed to eat little girls. So maybe a friend was just what he needed.

"Which way are we walking?" she asked.

Pedro looked around. "That way." He pointed his snout to the north.

"Why that way?"

"I don't think I've been there before. So maybe that's where Mom and Parisa are."

"Okay," she said. "Let's roll!"

And so they rolled. Or walked. Whatever it was, it was nice not doing it alone.

David sat back and frowned at his monitor. Children's books were mostly illustrations, with fewer than a thousand words, but he didn't work that way. He wrote the full story in prose and then illustrated the key moments, adding in new words as a complement to the visuals. It was like separating curds from milk to make cheese, or maybe a movie montage. He loved the feeling of it, converting words to images like visual alchemy. But this meant he thought of the story in images as he wrote, and they often swam together to form something unintended. Sometimes beautiful. Sometimes not at all for children. Pedro was somewhere in between, eyes too big, too afraid of the world, a white shadow in a white landscape, looking for form and identity in a harsh world ready to erase him entirely. There was too much anxiety in it, which meant there was too much of him in it. He wanted to help children, not scare them.

Maybe if you made the eyes bigger, he thought. And laughed. His inner voice was a tyrant lately. Well, always.

"Hey, you," Alicia called from the doorway.

David resisted the urge to close the laptop or hide the screen as he turned. She was in her usual house attire: fuzzy slippers (but no silly animals), silk leggings with a skimpy top and no bra. Attractive, with no sign of her maternity weight, and she knew it. He tried not to notice or let his body respond, but then again, maybe Kiaraa had a point. It might be time for something new. He didn't think it would change anything, but maybe it would increase the time between arguments.

"Hey," he said, forcing a smile. "You up for a movie?"

She canted her side. "Jason asleep?"

"Isn't he always? I put him down. He'll be out for hours."

She pursed her lips. "Okay. I'll grab a blanket and meet you in the living room." Which was big. She wasn't a fan of living rooms, so they usually watched movies in bed. Maybe she was trying, too.

"Wine?" he asked.

"Pfft," she said. "Of course wine."

*

ALICIA SNUGGLED UP on the couch in a heavy fleece blanket, wine in hand, leaning into him as he used the remote to pick the movie. The giant TV mounted over their fake gas fireplace suddenly showed a spider web at night, strands covered in dew, but far larger than any web should be. He hit *play* as her eyes narrowed.

"You're kidding," Alicia said. "You hate horror movies. When we went to that alien invasion one, you spent twenty minutes chatting up the teenager at the concession stand."

"Wow. That was years ago, and I was offering career advice." Then, pitifully: "I got us free Twizzlers."

"An inferior product. You need Red Vines to properly drink soda."

"Granted, but...I don't know. I've been seeing these things. Remembering them." He carefully omitted any mention of his visit to see Kiaraa. "Either way, I need to face it. So I thought I'd start by facing my minor and completely normal fear of scary things."

"You're such a little girl."

"But in a sexy way, right?"

She blinked, meaning *sure*. "What do you mean, seeing things?"

"I, uh..." He trailed off, shrugged. "Let's just watch the movie. Warning: there are spiders."

Alicia studied him for a second, looking for what was amiss. She knew he was hiding something, but was it worth digging for? He waited for the question that would make him admit he'd seen Kiaraa and turn the evening into a colossal shit-show, but instead she flashed her patented friendly shark/prosecutor smile and said, "Okay."

She Spins is a about a young single father who finds a giant spider in his garage. A man who looked strangely like James, if slightly less attractive. He tries to kill the giant spider when it goes after his son, and right when they're about to slaughter each other in a wild Mexican standoff involving axes and an improvised flamethrower, it speaks:

"Wait," says the spider, sounding like a sexy librarian. "I've got an idea."

Turns out, *She Spins* is like *Dexter* meets *Charlotte's Web*. The man makes a deal to bring her bad people to eat, well, any people, but he decides on the bad part. And soon he's out patrolling the city looking for badies while the spider gets bigger and bigger. Sometimes they chat between meals and she leaves him cute messages in her giant extraneous web. He talks about his dead wife while feeding her a man's arm. It's almost flirty. And then she lays a gajillion eggs and a flood of baby spiders comes out and eats her. At the end, he's standing in his open garage facing a horde of hungry baby spiders that have run out of mother and are looking for man food.

Spiders to the left of him. Spiders to the right of him. He looks pretty tasty.

"Wait," he says.

Smash close-up on his face.

"I've got an idea."

Fade to black. Roll credits.

"Well," Alicia said. "That was disturbing." She finished her third glass of wine. "Who recommended it?"

"I just heard about it," he lied. "I know you're not a fan of spiders, but..."

"No, it was good," she lied. She hated it. Why did he think she'd like a movie about spiders? She probably only tolerated it to see which one of them cringed more.

"Look," he said. "I'm sorry I called Kathryn. I was just freaking out about Jason. You know how I get since..." *Don't say Alex. Don't say Alex.* "...Alex." *Goddamn it.* "I'm so sorry. It was a mistake. Can we get past this?"

"Of course," she said in a husky whisper, meaning *never*, but I'm going to ignore the Alex thing so we can screw and pretend. She leaned in, eyes closed, mouth open, waiting. He closed his eyes too, which was rare, and imagined the old Alicia. The Alicia he had fallen in love with within minutes at a bar as the world came apart. The Alicia who giggled when you kissed her neck and loved bubblegum ice cream. The girl who danced in elevators and couldn't handle champagne and became the mother of his son. They never considered an abortion. They wanted that baby. Their SHAS baby. Her breath tasted like yesterday.

They kissed hard, both pretending, arms grappling at clothes, mouths on skin, hands reaching and probing, warmth flooding their bodies as they pressed together.

"Wait," he said, breathless. "I've got an idea."

And he put Kiaraa's marital saving plan into action.

Burning Man

DAVID COULD NEVER SLEEP after sex. Alicia's sweat and smell felt dirty on him—sticky reminders of something unpleasant, or at least uncomfortable. As usual, he put it out of his head by waiting for her to fall asleep, showering and going to sit with Jason. He walked quietly down the carpeted hall toward his son's room, wearing only a t-shirt and underwear, relishing the feel of cool evening air on his skin, and then stopped.

There was a sound, not quite a bump, but something soft hitting a hard surface, like a pillow *phumping* against a wall. He waited, listening, but it didn't repeat. It was an old house full of strange sounds and he had an active imagination, so he didn't think much of it, or tried not to, until he got to the door of the nursery and heard it again, softer, but definitely coming from inside.

His heart beat faster as he scanned the nursery, illuminated by only a nightlight and a white lunar glow that came in striped through the curtains. Nothing moved. He stepped into the room, squinting toward the crib, and that's when he saw it: something like a long black arm, maybe an inch in diameter, with one tip on the edge of the crib. Then it moved down over Jason, and he saw a fat black body through the bars of the crib, bigger than his son. Something…

Crack.

A delicate sound, like a breaking wishbone.

David took one step toward the crib in full panic and reached down for the black thing. It had to be his imagination. It was a teddy bear or pillow or shadow. But then why did the shadow *move*? He tried not to yell, somehow worried about waking Alicia, and grabbed for it.

Get off my son!

He got his hands around the smooth, bulbous body and the room lit up like ground zero at a nuclear blast, so bright he could see through his own hands and the thing was—

*

THE HEAT WAS STAGGERING, the sun blinding and the air was screaming. David was in a vast grassland with fine green-and-gold grasses up to his knees and out to the horizon in every direction. He turned around and around, but there was nothing but grass and the impossibly loud buzz of a trillion insects.

He assumed he was dreaming, but this was new for him. His dreams usually weren't this clear.

It didn't feel like a lucid dream. It felt like he was very much awake, but that was fine. Everything was fine.

Where were you before this?

But he couldn't remember. He was just tired. So he lay down in the grass and looked up at the sky until his eyes closed and the insects drowned out everything else.

*

DAVID SAT ON THE COUCH, facing the television and scratching at the burns on his arms. He knew they didn't really itch; it was just a nervous habit, so he forced himself to stop. It felt like ants were crawling down his forearms and over his hands, but he knew the feeling would fade. When he was seven, he'd started a fire in the backyard with lighter fluid, and he'd gotten it all over himself. If Dad hadn't rushed into the yard and covered him, suffocating the fire with his body and jacket, he would have died. As it was, he had a lot of scars and a phantom itch he shouldn't scratch.

How did he get to the living room? He must've fallen asleep. It wasn't unusual. He'd check on Jason and then stay out of the bedroom to avoid waking Alicia. He just couldn't remember anything after leaving her asleep in bed. He'd showered, pulled on a shirt and walked...where?

Huh. The TV was on, but he couldn't make out the dark image. It was almost like a reflection of the living room, but not the same living room. He squinted.

What the hell?

The image brightened until he was staring at an old black leather couch in an old living room he knew very well: the one from his childhood home in Fort Collins, when they were all still alive.

"Are you okay?"

Alicia was standing by the hall in a long nightie, looking concerned or annoyed, which was the same for her.

"Yeah," he said, pretty sure he wasn't. When he looked back at the TV, the room was gone and there was nothing but black. Was he hallucinating now? That was new. He must be more tired than he thought.

"Stop that," Alicia said, sharply.

He looked down and saw that he'd rubbed his forearm raw. He hadn't even realized he was still doing it.

"Sorry." He got up and walked over, pecked her on the cheek, as required, and they walked back to the nursery. Leaning over the crib, Alicia held her hand over Jason's thin hair, barely touching it, and he could see the love in her eyes. For all the things wrong with their marriage, this wasn't one of them; she was a good mother. Loving and kind, even if tentative and rarely there.

David leaned over next to her and inhaled, trying to pull in Jason's scent, but it was mixed with the sweat on Alicia's skin and something else, a smoky background, as if there had been a fire in the room and the carpet held onto the smell. Strange he'd never noticed it before.

"Come on," Alicia whispered. "Let's not wake him."

But David didn't want to leave yet. He wanted his time alone with Jason, even if that was impossible now. She'd make him come back to bed. So he lingered, running his eyes over Jason to capture every texture and color, every pudgy fold, the color of his lips, every tiny fingernail, until he noticed something wrong. Jason was missing another pinky tip, his left. His fingers were so small it was barely noticeable, but to David, it was glaring.

"What's wrong?" Alicia asked. She must have felt him stiffen.

Something *was* happening to their son. The thought infuriated him. The virus was back, eating him from the inside, but faster than he'd ever heard of. Jason was dying like Alex and—

"David?"

He shrugged off her arm, trying to get his rage under control. He knew it wasn't the virus. It wasn't natural. Something like this didn't just happen in a few hours without him noticing. This was being *done* to him, somehow, and the only thing he could think of was Alicia. He turned toward his wife in the crepuscular light, eyes full of hate and accusations he couldn't explain, and she leaned away from him, hands rising, as if expecting a blow.

Which made him laugh. The sound caught him by surprise and he stifled the noise with his hands. Is that how stupid he looked when she hit him?

All his rage and fear drained away. Jason had always been missing those fingers. Both pinky tips and one little toe-tip. Captain Peg Pinkies. Maybe he could only count to 9.33 on his fingers, but David loved him more than enough to make up the difference. He was just tired and imagining things, so he let Alicia guide him down the hallway.

"I'll be there in second," he said, pulling away by the door to his office. He'd remembered the printed pictures of Jason and just wanted to check. He pulled the photos out of his top desk drawer and studied them under the desk light. Sure enough, Jason was missing two pinky fingertips, but one of them was blurry in all the images, like the printer had selectively smudged that part. Sigh. He'd clean off the rollers in the morning and print another copy. This one, he crumpled and tossed in the trash. On the wall, Pedro's giant black eyes watched in dilated judgment. Did they make him feel paranoid, or was that why he drew them?

As he pulled the bedcovers up and murmured *goodnight*, he thought again about how the octopus mobile over Jason's crib would look from his perspective, like a dozen colorful spiders flying through the air. He'd have to get rid of the thing, no matter how much Alicia loved octopuses. Which he thought he'd thought before. Spiders could be terrifying to children. And that made him think of the movie and the giant talking monster in the garage. He was still thinking about it when he fell asleep, where he dreamed of an endless grassland under a sea of stars so bright they looked like fireflies just beyond his reach.

Salad Days

"I have lived eighty years of life
and know nothing for it,
but to be resigned and tell myself
that flies are born to be eaten by spiders
and man to be devoured by sorrow."

- Voltaire -

Eight-Legged Freaks

IT WAS A GLORIOUS DAY, a spring day, a glorious cloudless blue-sky spring-has-sprung day. There were birds in the air, rabbits in the grass, and fresh green trees fluttering in a slight but steady breeze. It was also Sunday, grilling day, and everyone was back on the patio. Alicia's lawyer friends had new Kandinsky ears, khakis for shorts, and their son remained fixedly fixated on his phone. James and Franzia chatted with them like old friends as Charlotte rocked Jason's swing-chair next to Alicia's vacant seat. The Balasubramanians kept to themselves in the corner, not shy or asocial, but clearly focused on the food. Did they not eat at home? The girls drew mandalas with chalk on paving stones in swirls of color matching their prosthetic ears. Padme saw David watching them and waved one fingerless hand, smiling at some joke neither of them understood. He had the urge to playfully flip her off, but wasn't sure they knew each other well enough.

Kathryn was there with Leslie, holding hands like young lovers and no doubt talking about their pending adoption. Kathryn's wheelchair had new spangles on it, tastefully sparkly, but David knew she just couldn't afford the new prosthetics. He thought for the hundredth time about giving her the money, but Alicia would never allow it and there's no way he could keep it secret. Kiaraa sat beside them, and they were all smiles and laughter. He'd almost forgotten they knew each other, both personally and professionally. Kathryn had interned with Kiaraa in college at his recommendation. Funny how it all blurred, the lines connecting everyone, like a network made of sand you had to rebuild every time the wind blew part of it away. He was glad they knew each other. Good people should know good people.

He smiled, momentarily content, and refocused on his chicken. Wings, drumsticks and small breasts sizzled over the low heat. He only bought organic chicken, free range if he could find it, almost afraid of the giant dry breasts they had to grow on angry, steroidal, factory chickens with anger management issues that were debeaked to keep from eating each other. He'd rubbed them with olive oil, kosher salt and ground black pepper. Grilled and then basted them with barbeque sauce, flipped and basted again. The smell was eye-wateringly delicious.

He glanced up to see where Alicia was with the serving platter just as an indistinct shrubbery by the back fence shuddered and opened to reveal a black cat slinking into the yard. That was probably slander; the cat was just walking. Who was he to judge? The cat walked across the grass, but his legs were blurry and strange. No, not blurry—perfectly clear but eight of them, four in front, four in back. It always took his brain a second to adjust. The cat sat and preened itself like fastidious Vishnu, licking and nuzzling, shifting and lifting. Franzia was watching with a frown. Charlotte's mouth hung open.

"Hey," David called out. "Check out the spidercat."

Everyone looked where he pointed with the tongs. Then some looked back like he was an idiot. Of course it had eight legs, their eyes said. All black cats born since mid-pandemic had eight legs and traveled in packs, or whatever you called a herd of cats. No big deal. Although Franzia's eyes were so wide, you could see the empty spaces inside her head. She looked at David for consolation. David shrugged and turned back to the grill. There weren't that many regular cats left, so they should have been used to the eight-legged variety by now, but they still freaked him out and he clearly wasn't alone.

"Spidercat, spidercat," he sang tunelessly as he turned back to the grill. "Who's afraid of spidercat?"

"You know, I heard they eat other cats." Alicia said from his side. Snuck up on him again, even with Jason asleep at her hip. Was there ninja training for prosecutors?

"I heard that one too," he said, losing track of his thoughts. "But only the four-legged ones." Cats of another color. Racist cannibal spidercats. He fought the urge to scratch his scars. Everything was fine.

The cat leaped into the air and took down a hummingbird that had been minding its own business by the feeder ten feet away. Alicia caught her breath. Kiaraa clapped—by the horrified look on her face, a surprised reaction rather than celebration—and spidercat trotted away with its twitching prize, leaving a single tiny feather floating in the air where it passed. Charlotte's jaw seemed unhinged.

"Have you seen that new show on Hoopla?" Alicia asked. "It's like *Amazing Race*, but you have to eat something awful on every episode. If you're the last couple standing, you get free sushi for life."

A *clowder*, that's what you call a group of cats. What about eight-legged cannibal cats? A disturbance? Sounded about right. A disturbance in the—

"David?" Alicia asked. "How's the chicken?"

"Hoopla?" he asked, confused. He had no idea what she'd said. He lifted the lid and inhaled the hot, heavy smell of cooked meat. Everyone turned toward him with expectant faces. What did you call a group of hungry people?

Dangerous.

"Just right," he said, reaching for the serving plate. Alicia smiled and bounced Jason on her hip, left arm relaxed at her side with Zombie Hand at the end. It was a beautiful thing, sculptured ultralight elegance that almost looked real in the right light. But then the hand blurred strangely, transforming to flesh-and-blood and back again like a three-dimensional flip-book illusion.

Alicia noticed his gaze and he jerked his attention back to the grill. Too late.

"What're you looking at?" she demanded.

Hadn't she pulled the shoe out of the wall with both hands?

"Nothing." He faked a smile. "I really like that top on you." She glanced down and smiled, taking the compliment with grace that always surprised him. He was terrible at compliments, always deflecting with sarcasm or a self-deprecating joke, while Alicia acted like compliments were invented for her. And it was a lovely embroidered floral blouse with whimsically voluminous sleeves. She had a few, but not in her favorite shades of blue. It was her birthday in a few days, and now he knew what to get her.

He plated the chicken and she took it over to their expectant guests, passing Kiaraa as she walked toward him. They exchanged brutally thin smiles as they passed, reminding David of why we drive on the right side of the road—so Roman soldiers could pass each other with a left-hand shield separating them from potential danger.

Kiaraa took Alicia's place at his side, inhaling deeply.

"You smell like all the meat," she said.

"I hope that's a good thing. I hear there are bears roaming the neighborhood at night."

"Really?" Pause. "Are you upset we all came? It's Kathryn and Leslie's anniversary, so they won't stay long, but I know…"

He shook his head vaguely, but he was more worried than mad. He always loved seeing them, but in the Venn diagram of his life, Kathryn, Kiaraa and Alicia were never supposed to overlap. The same diagram applied to planets, dinosaurs and meteors. Kiaraa understood that, so there had to be a reason she'd invited Kathryn and Leslie without telling him.

"I just wanted to see you and…" She gave up trying to explain. "God, that smells good. For an ex-vegetarian, you know your way around a grill."

"I always loved grilling. I used to watch Dad in the backyard, trying to figure out how he knew when to turn things, how it never burned. He was a magician. I'm not sure he would have liked me going green."

"At least you're not a *vegan*." Like she kept threatening to be. "You miss him, don't you?"

"Every day." What was with Kiaraa and her personal questions? It wasn't that kind of grilling time.

"So," she said.

"So?" he asked. He'd never seen her so hesitant before. This couldn't be good.

"So I called in a favor and broke the law, but please don't be mad at me."

He hesitated. "For what?" Was he hopeful or scared, and why did it feel like the same thing?

"You've been in the hospital three times in the last four years…" She said this quickly with no inflection, in a low voice, like a criminal confessing her worst crime. "…with serious injuries, including a broken hand."

That you know of, he thought. He knew he couldn't trust hospitals, so he'd learned to go to other clinics and private practices when he could. Probably something he'd learned from his mother. How many doctors had she taken him or Tommy to as a kid, always changing if one asked too many questions? The older the doctor, the better, which was his own insight: less suspicion, fewer questions and computers, and no shared medical records. He didn't bother to respond, but checked to make sure Alicia wasn't watching them. She was chatting with James, of course, gesticulating madly while Zombie Hand expertly gimbaled her vodka tonic without a ripple. James nodded politely while taking massive bites of chicken. The man could eat.

"The last examining physician thought you'd been hit with a high-heel shoe," Kiaraa said, almost whispering. "Hard, and repeatedly. They were defensive wounds."

"That's ridiculous. I just fell while working in the garage." He couldn't remember what really happened. Maybe he was drinking more back then. There had been a phase after Alex died when he did most of his writing drunk.

"If you were a woman, I'd say you were experiencing intimate partner violence and refer you to a hotline to get help. Maybe suggest a safe-house. You have all the signs."

His head filled with air. The sky grayed and he almost dropped the tongs. He didn't think she noticed—the episode passed quickly—but he still felt breathless. Panic attack? He flipped a burger that didn't need flipping. No, it wasn't panic. It was relief. Astonishment. Someone had noticed. Someone had spoken, so he didn't have to. Now the idea of not being in this relationship with Alicia seemed possible, if still infinitely improbable. It felt more than a little cowardly to realize it took Kiaraa saying it to make it real, but to hell with it. He wasn't a perfect man. That didn't mean he deserved to be slapped every time he overcooked the scallops. They were scallops. Blow on them too hard and they turned to rubber.

"David?" Kiaraa's concerned voice. "Are you okay?"

"Yes," he said, which was more true than usual. "But I'm not a woman and I'm not being abused." It wasn't time to admit it yet. Not out loud. "How could you think that?"

"You moving your desk?" She glanced at his wrist. "That was bull pucky."

He chuckled at her euphemism and shook his head, trying to hold the line, but he was a terrible liar. It amazed him he'd pulled it off for this long. After a while, he'd assumed everyone knew and just pretended not to. Or maybe they didn't understand. He was bigger than Alicia, and stronger. He had all his limbs. It's pathetic that he couldn't defend himself. If someone had asked why he didn't fight back, what would he say?

"I just...." Kiaraa glanced toward Alicia, who was watching them from the corner of her eyes. There would be questions to answer later. "Whatever's going on, David, you don't have to talk to me, but I hope you talk to someone. Kathryn loves you like a brother, and I can tell she's worried. These things always get worse before they get better." Pause. "If it gets worse, don't call the police."

He glanced over. "Out of curiosity, why not?" He'd thought of befriending James for this very reason. Not the only reason, of course, but he really should have taken him up on that beer.

"Let's just say that while law's nominally gender neutral, enforcement is...uneven."

"Well, that's good to know." And not surprising. "But I'm fine. Just a little clumsy, like I said. I assume you're the Impossible meat burger? I'm not too experienced with these. How do you like it done?"

"Medium rare." She put her hand on his, careful to make sure the gesture was hidden from Alicia by the grill. "I'm sorry, David. Whatever it is, I'm sorry. I don't know how to help, but I will if you'll let me in."

She sounded like his father. *Don't worry, everything will be fine.* The lie that keeps on giving. He pulled his hand back before she could feel him shaking. The only thing that mattered now was protecting Jason from Alicia. Nothing else came close. And even if it did, well, people said they'd listen, but they were fooling themselves. Human beings are just made a certain way, and anything else is an act—learned words, like scripts we told ourselves to feel civilized. You see a woman getting slapped and you flinch in horror. You see a man being brutally beaten by a woman and you laugh and laugh because it's funny. Sometimes, he looked at himself in the mirror and laughed until he cried. It was hysterical. There was no help, not for him. There was only Jason.

But.

"You're not alone," she said, or maybe he imagined it. He wanted to scream. Instead, he carefully laid the burger on Kiaraa's towering Jenga-assembly of bun and condiments—typical vegetarian overcompensation—and glanced toward Alicia again. She was standing close, but not too close, to Kathryn and watching him with Kiaraa, wearing a tight little smile like a string to hold up her mask.

Oh, well, he thought, turning back to the grill. Kiaraa left, mumbling something he missed, and when he looked up again, the spidercat was back on top of the fence this time, looking at him with hungry eyes. Which made him wonder, if he wasn't crazy, if Jason and the rest of the world really were being eaten and all of them were just food, did it cook them first? Were they grilled meat or sashimi, or flash-fried like scallops? What was the right internal temperature for cooking a human arm or calf, man-shank or lady-flank, and did you use a marinade or rub?

The spidercat turned its focus on Franzia, who stared back with such unblinking intensity that the cat finally surrendered and dropped into the neighbor's yard. Impressive. He turned back to the burgers, each sizzling enthusiastically and just as glad to be of service as the talking cows from *Hitchhiker's Guide the Galaxy*: 'I am the main Dish of the Day. May I interest you in the parts of my body?' Sizzle and spin. Do some fancy pageant-walking to seal the deal. 'An excellent selection, sir. Ground beef, coming up.'

He snorted. Sometimes his mind went to weird places, but that was always how he escaped: sarcasm and fantasy. Which probably started with *Star Trek* when he was a kid and stuck in bed, too tired to move for months at a time. There were no angry mothers or sick children in space. Everyone was good and smart and if they weren't, they always lost. He liked that better than cartoons, where nothing had consequences. Squished things un-squished. Blown up things reassembled. In space there was risk and fear and pain, but you worked together. You were a family because you had to be.

And you had lasers.

Happy Birthday

DAVID COULDN'T PLACE HIS ANXIETY. Birthdays were always hard with Alicia. She didn't like the reminder of her mortality, or maybe that she was spending so much of it with him. And presents were a thing. Too expensive and she'd go off, pointing out that she knew he made more than she did and he didn't need to rub it in, too cheap and she'd think he was devaluing her. Too personal was risky because it was hard to interpret, too generic and she'd think he didn't care. He spent months thinking of the one right gift, looking for the safe choice, but it always came down to a last-minute panic buy. This year, finding new designer blouses in her preferred colors online had seemed like a godsend. They were her size, her style and aesthetic. She already had a few. She'd love them, guaranteed.

Except.

He'd made dinner—seared ahi, her favorite—put up balloons and bought a chocolate mousse cake that she would eat in late-night fridge binges he pretended not to notice. It was a weird game—she never gained weight and he wouldn't have cared if she had—but seemed harmless enough. There were no obnoxious candles or happy birthday songs, none of the things that set her off. But something was still amiss.

As she pulled the box across the dining room table and carefully slid off the ribbon, not tearing it off like he would, he wanted to snatch it away from her. *Not this one! That's the wrong gift.* But it was the only gift. Neither of them was materialistic. While Alicia loved her some luxury, it was more about status than volume. For personal gifts, it was the thought that counted. Allegedly. How could it be wrong?

She pulled up the top of the box, unfolded the white crepe paper, and pulled out the first blouse. It was a diaphanous blue, trimmed in topaz and turquoise, delicate as tissue and even lovelier than on the site.

"It's beautiful," she said, draping it over Zombie Hand, brushing her fingers across the silky-thin fabric and toying with the tiny buttons. So many tiny buttons.

Oh, shit.

Her smile trembled. He wanted to snatch the blouse away from her and shred it. How could he be so stupid?

"It's really beautiful, David, but I can't wear these anymore. I haven't worn the ones I have in…"

"Alicia, honey, I'm sorry. I didn't—"

Her look cut him off. Eyes were like knives, her lips a cutting board. He was screwed.

"How the hell am I supposed to fasten this?" she asked. She didn't raise her voice. She didn't need to.

"You have others, so I… I'll help you."

"Oh, that's what you like, is it? Helping me? Making me feel helpless? Reminding me how useless this is?"

She raised her prosthetic hand like an accusation, and for some reason, he thought of a movie about a man who lost his hand in a cooking accident. *I lost my hand! I lost my pride!* He almost laughed, not that it was funny, but he was beyond anxious and he knew he'd screwed up. He just didn't understand how he could be so stupid. He knew her thing about buttons. Of course she was sensitive about it. How could he have forgotten about her 'utterly fucking useless' hand? Zombie Hand was beautiful and Zombie Hand was strong, but it wasn't great at the little things.

"Babe," he pleaded, a deer frozen in the headlights. "I'm so sorry. I didn't…"

She reached over and slapped him across the face with Zombie Hand, a glancing blow that still stung. Turned out, it wasn't useless after all. His hand flew to his face, but his first thought was, *is Jason down?* Of course he was: asleep in his crib, door mostly closed and safe.

The next slap made his eyes water. Her aim was getting better.

He deflected the next blow involuntarily, another mistake. Defending himself just implied he didn't deserve it, when he clearly had it coming. Which escalated things.

He was never sure how he ended up on the floor with her straddling him, Zombie Hand raised like a blade, ready to drive through the chest of a nearly vanquished foe. The moment froze in time, recorded in perfect full-color resolution to his otherwise fickle memory, the evening light behind her the crimson radiance of a vengeful god.

He didn't even turn his head to the side. He just thought, *Pedro wouldn't take this shit*, and then she knocked him unconscious. Which was a first; Zombie Hand packed a punch.

*

DAVID WAS BACK in the grassland, but the insects were quiet. It was evening and the sky was turning red.

"It'll be okay," the air said in his father's voice.

He stood up and looked around. He was still alone.

"Who said that?"

"You know." The voice came from nowhere. David turned and searched, but there was no one else.

"Dad? Where am I?" David asked. "Am I dead?"

Because it was the only thing that made sense. Alicia had finally gone too far. He didn't think this was heaven or the spirit of his father was waiting for him somewhere just over the horizon. He'd never believed in such things. He just thought his brain was dying and this is where it decided to take him. Which meant he'd failed Jason and left him alone with Alicia.

"I'm sorry, Jason," he said. "I'm so sorry."

He would have screamed to be let out, to be revived, to live, if only for his son, but his invisible father was laughing.

*

"ON THE COUCH AGAIN," David hummed as he pressed an ice pack against his face. His jaw was screaming, but probably not broken. There was blood in his mouth—he'd bitten his tongue again—but none of his teeth seemed loose. Not bad, all things considered. Better than dying in some weird grassy purgatory while his dead father laughed at him. Except Alicia was crying. She sat on the coffee table facing him, knees between his, tears dropping freely onto her buttonless shirt. He hated sitting across from her his way; it was invasive. He wanted to knee her in the face, which he never would, but mostly he just wanted her to go away. He'd taken his beating like a good little dog. Why was she still here? He was in no condition for makeup sex.

"I'm so sorry, honey," she said, hand reaching for his knee. He jerked away. "I don't know why I get so angry."

He snorted, grimaced, tried to think of the fastest way to escape her presence.

"It's okay," he said. Just like the last time. Just like the next time.

"Really?" she asked, surprised or confirming or just playing the game.

Really? he asked himself. And for the first time, he wasn't sure. Not that it was okay or he could forgive her—there was no forgiveness in his heart—but that he could keep playing the game. Keep pretending. He saw himself growing older with her, becoming colder, quieter, losing his creativity, hiding behind Jason until Jason was too old to want him around anymore. Years of quiet indifference turning to gray, passionless nothing. Like dissolving in acid made of his own shame and regret. How could he have thought that was tolerable? Jason would grow up like him, afraid and quiet and trapped in his own skin, a two-dimensional man turned sideways to hide from the world. That wasn't what his son deserved.

"I'm so sorry, David."

She was always sorry. She always cried. At some point her boobs would come out, the answer to everything. God forbid he didn't reach for them. God forbid he make her feel unattractive. She loved her some makeup sex. Loved it long and loud and hard. *Spank me, baby!* Like she wanted them to be even. He was always surprised when his penis responded, powered by some frog-brain instinct to screw no matter what, and he couldn't tell if he felt betrayed or grateful. Being inside her was like basting meat without the hope. After his shower and visit with Jason, she'd be curled up in bed like a child, and as he got into bed next to her, quietly, careful not to wake her, he'd think for the umpteenth time about a movie with a girl who had teeth in her vagina. One wrong move and you were a screaming, dickless mess. It sounded nice.

He just couldn't do it. He couldn't do *her.* Not now, not that night, and maybe never again.

"Babe?" she asked. "Are you really okay?"

He decided he hated the word *babe.* It was just more falsely intimate four-letter fuckery.

"I'm fine," he said. God, his jaw hurt. He opened his mouth and it popped like a firecracker. He was going to need all the ibuprofen to sleep tonight. "It's not that bad." Which cracked open his lip and blood dripped onto his shirt, matching the tears on hers. He reached across and patted her good hand. "It's fine."

And strangely, it was. Because Kiaraa had seen him and now he saw himself, and he didn't like what he saw. It was time to change. It was time to *leave.* He just had no idea how to get Jason away from her. She was the lawyer. She was the mother. He knew Kiaraa was right and the system was against him—and he understood why—but there had to be a way. Maybe he could ask James.

So he nodded and stood, wobbly on his legs, and forced another smile.

"I'm going to take a shower and see about my face. Can you check on Jason?"

"Are you sure?" she said. "Maybe we should—"

"I'm sure," he snapped. He'd never been more sure of anything in his life.

*

WHEN DAVID WAS EIGHT, his father took him and Tommy camping in Rocky Mountain National Park, just south of Jackstraw Mountain. It was a nearly perfect road trip and adventure, the first one that really stuck in his mind, but not for the trees or lake, mountains or snow. Not even for hot chocolate in the morning or the pain of his feet slogging his tiny pack up the endless, stony trail below Mt. Ida while Dad alternated between carrying Tommy and dragging him along. What he remembered was the second night in the campground, all three of them nestled together in one smelly tent, Dad in the middle, while something big moved around the campground.

"What is it?" Tommy asked in a hushed whisper. There were snuffling sounds and something like a cough.

"Probably a marmot or squirrel," Dad said, just as quietly. "Everything sounds bigger at night." But even he could tell he wasn't sure. Something stomped on the ground outside the tent on his side. That was a big squirrel. David shimmied away from the tent side, that little layer of fabric that protected them from the world, and Dad pulled him even closer. Then he put his finger to his lips and turned off the flashlight.

In the sudden darkness, there was nothing but the sound of a very large something sliding across the tent fabric, a rasping slide that caught occasionally as if something sharp got stuck. Like a claw or fang. Something that wanted inside. Something hungry.

"It's okay," Dad whispered in David's ear. "Everything will be fine."

The unnamed thing pressed against the side of the tent, pushing the fabric against David's sleeping bag. Then it pulled back and the thing, whatever it was, exhaled and coughed again. He knew what it was then, and Dad did too, even if he wouldn't say it: a bear. A *big* bear. In David's mind, the biggest bear in the world. One bite and it could swallow him whole. One claw swipe would send Tommy flying into the trees. There was nothing Dad could do, and that was what scared him most; Dad, who always seemed so huge and powerful, was as helpless as they were.

Everything would not be fine.

But, somehow, miraculously, it was. The bear tired of snarfling around the tent and shuffled off into the woods. For a few minutes, all they heard was their own breathing, the rush of wind through the pines, and nylon sleeping bags sliding away from each other.

"Is the squirrel gone?" Tommy asked.

Dad burst out laughing and David did too. For a second, everything *was* fine.

And then there was a snap, loud, like a gunshot, and they froze in their bags. The sound of wind vanished and they heard something else, a dragging sound, and then another grunt or cough. The bear was back, and it had brought something with it.

"Shh," Dad said for no reason; they were all quiet. David thought he could hear breathing, fast heavy breaths, or maybe just branches rubbing against each other. The next sound was unmistakable. Something *crunched* into meat and bone and started chewing loudly, grunting and biting its way into whatever dead thing it had dragged into camp. There were loud licking sounds, and David could almost feel a giant, bloody tongue sliding over his body. Some more crunching and tearing. This went on for what seemed like hours, and the whole time, none of them spoke or moved. Even Tommy, normally a squirmy ball of energy, was petrified in his bag, though it later turned out he'd peed himself and was afraid Dad would notice.

Crunch. Lick. Grunt. Snarfle. Cough.

Hours later, or maybe just minutes, the dragging sound came back, and then there was silence. The rain fly flapped in a gust of wind. David heard Dad breathing in long, slow breaths, like he'd taught David to do when he was scared. It was Tommy who broke the silence.

"Do you think it was Mom?"

David almost laughed, but Dad was silent, frozen in his bag, until he exhaled and took us both in his arms. The bear didn't come back and everything was fine. Somehow, David never wondered why Tommy would think the bear was their mother, though that was one thing that came back to him when Tommy was dead and buried. Had she started on Tommy earlier than he realized?

In the morning, they found blood and ratty balls of short brown hair near the fire circle, and they could see where the bear had dragged a deer carcass back into the woods. Dad cleaned up so they wouldn't see it, but the smell was what David remembered. He could still smell the coppery tang of blood on the rocks. But it was a beautiful morning. The lake below them was blue and glinted in the light, like the surface was made of diamonds. And Dad made hot chocolate and eggs while telling silly stories very loudly, so everything was fine. Everything was great. Though he didn't cook the sausage.

That was twenty-eight years ago, and David hadn't thought of that trip in more than a decade. Not until he woke up in his bed next to his wife in the pitch-black to hear the same sounds he heard that night in the tent.

Crunch. Slurp. Swallow.

Well, not quite the same. There was no coughing or snarfling, but something was definitely eating something else, and there was no tent wall to separate him from whatever it was. The sounds were so close he was afraid to move an arm or finger. He was afraid to breathe.

Crunch. Crunch. Suck. Swallow. Crunch.

Teeth biting through bones. *Slurp* as blood was sucked off meat. And the hot smell of blood.

It was right next to him. Something was eating his wife. Something was chewing on Alicia's *bones*.

He snapped out of it and reached for the lamp on the bedside table. It had to be a dream. His fingers found the archaic plastic knob, pressed on the ridged surface, took a deep breath—

You're just imagining things. Don't be such a coward.

—and twisted.

*

IT WAS DAWN on the grasslands. Behind him, red light blood-tipped the grass and silenced the insects. He was sitting on the rocky beach of a lake with his toes in the water. His father sat next to him, boots pulled safely under him and away from the water. Ben Chambers hated getting his boots wet. He was in a golden plaid shirt and jeans, his usual, and he was the same age he died but lacking the hole in his head that was usually present in nightmares about his death.

Nightmares that always stopped the second that hole appeared, which was exactly where his memories ended.

"Dad?" He wanted to reach out and touch him, but was afraid to break the illusion.

"Listen," he said.

The sounds of crunching came from behind him, like lions tearing into a fresh kill. The air stank of hot blood.

"What's happening?" David asked, afraid to turn around. "I feel like I'm losing my mind."

Snap!

He winced, but the crunching stopped.

"What's happening?" he asked again.

His father rested a hand on his arm and David put his hand over it, feeling the warm, dry skin and tiny gray hairs. God, it was real. It didn't feel like a dream. It felt like him.

"You'll see," his father said.

*

"OKAY," DAVID SAID. "This again."

He was in the living room in his underwear, sitting on the couch directly in front of their TV, where his childhood living room waited to be explained. Someone had turned on the gas fire, so it whispered out a cool blue flame that snapped orange and yellow at the tips.

He shook his head. His jaw pain was almost gone. He touched it. Strange. There was no swelling and he couldn't find the cut on his lip. How did he get back into the living room? He really was losing it.

And then he remembered; something was eating Alicia. His heart jumped and adrenaline flooded his body. He almost stood and ran to the bedroom, but he couldn't seem to move. This still had to be a dream. What was on the television made no sense. He rubbed absently at the burn scars on his arm. He looked around for something that made sense. What was happening?

He squeezed his eyes shut.

Wake up, wake up, wake up.

But he knew he wasn't asleep. He'd never had dreams that could be mistaken for reality, never confused the two, and he didn't now. So he wasn't asleep. He was just insane.

On the TV, on a channel that didn't exist, was the room where he'd played chess with his father or watched Tommy throw chess pieces across the room in frustration.

Well, he thought, *at least the wall isn't covered in brains.*

Instead, there was just the old black couch in a room that didn't exist anymore. They couldn't sell the house after what happened, so the insurance company paid out to his estate, a pitiful sum that barely covered his college tuition years later, and then tore the house down. There was a park there now, with swings and a sandpit, benches and a tiny memorial to his family that omitted how they died. The warm smell of leather and sweat reminded him of his father, but how could he smell something on television?

Jason cried from the nursery and David jumped. He was in the nursery and over his son in seconds, but Jason was fine, mouth moving as he dreamed about something that probably wasn't snarfling bears or vast grasslands. David kneeled down and smelled his son's head, letting the scent fill him with quiet comfort: the best drug in the world.

He checked Jason's fingers and toes and they were all there, or as much as ever had been. His little feet kicked, but not much. He was the quietest of babies. David had no idea what they'd done to get such a perfect child. Maybe it was recompense for Alex. Even with his two missing pinky finger tips and one little toe, he was perfect. The perfect pirate baby, *har, har, har.*

When he went back into the living room, the TV was a blank black stare. He had imagined it. He had imagined everything. So why was he so reluctant to go into the bedroom?

Now that the adrenaline was gone, his limbs felt like lead. He was still a little bruised from earlier. It was hard to inhale deeply, so maybe she'd broken a rib or two. Greenstick fractures. Nothing serious. She was careful like that, well, she was careful like that sometimes.

Come on, David. Nothing's eating Alicia.

He shuffled down the hall and pushed open the bedroom door. The bedside light was still on, and Alicia was curled on her side with the covers pulled up to her chin, sleeping peacefully under the ridiculous clock. He always envied how she slept, fast and hard, without dreams or trouble. There was neither blood nor shards of chewed bone. There was no sign or smell of blood. There was just Alicia, his wife, this strange, angry being to whom he was bound, safe and sleeping and uneaten, with her Zombie Arm leaning on the bedside table.

For a second he would have denied a second later, he felt the strongest surge of disappointment.

Kathryn the Carrot

DAVID WATCHED JAMES sip an IPA from a frosty glass across the roughhewn table at the Acreage, a stylish bar filled with the young and drunk on a rise overlooking the Flatirons—massive granite slabs leaning into the western mountains like an abandoned collection of titanic arrowheads. It was a long drive for a beer, but when James called, David hadn't hesitated to say yes. Anything to get out of the house and away from reminders of Alicia. Thank god he'd found a last-minute sitter for Jason. When was the last time he had a beer with a guy? A long damn time.

James looked up and wiped his lip. "You don't like yours?"

David glanced down at his hard cider, shrugged. "Just haven't been out in a while, you know?"

James nodded. "I do. So, you sounded a bit…something…when I called. Everything all right?"

David thought about it. What he wanted to say, what he wanted to scream for everyone to hear, was that he was trapped and he wanted out, but of course he wouldn't. He'd say nothing and pretend everything was fine, and in a way that's what he truly wanted—to be around someone almost as repressed as he was, both knowing but not acknowledging it, just drinking beers and whistling past the graveyard of their marriages. Or something like that. Maybe he was seeing what he wanted, what he hoped was true, so James would be more sympathetic later on.

"Yeah…" David said, shrugging. "Just one of those days."

James held his gaze. "I'm glad you agreed to meet. It's been a while since I've gone out with one of the guys."

David took a drink of his cider, closed his eyes and felt himself relax. Was he one of the guys? That was new.

"How long?" he asked.

"Forever? Not really my scene. The guys go out after work and talk about cases. The women sit separately and talk about what assholes they are. It's like high school with bad suits and guns." He shrugged. "And I can't wait to get home to see Char anyway." He took a sip. "And Franzia," he added quickly. "How's Jason doing?"

Not Alicia, David noticed. Did he know too? If so, maybe he could talk to him without really mentioning specifics. Something about how cops respond to domestic violence calls from abused men. You know, *subtle*. He had the feeling he could trust James. He felt the connection, the bond between them, even if it was eighty percent desperation.

"David?"

"Sorry." David took a long drink. "Jason's great. Happy, healthy and unbelievably cute."

James smiled broadly. "Right? We do have good-looking kids."

David smiled, thinking about Charlotte entertaining Jason with her missing pinkies. Jason's bright and happy laugh. They were undeniably cute together. He looked around the open room full of picnic-table seating filled with young couples and families, kids tearing into sliders, parents chewing on short ribs and long brats, everyone smiling or trying and oblivious to the fear and hate he assumed they all hid inside. It was a great illusion, like an expressionist painting of *people pretending to be perfect*. He tried not to think of the men who beat their wives, kids who tortured their siblings, those on the verge of bankruptcy, having affairs, thinking of killing their in-laws or poisoning the neighbor's parrot, all chewing and spitting and laughing like—

"David?"

David snapped out of it. That was a dark moment. "Sorry," he said. "How did she like the ears?"

"Loved 'em. Now she's wearing different ones on each side. She has devil ones that are a little weird, but they make her laugh every time."

That's right. Charlotte was missing both ears. He'd almost forgotten.

They talked about their kids, their work, places they'd been, things they wanted to do, and for a half-hour or so, the world seemed normal again. Just two dads shooting the shit over beers. James told him he'd once been a competitive triathlete. David told him he'd thought of being a guitarist before the writing took off, a skill learned while singing terrible songs with Kathryn. It was a much easier market now that everyone was missing fingers. They laughed too long at that, and David decided he might actually have a male friend. His first one since, well, if he was honest, his first one ever.

"This place is great," James said, sitting back. "But we probably need to get home."

The eastern sky was dark, and the mountains glowed red and purple to the west. The dinner crowd was filling the window tables. David had the lightest buzz, more like a tickle in the back of his mind, and felt something like…happiness. Not real happiness. Not joy or ebullience or anything you'd make a movie about. Just a nice loose feeling where his acidic stomach usually was.

"Do this again sometime?" he asked as they shook hands on the street and David fought an urge to hug the man.

"Soon," James said. "I mean it. You headed home?"

"No, I'm going to get Jason from the sitter and go see Kathryn at the hospital."

"Kathryn?" James asked.

"Kathryn Thorn," David said. "From…" He frowned. He knew they'd met. Hadn't they met?

"Sorry," James said, looking uncomfortable. "I don't know who that is."

Of course he didn't know. Kathryn had been in the hospital for years. How could they possibly have met? And yet David had a clear memory of James pushing Kathryn's wheelchair over a hump in the backyard. A wheelchair she'd never had in a yard she'd never seen. What the hell was wrong with him?

"My bad," David said, forcing a smile.

By the time James got in his black 4Runner and drove away, David's happy feeling was long gone. He stood at the side of the road as the sky turned black and the stars winked on, as his body shook and the cold seeped into him, and he wondered if maybe, just maybe, he really was losing his mind. It was a disturbing thought, but then again, if he was taking a trip to the loonies, he hoped he'd pick a better fantasy life for himself. Maybe something with polar bears.

*

KATHRYN WAS DYING. Of course, she'd been dying for a long time—she was by far the longest-term SHAS end-stager in the hospice—but the longer he stayed away, the more he saw the signs. She was thinner, paler, with more of everything you wanted less of and less of everything that mattered. David sat in the rock-hard chair in her room at the clinic for those 'on the cusp,' basically a storage facility for those so consumed by the disease they couldn't function in society and no one could take care of them at home. Sometimes they called them vegetables, which wasn't right because they were rarely in a coma (as if that was the problem with the label), but they'd taken to calling Kathryn "the Carrot" due to her hair, and it didn't bother him as much as it might have otherwise. He'd called her Carrot-top when they were kids, and it was her team nickname when she ran at CU. Maybe it was the intent that mattered, or who said it.

"Hey, Carrots," he said. He bounced Jason on his knee and pulled him closer to the bed. Kathryn was in one of the oldest parts of the hospital, the wing reserved for conscious end-stagers, thinking, aware, but utterly helpless and often ignored. He tried to visit her every month, or more, but it was hard despite Alicia's reluctant permission; even Alicia couldn't be jealous of a woman who wouldn't survive without constant medical support.

Jason drooled, and David wiped his face. More drool. More wiping. Still more drool, and that was just how it was going to be. Some days were drool days. He wished he could've gotten their regular sitter to keep Jason longer, or even a nanny, but the one girl (Olivia, he thought, but he wasn't sure) they'd liked months ago had died of SHAS, suddenly, which is to say she'd vanished. Fast-moving SHAS was like the rapture; one day, you just walked in and the person was gone but their clothes were still there. No flesh or bone left, nothing but questions where there had once been a person. People called it being *vacated*, like they'd just checked out of a hotel one night. They'd always made do with sitters, but last-minute scheduling was nearly impossible. And it wasn't like he minded; he was so paranoid about Jason's missing fingers and toes, he could hardly stand to let him out of his sight.

David rested a hand on Kathryn's shoulder and told her how much he missed her. Her only response was a smile. Thank god she still had her lips. No teeth or tongue—he could never understand what SHAS did with the teeth—but perfect lips.

"Say hi, Jason." Jason burbled and smiled. Kathryn smiled more.

David wiped his eyes and tried to keep any sadness out of his voice. One thing she had left was hearing.

"Hah aah ooo?" Kathryn asked. *How are you?* She had few vocal chords left. No eyes, outer ears, arms or legs. It was hard to look at her.

"I'm great," he said, like he always said. No matter how bad he felt, he knew she had it worse.

After high school and a two-year break (where she'd worked and trained and he'd flirted with homelessness), they'd gone to the same junior college and then CU Boulder. David played intramural sports, but Kathryn was a nationally ranked track star, blazing in the 5,000-meter races and being recruited hard by Division I schools. And then she got sick.

One day David had come back from his appointment with Kiaraa, who he still found strange and off-putting but at least honest. She didn't try to tell him he was wrong or right, but only tried to help him understand what his dreams about Tommy meant and how to live with them. Kathryn interned with her when she wasn't running, and having the two of them to talk to was making a difference. For once, he felt not necessarily safe, but less afraid.

When he got back to his apartment, there was a message from Kathryn. She'd checked herself into the hospital and they'd sent her to the quarantine wing, suspected of having SHAS, which, at the time, was thought to be caused by a mutated form of the same group A Streptococcus that caused other flesh-eating disorders. Which was wrong, like every other suspected carrier, but that didn't change the outcome.

"No, no, no…" he said to himself, calling the number she'd left. Kathryn couldn't have SHAS. She was healthy and ate organic and how could she be sick?

"Intensive care," the nurse answered. He sounded tired.

Intensive care? "Hi, my name's David Chambers. I'm trying to reach Kathryn Thorn."

"Just a second. Oh, here…are you family?"

"I'm her brother," he said. Which was true in every way that mattered.

"Different last names?" the nurse asked, not buying it. "She can't talk now. The doctor's in with her. If you want to talk to her, you'll have to call back in the morning."

"Is she okay? Just tell me she's okay."

A long sigh. "I'm sorry, Mr. Chambers. I really can't say anything."

David had taken a rideshare to the hospital and spent the night in the hospital lobby, as close as they'd let him get to the ICU in the quarantined section. There were so many people there, all asking questions about their families. All getting nothing. He stayed that day. Then that night, another day, and another night, and finally a doctor came out just to get rid of him. He could still remember her, a heavyset Black woman with tired eyes and a shell necklace that made him wonder if he'd ever see the Caribbean.

"I'm sorry," she said, and then he just broke down and cried. Not because Kathryn was dead, but because he knew she wasn't and she'd never run again, and how was that fair?

No one really understood how the virus worked. It ate away at you like a flesh-eating virus, but strategically, keeping you alive, one limb or extremity at a time and then working inward, but it left no outward sign, no bleeding, no wounds. A person just got smaller, reduced, until they reached some lesser size and it stopped. Or it didn't and the virus finally took something they couldn't live without. It stopped at Kathryn's inner ears. She could hear and move her head, kind of whisper, but it even took her stomach muscles. She was a head and torso now, with pretty token lips, though they had given her very nice glass eyes.

"Hah aah ooo eee-eee?" she said from the bed—*How are you really?*—straining to get the sounds out. Someday they'd have the money for the new computers that could interpret brain patterns and help her speak, but they were in such high demand it was hard to even get on a list. A guy down the hall named Rothman had one, but refused to share. Arms and legs and ears they could do, easily, cheaply, but not simple human speech. It made no sense.

"Good and bad. I'm thinking of leaving Alicia," he blurted. Jason hiccupped in surprise. Kathryn's mouth opened in an 'Oh' and then she smiled and nodded vigorously. Well, vigorously for her.

"I've been saving up for a while." Which was kind of true. He'd been stashing money in a private bank account, largely so Alicia wouldn't get irritated about how much more he made than her, so the money was there. "And Kiaraa is going to help me." Was that hope in his voice? Couldn't be.

Kathryn smiled and nodded more. He wished he could take her with him, some place better than this shithole warehouse for lost souls, and his smile faded. He knew she wanted to die. He had tried to get legal permission to let her die with some dignity, but it wasn't that kind of state since most death-with-dignity statutes were repealed, and he didn't have that kind of power. So she was here and she'd never be the social worker she wanted or the athlete she hoped or anything but this lonely stub of the person she was meant to be. He hated it.

"Well, I brought a new book." He pulled out the third book in The Expanse series, *Abaddon's Gate,* and flipped open to the first page, just out of Jason's grabby reach. He hoped she still liked science fiction, but he wasn't sure if she'd tell him if she didn't. When they were younger, they'd both liked the hope of it, the idea that things could be bigger and better than their little world.

"'When he'd been a boy back on Earth…'"

David read aloud as Jason grabbed for the book and his attention. He read to her about the wonders of space, alien technology and human politics for an hour, stopping now and then to help her sip some water, and until he had to change Jason and his eyes blurred too much to keep going. God, he wished he could talk to her. Instead, he shifted Jason to his other leg and ran his hands through her bright red curls, the liveliest part of her, and hummed one of the morbid Irish ballads she'd sung to him (out of tune, of course), when they were first in care and they both had mommy issues to work through:

About a maid I'll sing a song
Sing rickety-tickety-tin
About a maid, I'll sing a song
Who didn't have her family long
Not only did she do them wrong
She did every one of them in, them in
She did every one of them in

Her mother she could never stand
And so a cyanide soup she planned
Her mother died with a spoon in her hand
And her face in a hideous grin, a grin
Her face in a hideous grin

And when at last the police came by
Her little pranks she did not deny
To do so she would have had to lie
And lying she knew was a sin, a sin

Lying, she knew was a sin

They left out all the verses about brothers and sisters and a dozen more they'd found over the years, and as he trailed off, he noticed Kathryn looked almost happy. He wondered if the song reminded her of being young, being able to sing or something else. How did you spend day after day of darkness without going mad?

"I miss you," he said. She was his best friend and, for many years after he lost his family, his only friend. He missed her like a limb.

He had the sudden urge to tell her about the dreams and the strange clock and ask her if he was the one losing his mind. *Something's eating Jason*, he wanted to say, *but no one believes me*. He wanted her to have eyes so he could show her the scars on his arms and Jason's missing pinky fingers and toe and try to explain why they hadn't been missing before when clearly they had.

"What…" He shook his head as the room spun, clutching onto Jason so he wouldn't drop him. The book fell closed in his lap. He was suddenly back at the spidercat barbeque, serving Kiaraa her fake burger, looking over the grill at Kathryn. Kathryn in a wheelchair with a hamburger half-eaten on a plate in her lap, talking with Leslie and checking her watch as Charlotte ran frantic circles around the yard.

"Leslie," he said out loud. Kathryn caught her breath. "You were going to go out with Leslie. It was your anniversary. You were going to adopt because…" Because the only things she'd lost was a finger in college and her uterus much later. Her SHASterectomy. Not that that was a little thing, but it wasn't all of this.

He shook his head and the memory was gone.

Kathryn was never at the barbeque. She never left that hospital in college, not really.

And who the hell was Leslie? There was no such person.

"Kathryn, I'm sorry. I'm tired. I don't know…" he trailed off, surprised. Kathryn was crying, tears running from under both glass eyes and dripping onto the pillow. He didn't even know she could cry. "Kathryn. What do I do?" Why was she crying? Was it the idea that she had a date with some girl, or that she could adopt a child? How could he say such cruel and impossible things?

"I uuu huh," she said.

"I'm sorry, Kathryn. I don't understand."

"I uuu huh," she said again, and then he understood. *She loved her.* She loved a woman that didn't exist. She was finally losing her mind, or maybe she was so lonely she'd believe anything. David wanted to punch himself for being so irresponsible and stupid—his jaw didn't hurt at all anymore, so he was ready for another round—but he put his hand on her shoulder and cried while she cried and Jason drooled as if everything was just fine.

"Ehh-eee," she said, again and again. *Leslie.* "I uuu huh ooo uuu…" *I loved her so much.*

*

DAVID PLUGGED ALICIA'S AUGMANITY TECH fully automated, third-generation, machine-learning-enabled prosthetic arm, aka Zombie Arm, into the USB port on his laptop and waited for the customization interface to appear on screen. He checked his phone again. Still no number for anyone named Leslie. No record Kathryn had ever known anyone by that name. He scratched at the scars on his arms, half expecting them to just peel off like fake laminates, part of some bizarre illusion. Because something was wrong. How could Kathryn have remembered someone who didn't exist? That was no planted memory, no hypnotic suggestion; she clearly remembered loving someone they'd never met. He wasn't even sure how he knew the name, or if he'd just imagined it.

Zombie Arm pinged for attention and he looked up.

"Manufacture date," he said. The date came up, years ago, which wasn't helpful; it could have been in a warehouse.

He glanced at Pedro's watchful eyes and felt a chill. The walls were watching.

"First interface date with Alicia Chambers."

Instead of answering directly, the computer displayed a change log, showing every date and time from manufacture to purchase, right up to bonding to Alicia's shoulder implant and her detachment of the arm to take a shower ten minutes ago. She didn't have to take it off—it was waterproof and rated down to thirty meters—but it was too valuable to take the risk.

He looked up and listened. The shower was still running. Alicia loved long showers after her runs.

The date log showed she'd had the arm for years, and the ID of the prior version it had replaced.

He closed his eyes and tried to remember seeing her arm. What always came back was violence. That time she'd hit him. The time she'd kicked him. Pulling the shoe out of the wall. Then, grabbing bacon off the counter and tossing it from hand to hand.

Ouch-ouch-ouch.

Why would hot bacon hurt a synthetic hand? Was that a programmed response?

And then that memory faded as if purged. He opened his eyes and caught his breath. Something was very wrong.

The change log updated, showing a new entry: a location request from thirty seconds ago. He turned and Alicia was at the door in a towel, scratching at the stump under her shoulder and picking at the implant where the arm mounted. Just like he scratched his arm—like a habit she hadn't learned to break because it was new but couldn't be.

But it was her eyes that concerned him. Calm, watching, like rage preserved in amber. He unplugged the arm and held it out to her, fighting the urge to apologize. She walked in and let it attach itself without taking her eyes off him.

Behind him, the computer pinged with each update.

Zombie Arm is home! Zombie Arm is happy!

He refused to drop his gaze. He wanted to scream at her. The world was broken. Kathryn was dying. He was losing his mind. And he was done with her. He was taking Jason. There was nothing she could do to stop him.

But.

And it was the weirdest but.

He didn't hate her, not completely. It wasn't that simple. And that was the first time he knew you could feel hate and love at the same time, wrapped around each other, layer after layer melted together by seething fury until there was just heat and it burned. It burned to look at her.

"David?" Her voice trembled. "I'm sorry about…" She reached for him with the fake arm and he recoiled.

There was a spark in her eyes. The point of ignition.

"How long have you had that arm?" he asked, ignoring the danger.

Her hand dropped back to her side. "What?"

"How—"

"You bought it for me. You even got the pearl inlay." Pause. "How was your man-date with James?"

"Good," he said. Was she jealous or afraid of losing control? "So, you've had the arm…"

"It was an anniversary gift. How could you forget that?"

"So, two years ago this May?"

"Yes." She nodded, clearly trying to work out where this was going.

"No," he said. "You had your real arm just the other day." He knew he shouldn't say it, but he couldn't stop. "You had a prosthetic hand, but—"

"Oh, for fuck's sake," she said, rolling her eyes. "Not this crap again. You think I'm eating myself now?"

He snorted at the unintentional sexual imagery. That would solve a lot of problems.

"No, you're not eating yourself." But something was, right? Isn't that what he really believed? "Never mind." She clearly had no idea what he was talking about, and it didn't matter. Whatever was wrong with the world, the Dave & Alicia show was coming to an end.

"Why are you smiling like that?" she asked.

"I was thinking of the night we met. How we ran into each other at that bar, drunk, unmasked, risking SHAS for a few moments of freedom. Five minutes sooner or later and we never would have talked."

"Oh, that's..."

He knew the next word, *sweet*, treacly sweet, and he almost laughed out loud; he wasn't smiling because they'd met. He was smiling at all the other universes where they hadn't met or they hadn't fallen in love, a trillion-trillion possible versions of himself that never knew the shape a high-heel shoe left on your temple. And even because he was this one David in this one timeline and he was going to save his son. He was finally going to act instead of being acted upon. There would be no more Tommys, no more Dads, no more moments wishing he'd *done* instead of *been*. He smiled so broadly he must have looked like a clown, the unrepentant freak that he was. He kept smiling until the fire died in her eyes and she looked away, and then he smiled even more.

When Alicia had left, David turned off the Augmanity activity log—it felt invasive, like he was tracking her around the house—and turned in his chair. Pedro eyes. Doorway and more eyes. Bookshelf and family photo. Desk and Pedro eyes and Jason print-outs and other scribbles. Around again, and again, until he came to a stop looking at the photo of him with his dad and Tommy in the woods. Even that felt wrong, and it wasn't just the phantom hand of his mother or what happened to them a few years later. There was something wrong with the world. Or with him.

Because it was far more likely he was crazy than that something was eating Jason or anyone else. Infinitely more likely he was losing his cheese under stress than that Kathryn really remembered someone who didn't exist. Leslie was a common name. He couldn't be sure what Kathryn had actually said. And god knows she might be dealing with her own crazy, stuck in that room all day and night while her body shrank around her.

The only thing he was sure of was that it was time to get out.

Crazy or not, he had to get away from Alicia.

And now that it seemed possible, he couldn't stop thinking about it. There was a world out there without her, without being insulted or beaten every day. A world with friends and family and a real life. Something he'd only fantasized about until now. He wanted it so badly he could taste it.

He picked up his phone and scrolled down to Kiaraa's number.

His finger trembled millimeters from the screen.

If he did this, there was no going back. Alicia would find out. There was no hiding it. Alicia probably had a tracking app on his phone. Meaning another one. He could never get them off as fast as they appeared.

He took a deep breath and closed his eyes, imagining Jason as a grown man who knew how to smile without lying.

He glanced at his father's picture.

It'll be okay, he whispered. His usual lie that maybe wasn't.

He hit *dial* and listened to it ring.

Please, please, please.

Her voicemail picked up. "You've reached the office of Dr. Kiaraa…"

She wasn't there, so it wasn't too late. He could just hang up. Why was he shaking so badly?

"…please leave a message." Silence. A vacuum waiting to be filled.

He inhaled and closed his eyes again.

"Hi, Kiaraa." *Oh, Jesus.* "This is David. I need to talk."

The Clock Strikes Back

JAMES ANSWERED THE DOOR in trim-fit black velour jammies and flip-flops, with Charlotte standing behind him, arms wrapped around his leg and peering out from under an unruly puff of tightly curled hair. James looked like a fashion model waiting for makeup. Charlotte looked like a cute but normal human child. David felt like an idiot. He should have called first. He shouldn't have come at all. Maybe he could crawl inside himself and roll away like a potato bug.

"Morning, David." James smiled, all white teeth and warm welcomes. "What's up?" Then he eyeballed David's hands, in which David nervously clutched a Tupperware container of baby blueberry muffins (nervous baking) and a laminated flyer (nervous social networking) in his sweaty palms (nervous existence).

"Sorry to come over without calling," David said. "I'm on the way to an appointment." To tell Kiaraa he was leaving Alicia, taking Jason with him, and hopefully not getting beaten to a pulp in the process. And maybe come out of it with his finances intact, or maybe not, but either way—

"No need to apologize. Are those for us?" James' stomach growled loudly. They laughed and Charlotte giggled. That broke the tension.

"Yes." David handed over the muffins. Charlotte snagged them and ran back into the house.

"Save some for me and your mother!" James called after her.

"Some of what?" she called back.

James turned back, chagrined. "Well, they smell delicious. You okay? You look…"

"Yeah, yeah, I'm fine. Just a little amped on coffee, I guess." He hadn't had a drop. "I'm having a book signing next week at Barnes & Noble." James took the offered flyer. "I thought maybe you or Franzia could bring Charlotte? Love to see you there, and there could be free—"

"Yes. Absolutely. She'll love it. I mean, we'll love it. We all love your books."

"Really?" David blinked, surprised. "I mean, I understand if you're on duty or whatever."

"No, consider it done. We'll be there."

"Great," David said, feeling like a kid who just asked the popular girl to prom. It was ridiculous. "Well, you better go rescue your muffins."

"Soon enough. Where are you off to?"

"Nowhere important." Why did he have a sudden urge to tell James everything? "Have a great day. I'll see you at the signing."

"Okay, see you. Call me for another beer if you want."

The door closed. That went better than expected.

Then his eyes locked on a spidercat watching him from the branch of a white oak in the neighbor's front yard. No, two cats, then another. Three mutated black cats stared at him without blinking as he turned and walked back to his car.

"You lookin' at me?" he asked, loudly, trying to sound as tough as Robert De Niro in *Taxi Driver* while his voice cracked and he stifled a cough. One spidercat chewed methodically on a mouse, tiny tail twitching as it hung from its mouth like an errant noodle. Chew. Crunch. Stare. The tail very slowly disappeared.

That wasn't ominous at all.

*

DAVID FIDGETED ON KIARAA'S COUCH, folding a leg, tossing an arm over the back, deciding that was too comfortable, folding another way, and then somehow ending up slumped down like a mopey teenager. His hands fussed in his lap, beyond his control. The octopus clock ticked, watching him with a big black eye full of watery wisdom as he fought the urge to run. This was a terrible idea, but he'd gotten a sitter and Alicia would know he was out, so no matter what, he was going to face some questions.

He glanced at the table next to Kiaraa's chair. Her container of muffins sat there, untouched. Didn't she like muffins? Who didn't like baby blueberry muffins? *That* was crazy. Maybe this was a bad idea.

"You're nervous," she said.

He trapped a sarcastic *no shit* behind tight lips. This was a big day. This was the first day of his plan to escape, to run away with Jason, to somehow end up somewhere in a life where no one kneed him in the groin for overcooking scallops. Fucking scallops, hemophiliacs of the kitchen, easily wounded, hypersensitive mollusks that he called *resting bitch meat* and Alicia called *heavenly* unless they were chewy and then *bam*, knee to the balls. Okay, that was melodramatic. She never went for the genitals. That would get in the way of making up later.

Octo-clock octo-ticked and he grimaced. It was too much like being at home in bed, which was too much like being in prison, which was—

"David?"

He exhaled dramatically. "Sorry."

"You don't have to be sorry."

"Sorry."

She smiled. "On the phone, you sounded a little, let's say, excited."

"Excited?" That was a nice word for terrified. "At the barbeque, you mentioned…" God, it was hard to say it out loud. "…it was hard for a man to go to the police in cases of domestic violence."

She nodded. "Hard and dangerous, yes."

"Why?"

Kiaraa cleared her throat, as if getting ready for a great lecture, and maybe she was. "Most police forces are trained to respect domestic violence against men as much as women, but in practice it doesn't always work that way. Women, many of them, know if they claim it was the man who was violent, they're more likely to be believed. It ends up in a *he-said-she-said* situation where men rarely win."

"Because men are usually the abusers."

"Most often, yes, but not as often as you might think. From what I've read, around forty percent of all violent domestic abuse is by women against men—though that's highly contentious and could be higher or lower—but men are of course stronger and thus more lethal. Are you being abused, David?"

"Um…" He inhaled and glanced at the clock to see how long he'd been there—just a nervous twitch—but the clock wasn't there. Well, it was there, but *there* was somewhere else. The clock was several feet farther away, close to the far corner of the room. He frowned critically. This wasn't normal clock behavior.

"Yes?" he asked. He meant to say *yes*, affirmatively, committing to it, but the clock threw things into question. Was he just crazy? What if he was imagining all of it, the eating and the beatings? No, Franzia had seen the bruises. So had Kiaraa. That's why he was there. "Yes," he said, trying to sound more certain.

He blinked and the clock was now in front of the bookshelf behind Kiaraa, hanging from nothing like a hover clock. Was that a thing? Maybe Dyson had redesigned clocks so they looked at you instead of the other way around. *The first octopus clock that doesn't lose facial suction.* He wiped his eyes and tried not to giggle.

"How long has it been going on?" she asked.

"Is this private?" he asked. "Just between us?"

"Unless you're in imminent danger, or planning self-harm or violence of your own, yes."

Planning violence of my own, David thought. Strange that it never occurred to him. Dad had kept a gun in the bedroom to protect them from violence. That hadn't worked out so well.

"Since just after Alex was born," he said.

"Alex?" Kiaraa looked confused. "I thought your son's name was Jason."

That's right. He'd stopped making his yearly appointments right before the first pregnancy, another thing Alicia hadn't approved of—*What are you saying to her? Do you talk about me? You're talking about me, aren't you?*—and gone only once since then when, if he recalled correctly, he'd talked primarily about new book ideas.

The clock had moved further to David's right, like it was trying to sneak behind Kiaraa and run away.

"Our first son was Alexander, named after Alicia's grandfather," he said. "He was born about three years before Jason." He inhaled, exhaled. "We don't talk about it much." At all, ever. "The pandemic got him. Every day, he was missing something new and then..." He just dissolved before their eyes. It was like cutting into his own guts, it hurt so much to even think about. "...he died. The hitting thing started after we brought Alex home."

"I'm so sorry, David. I had no idea. Do you know why it started, the abuse?"

Good damn question. Had Alicia always been this way and he'd missed it, or had he sought it out somehow, looking for a woman like his mother? All he knew was the pregnancy was harder than anyone expected—brutal, exhausting, and afterward she was depressed and tired. They both were. Alex wasn't like Jason. He was a crying-screaming-crapping demon who only slept in the wreckage between tantrums. But Alicia was still the Alicia he loved, and they were figuring it out together until he screwed up a diaper change.

The clock had moved again, another foot to his right.

"Diapers were hard with Alex because, you know, no legs. Even custom ones for amputees were a challenge. I couldn't get this one diaper to stay in place. Alicia was hovering over me, and I was nervous because she was better at it than I was. And then Alex peed on her." Which was an understatement; a laser of urine shot from his son's loins, blasting her in the face. Went right up her nose. "I laughed." He couldn't help it, but then he focused on getting the laser cannon under wraps. "When I was done, I picked up a hand towel and turned to help her clean up. And she hit me in the face with a book." A hardcover tome on parenting, *Perfect Parenting for*

Imperfect People—three hundred pages of hardcover drivel smashed across his left cheek with a slap so loud it surprised Alex into a rare moment of silence.

"You think this is funny!" Alicia had screamed, and then she hit him again, and again, and that was how he ended up in the hospital the first time with a broken cheekbone. Fell down the stairs, he said. Got to fix that light in the basement, he said. Nobody asked or cared. They didn't have a basement. It was weeks until he could chew without pain.

The clock was another foot to the right, blocking Kiaraa's *Silence of the Lambs* nook.

"Anyway, that's how it started. Alex was dead three months later."

"I'm so, so sorry, David. About all of it." She exhaled, showing more emotion than usual during a session. "Have you ever fought back?"

The clock was directly behind her head, octopus legs spread above her hair like an aquatic tiara. She looked like the cephalopod Statue of Liberty. He knew what she was asking; had he ever hit her?

"No," he said. Was the clock glowing? Her hair lit up like an angelic halo. "I've never hit anyone." He was a terrible wingman in a bar. If you got hit standing next to David, you got hit and that was end of it. It wasn't that he was a coward or pacifist; he just found physical violence so strange that he couldn't take it seriously. "Oh, except that one guy, well, you know. John?" He could barely remember the kid's name—just some asshole homophobic teenager who went after Kathryn in high school. David had lost it and blacked out. Done some things he regretted and almost went to jail for, or juvy, whatever you did with sixteen-year-olds.

"I remember," Kiaraa said, because of course she did; she was his court-appointed psychologist. That's how they'd met. "But nothing since then?"

"No, nothing. Ever." He still couldn't believe that much anger lived inside him, but inside is where it stayed, no matter how much Alicia tried to drag it out into the open. At first, her lesser beatings were oddities, things he looked at from outside his body with a sense of bemusement, but that just encouraged her. She wanted to see his pain, and eventually she did. It was amazing how much damage she could do with skinny arms and boney knees. Thankfully, she'd never engaged Zombie Arm's defensive mode, though that was probably more of a legal liability issue given the prosthetic's cloud-archived activity logs.

"We don't have to talk about this now, or ever, but it would be good to examine why."

"Why?"

"Why you let it happen."

"You think this is my fault?"

"No," she said, surprised. "*Never.* But I've known you a long time. You have a habit of…"

"Tolerating the intolerable? Playing peacemaker? Trying to fix broken things?"

"…blaming yourself for things that aren't your fault."

"True," he said. No denying that. "But what's that got to do with Alicia?"

The clock throbbed like an impatient heart, pulsing yellow-and-white. Kiaraa was queen of the rave.

"Sometimes we punish ourselves for things we've done, or not done. Or we let others do it for us."

He didn't ask himself what he was punishing himself for; the answer was obvious even if he'd never admit it.

"Let's table that for now," she said.

He nodded and the clock face lit up like the sun.

"Let me tell you what I think we should do."

Her hair was golden fire. Was this really happening?

"First, we'll need to document all of your hospital visits, clinical check-ins and how you got your injuries. This isn't something I've done before, but before you talk to an attorney or anyone else, we'll need to create as much supporting documentation, including pictures, as possible. Did you keep pictures of your injuries?"

"No." Well, not all of them. There were pictures from the hospitals. A few others from gatherings where you could see his bruises beneath makeup or skewed shirt collars. She got careless sometimes. "I mean, some, yes." When he finished the last sibilant and the *yes* was stretched out in the space between them, the clock's octopus legs vanished and he realized he couldn't move. Not his hands or his arms, feet or mouth. The only things that worked were his eyes.

There was a movie he'd seen years ago about a young Black man trapped by a white woman in a chair, hypnotized, thrown out of his body and down into the basement of himself. What was the name of that movie? His brain wasn't working. He just knew he didn't like the feeling. It was like being pinned under an immovable object, claustrophobic, breathless and helpless as a child.

"Okay, get those together," Kiaraa continued, oblivious to the clock or his paralysis, "but make sure Alicia doesn't know what you're doing. Don't tell her you're thinking of leaving. Don't change anything in your behavior or patterns. That's important. And…"

David was so grateful for Kiaraa's help and the fact that she'd clearly read up on how to handle his case. He really wanted to pay attention. But her voice faded to a distant subterranean echo full of hollow droning sounds. The light was gone, but there was something on the arm of her chair, a blur, like a desert mirage where superheated air made the cacti dance. The blur moved over her right hand, and then parts of her fingers disappeared. There was blood and bone, shreds of skin, but all trapped inside the blur.

What the hell?

His eyes snapped back to Kiaraa's, but she hadn't noticed that something was ripping her hand apart.

"I know you're a friend of Franzia's detective husband, James? Yes, James. It would be ideal if you can trust him and get some inside information on how the system works when a man comes in, but I doubt it'll come to that…"

Kiaraa! he screamed in his mind. Her hand was gone now to the wrist and blood dropped on the floor *pit-pit-pat,* but she still didn't notice. *Kiaraa!*

"That reminds me, I have a friend over at the women's shelter. Maybe I can ask her. Anyway…"

The blur moved faster now, working its way up her arm. Kiaraa's forearm was gone in seconds, shirtsleeve and all, then her upper arm to the shoulder. Blood splattered on the dour beige lampshade on the table next to her, coating the blueberry muffin container, and then somehow the shoulder skin closed up on itself and the bleeding stopped. It was as if a skilled butcher had tied off the end of a sausage. It looked just like one of Kathryn's stumps.

This isn't happening, he told himself. It's just like the dream that something was eating Alicia but nothing was eating Alicia but then where was her arm she used to have an arm or how else did she hit me and what about Kathryn?

Oh my god, Kiaraa. It's eating your foot.

"You know what I'm going to do? I'll make a checklist. I love checklists. I know it's compulsive—self-diagnosed, of course—but I really think it'll help when…"

Her leg was gone at the knee, then her thigh, until there was just bone and muscle, and then it sealed up again, skin growing over the stump like it had always been there, and the blur moved to her other foot. Where the hell were the clothes going? Was it eating her shoes? And what was it? What the hell was eating her?

"I'm just guessing, but I think if you're willing to work on this for a few weeks, again without breaking your daily routine, we can be ready to do something within a month. Maybe two at the outside. I know it's hard to stay in the house, and you're worried about Jason, but if you take him now, you could look like a kidnapper, but…"

Both of her legs were skin-covered stumps when the blur moved to her right arm.

Kiaraa, please, please, why aren't you seeing this?
Because it's not real!
But what if it is?

When her other arm was gone, he thought it was over. Kiaraa was a quad amputee now, just like Kathryn, like little Alex when he came home, and that's when David got it, all of it, like a small bomb detonating in his cerebellum. There was no pandemic or SHAS. There was no disease. Something *ate* Kathryn. Something ate Alex. Something was eating all of them. And that same something had eaten Jason's fingers and toes.

Jason.

His mind locked on his son's name and for a second he forgot all about Kiaraa and the octo-blur eating her, Alicia and the world of limbless people.

Jason.

Whatever this was, why ever it was eating them, he had to save his son. Alicia didn't matter anymore. *He* didn't matter anymore. He just couldn't let this happen to his little boy. Not again.

"I don't know. I wish I knew more, David, I really do. It's just…"

He squinted at the blur, staring, trying to make sense of it. It was on her stomach now, not eating, but frozen as if it had paused to watch his reaction. He had to communicate, say something, tell it he'd do anything, anything at all.

I'll do whatever you want. Just don't eat my son.

The rest happened in stop-motion, atrocity in lapsed time. One moment Kiaraa had a body, the next she stopped talking because she was just a head and heads couldn't talk without lungs or diaphragms to pump air. Before that, something exploded from inside her. Blood dripped off the ceiling and down his face. He could taste her blood sliding across his gums and tongue, but he still couldn't move. Kiaraa looked so surprised, eyes wide and frozen in that last moment, and he wondered if she finally realized what was happening to her or it just ended in a painless second. He hoped that was it.

Her head wobbled on the blood-soaked cushion and then rose a few feet, hovering in the air over the blurry nothing. And then her mouth opened like she was going to speak and he almost lost it then, however you lose it locked in your own head, because no way could he deal with a disembodied talking Kiaraa head floating around the room like a loose balloon.

Instead, two fat hairy black things slid out of her mouth and descended several inches below her chin. Shiny black talons or claws, no fangs, twitching at the end of each hairy part. Then her eyes bulged and turned jet black and she had four eyes, no six—two at her temples and two partially covered in hair—and David could see himself in all six, tiny and lost in the black. He still couldn't see what was holding her head up, but he had the strangest impression it was a spider. A spider wearing Kiaraa's head or face. And it was looking at him.

Maybe it was coming for him next, and this was just a break between meals.

I'm sorry, Jason, he thought, wishing he could close his eyes.

Kiaraa's mouth stretched around the hairy arms—*no, he thought, chelicae, that's what they're called, which is really helpful, you fucking dork*—and he waited for her face to rip in half but instead the spider leaned forward and said:

"Hello, David," in his dead father's voice.

At which point, he could move again. He grabbed the nearest thing on the side-table, a snow-globe from one of Kiaraa's trips to visit family in Germany—*Wilkommen!* it said. *Welcome to Bavaria!*—and raised it to bash out spider-Kiaraa's head with a kitschy reproduction of Heidelberg because it wasn't her, it couldn't be her, so it would be a mercy, and then she-it waggled two blurry front legs and said:

"Wait! I've got an idea."

And the world vanished.

Greetings & Salutations

THE SUN BLAZED DIRECTLY OVERHEAD *and there was nothing but grass in every direction. The insects were screaming again, but he couldn't see them. He wasn't even sure they were insects. Why were they so loud?*

"What is this?"

He looked at his hands. They were covered in spots of Kiaraa's blood. He closed his eyes and saw the spider-thing eating Kiaraa and her head growing fangs. He opened his eyes and saw grass and sky forever.

"What the hell is this?"

He had finally lost his mind. Alicia must have hit him too hard this time. Or was it a stroke?

"It's okay, David."

He spun and faced his father, who was now dark and hairy for some reason, like he was changing into another man with a better tan.

"Dad?"

"It's okay, son." His father reached around his neck, as if he was adjusting David's collar. He smelled like smoke. He always smelled like smoke. "But this will hurt a little."

Pain exploded in David's neck, and his mouth opened in a silent scream. Pain shot down his spine to every extremity. His hands were on fire. His teeth burned in his jaw. The pain rose in waves, impossibly high, and then soared higher again, and again.

Dad, please stop whatever you're doing it hurts…

Then the pain was gone and he could hear the insects again.

"See?" Dad said, resting his huge hands on David's shoulders. "That wasn't so bad."

*

DAVID STARTED GETTING SICK after his ninth birthday. He'd wake up feeling fine and then eat breakfast and start throwing up. Day after day, month after month, until he was too weak to go to school. Sometimes when Dad was at work, Mom would look down at him and shake her head in disappointment. Why was he so weak? Why wasn't he more like Tommy? Why was he *doing this to her*? And he'd cry and say he was sorry and crawl out of bed to go play in the living room or yard, or try. His skin ached. His joints screamed. When she was out of sight, he'd lie in the grass and stare at the sky, panting. He couldn't understand why he felt like this. Doctors didn't help. Medicine didn't help. There was just something wrong with him. He was a broken kid and a burden to his mother and family. Even Tommy stayed away from him now, afraid to touch him and catch what he had. That was one reason he stayed outside: to protect them from him.

He'd be ten in a few months, then eleven and soon a teenager, in middle and high school, and all he could see was a sick version of himself slumping around and scaring everyone away from him. David, the sick kid. David, the pukey kid. Bullied and hated and pathetic. He cried just thinking about it. He cried a lot when his mother wasn't watching. And they'd make fun of him for that, too. Maybe it was better if he just died.

Which is exactly what might have happened if Mom hadn't gone to work at the hospital one night—she worked three nights a week as a neonatal nurse—and left him with Dad and Tommy and a new streaming subscription. Tommy curled up on one side of Dad, head in his lap, David on the other, and watched Dad scanning for movies to watch. Dad wanted something about nature. Tommy wanted something with bears or dinosaurs or, for some reason, penguins. David barely cared as long as he could stay next to his father, but he liked horror movies, and when Dad hovered over the *Sixth Sense*, David grunted, "That one."

"Boring," Tommy said, which is what he said about anything that wasn't cool.

"You sure?" Dad asked. There was something in his voice, which David assumed was: *should the sick kid watch a scary movie?* Maybe it'd be better to watch a happy movie with dancing unicorns. David hated unicorns. And dancing. And happy anything. Life sucked. The world sucked. The movie looked dark and dark is what he wanted.

"Yes," he said.

"Groan," Tommy said.

"Okay," Dad said, resting his free hand on David's shoulder. "Next one is Tommy's pick."

Which sounded fair, but they never watched another movie together after that.

The *Sixth Sense* was about a psychiatrist helping a kid about David's age who saw ghosts. It was pretty cool, as Tommy admitted later. One of the ghosts is a little girl who's always sick and throwing up and then dies. Dad's hand stiffened on his side when he realized where the story was going. David sat up to watch more closely and make sure Dad didn't stop the movie. The girl got sicker and sicker and then, of course, she died. You couldn't be a ghost without dying. And David thought, *it's about me. I'm sick. I'm throwing up. I'm dying.*

But that wasn't the thing that mattered.

What mattered was what the girl ghost showed the little boy: that she wasn't a broken girl. That it wasn't her fault. Her mother was poisoning her. Which was when David realized he was sick for the same reason. It was the only thing that made sense. His mother was making him sick. He just knew.

He glanced up at Dad. Dad looked down at him, eyes warm but not wide or full of realization. Just sad. It was the first time David wondered—*How could he not know?*—but then he turned back and watched the rest of the movie. He watched to the very end, long after Tommy fell asleep, and then Dad carried them to bed without saying a word. David stared at the ceiling as Tommy tossed and turned on the other side of the room.

His mother was poisoning him.

He had to stop her. Or get Dad to stop her.

But what if he was wrong? Or what if, and this kept him up for hours, he deserved it?

Mom loved him. Moms always loved their children. So he must have done something wrong. He thought back. There were a hundred things to pick from. He hadn't cleaned up the table when it was his turn. He hadn't rinsed off his plate before putting it in the dishwasher. He didn't clean his room. Was he just a bad kid?

He looked over at Tommy in the darkness.

Maybe. Maybe he was a bad kid. But maybe he could be better. If she told him what to do, he could fix it. And then maybe she'd never do it to Tommy. Because Tommy wasn't perfect either. He hated cleaning anything. Tommy was a mess. Which is what decided it for him. He had to ask her so he could tell Tommy and they could do better. And then she'd stop and things would go back to how they were.

He fell asleep, hopeful for the first time in months.

His mother loved him. He just had to do better. He would do better.

Tommy was already gone when he woke up. Mom was at his bedside on a stool with a plate in her lap, hand on his forehead to check his temperature.

"How are you feeling this morning?" she asked.

"Okay." He sat up. She dug a fork into a plate of scrambled eggs. He shook his head. "I'm not hungry."

"I know, honey, but you have to eat." She sounded so worried. Maybe he was wrong.

"No, Mom. I'm not hungry."

"You have to eat, David." She pushed the fork against his lips. He leaned back. Her eyes darkened.

"David, stop acting like a baby."

"I'm not a baby. And I know what you're doing."

The fork hovered in midair, trembling. Egg fell on the bed. David swallowed. She hadn't spanked him in years, but she looked ready to now.

"Mom…"

She put the fork back on the plate and sat up straight.

"What am I doing, David?"

And so he told her about the ghost girl in the movie and the poison and didn't stop talking until he said he knew she was poisoning him but she didn't have to because he'd be better if she just told him how. He was breathing hard when he finished. Mom didn't say anything, so he opened his mouth to start again.

"Who picked the movie?" she asked.

"What?" David asked. Why was she looking at him like that? "I did."

"Not your father?"

"No…" He thought back. The icon had hovered over the movie thumbnail, shaking. Was he hoping David would pick it? Did he already know about Mom? Was that what she was asking? "No," he said again. "It was me."

"Good," she said, smiling with cookie-cutter lips used to slice words from the air. "Then you have a choice."

"I want you to stop. Just tell me what to do."

"It's up to you, David. You're almost ten now. A big boy." Pause. "You or Tommy."

"What?"

"You or your little brother." She picked up the fork again. "Your choice."

"But—"

"You or Tommy. Your father will never believe you. He's weak like you, David. But Tommy will never know. Just tell me and…"

He was crying. Or maybe he had been crying. He didn't understand what was happening.

The cold eggs were back near his mouth.

"You or Tommy," she said again. "Choose."

He wiped his eyes and looked at Tommy's bed. Tommy was happy. Tommy was a goofball. Tommy didn't deserve this, and maybe David did, even if Mom wouldn't tell him why, so it wasn't really a choice.

"Me," he said, opening wide. She shoved the fork in his mouth and he swallowed without chewing.

It was the same every morning after that. She didn't talk to him anymore. She just fed him and he got sick and it never occurred to him to try to throw it up or not eat because she'd just do it to Tommy and he couldn't let her. And he threw up later anyway. He slept more. He watched the sky and the clouds and felt nothing. Sometimes he wondered if he could do something. Most of the time, he was too tired to care. At least Tommy was safe.

Occasionally, they all ate breakfast together, Dad smiling and talking about their next camping trip like everything was fine or would be, Mom scanning each of them with her lighthouse gaze and humming a tuneless nothing. Tommy happy and oblivious and eager to get out and play away from his sickly brother.

David remembered looking at his father. His *strong* father, no matter what his mother said. His kind and loving father. And he wondered: *How could he not know?*

Which is why when David woke up on the couch in his living room facing his father, he knew something wasn't right. His father was on TV, sitting on the couch in their old living room, face calm as the Buddha, unaged, wearing one of the blue plaid shirts that made him prone to lumberjack songs and spontaneous sea shanties. David scratched his neck, wincing at the fading memory of pain. His father blinked under bushy eyebrows beneath a forehead lightly lined with worry. He knew, somehow, that Alicia was still at work and Jason was asleep in the nursery and this man wasn't his father. For one thing, he hadn't aged in nearly thirty years. For another, there was no bullet hole in his forehead.

"Hello, son," said his impossible father.

David squinted, checking the rest of the room for hideous clocks or blurry signs of impending violence. Nothing seemed out of place. It could have been any other day except for the blood spatters on his pants and the virtual father thing. Oh, and the mutilation of Kiaraa. He kept seeing her head dance in her office chair as hairy fangs clicked in time. He checked his hand for the Bavarian bauble, but his hand was empty. How did he get home?

"David, hello," his father said, sounding impatient.

David cleared his throat. "Are you…it?" he asked. Are you the thing that ate Kiaraa? Did you bite off my son's fingers? Are you real? Or was he just insane? It was still the easier thought.

"I'm not…him," his father said. "He thought you might have some questions, and that my appearance would be less jarring." His voice was warm and full of oak and timbre. It sounded exactly like the Ben Chambers, born in Victoria, Canada, died in Fort Collins, USA, cluelessly happy father every moment in between.

"Him?" David asked. "You mean the thing that…" He couldn't finish the sentence.

"Yes," Dad said, smiling like he had a great secret he just couldn't wait to share. He was terrible with secrets, or had been before Mom shot him. Now he was unparalleled.

"What happened to Kiaraa?" David demanded, sounding more courageous than he felt, and then the words poured out: "What was that thing? And who are you? You're not my father. My father's dead. What's with that grassland and the pain in my neck? Why is it eating my son? What the hell is going on?"

"You mean, are you crazy?"

"Of course that's what I mean."

"No, you're not crazy, son."

Which is exactly what your dead father would tell you when you were mad as a rabid wombat.

"Stop calling me that," David said. "Whatever you are, I'm not your son."

The antenna twitched above the TV screen, but David couldn't be bothered to look away from his non-father's vaguely offended face. Besides, his TV didn't have an antenna any more than it had UHF. This wasn't the seventies.

"Dad, I'm…"

"No, that's fine, David. You're right. I'm not your father."

"What are you?"

"You'd call me an artificial intelligence. An avatar? He thought it would be easier to talk this way. You look good, David. I always wanted to know what you'd look like as a man. You're skinnier than—"

"Stop it. Who is he?"

The antenna twitched again. David looked up this time, and watched as a head with two, no four, then six giant black eyes rose from behind the TV. He wanted to run screaming from the room, but it couldn't be real. There was no room between the wall and TV for anything, let alone a spider that ate psychiatrists, but at least it wasn't wearing Kiaraa's face.

The spider-blur slid into the TV and Dad's eyes turned obsidian-black and shiny as oiled glass.

"Hello, David," Dad said. "My name is Arachniss."

David snorted. "Really?" Maybe Alicia was poisoning him the way Mom had, and he was seeing things. Monsters should have names like Cthulhu or Godzilla, not sound like spider princesses at a tea party. "What are you?"

"You seem upset," his father said, or the spider-thing said, using his father's face.

"I just watched you eat my friend and wear her head like a Mardi Gras mask, was burned from the inside out in a dream that maybe wasn't a dream, and now I'm talking to my dead father so, yeah, I'm a little upset."

Dad vanished and Tommy was on the screen, still barely eight.

David caught his breath or just forgot to inhale. His heart stopped. Blood stopped flowing through his veins. Tommy stared at him with big black eyes full of accusations. The room spun.

"Is this better?" Tommy asked.

David couldn't speak. He opened his mouth, but nothing came out. He closed his eyes and willed his lips to move.

"No," he whispered. "No." And he could breathe again.

Now Tommy was Kathryn when she still had eyes and could talk.

"This?" she asked.

"No," he said, trying not to scream it.

Then it was James and his perfectly symmetrical face.

"No. Just go back to Dad."

Dad relaxed on the screen and David with him, exhaling and sinking into the couch. No matter how fake he was, or what he was, just seeing him made David feel lighter, safer, like a little boy leaning against him as he read one of his hiking magazines. Though the black eyes didn't help.

"David," he said, "I'm sorry about what happened to Kiaraa, but you had to see it."

"Why?"

"Because the things you've been seeing are real, your memories, all of it."

"That's impossible."

"Then you think you're imagining everything?"

Jason. He's talking about Jason. His stomach lurched. "My son. His fingers. You're eating my son?"

"Not recently," Dad said, shrugging.

So that was a yes. "And Alicia? Her arm?"

"Yes."

"Kathryn?"

"No, that's not me."

There are more of you? Wait, he hadn't said that out loud. "There are more of you?"

"Of course there are more of us."

"What are you?"

"We call ourselves Arach in your language, but that means the same thing to us that 'humans' does to you."

"The same thing that..." He closed his eyes. *Humans.* Opened them. Looked at the fireplace and back, searching for something to hold on to, something solid, like the Rock of Gibraltar or the Himalayas, but his eyes just slid back to his father's face like he was at the bottom of a visual gravity well. This couldn't be happening.

"You're aliens," he blurted. There. The crazy was out. Because he was pretty sure humanity would have noticed giant man-eating spiders running around if they were from Earth.

"Bingo," Dad said, just like he used to say it, too happy and excited about something that didn't matter because he was always covering for Mom. *Bingo!*

So this is first contact, David thought. Well, his first contact. First awareness of contact? It was disappointing but also not; he'd never understood people who thought aliens would be advanced and intelligent enough to travel across the vast reach of space just to fumble around in cornfields making pretty shapes. If they invaded, it would be like slaughtering insects. If they didn't, their arrival would be humbling to the point of humiliation no matter how highly humanity thought of itself. But it never occurred to him they were already here and eating people. There was a very old Twilight Zone Episode, *To Serve Man*, but there the aliens arrived, abducted a few people, and left behind a disturbing cookbook. They didn't stay. And they sure as hell weren't giant spiders.

"Why are you here?" David asked. He'd always believed in aliens, but not the bug-eyed monster kind. Somewhere in the whole universe there had to be life—intelligent life, evolved life, gods of space and time—but apparently the bug-eyed thing was closer to the truth. Which was, again, disappointing.

"I think you're figuring that out, David, but I can't answer all your questions right now. I've created this simulation of your father so you can ask him what you need to know. He has access to any information he's allowed to share with you. He's in your phone, or you can email him. He'll be available day or night."

"Like a chat bot? You ate Kiaraa and bits of my son and you're leaving me with Dad-bot to discuss my feelings?"

"Places to be," Spider-dad said. "People to eat."

And then he was gone. Dad's eyes returned to normal and he looked around his virtual living room like he was surprised to be there.

"I think we're alone now," he said.

"Fuck your alone," David snapped, and turned off the TV.

Now what?

He turned the TV back on.

"David!" Dad said, happily, like his big boy just got back from summer camp.

He shut Dad off again and called Kiaraa.

"The number you've dialed is no longer in service," said a sad lady voice, and David wondered if it was some poor women-bot trapped in the phone like his dad. He hung up and suddenly remembered that Kiaraa had died last month in a car accident. He'd gone to the funeral with Alicia and told Kathryn about it afterward. They cried together and he ran his hands through Kathryn's remaining hair to relax her and then they cried some more. Arachniss had eaten Kiaraa right in front of him, but he knew that if he asked Alicia when she got home, she'd remember the funeral perfectly. And then she'd hug him with Zombie Arm (hug mode was nice, if a little stiff) and pat him on the back with electronic fingers until he pretended he was okay and she could go do whatever she really wanted to do instead of dealing with his feelings.

So the Arach could change memories. There was no way to know how many of them there were or how long they'd been there. No way to tell anyone or show them the truth. So what was the point of telling him at all? None. There was no point. He was nobody. This was absurd.

He went into the bedroom and, of course, the octopus clock was gone. Maybe it had never been there, or maybe it was just Arachniss watching them as they slept. Creepy alien spider cannibal. Well, Arachniss wasn't eating other spiders, so not a cannibal. What would Dad-bot say? *He's not creepy once you get to know him.* Always the peacemaker. And—David checked—he was in his phone under 'David's Dad,' like there was another one. He'd never met Alicia's parents and wasn't sure they even existed. Maybe she was an alien too. No, he wasn't that lucky.

He walked into the nursery and checked on Jason. His son looked up with happy blue eyes and made little spit bubbles while he played with David's finger. He was in a short sleeve bodysuit that said "I Love Boobies" that Alicia had gotten him right about the time she stopped breastfeeding, meaning he loved boobies a little too much and her nipples kept bleeding and she was over it, but whatever the ironic sociopolitical overtones of his clothes, Jason was still insanely cute. Tiny spider shadows circled around the crib, crawling up and down blanketed hills like a miniature arachnoid invasion. He pulled his finger out of Jason's grasping little hands, tore down the mobile, dumped it in the trash, took another look at his son, fought the urge to snatch him up and hug him until the world made sense, and found himself back on the couch with the remote.

"David!" Dad said when he appeared, now in a different plaid shirt, gold and brown, harvest colors. One of David's favorites. He'd kept that shirt in a box of his belongings for years until the moths got it and it smelled like rat poop and one of his foster parents trashed it when he was at school. That was the third home he left due to 'behavioral issues,' which apparently included rummaging through neighborhood trashcans in search of his dead parent's clothing.

"Okay," David said. "What the hell is going on?"

So Dad showed him a movie.

Earth span slowly in space as a woman with an English accent narrated:

"Locally called Earth by its dominant semi-sentient species, Earth is a class-four, free-range certified ranching planet cataloged as planet X-23-4AX14 in the Trans Nebulonic farming cluster managed under Section 34a of the galactic virtual meat and sub-species experiential entertainment compact, subject to and compliant with all regulations and codes therein—including one of the lowest rates of cross-contamination in its class."

Aerial view of a London street. Close up on a woman's face, then a man and others.

"Earth's primary herd is the 'human' species, homo sapiens in the dominant local dialect, which comes in two-plus gender configurations, numerous aesthetically pleasing skin tones and hair colors, including related ocular morphisms, and boasting a full spectrum of meat cuts from muscled shanks to some of the fattiest pate-ready livers available in the galaxy today."

A group of heavy-set people.

"Think pate that stuffs itself."

Shot of tropical paradise with thatched tourist huts over pristine blue-green water.

"If you're planning to visit Earth, luxury accommodations are available in all climates and customizable to all tastes. And because we've seeded the planet with 'spiders' that look very similar to our primary local hosts, it's simplicity itself to maintain the illusion that you're not even there."

A naked man running down a village street somewhere in rural England, chased by two giant, tarantula-looking spiders, one of which wore jewelry.

"Unless you want them to see you, of course, in which case, chase-a-petit! We'll erase all memories to prevent cultural contamination or global panic."

Flash of an Olympic-sized swimming pool—

"Okay, sorry," Dad said, back on screen. "I thought that would be more helpful. I skimmed the rest and it's a bit graphic. You okay, son?"

David let the son thing slide. Right at the end, there was something black and spider-like swimming in the pool of blood and human parts. That would be hard to forget.

"David?"

"We're a farm." He said this to himself as much as Dad. "Earth is a farm for meat-eating spiders?"

"Well, they're not really spiders."

"They sure look like spiders."

"Oh, the movie? That was for your benefit. Why else would they have English marketing videos? Anyway, they're not—"

"Why's it in England?"

"Americans find English accents believable and English settings comforting."

Was he screwing with him? "We're a farm?"

"A ranch, yes. It's not that uncommon. There are high-density production facilities throughout the galaxy, though almost all of them grow synthetic meats hydroponically. Doesn't make sense to ship bodies all over the galaxy, I guess. This free-range situation—having your own lives and society—is pretty rare. You're incredibly lucky."

David couldn't tell if this was Arach propaganda or his dad's positive spin, but either way, it made him twitchy.

"How long?"

"How long what?"

"How long have we been a spider ranch?"

"Always?" He frowned. "Oh, I see. No, they're not invaders. They created you. Bred you for compatibility with their biological needs. Human beings are one of the most popular meat crops in the galaxy. I'm looking through some of the data now. It's quite—"

"You're telling me god is a giant black spider?" David asked.

"God? No, just, well, there's a lot more to the universe than we knew, and we're a pretty small part of it."

"'We?' Never mind. They're eating us. SHAS is a cover. There was never a pandemic. They change our memories so we don't see it, but we're being eaten."

"That's right. Sorry?" The upward inflection turned his apology into a question. Maybe he was sorry. Maybe he was just doing his job appeasing the meat.

"Why is it showing me this? I assume most people can't see them."

"No one's supposed to, but some people are more resistant to the, uh, reprogramming. The implant in your neck should make that impossible, but some people develop a resistance. They're not sure how or why. I'm not sure they care. They think it's…"

"What?" David remembered the pain he'd felt in the grassland dream and felt his neck for any sign of the implant. There was nothing but a small scar he couldn't remember getting, no, wait, it was from the same fire that burned his arms. His shirt collar had seared to his neck.

"Funny," Dad said. "Amusing, maybe. Their humor is hard to explain."

Maybe they were German spider aliens. "So, what do they want from me?"

"I don't know. I mean…" He trailed off. "I'm sorry about this."

Before Dad finished the apology, David turned toward the hall to see Jason floating toward him. He tried to get off the couch and race to his son, but he couldn't move. Jason hovered more than a foot off the floor in his panda onesie, pudgy little hands reaching for the ceiling. Of course, he was smiling. He was always smiling. Beneath him, something blurred, like air was smeared or flowing around the vague outline of a spider, or maybe David was imagining it. Either way, Jason's hover-trip ended with him resting on the coffee table.

"What is this?" he demanded, at least able to speak. Dad looked down at his lap. David tried to reach for Jason, but still couldn't move. "Leave my son alone."

Jason started to bleed. A fine line of blood traced around the tip of his remaining pinky toe in a perfect ring.

"Stop it!" David yelled.

It didn't stop. The only change was Jason turning toward David in surprise. Had he ever yelled in his son's presence before?

The tip of Jason's toe slid into the smear.

"Please, please stop. Whatever you want…"

Snap!

The toe disappeared. Jason didn't react. David's mouth hung open in something worse than horror: helplessness. This thing was eating his son like it had eaten Kiaraa, and there was nothing he could do about it.

"Please," he said again. "I'll do anything." If it made him watch his son die, he would lose it forever.

The blood-and-bone wound on Jason's toe vanished, leaving perfectly healthy pink skin with no sign of injury. Just another stump toe for Pirate Baby. Now he could count to 18.67.

"Anything?" his father asked. David looked back at the screen. Dad was watching him and his black eyes were back. This wasn't the bot anymore. This was the thing. Arachniss.

"Anything at all?" it asked again.

David nodded without hesitation. "Anything." Though he had no idea what the spider wanted or could want from him. "Just leave my son alone. Please." Silence. "Why…" He looked at Jason and forced his breath back under control. "Why are you doing this?"

Dead black-eyed stare. No response. Nothing.

"Please," David begged. "Just tell me what to do." More silence. "What do you want from me?"

"You'll see," he said.

"When?"

"No. You'll *see*." The black emptied out and David assumed Arachniss was gone, or that's what he was supposed to think. Dad blinked as if waking up, green eyes back and full of concern.

"I'll see what?" David demanded, more confident now speaking to the avatar, which made no sense. Arachniss could still be in the room. He could be anywhere.

"You'll see the real world," Dad said. "No more illusion. No more changed memories, well, nothing you can't see through except the hosts themselves."

"The hosts?"

"That's what the Arach call themselves on Earth. Listen, this is important. You'll still know what you should be seeing, what others are seeing, because you have to play along. But no matter what you see, no matter what you hear, you can't react. You have to pretend you see nothing at all or at least nothing that others don't. If you don't keep up the act, he can't protect you."

"Protect me from what?"

"From the others."

"Other spiders?"

"Arach, David. They don't like being called spiders."

"They don't…" *Fine.* "How many of them are there?"

"On earth? Thousands. Sometimes millions. It varies."

"Millions?"

"They're everywhere. You just can't see them. Well, you mostly can't see them. Go for a walk downtown and you'll understand."

"Go for a walk? This is…" What was the word? Insane? Impossible? Incomprehensible. All the I-words and none of them were enough. Although the insane part would make things easier.

"You're not crazy, David," his father said. "Pretending this isn't happening will just put Jason at risk."

"You can read my mind?"

"I know my son."

"I'm not your…" He couldn't even finish. He felt so tired he wanted to pull Jason into his lap and sleep until the world ended or Alicia came home. Instead, he turned off the TV, picked up Jason and walked into his office. Jason was soon sleeping against his hip, quiet, happy and perfect if slightly more stubby. David kept grabbing Jason's foot, examining the skin to find some evidence of recent mutilation, but his newly truncated toe looked like it had been that way forever. No, that couldn't be. He squinted at the toe again. Still nothing to see.

Pedro's giant eyes were right; something had been watching him. Something was watching everyone. He wanted to tear them all down, every drawing, rip Pedro and his accusatory eyes to shreds, but instead Jason woke up and started crying. The sound surprised David so much he jerked in the chair, and Jason cried even louder. Jason never cried. Could he tell how scared his father was? Because he was terrified.

"It's okay, Jay. It's okay. Daddy's got you." Which were meaningless words. What could he do to defend Jason from millions of…whatever they were. Did anyone else know? Was anyone else lying to their children right now, pretending they could protect them when they knew they couldn't?

He rocked his hot little son until the crying stopped and he fell asleep.

"Wait…" He pulled out the photos he'd printed of newborn Jason. In every one of them, Jason had all his fingers, no pinky stubs, no pirate baby. So he'd been right about that too; something was eating his son, and presumably everyone else. He thought of Charlotte's ear, Padme's fingers, Kathryn's everything and a thousand more missing limbs and body parts. All eaten by aliens and then made to look like part of a pandemic. Memories were changed or erased. But he guessed it wasn't worth the effort to change photos, so they just made people see what they wanted them to see.

"SHAS," he scoffed. It was so suddenly and obviously absurd.

Unlike necrotizing fasciitis, the SHAS virus had allegedly consumed you from the outside in, pulling parts in and dissolving them until nothing was left, not blood or bone, all within a neatly sealed skin like someone deflating a balloon animal, retracting its limbs until nothing was left but a lumpy body and a useless head. He had 'researched' extensively online about what you could live without after Kathryn lost her legs, what parts of your body could be removed without necessarily killing you. It laid out a familiar map, printed in the collective consciousness by decades of disease and loss. With no support or artificial replacements, you could lead a good life without your appendix, of course, but also your spleen, adenoids, gall bladder, tonsils, a few lymph nodes, one of your kidneys or lungs and even part of your intestines or rectum. This was where he was on that map, in a safe zone of missing extraneous organs, minor things that we hardly noticed or, in Alicia's case, benefited her notoriously unrestrained eating habits. None of this seemed unusual until that afternoon. It all made sense, right?

But of course others lost more personal things, breasts and ovaries, testes, prostates, uteruses, clitorises, strips of labia and lengths of cock, leaving feelingless nubbins and stumps, dependence on hormonal therapies and forgiving partners, but still mild in their physical if not social impact. He knew a few people on this part of the map, a quiet tribe of downcast eyes and frustrated sexual pantomimes. If they were to take any part of him on this list, he wouldn't mind a groin smooth as a Ken doll, useless to man or woman, like a get-out-of-obligatory-sex card, free of performance anxiety and the mess of ejaculation, though he would miss peeing standing up.

Wait, wasn't that the old thinking? He was supposed to be leaving Alicia, but that plan felt like a fantasy that died with Kiaraa. There was nowhere to run now, nowhere to go. Alicia was at least familiar and human.

Jason was in another part of the SHAS map, though barely, like a pretendian, only one-thirty-second Navajo and never once on the reservation, missing mere bits of finger and toe. But of course you could lose far more if you had the support of friends, family and medical science: all of your fingers and toes, hands and feet, every inch of limb, eyes and ears, nose, larynx and tongue. But there's not one of those things you wouldn't miss at least a little, no matter how accepting society was, and losing all of them left you little more than a lukewarm vegetable, appealing as overcooked asparagus—or carrots, in the case of Kathryn. She was at the edge of the map with the dragons, one gust of wind from an endless drop into the void. He supposed the soul was in there somewhere, though he doubted it was edible.

What struck him most about this map of SHAS was how strange it was that they accepted such a nicely behaved virus, which navigated by a compass anyone could see. True north, uneaten, and true south, where nothing was left but essential meats and empty thoughts. The SHAS virus allegedly worked from the outside in, little to big, vestigial to essential and only then, when nothing extraneous was left, the final step that was death. Like a great finishing chomp of ground bone and marrow, hearts and livers, and then our fat brains pickled in darkness and desperate for the peace of sharpened teeth. This was an Eagle Scout of viruses, a trained survivor that navigated the body with perfection, which meant it was no virus at all. He couldn't blame the Arach for the illusion, or even resent it; people would believe anything to hold their place on that map among the living, the higher the better. And the Arach had to know it. Would people even want to know the truth?

He glanced over at his family photo on the bookshelf, half expecting to see a spidery blur behind his brother and father, but there was nothing but the disembodied hand of his mother to turn his stomach.

They were being eaten. Earth was a farm, and he couldn't tell anyone. Well, he probably could, but who would believe him? He still thought he might be crazy. He'd never felt more alone in his life. He wanted to talk to someone, anyone, which reminded him about Kiaraa and then he cried, and Jason joined in until they were a rocking, sobbing mess. Of course Jason stopped first, shaming David to wipe his face and pretend to get his shit together.

"Okay," he said, flinching from Pedro's unwavering gaze. "Okay." It was time to get out of the house. He started to stand, then stopped. Maybe that wasn't such a good idea.

'You'll see,' Arachniss had said. Dad told him to go for a walk, but now he just wanted to stay inside. It had to be safer in his home than outside. He looked down at Jason and his missing fingers. *Safe?* What a joke. No one was safe. Nothing and nowhere was safe. He couldn't protect his son if he didn't know what was going on.

Dad had suggested going downtown. It was a nice day for it. What's the worst that could happen?

He snorted. He could be eaten alive and no one would even notice.

You shouldn't take Jason, he thought. *Call Olivia.*

Who the hell is Olivia?

Hadn't she been their…something? Was she a baby sitter? No, he'd remember the name at least. Probably something else Arachniss had purged from his memory. He touched his neck again. Was there a lump there? Had they removed the implant or just changed it? His fingers traced over the scar. There was definitely something, a tiny lump on his cervical spine. He looked over Jason's neck, feeling carefully along his son's spine, but there was nothing there but soft, warm skin. Jason was helpless, innocent and just so damn tiny. How could anyone or anything threaten something so defenseless?

It was definitely time to get out of the house, but Jason was coming with him. David wasn't sure he'd ever be able to let his son out of his sight again.

David Goes for a Walk

BABY CARRIER, HAT AND SUNGLASSES. Mental inventory of science fiction apocalypse scenarios. Baby go-bag with diapers and a hundred other things that were never quite what you needed. Shoes. He should put on shoes. What was that book about cannibalism? *Tender is the Flesh*. No, that wasn't the same thing. That was people eating people. Where were his shoes? Oh. He was in the bedroom staring at a pile of shoes on the closet floor, mostly deck shoes and running shoes. What was the right footwear for man-eating aliens? Panda slippers were tempting. Running shoes it was. Back in the kitchen for formula, water and snacks, because he didn't want to die hungry. There was another book, *The Road*, but that was just more human-on-human post-apocalyptic cannibalism. Nothing unusual there; people ate people when food got scarce. That wasn't even fiction; that was Donner Party fact. Wasn't there something with aliens? Trip to the bathroom.

He was at the front door looking like a very clean hobo with his entire life on his back, but still missing something. His hand rested on the doorknob. Was it always this cold? In *War of the Worlds*, aliens mulched humans as fertilizer, but they didn't *eat* them. Oh, *The Blob* was about an alien eating people, but the alien was a formless glowy lump, not an advanced alien species that spanned the galaxy and made personalized promotional videos.

He tried to catch his breath. Why would aliens even eat human meat? Why didn't they eat their own farm animals? The hall spun and he had to press a hand against the wall to keep from falling over.

Okay. It'll be okay. Okay is what it'll be. Stop freaking out.
I'm not freaking out.

He was totally freaking out. There were aliens on Earth. Spider aliens. He wanted to call Kathryn, because she'd know what to do, but he couldn't call Kathryn and that just pissed him off. They were *eating* his best friend and had already eaten most of what made her life worthwhile.

What was he forgetting?

They're eating all of us. No, he wasn't ever forgetting that.

He opened the door. The sun hit him in the face with the big warm snap of a towel fresh from the dryer and he squinted suspiciously into a blinding blue-green world. He got his breathing under control. If they wanted to kill or eat him, they didn't need to trick him into going outside. They just wanted to show him something.

"It'll be fine," he told himself, fighting the urge to giggle.

In *Tomorrow War*, didn't the aliens eat people? Yeah, but they were idiot aliens: violent bugs with a thirst for human blood. What did it matter? It wasn't like he was going to find an explanation for the Arach in one of his science fiction books.

We're a farm. He blew out a long breath. Maybe the Arach didn't allow anyone to publish a book saying that. Or maybe it was exactly as unbelievably crazy as it sounded.

Time to go for a walk. He stepped out onto the porch.

And then he realized there was no baby in his ergonomic and highly adjustable front-hip-or-back baby backpack, and went back to get Jason.

*

DAVID STOPPED AT THE SIDE of the street and looked both ways, then up at the sky, repeatedly. He was expecting to see vast starships plying the morning skies or hordes of spider aliens hanging out on the corner like delinquent teenagers looking for some action, but there was nothing but a gorgeously normal Boulder afternoon. And there was nobody on the streets of his Flagstaff neighborhood. No one on the occasional sidewalks. No cars in the street or birds in the air. Dad-bot had suggested a walk downtown, presumably toward more populated areas, so David took a breath and turned left.

The world looked perfectly normal. Maybe he was just losing his mind.

You just wish you were losing your mind.

Which was true. The more he thought about it, the more he realized all his science fiction books and movies had prepared him for one of two eventualities: one, aliens would come and there would be hilarious hijinks. Oh, you crazy alien you. So cute and misunderstood. Or, two, exactly the opposite: horror, invasion and death with blood in the streets and cities burning as the brave people of Earth mounted a heroic last stand. The far more prosaic concept that aliens were here, always had been here, and just enjoyed eating people without panicking them was...was...

Pretty funny.

He started giggling and, once started, couldn't stop. Soon he was bent over, one hand on Jason's head to keep him steady, while he laughed and laughed until he cried and then laughed some more. Kiaraa was dead. Kathryn was little more than a torso. Aliens were eating the world. Humans were food. They were *food*. It was horrifying, beyond understanding, staggering and hysterical. Not the Kathryn and Kiaraa part—that was too much to even comprehend— but the part where humans were just meat for spider aliens. That was funny as hell. How many times had he wanted to scream about the horrors of eating sentient animals, of taking pleasure from the death of other thinking beings, about how they would feel if it happened to them? It went beyond ironic to seem just and fair.

And yet it also wasn't funny at all. Once the flush of hysterical irony had passed, he was back to being terrified. It didn't matter if it was fair or they deserved it. It was real and they were being eaten. He shook his head. Insanity.

He detoured down Gilbert past Smith Park on the way to 6th St., stopping in the shade to give Jason some formula. There was only one family in the park, two young boys screaming and running circles around parents who watched them with exhausted amusement.

There was no sign of aliens or spiders. Every human being was missing something, whether fingers and hands or ears and a nose, but that wasn't new.

He turned as a teenage boy rode his ebike down the street with an old-model metal leg pumping away under baggy cargo shorts, and suddenly he knew this kid: His name was Ansel and he liked to cruise the 'faggoty liberal' neighborhoods looking for animals to chase on his bike. There was a clear memory of the last animal he'd hunted down on foot before losing his leg, a three-legged black lab (which was rare to see outside at all) and how he'd called the dog over, and then kicked him in the stomach as hard as he could. The dog yelped and stumbled away as Ansel laughed at the stupid cripple dog and then flipped off a woman watching him from the doorway of a rundown bungalow across the street.

"Watch it," Ansel said as he raced.

"Asshole," David whispered under his breath.

Ansel looked back, probably wondering if he'd really heard the old man say that and maybe he could use a good kicking with his bad-ass metal leg, and then glided away like David wasn't worth the effort.

I just read that kid's mind.

No, that wasn't it. He'd seen part of Ansel's past because Arachniss wanted him to. But why?

He shook his head, checked on Jason, and continued walking down Gilbert to Euclid and 6th, turning north toward downtown. Along the way, he passed several people. Each time, he suddenly knew more than he should. This man was worried his wife was cheating on him. This girl was off to steal expensive makeup with her friends. One woman had just been laid off and was trying to figure out what to tell her parents. This guy had slapped his son and was almost glad SHAS had taken his hand as karmic punishment. This little girl wanted the cool shoes her friend had. Sometimes it was the past, sometimes the present, and while the memories frequently coincided with a missing body part, they didn't always.

He didn't see any spiders or spidery blurs, though there were more spidercats than he realized—black cats under bushes, packs of them running down side-streets, others watching from the trees. Had there always been this many and he was just seeing them now? Either way, they unnerved him, and he looked down at his feet as he walked on, which gave him a better view of Jason. He was carrying his son on his hip facing inward despite him preferring to face outward now. Jason blinked at him with big wet eyes or dozed against his side. Whenever panic set in, he'd look down at his son and calm down, at least a little.

He walked down Sixth Street past house after house, eyes down, afraid of what he'd see. Farther, past Arapahoe and over Boulder Creek until he turned right on Pearl. He raised his eyes when blurry things flashed by or stopped near him, like heat mirages with legs, then quickly looked away and pretended there was nothing to see.

Dad was right; they were everywhere around downtown.

Boulder's most famous manmade tourist attraction was the Pearl Street Mall. David walked down Pearl until the street was blocked off for pedestrians only at 11th Street, and then into the crowded shopping plaza. The blurs multiplied along with the people, mostly moving, some still, not appearing to do much but make his heart jump each time they came close. He put his hand on Jason's head, felt his temperature and whispered calm things that were meant for himself, until he came to a stop outside of an ice cream shop as a double-scoop sugar cone floated by and then vanished.

He lifted his phone. "Dad-bot, do the Arach like ice cream?"

"They like new experiences," his father responded instantly. "And ice cream is a popular one."

Dad's tone was playful, like, *of course the Arach like ice cream; they're not savages.*

David was about to say something snide when a seven-year-old boy on a skateboard slid into the space where the ice cream had been and exploded in a fine red mist, like he'd fallen in a tree chipper. David nearly dropped his phone, but no one around seemed to notice. The skateboard blurred for a second, passing behind a nearly invisible Arach (he assumed), and slowed to a stop a few yards away. A spidercat ran into the bloody area and began methodically tonguing everything red. More cats joined in, and more, until the walk was aswarm with licky-sticky black cats and the smell of blood.

"Jesus..." David whispered, resting his hand on Jason's chest. He couldn't take his eyes off the space where the boy had vanished. Already the blood had settled or melted away, but the blur didn't move. In fact, he had the distinct impression it was watching him. Which wasn't good.

You can't react. You have to pretend you see nothing at all.

The blur swelled as it moved toward him. David fought every urge in his body to turn and run. Instead, he calmly rested his hand back on Jason's head and told him he'd be old enough for ice cream soon. Jason burbled in excitement and David walked calmly down the mall as if everything was just fine. Nothing to see here. But there was no way the Arach didn't hear his heart beating against his chest.

Don't look back, he told himself. *Just don't look back.*

He walked until his legs were shaking and he had to sit on a bench, head down, trying not to see, but he could still hear and feel them everywhere. He had no idea if that feeling was real or paranoia. Probably paranoia. But that didn't explain how he knew so much. Every time someone walked by, David knew something about them. Their age, their love life, their career, not everything, but snippets of lives lived well or poorly. Who they loved and how, what they hated and why. And what limbs or parts they'd lost to the pandemic or other random events.

He coughed. *The pandemic.* What a joke. Arachniss had opened his eyes and his mind with them, apparently. Dumped in a whole world of ugliness he couldn't keep out.

He shook his head, trying to focus on Jason. Around him were sporting good shops like Patagonia and Mont*bel, catering to Boulder's young and fit. Along with trendy restaurants, coffee shops, knick-knackeries and tourist traps. Hundreds of people shopping and talking and eating. A very few dogs on leashes, numerous babies in strollers, and at least a dozen Arach blurs circulating among them that he could *almost* see.

"Jesus," he whispered. What was he going to do?

A severed arm floated by, still adorned in green plaid. It was from a middle-aged man by the skin of the hand, but white-collar. Nothing too dirty. Then he knew the arm once belonged to Peter Tifton, Esquire, a local ambulance chaser and womanizer who now thought he'd lost the arm to SHAS more than a year ago.

He covered Jason's eyes and watched the arm bob along two feet off the ground. Big spider taking lunch to go. No one else noticed the arm. No one was missing an arm. Well, lots of people were missing arms, but none appeared to be recently or violently misplaced. True to Boulder, more than a few people proudly wore ruggedized outdoor prosthetics decorated with forest silhouettes or marijuana leaves, but there were none in plaid.

A girl walking by glanced at him and he knew her name was Tiffany, who went by Tiff or Iffy and had lost one of her kidneys the night before while taking a post-coital nap. Her lover had lost her everything, vanishing from the bed next to her and leaving her with a vague sense of bliss and melancholy she quickly dismissed as she thought of the many lovers she had cosseted about town. A man walking by, Thad, had lost everything between his legs during a game of poker where he systematically bankrupted two addicts he'd met at Gamblers Anonymous. A young woman in Patagonia trekking pants and a puffy Patagonia vest shaded under a Patagonia hat pushed her running stroller to a stop next to him. David looked in the stroller for a Patagonia-sponsored child, but there was only an ambiguous tumble of fleecy blankets wherein a child was hiding or had melted, and a shockingly brutalized teddy bear.

"He's so cute," the woman said, nodding toward Jason's barely visible head. "How old?"

"Eight months. Yours?" He looked back at the blanket-filled stroller. There was a single brown stain on one fold of fabric. Blood or chocolate?

"Oh, I haven't been blessed with children yet," she said. "I just use it for shopping."

At which point David recalled her name was Janice and she had, in fact, had a five-month-old daughter named Eva when she started her afternoon jog down the mall. Now she had an empty athletic stroller, some stained blankets and a traumatized teddy bear she told herself was for 'the baby, whenever it comes.' Arachniss was sharing again.

"But I hope, you know, someday…" Janice trailed off and stared through him, apparently frozen in place, a single tear gliding over the rise of her cheek.

"Of course," David said, because that's what you're supposed to say. "Someday…"

She nodded as he clutched Jason to his chest to make sure he was still there. Could he forget his own son? Could he forget Jason had even existed?

"Wait," he blurted. "Did he eat Alex?"

"What?" The woman's eyes widened.

How had that not occurred to him before? The Arach hadn't eaten his son. It wasn't some unknown spider alien out there in the vast unknown; it was Arachniss, the thing in his house.

"Alex?" he asked the air. "Did Arachniss eat my son?" The flaming surge of rage he felt could have melted the town of Boulder to slag if not immediately doused by confusion and doubt. Who eats a child? It was incomprehensible.

"Well," the woman said. "I'm sure I don't know." Which seemed like a perfectly valid answer. She fled before he could ask anything else. In her wake, she left a vague scent of fear and the shredded leg of a teddy bear.

"Jesus," David said again, trying not to squeeze Jason too hard. A blur drifted over his head, blurring the sun.

They can fly?

Of course they can fly.

What the hell am I going to do?

*

ALICIA SLAMMED THE DOOR to the garage, kicked her shoes somewhere in the hall—where he'd find them later and grudgingly put them aside—and stopped at the entry to the kitchen with her arms akimbo in unusually short sleeves, an impatient cowgirl with one bone-white prosthetic arm carved with fine patterns like art on ivory. Zombie Arm was beautiful in design, positioning less so. What had he done this time?

"Rough day?" he asked, because he couldn't wait to hear her complain about what a bastard her boss was or how the system was stacked against justice.

"What's for dinner?" she asked.

We are, but what he said was, "Pasta and vegetables."

"No meat?"

He shuddered. "No meat. White sauce over orechiette." Which he remembered meant *little ears* in Italian, because of course it did. "Grilled asparagus," he added, sounding bored even to himself. "And dessert!" That was overcompensation. Her Zombie Arm quivered in irritation, but she didn't know aliens were eating them, so whatever.

"That sounds…good," she said, slowly cutting him with an ellipsis, then walked over to kiss Jason on the head, where she left lipstick like planted evidence of her love. Jason slapped at the plastic tabletop and nodded happily. God, he was an adorable kid. They had made him together. Two human beings who once loved each other had made this gorgeous child. He wanted to grab her and shake her until the old Alicia came out. He needed her. He needed someone. Kiaraa was gone. Kathryn was helpless. And there was no way he could do this alone.

"Have you noticed?" he asked. She waited for him to be more specific. He struggled to get the words out. "How SHAS is so much worse now?" It was hard to say SHAS without giggling, but what he saw downtown made no sense. At that pace of consumption, the human race would be nothing but body parts and bad memories within months—but the pandemic had lasted twenty years.

"It comes in waves," Alicia said with a shrug.

Which was true, but this wasn't a wave; it was a tsunami.

"Are you okay?" Alicia asked. "You look like you've seen a ghost."

He started laughing and, just as out on the street, realized he couldn't stop. She backed away, perhaps sensing how close he was to the edge and not wanting to set him off, or maybe hoping he'd fall and she could be done with him. David didn't care. Flesh didn't concern itself with the motivations of knives. It just tried to avoid the blade.

Jason giggled until they both ran out of breath and watched each other with big, wet eyes.

"David," his father called from the living room. "You're not alone."

And then he was laughing again.

Benny and the Pet

PEDRO SAT ON THE ICE, staring at nothing. Wasn't he going to walk somewhere?

Shyla danced in circles like a Peanuts cartoon, Lucy around Linus at his toy piano. Pedro didn't even notice her for the longest time. He looked at the sky. At the ice. And finally, down at the little girl and her endless gyrations.

His stomach grumbled.

Didn't he used to eat little girls?

David sighed, hit *Delete* and stared at the blinking cursor. Something about finding out the human race was meat for aliens had interrupted his creative process. He'd never had writer's block before, but he supposed the threat of being cut into little pieces for smart-ass invisible spiders was a good excuse. He knew it was stupid to be working on a children's book, but he needed something to calm down and his only vice was verbal diarrhea. It had saved him from crushing depression after realizing what Alicia was. Surely it could save him from the Arach.

One more try:

Pedro watched the massive ice spider crawl out from under a slanted hummock, a slab of ice forced above the pack ice by wind or pressure. He stayed downwind, behind the broken walls of ice, letting the hairy black monster drag itself into the sun. It was a hideous and unnatural thing, stinking of death and decay. When it stood on all eight legs to its full height, Pedro leaped on its back and crushed it, exploding its hairy abdomen with the weight of his four-point landing. It screamed and struggled until Pedro bit its head off and spat it across the ice. Then it didn't do much of anything but leak thick blue blood onto the snow.

"Better," David told himself, but maybe he wasn't in the best headspace for a children's story.

"Aren't you going to be late?"

David hit *Delete* instinctively as he jerked around to see Alicia in the doorway, wearing casual slacks and a deep V-neck blouse, Jason under her arm. She was doing her Lawyers who Lunch brunch in Denver and looked amazing for a woman who'd had two children and one quite recently. Maybe she was an alien. He wanted to snatch Jason away from her, but that probably wouldn't go over well.

"Late?" he asked.

"For your book signing."

"Oh, that's right. Thank you." He hadn't forgotten; he was just reluctant to walk past the living room.

She waited for him to get up. He waited for her to leave.

"Are you okay?" she asked. "You were talking in your sleep last night."

He caught his breath. He hadn't done that in years.

"Something about spiders," she said.

He forced a smile. "I guess the movie was a bad idea."

She pushed Jason's hand away as he made another grab. "It wasn't all bad."

His smile stretched thin. She waited for more, probably agreement, but he couldn't do it. At some point, she left and he stared at the space where she'd been until he heard the throaty grumble of her Porsche Cayenne pulling out of the driveway. Only when he was sure she was gone did he grab his satchel and make for the door.

"David!" Dad called from the living room as he passed.

Damn it. David stopped and turned toward the TV. "Morning, Dad."

"Good luck at the book signing today," Dad-bot said.

"Thanks?" A week had passed since his trip downtown, and he'd avoided his TV Dad and Arachniss the whole time. He watched Alicia move through their lives like a ship indifferent to the sea, having no idea what shallow reefs passed under her beaten keel or other wrecks that lay beneath. Jason remained whole, unchanged, beautiful, but he wondered, what was the price? What had he agreed to? Because he had no delusions; by saying he'd do *anything* for Jason, he'd gone to the crossroads to sell his soul, and the devil was coming. He knew it. He saw it every day.

At the supermarket, Alex the checkout kid, was missing three fingers instead of one, but it didn't slow him down. He scanned like a champion. *Beep. Beep.* Red lines passing over his hands as if measuring his weight in meat. The world was filled by adults without fingers or arms, an endless parade of diminished people as happy as cows. It was hard not to despise his entire species. They weren't humanity, elevated and glorious. They were meat on the hoof, walking burgers and steaks, food for the gods they didn't have eyes to see. But at least David couldn't read their minds anymore; whatever Arachniss had done for his trip downtown to share everyone's backstory, that was over.

On the way back from a visit to Jason's grumpy *why-would-you-bother-me-when-I'm-golfing* pediatrician—Jason was healthy as could be, and David had to keep himself from silently thanking Arachniss for keeping his word—he noticed the number of elderly people out on the streets, vastly outnumbering the young. The old had been spared, largely untouched, decrepit, slow, now giving up their seats on buses to those who could not stand on their own. David assumed they just didn't taste that good after sixty-five. The AARP was humankind's oblivious senescent resistance.

He'd talked to a woman missing her nose, but with a very nice prosthetic as they had these days, and rudely asked how she'd lost it just to see what she'd say. After a flush of embarrassment, she told him it was flesh-eating bacteria from swimming in Florida. Then she shrugged it off as if that was just the way of the world. Which was fascinating to David; so many memories of loss weren't about SHAS, but some other random accident or disease, as if the Arach knew there was a limit to the illusion and they wanted to spread the blame around. Even more interesting was how casual everyone was. Limbs or organs lost to SHAS or other incidents weren't terrible tragedies, but just part of life. Horror wasn't what happened to you, but how you felt about it. And if everyone was losing bits of themselves to the pandemic or other common events, then there was nothing to be afraid of. You just dealt with it and moved on.

At the last backyard grilling, Alicia's attorney friends wore new and fanciful prosthetics, but their son seemed to have vanished. Probably young and fatty and delicious. Padme had a prosthetic arm like Alicia's, but with subtly beautiful artwork etched in the surface. The twins seem unchanged, but spidercats prowled the perimeter looking for scraps. They were everywhere now, or maybe now he was just allowed to notice; he couldn't tell where reality ended and illusions started. Everyone seemed content with the fantasy.

Every day he passed the living room and turned his eyes from the TV. Every day, he expected his father or Arachniss to call him back and tell him the cost of protecting Jason. He knew it wouldn't last forever, but there was no reason to engage. Jason was safe, and even Alicia was strangely subdued.

But two things ate at him: first, the pace of human consumption was insane. Limbs were vanishing. People were disappearing. It wasn't sustainable for a year, let alone the two-decade span of the pandemic. Second, the movie Dad had shown him started with the phrase '...virtual meat entertainment compact...,' which were a lot of words that made no sense together. There was nothing virtual about what was happening to people. Being eaten alive was about as real as it got. He had to fight the urge to ask Dad-bot what was going on, partly for fear of the answer, partly for fear of what came next.

He'd looked online for any sign the world knew about the Arach, on bulletin boards, social media and conspiracy sites. His browser search history was an NSA wet dream, but there was nothing to find. There were plenty of conspiracies about alien abductions, saucer landings, Area 51, and so on, but no one seemed to think the human species was just meat bred for alien consumption. Which just meant the Arach were good at their jobs.

Ask Dad, he kept telling himself. It was the obvious answer. Dad would tell him.

He's not your father.

Which was technically true but hardly the point; David had to know what came next, even if it was terrible. And it was probably terrible, given the conversation he'd had with Dad the night after his trip to the mall. The day Kiaraa died, when Dad told him he wasn't alone.

David had taken the bait and gone into the living room.

"What do you mean, we're not alone?"

"I mean you have me…" Dad said.

David snorted. Was he kidding? "Okay, thanks." Then he had a thought.

"In the dream. The grass world. Was that real? And what did you do to my neck?"

"Lucid dreams like that are often cognitive shunts, pleasant delusions used to occupy your mind while things are happening to your body. Sometimes it's…"

"Being eaten?"

"Yes, but not always. Bodies have to be moved. Things cleaned up. They need time."

"Okay, but why do they care? If they can change our memories. Why care about pain we'll forget anyway?"

Dad sighed. "Are you sure you want to know?"

"Yes." *No.*

"Fear and pain cause surges of chemicals in the human body that ruin the flavor. That's one of reasons for humane animal dispatch in your slaughterhouses. It's no different for human beings."

"Well, that's terrible."

"Want to hear something funny? Almost all wet dreams are shunts, fantasies so they can eat you without ruining the flavor with too much chemical sedative. The next time you dream about great sex, you'll probably wake up missing a testicle." Dad frowned. "Sorry, that sounded better before I said it."

David suppressed a smile. Dad-bot was getting better at acting human; Dad had always been terrible at jokes.

"So what was he doing to me while I was stumbling around on the savannah? That was the savannah, right? Somewhere in Africa?"

"I have no idea, but he wasn't doing anything bad. He just needed time to reconfigure your implant."

David fought the urge to check his neck again. "What's the implant for, and what did he update?"

"It's for monitoring behavior, implanting the grand illusion, and so on. Nothing too invasive."

"So tracking and pacifying the herd. We're tagged like cattle."

Dad shrugged, meaning yes.

"And what did he do to mine?"

"You are not his property, per se. He can't protect you without reason; meat is a commodity and his job is to maximize productive value, not protect herd members from their intended purpose. So he overrode the administrative privileges on your implant to reclassify you as a pet."

"A pet? Like a dog? Wait, early in the pandemic, dogs and cats were the first victims. What do you mean by 'pet?'"

"It's not that literal. A pet is just a usage license, like easement on a property. You're not a dog. You're more like a horse on a long-term lease."

"And that's better?"

"For now. It allows him to protect you without bureaucratic processes he hates and costs he doesn't want to incur. Don't be offended. It's quite an honor."

David blinked. That word must mean something else to spiders.

"Maybe companion is a better word than pet?" Dad offered.

"Sure. If I'm a good companion, is Jason really safe?"

"Yes. If you do everything he says, Jason is safe."

Well, David thought, maybe this isn't so bad.

Then he remembered Kiaraa. Everything could mean anything, and anything seemed to include some pretty horrible stuff. Would Arachniss make him take part somehow, make him part of the slaughter?

What else could he want?

He would do anything for his son if that's what Arachniss demanded. He said it. He meant it.

But anything?

The word was a poltergeist banging around in his head, tearing out walls and demanding attention. What did anything really mean, and was he capable of doing it? And what kind of man would he be if he did? Dad waited with the answers. Dad would tell him the cost of Jason's life in calm, soothing words that would make the horror tolerable.

So when Dad finally spoke to say, 'Good luck at the book signing,' David expected more than casual pleasantries. He expected to be told to sit down and learn about all the terrible things to come. Instead, Dad smiled and turned himself off, leaving David alone in the hall sweating far too much for the temperature. Maybe Arachniss had forgotten about him. He was just a pet after all.

He checked his phone. He really was running late.

*

DRIVING WAS AN EXCITING EXPERIENCE. In the past, David looked forward to a trip out of the house and a little sight-seeing. He was amazed by what people did when they were supposed to be guiding thousands of pounds of metal down the road. Women putting on makeup. Men screaming at their phones. Children shouting until their parents wanted to drive off a bridge. Frequent off-pitch singing, road rage, hard-core nose picking and the occasional discrete but obvious blow job. Anything but watching the road. It was entertaining, if nothing else.

But on his last trip to the pediatrician with Jason, David got to watch a spider-blur eat the face of a young girl in the car next to him at the stoplight while her mother hummed along to something on the radio. That took the fun out of it. So when David pulled into the

Barnes & Noble parking lot, he let out a sigh of relief. He'd made it without seeing anything horrible. Now he just had to face a herd of edible people in a crowded store.

He got out, nearly hitting Charlotte with the door. She *eeped* as James yanked her back.

"Whoa there," James said. "Watch where you're going, Mr. McSwizzle."

"Whoa there?" David asked, checking out James' cowboy hat and snazzy-lookin' boots. Charlotte had a matching set in pink. Then he got it: one of his books was about an armadillo named Armando (of course). There were lots of hats and western references. "Sorry about that."

"No harm, no foul." James grabbed his arm. "You okay? You look a little…"

"Gross," Charlotte said.

"…sweaty," James corrected. "Be nice, baby-cakes."

Charlotte frowned and tugged at one of her fake ears.

"It's okay. I am a bit sweaty. Thanks for coming." David looked around the vast parking lot. There was a Whole Foods at the other end. Ansel would love this place. "No Franzia?"

"Working overtime on top secret projects," James said. "So it's just us. Alicia?"

"Lawyers Who Lunch. Once a month on Sunday." Not that she'd come anyway.

"Sounds important," James said.

"Doesn't it?" It suddenly occurred to him that she could be cheating on him and he'd have no idea. Would she do that? Would he care? Probably not, though it might help in the divorce. He hated thinking that way, and he wasn't sure it mattered anymore; he needed to focus on Jason, and Jason was safer with both of his parents for now.

"Dad…" Charlotte tugged at James' arm, bored.

"See you inside," James said. David followed along behind them, smiling. James seemed like an amazing dad. Whatever happened, he hoped Jason got to grow up with him around.

*

DAVID ALWAYS PASSED through the children's section to look at his books on display before a signing. It wasn't a vanity thing, at least he didn't think so; he just couldn't believe he was able to do what he loved and make a living at it. Sometimes the power and beauty of the cover illustrations shocked him, and he thought someone else must have done them. That couldn't be him. He wasn't that talented.

But mostly he hoped he'd see a child flipping through one of his books, eyes wide, and then run to his mother or father and ask to take it home. That was the best feeling in the world.

"Mr. Chambers?"

David turned to see an earnest young woman named Lysa, according to the name on her shirt. They'd talked on the phone and probably met before. He did the usual cursory check for missing parts. Nothing more than the sadly antiquated prosthetic hand where she tentatively clutched promotional bookmarks and flyers, each bearing his formal headshot. Why was he wearing tweed?

"Yes," he said. "Hi, Lysa."

"Are you ready to get started? We have quite an audience today."

"How many?"

"Twenty or thirty, maybe more. They're still coming in."

"Why?" he asked, because that was quite an audience. They both laughed and she shrugged; it was so random, there was no way to tell. It could just as well have been one mother and child and no one else for the entire hour. He'd once read to a service dog for thirty minutes, which he'd loved, because there were so few dogs left. He half expected Charlotte and James to be the only ones to show up.

"Okay, I'm ready."

He took a seat as Lysa announced him, and then quickly headed behind the seating area. There was light applause from a dozen mothers, a few fathers and two dozen children, most of them holding their favorite books or all nine of his books in a big rainbow stack, which made him smile like an idiot. James and Charlotte were in the front row, Charlotte in James' lap, smiling right back. He loved this part of his job.

"Hi, everyone. Thanks for coming out. I'll be reading *Snyder the Eider Spider* today…"—more applause and one *woot*—"…and then taking questions and signing books. As always, participation is encouraged if you want to make the animal noises." A little boy *cawed* loudly and everyone laughed. "Perfect, so let's find out what's going on in the rainforests of Brazil." He opened the book, took a breath, and started reading…

"Once below a tree in a place you'll never see, was a spider spinning silk in the shade of the canopy…"

By the end of the book, children had roared like leopards, squawked like macaws and chittered and knocked like a wandering spider might if anyone listened closely enough. He turned the book to show them Snyder flying on new silk wings, up, up and away on his new adventure to another day, and then closed the book to applause and a little gratuitous cheering. Not once when reading about Snyder did he think about Arachniss or his father or whether people tasted like chicken. It was awesome.

Then a pale, gaunt older woman he hadn't noticed sneak in cleared her throat from the back row.

"Patricia," he grumbled under his breath, but not quietly enough. Everyone turned to look at her.

"Is Snyder a metaphor for trans-*sexualism*?" she asked, dragging the *sexual* part out way too long. There was a collective grown from some mothers, confused glances from the children, and a token shrug from Lysa, who clearly wasn't interested in playing bookstore bouncer. It wasn't awesome anymore.

"Go home," one father said. Patricia didn't notice. But then Patricia didn't seem to notice a lot of things, including social etiquette and freedom of speech. She was a self-appointed morality troll guarding the bridge to children's fragile minds. She usually spent her time posting hateful comments online or leaving him one-star reviews for books she'd never read, but every once in a while she'd show up in person. It was always a treat.

"This is for children, Patty," he said, calmly, knowing she hated the name. "Why don't you talk to me afterward?"

"Afraid of the truth?" she asked. "Is Snyder a—"

"No," he said, bluntly. Which was a lie. *Snyder's* transformation was absolutely a metaphor for transsexual transitions, but he'd never meant for children to understand the allegory, especially not his younger readers. He'd made it subtle, but obviously not subtle enough. Patricia had eviscerated his 'commie-sexual' politics on every Christian and conservative blog in the region. Then she doxed him, posting his address online, and Alicia ended up suing her and winning a token judgment, but failed to get a restraining order or any takedowns. Now Patricia stalked him like the ghost of morality past.

"Really?" she asked smugly.

Lysa had moved closer and leaned in, asking her to leave. Patricia waved her off.

"Then can you explain the *backstory* of *Benny Beau Beaver*?"

So punny, David thought. Parents moaned. Some started leaving. B.B. Beaver used fallen trees and other things on the forest floor to make art that had no place in the world of serious industrial beavers. He was like Rudolf without the body shaming, but mostly he was an excuse to make a lot of terrible beaver jokes for the parents. And talk about all the things his father had taught him and Tommy on long walks in the woods of the Front Range. It wasn't a great work of western children's literature, but backstory? It wasn't like *Snyder,* there was no backstory.

"It's about beavers," he said. "And bullying." And there were some terribly great sex puns.

"Homosexual beaver abominations," Patricia spat. There was a gasp. Lysa flinched. One mother covered her mouth, laughing, but more than one sat up straight as a meerkat as in, *what did I miss?* Were the beavers fornicating? Was there sodomy in the sod? Splendor in the ender?

"Do you deny that Benny was, in fact, gay?"

All eyes turned to David. Some rolled, some squinted, but all were wide and focused. Did he? Did he deny it?

"I don't," he said. "Nor do I confirm it. It never occurred to me. He was creative and different. It wasn't code for anything. He was just an artistic little guy trying to get along in a regimented world." He turned to the kids, who were by this time baffled, distracted or crying. Even Charlotte looked confused. He didn't envy James' conversation that evening, but at least he hadn't made things worse by playing the cop card and trying to shut Patricia down.

"But if he was gay, and maybe he was, I don't know—he doesn't tell me everything—I'd be fine with that." And that reminded him of a line from an eighties movie where one character is caught in a compromising position with a mannequin—'I wouldn't want to keep a man from getting some wood'—which was apropos to nothing, but it made him smile, and that was a mistake.

"You think sodomy is a joke?" Patricia barked. James coughed out a laugh and David cracked up. He just couldn't help himself. Some mothers joined in. Some didn't. It was time to make an early exit.

"Sodomy is an abomination against god!" Patricia proclaimed, standing, fist raised. Was she going to smite him? He'd never been smited before. Smitten? No, that was too romantic. Smote? No. Smoten, maybe? That couldn't be right. He wondered if it tickled.

Then a spidery blur moved behind her, and he stopped laughing.

"Okay, ma'am, I think it's time to leave," Lysa said, reaching for Patricia's raised arm. That was a mistake; never touch an elderly white woman mid-smite.

Patricia pulled her arm back, jerking Lysa off balance. Patricia tried to defend herself from the falling staffer with her other hand, instead face-punching her with a tightly clenched bible. Lysa let out an audible grunt—smiting didn't tickle after all—and mothers scattered with their children, loosely attached prosthetics flying or left neglected on the floor. Patricia and Lysa released each other and fell into collapsing chairs under a rain of books, bookmarks, business cards and other confetti-like detritus Lysa had been holding in her third-rate fake hand.

David pushed his chair back and fought conflicting urges to help Lysa, run, or at least see what happened next, which froze him indecisively in place. And then the blur moved over Patricia's fallen form, her arms and legs up in the air like a capsized beetle, and her entire body seemed to vibrate at an impossible frequency. David thought about calling out, but he didn't.

Boom! A wet red bomb went off and everyone in twenty feet was coated in bloody mist.

Patricia was gone. Her clothes, her body, everything.

David wiped some of Patricia off his face. James and Charlotte were coated in it. But neither they nor anyone else, not one person, mother or child, noticed anything other than a loud noise that could have been a firecracker (it wasn't). One little girl licked her red cheek nonchalantly, like it was snowing and snowflakes were delicious. Lysa sat up and looked around, confused and drenched in blood.

"Where did she go?" she asked. She had a bookmark stuck in her sticky red hair.

And then the spidercats arrived, swarming over bookshelves, chairs and people like a feline Hoover of tongues and blackness. In a moment, the blood was gone and the chairs cleaned. Not even the blur remained.

And no one noticed any of it.

Well, David noticed. He noticed specifically that Arachniss—he assumed it was Arachniss—had eliminated his arch enemy. Vaporized her. Erased her from the world. David could already remember reading her obituary, about how she died tragically in her apartment from a stroke and no one noticed for days. There was no mention of her cats or what they did to her, but it was implied. *Crazy Christian Crackpot Consumed by Cats.* Now that was a smiting.

He tried not to smile. He really did.

But come on.

Welcome to the Club

"I'M GOING FOR A RUN," Alicia said, dumping Jason in David's arms at the front door. She didn't ask about the signing or tell him about lunch, for which he was grateful. He held his son at arm's length and watched his wife jog to the street and vanish north toward Chautauqua Park. He had no idea how she had so much energy or, for that matter, how the Arach made it so Alicia missed the fact that he was still spotted with Patricia's blood.

"How you doin', little buddy?" David asked Jason. Jason answered with a hiccup and impressive drooling.

"I know what you mean. I've had a bit of a day myself."

He carried Jason into the nursery while trying to keep him from getting bloody. There followed a quick feeding and diaper change. Then he checked his phone. He had a missed text from James—
THAT WAS FUN! LOL—
And thirty-five more from Dad-bot. That probably wasn't good. He'd avoided his digital father long enough. He just needed to clean up before getting down to it.

Quick shower. Fast shave. New clothes. Back to the nursery to check on Jason.

"Who's the best pirate baby?" he asked as he leaned over the crib.

But Jason wasn't there.

David looked under the blanket, under the crib, spun around the nursery checking under things you couldn't hide a wallet behind, then raced to the living room. Where Jason was on the coffee table again, perfectly happy, but definitely not where he was supposed to be.

David picked him up, examined every square inch of his tiny body in a way that would make him feel nostalgic during future TSA pat-downs—nothing new was missing, at least nothing on the outside—and rocked him for a moment. Then he jabbed at the TV remote.

"Long time no talk," Dad said, smiling his standard smile.

"You don't have to use Jason to get my attention."

"Apparently, I do." Dad put a finger up to the side of his right eye. "You missed a spot."

David followed suit and came away with a smear of red. *Great.* He wiped his hand on his jeans.

"That's better. I imagine you have questions."

David wanted to laugh. He had *many* questions. He just wasn't sure what was allowed. Would the wrong question get him killed or Jason cut to pieces? He didn't know where to start.

"Just ask," Dad said. "It's not a trick."

"Okay." David looked down at Jason. Forced himself to relax. "What are you?"

"Meaning the Arach?"

"Meaning *you*. Are you just a front for Arachniss, or…"

"Oh, no, I'm a separate entity. I have my own thoughts, based on your father's reconstructed mental framework, but Arachniss knows everything we talk about. So we're different, but our conversations are not private. Does that help?"

"Yes." Not really. "So you're an AI?"

"Hmm." He puffed out his cheeks and exhaled. "In terms of technology you'd understand, close enough. I'm considered a semi-sentient virtual entity, technically alive, but with no legal protections or rights. Not a person as such." He shrugged. "Too much information?"

"No, that's fine." *Semi-sentient virtual entity?* "Why did you kill Patricia? She was a terrible person, but she didn't deserve to die that way." No matter how momentarily gratifying it was.

"I didn't kill anyone, David. I can't interact with the physical world. But neither did Arachniss."

"Then who did?"

"I told you Arachniss is one of many Arach hosts on the planet. Host just means he has a territory, and that territory includes your neighborhood and several others. He's responsible for what happens to the herd, meaning you, in this neighborhood. He can't go outside of that territory or interact with any other herd without permission of the other host. So Arachniss made a trade to have her harvested at the signing. Another Arach did it. Arachniss just picked the timing."

"What did he trade for?"

"I think you can guess."

"He had someone else killed in this neighborhood?"

"Not killed, no. Patricia was older and of relatively low value. It's not one-for-one. The trade was for a few limbs of a younger and healthier person."

"A *child?*"

"A teenager."

"Who was it?"

"I can ask. You've probably never met them. Are you hoping it's Ansel?"

"You know about…never mind. No. I don't want to know." He should, but how would that help? Even Ansel didn't deserve to be dismembered by aliens. He looked down at Jason. This wasn't an academic discussion. He needed to focus on what it took to protect his family. The rest could wait.

"But why do it at all?" Meaning, what was the real cost of that trade?

"He wants something from you. And he thought you'd appreciate the gesture."

"He thought I'd appreciate having a woman murdered at my book signing?"

"Didn't you?" The TV showed David at the signing, face spotted with Patricia's blood, his look of horror slowly turning to a slight but undeniable smile.

"You recorded that? I was surprised." He shook his head; he could search his soul later. "What does he want?"

Dad came back and his eyes flooded with black.

"I want you to fetch something for me."

David flinched back into the couch, covering Jason's eyes instinctively. Jason giggled and grabbed his hands.

"Like the good little dog I am?" So much for Dad's rationalizations.

"Exactly."

"What?"

"We'll get to that. Ask me."

"Ask you what?"

"Ask me the question you've been avoiding."

He swallowed. "Did you eat Alex? Did you kill my son?"

"Yes." No hesitation. No remorse.

Rage flooded David like it hadn't in years. Nothing Alicia had ever done brought this out. Nothing had since that kid attacked Kathryn in high school. What he remembered was losing all control. He blacked out and started beating the kid with everything he could. He'd have killed him if campus security hadn't pulled him off. It was one reason he tried harder to understand Alicia than he should; maybe she blacked out. Maybe she had never conquered her rage, or learned to force it down. It might be they were more alike than he liked to admit. Because at that second, he wanted to reach through the TV screen and beat Arachniss to death. Rip him spider-leg from spider-leg until there were just parts and guts and nothing else. And he would have tried, but he couldn't move.

"Let me go," he demanded.

"You want to know why?" Arachniss asked.

"I don't care," David spat. "You murder children. You can't explain that."

"Children are veal, David. Soft and fatty and highly prized throughout the galaxy. I don't have to explain it. They're delicious. Now, calm down or Jason can join Alex on the menu."

David closed his eyes and focused on his breathing. On Jason, his living son. Inhaled. Exhaled. The rage drained slowly, far slower than it had come, leaving him sick and exhausted, but it left. That's what Kiaraa had taught him after high school and throughout college; how to control it. How to live with a sea of rage that would drown him if he let it. And now she was dead, too.

"That's better," Arachniss said. "I harvested your son, but I didn't select him. The difference might not mean much to you, but you are not mine to eat at will. I serve a market, and when that market demands a certain type of meat, that's what I deliver. I take no joy in it."

"So you're just following orders?" he sneered.

"Do you think equating me to a Nazi is going to help you save Jason?"

Inhale. Exhale. "So it was random, just one child on a list of children to be slaughtered?"

"No, not random. There are a lot of things you don't understand yet. Nothing is random. But it wasn't my choice and the reason I'm here, the reason Jason is not on that list right now, is because I saw how it affected you. I saw how you loved your son. And that affected me."

Alex's death touched Arachniss' cold spider heart more than the death of every other child before? David shook his head. *Bullshit.* "And?"

"And Alex was going to die no matter what. It could have been painful. There's a market for that. I made it painless."

"You want me to thank you?"

"I want you to understand how much worse it can be. Would you like me to show you?"

He didn't wait for an answer. Jason screamed. *Loud.* Screamed like never before.

"No! Please. Please don't hurt my son."

The screaming stopped.

"What did you do to him?"

"Nothing. Pain can be simulated. There's no need for real harm to make him feel pain you can't imagine. I let you see some of the real world and what happens to people, some of whom probably deserve it, some of whom most definitely do not. But I'll show you far worse if you don't do what I tell you."

"Okay," David nodded forcefully. "I'll do anything." That word again. "I told you."

"Good. Now ask me something else."

"I don't—"

"Put your emotions aside for a second. You're talking to a being who's lived thousands of years and traveled the galaxy. You must have one interesting question."

He frowned at his black-eyed father. "Why do you care?" And decided he needed a better name for Dad-possessed-by-Arachniss. *Dadrachniss* was obvious enough.

Dadrachniss shrugged. "We're going to spend some time together. It can't all be threats and screaming. Just one question. Humor me. I'll answer if I can."

"Okay, just..." He had a thousand questions. What kind of messed up society has a market for human meat? Why had he shown him what others were thinking and what happened to them? Why didn't they like being called spiders?

"Ask, David. It's not a trick."

He knew what he should ask: what was the cost of protecting Jason? But he knew the answer was going to be ugly.

"There's too much killing," he said. "I went downtown like Dad suggested. There were dozens of you. At the rate you're killing us, we'll all be dead in months. Or is it just in highly populated areas? And I thought you had specific territories?"

"Some public spaces are akin to open season." Dadrachniss shrugged and smiled. "Why do you think the death rate is so high?"

"I don't know. It feels frantic. Almost out of control. It's been twenty years and SHAS was never like this. Things are escalating. I have no idea why."

"It's very simple. The harvest is coming to an end."

"The harvest?"

"We're not here all the time, at least not most of us. We return every few generations to take what we want, and then we leave you to recover."

"This has happened before?" He knew the question was stupid before he finished. Of course this has happened before. Earth was a farm. That's what farms are for.

"Of course. All the great pandemics were harvests: SHAS, COVID, the Spanish Flu, the great Black Death, the Plague of Justinian and many more. Every die-off of your species, and every species before that, back to the dinosaurs and long before. That was us. We feed and then leave. We'll be gone before you know it. Humanity will go on. Think of it like crop rotation on a galactic scale."

"Wait, the dinosaurs?" Amused nod. "You dropped a meteor on the dinosaurs?"

"It was nearby. We just gave it a nudge."

"A nudge? I mean, what?" He wasn't processing this well.

"That's your real question, isn't it? How long does this go on? Is there a chance for any of you? Can you protect Jason? The answers are: a bit longer, yes, and absolutely. You can protect your son."

"Okay." Thank god. "When is it over? When do you leave?"

"Soon. And that brings us to what I need from you."

"Wait, I have—"

"One more question, David. Save the rest for your father. That's why I created him."

"Um." His brain had suddenly gone blank. They'd killed the dinosaurs? "How many of you are there?"

"It depends on how you count. There's a host like me for every ten-thousand people on Earth, but it's all dependent on current tastes and needs. Sometimes we stay for years, sometimes far less."

"But you've been here for decades."

"This time, yes. There was a debate about what to do with you. You've become advanced enough to be evaluated as something more than meat, semi-sentient at least, and the demand for your product has waned over the past thousand years. Some wanted to exterminate you—"

"What?" David leaned forward. "You mean kill *all* of us?"

"Of course that's what I mean. I suppose we'd keep a few of you as pets. Please don't interrupt. Some wanted to exterminate *all of you* in favor of a new, more marketable species. Some wanted to offer you a place in Arach society. We reached a compromise. You're still meat, but we won't exterminate you for now. Congratulations."

"What?" David was still processing being meat. The idea of being eradicated was a bit much. Dadrachniss waited for him to calm down. It took a moment.

"Okay," he said. Back to the original question. "How many of you are there in the universe, not just on Earth?"

"Trillions. We're the most populous sentient form in what you call the Milky Way."

"Trillions? Why haven't we seen any evidence of you?"

Arachniss hesitated, and David wondered why he was being so patient. Why waste more time with his pet?

"Some sort of Dirac equation question?" Dadrachniss asked. David knew the Dirac equation was a popular if controversial way of estimating how many intelligent species were in the universe, and nodded. "You do see us, all the time. Our galaxy is dense with communication and remnants of prior civilizations. We just don't allow you to remember what you see. Just like you won't remember us. There's always a caretaker on the planet, sometimes several, though more often automated than live. They only allow you to see what we want you to see, and feed enough confusion and idiocy to distract from what leaks through to people like you."

"And other galaxies?" As if that mattered. But still. The universe had just gotten a lot more crowded.

"That's a question for another day. From our experience, every galaxy is dominated by one species or dead. It's too easy to kill others off with relativistic weapons, which inter-galactic distances protect us from. Well, mostly."

"Mostly? You're at war with other species?"

Dadrachniss shrugged. "Not currently. And you should concern yourself with what's happening far closer to home. I did you a favor. Now you're going to do one for me."

"You mean Patricia? I don't owe you anything." Not for killing a woman, no matter how he hated her.

"True, but I don't have to ask nicely. And Jason is looking delectable this evening."

David froze. It was hard to remember how powerless he was.

"Sorry," he said. "Sorry." *I'll be a good dog.* "What do you want me to get?"

"There's a woman nearby, but in someone else's lot. Like you, she can see more than she should. I'd like you to bring her to me. If she agrees, I can protect her and her daughter."

"Like you're protecting me? I mean, you are, right? Being untouched is unusual."

"Yes."

"But not Jason. Why?"

"Leverage. You need to bring her here tomorrow night." He was losing patience.

"Leverage for what?" Silence. "Okay, I'll do it, but…"

"Am I going to eat her?"

"Yes."

"No. She's not mine to eat. Not without compensation. And I just want to talk, in private. That's why I need you."

"Can I tell her about you?"

"You can tell her anything you want as long as she's here tomorrow night."

"Okay. Who is she?" The thought of having another human being to talk to was absurdly exciting. He'd do it just to keep from losing his mind. "Where does she live?"

"You know her already."

He instantly knew who he meant. "Franzia."

"Good dog," he said. "Now, before you go."

"What?"

"Your neighbors two doors down have triplets."

"The Connellys?" He caught his breath. The Connelly kids were barely three.

"Yes. They're a rare treat and I like to keep them symmetrical. What should I take next?"

"I'm not doing that," he mumbled. Of course he was. That's what *anything* meant.

"Them or Jason. Your choice."

"Their pinky tips," he blurted, instantly hating himself for it.

"Oh, good choice. Like little bird bones. Snap-snap."

And then Arachniss was gone and the TV turned itself off.

David closed his eyes and tried not to think. Maybe Arachniss wasn't down the street eating Oliver, Olivia and Olivander. And even if he was, it wasn't David's fault; Arachniss would have done it anyway.

Olivia? Why was that name so familiar?

Snap-snap-snap.

*

THE NEXT NIGHT, Franzia Faizan came to the door in a thin robe, breasts barely covered, that exhausted not-young-enough-mother look, like the haunted stare of a soldier returning from war. He found himself distracted by her breasts and then by the thought that he even noticed breasts and then by the weird realization that he might not be dead inside, which was surprising—and unfortunate timing—but he probably shouldn't stare and what the hell was wrong with him; he was a married man. What he should have noticed more quickly was how puffy and bloodshot her eyes were, and the smears of mascara on her sleeve. She'd been crying. He probably should have called.

"Everything okay?" he asked, trying to focus on her mouth.

She frowned and pulled her robe tighter. "You're not my pizza."

He laughed. "Did you order pizza?"

"Of course not."

"Then—"

"Like any rational person, I assume that the rise of the machines will be preceded by a brief period where they lull us into compliance by predicting our every need. And I'm craving pepperoni."

"You think they're machines?" he asked. Why would machines need to eat people?

"What?" She looked baffled and he felt like an idiot. Apparently, she didn't know about the Arach yet.

"You thought Siri had ordered you a pizza?" he asked, pretending he hadn't said anything idiotic.

"Alexa, Skynet, whatever. As long as there's no pineapple." She shrugged and took a sip. "What's in the bag?"

"Pastries."

Eyebrows raised. "What kind of pastries?"

"Tarts. Lemon for Charlotte, key lime for James, and tarte à l'orange for you."

Eyebrows furled. "You are a machine. I was right."

"I just—"

"Seriously, how do you know what kinds of *tarts* we like? Did you hack our email?"

"You told me at the last barbeque. You were trying to prove you weren't totally white trash because you liked, uh, *bougie* desserts."

"I have no recollection of that." She sighed and glanced at David's Outback parked at the curb, searching for Alicia or Jason. "What's up, David? James is asleep upstairs. He's working graveyard too this week, because apparently working one shift isn't enough."

"Working off all the meat?"

She blushed, the slightest flush of red. "Yeah, he seems to lose control when you grill."

"It's fine," he said. "Flattering, actually, but I came to see you." That seemed to be the wrong answer. "Sorry. I can come back tomorrow." Which was idiocy. Why was he so nervous?

"Oh, no. You're not going anywhere with my tarts. Come in, come in. I'll make coffee."

David gently laid the tarts out on miniature individual paper plates on the dining room table while Franzia banged around in the kitchen, apparently searching for coffee under the floorboards. The personally sized tarts were flawless as art, each with a lightly browned crust, fresh cream on the lemon and key lime, torched sugar on the orange. And there was the tiramisu one for him, with dark chocolate curls and a dusting of cocoa. It occurred to him he had more than the usual number of tart pans for a heterosexual man, which wasn't exactly a politically-correct thought. But Alicia had pointed it out frequently enough, even if it was never clear what the right number was. Zero, he supposed. Once he'd put the set around his penis and walked around the house sounding like a muffled snare drum while Alicia frowned at him over a printed copy of *Colorado Lawyer*. He wasn't sure it had the desired 'this is manly' affect, but she did golf-clap at his little dance and he loved his tart pans. Damn it.

Franzia reappeared with a light puffy jacket over her robe, coffee, and tiny little dessert forks. David smiled and pushed the orange tart over to her. She dug in immediately, taking a bite, sucking air in surprise, her eyes rolling back in exaggerated pleasure.

"Sweet Jesus," she said. "Forget the meat. This is your calling."

"Thank you." He sipped the coffee. French pressed? It was fantastic.

"James said there was a riot at your book signing."

"Riot's an exaggeration. Someone set off a firework in the back row. People panicked." Which was exactly how he remembered one version of it. So sad that Lysa fell over and hurt her arm. "It was great for sales." After word of the 'riot' got out online, people flooded the B&N website for copies of *Benny* and *Snyder*. There really was no such thing as bad publicity. "I hope it wasn't too scary for Charlotte."

"Scary? She loved it, but she didn't get her books signed."

"I can do that anytime. Now, if you've got them out."

"Maybe another time. So, what's up, non-biblical David? How's Alicia?"

"Good. She's, well, that's part of why I'm here."

"No."

"No, what?"

"We're not swingers. Don't even ask."

"Why would I ask that?"

"Why wouldn't you?" She looked offended. "You don't find me attractive?"

He took a bite of his tart. Maybe he should just let the spiders eat her.

"Sorry," she said. "Sometimes I'm all ass and no smart. Did you know James and I are in an open marriage? No? Of course you didn't. Well, now you do."

"An open marriage?" he asked, meaning, *that's a real thing?*

"It's less exciting than it sounds. I don't think either of us has done much more than flirt with anyone else." She shrugged, a strangely sad gesture. "So what's up?"

David chewed longer than necessary, then just spat it out: "So, I've been having these weird dreams lately."

Raised eyebrows. Slight turn to the side. Defending herself from the crazy.

"Nightmares, really," he continued, speaking slowly so he could watch her reaction to each word. "About Alicia and Jason." It was all he could do not to mention Alex. "Sometimes I wake up and it feels like there's something else in the room with us."

Her coffee cup was perfectly still, balanced on her bare leg. She had completely frozen, her face blank, the poker face of a mannequin.

"Charlie!" she shouted. He nearly dropped his coffee.

"Coming!" Charlotte yelled back from upstairs. A second later, she ran into the kitchen and pulled up short when she saw David.

"Hello, Mr. Chambers," she said, surprised. "I liked your signing."

"Look, Char. He brought us pastries. Want one?"

She noticed the remaining lemon tart, and her eyes widened. In a flash, she'd grabbed it up in her left hand and hid it behind her back like something she'd shoplifted, but it was enough. Her right hand was now fingerless, just a palm and nothing else, more like a flipper than a human limb, like Padme's.

"Take it up to your room," Franzia said. "And don't get crumbs everywhere."

"Okay." She smiled brightly and waved her flippity-flappity hand. "Thanks, Mr. C." And then she was gone.

"You shouldn't stare like that," Franzia said.

David turned back. "What?"

"At her hand. It's rude." There was so much gravel and anger in her pronunciation of the last word it sounded like the victim of a sex crime trying to dig herself out of rocky earth. And her eyes were wet, like she was on the verge of tears again. Charlotte's finger loss was a recent thing, but he didn't know what Franzia knew and he wasn't sure what to say, so he defaulted to the usual:

"Sorry…" he mumbled.

"You were saying. Someone was in the room with you?"

"Not someone, some*thing*."

"Like an animal?"

He studied her, wondering if she was really this clueless and Arachniss had been wrong, or if she was just testing him. He had no idea. He thought Alicia was good at blank expressions, but Franzia set the international standard for inscrutability.

"Like an animal," he said, "but also…not."

She was silent. Unmoving. Eyes like white holes. It was unnerving.

"And, I, well, sometimes I think that it's, whatever it is…" *Just say it.* "…is eating them."

Nothing. No reaction. No blinking. Could he tell if her pupils dilated? He squinted. She leaned back.

"Franzia?"

Her coffee cup was shaking, like the tremor of someone with palsy or alcohol withdrawal. Or fear. Did she already know? She cleared her throat, took a sip of wine, then coffee, and then her face changed to a mask of rage. It wasn't like she got merely angry, but that she adorned the cloak of fury and all its manifest violence. She *became* fury. The transformation was so sudden and violent, he almost fell out of his chair. Was this what he was like in high school? It was terrifying.

"You should leave," she said, her voice low and menacing.

"Franzia, I—"

"You think something is *eating* my daughter? What the holy fuck is wrong with you?"

"I just thought—"

"Get. The hell. Out."

"Uh." This wasn't what he expected. Hadn't Arachniss said she was like him? Was this—

"Get out!"

He stood and backed toward the living room, Franzia following.

"I know you're having trouble with your marriage, David. I know you're worried about your son. But don't bring your crazy here. We're all full up with our own shit. Now get out, or I'll have James throw you out."

David had no desire to be evicted at gunpoint by an angry cop or spend the night in the crazy tank. He assumed there was a crazy tank next to the drunk tank. Or maybe everyone went in the same one, like a prisoner stew. Franzia stepped toward him. He stepped back, turned, and fled into the night.

I'm alone again, he thought as he sat in the driver's seat of the Outback and pushed the *Start* button. For a second, he thought she'd believe him. That he wouldn't feel as alone with the madness of Arachniss or the violence of his marriage. That someone would believe him. See him. That maybe he'd have an ally. More stupid fantasy. He wrote children's books. He didn't live in one. No matter what people said, everyone was alone. Always and forever alone.

And he'd failed Arachniss.

Bad Dog

PEDRO LOOKED UP AT DAVID, all eyes and no answers.

"She's not coming," he said. Would Arachniss kill him or Jason? He had no idea what to do. The cost of failure could be anything, and there was almost nothing he could stand. Even another digit sliced off Jason's fingers was too much. There had to be something he could do. Alicia was asleep. Kathryn was mute. Franzia thought he was crazy. There was just him and Pedro, and Pedro wasn't answering.

"What am I supposed to do?" he asked the bear. Pedro looked at him with pity. David ground his pencil into graphite on the bear's eyes, smearing them across the paper. Then he used charcoal to blacken the page to utter darkness and tossed it in the trash.

He looked around the room. Pedro's infinite eyes glowered with pity and contempt.

"Sorry," he said to the bear and the air. "Sorry."

Maybe he could ask his father?

They're the same thing, Arachniss and Dad. They're the same.

Maybe not. If he's the same, what's the point of him?

What's the point of you if you can't protect Jason? You had one job. And you screwed it up.

Why did he look at Charlotte's hand? Why did he say 'eating?' He could have just invited her for drinks. But he'd assumed she knew more. Why else send him there? Was it a trick?

*

"DOES HE KNOW?" DAVID ASKED Dad-bot. "Franzia's not coming. She didn't believe me."

"It's okay, David. He knows. I'd have been surprised if it went any better."

David clenched the remote, wondering how it would look embedded in his father's face. Probably better than a bullet, but equally unhelpful. He was losing control. He forced himself to exhale slowly and put the remote down.

"What?" he asked, as calmly as he could without cracking teeth.

His father quirked his lips to the side and shrugged. "She already knows, David. She's just scared."

He thought back on her frozen mask of indifference. Scared wasn't the word he'd choose. In denial, maybe. Suppressing serious rage, definitely. Maybe she just processed fear differently.

"Maybe," he said. "But what does this mean for me?"

"You mean, what does your failure mean for you and Jason?"

David nodded. "I can try again and—"

"Arachniss knew she wouldn't come. But the seed's planted. She'll come around."

"He knew…" That was annoying, like some game Alicia would play: bait a trap and wait for someone to fall in. Usually him. So the next part sounded more terse than was advisable: "I don't understand why you're like this."

"Like what?"

Something in Dad's voice set him off. The condescending calm. The feigned innocence. "All of this. You're a powerful, technologically advanced species that spans the galaxy. You have infinite power. You could do anything. And what you do is eat human beings. You're sadistic and violent and just so…disappointing. Why does it have to be like this? What the hell is…?" David's words stuck in his throat. Dad's eyes were black as pitch.

Arachniss had arrived.

"What the hell is…?" Dadrachniss left the question hanging.

"I'm sorry, I just. I don't get it. I don't get any of this."

"You mean you failed and now you're trying to avoid the consequences of your failure."

"No, I…" Yes.

"Why aren't you a vegetarian?"

"What?"

"You were a vegetarian. For as long as you could choose what to be, that was your one choice. From high school on, you were a quiet but strict vegetarian. Now you're the god of brisket and you hate it. You hate yourself, but you keep doing it. Why?"

"It just got too complicated." And now the spider alien was psychoanalyzing him.

"You mean Alicia made you and you're too weak to stand up to her."

"Meaning my family is more important than my dietary choices."

"What family? Your wife has nothing but contempt for you, and you let her take away the only part of your identity that you were truly proud of. You're ashamed of your own shadow and the balls between—"

"Stop it!" He froze. He'd just yelled at the alien.

"Am I wrong?" Dadrachniss asked.

"No, you're right." David spoke slowly and carefully, keeping all emotion out of his voice. "I gave in. It's not hard to figure out. Kathryn and Kiaraa remind me, reminded me, every time I saw them. But you know the answer. Alicia would never allow it."

"So you're okay with killing animals for pleasure?"

"No." But he saw where this was going. "And it's not the same. My son needs a mother."

"Your son needs a father who doesn't despise himself."

David snorted. "Fine. I'm a coward. Is that how you justify slaughtering millions of human beings? You're an advanced galaxy-spanning civilization that eats us just like we eat cows or pigs. No matter how advanced or powerful a species gets, it's still just this. It's pathetic." God, why couldn't he stop insulting the alien?

"You're not wrong."

"What?"

"Let's take a trip."

*

DAVID AND DADRACHNISS WERE STANDING on a walkway over dark-gray concrete prison yard, where massive tattooed men worked out and eyeballed each other like prey and predators, heads on swivel. He could smell the tension, fear and sweat. David shook off the disorientation quickly—it was obviously an illusion— but couldn't resist the urge to put his hand over his father's, pressing it to the cold metal railing. It felt real, warm, bone and skin *real*. Like he was really there. Then he saw his father's black eyes and remembered that none of it was real. He pulled his hand back and wiped it on his pants.

"Look," Dadrachniss said, not even acknowledging the touch.

"At what? Why are we here?"

"This is how you house your poor. Trapped, forced to fight for survival, fearing for their lives every day and night. You let them kill each other. You let them rape each other. This is your society. How are we any worse?"

"Seriously? For one, these men did something to be here. For another, no one's eating them."

"So you think they deserve it?"

"No." *Not all of them.* David watched a man slide a shiv into another man's side, then stab him a dozen times. Others blocked the guards' view, then melted into the general chaos. Someone put a hand over the man's mouth to keep him from screaming as black blood pumped from multiple wounds. No one deserved that. "No," he said again, pointlessly. Was this a morality lesson? "Enough."

*

THEY WERE ON A BUS in India, watching a group of men rape a woman. No one helped her. David strained forward to stop them, but they were suddenly in Africa. Child soldiers butchered a group of men using machine guns as big as they were. Then they watched children picking over mountains of garbage in a landfill. In a chicken factory, a belt funneled baby chicks into a chute where they were grabbed up by mechanical claws and then had their beaks snipped off—some clean, some bloody, but all fast and efficient. In the Middle East, a drone strike killed dozens of women and children as they slept on mats in the dirt. Hunters in Africa slaughtered an elephant for ivory so someone in China could get an erection. In Brazil, the rainforests burned. In Japan, a bay was filled with the blood of dolphins slaughtered for their meat. Somewhere on the Pacific, a container was filled with women being trafficked to men in Canada. On and on in an endless montage of human failure.

"Please," David said. "Please stop this."

*

THEY WERE BACK in the living room. David bent over and did everything he could not to throw up on the carpet. When he looked up, sweating and nauseated, he was angrier than ever.

"So that's your rationalization?" he demanded. "You're no worse than we are?"

"No," Dadrachniss said, back in the TV. "I'm a lot of things, but not pedantic."

"Then what's your point?"

"Violence is the universal background radiation of biological life, David. You eliminate everything else, and you can't get rid of the constant, ubiquitous chatter of petty hatred and destruction. It's not your fault; life itself is a form of abuse. You're born into it. You bathe in it. You die in it. There is no life without violence. There is no violence without life. You think there's some saintly place separate from violence, but there isn't. There is no sanctity or perfection. There is only the best you can do. No one expects perfection from humanity or any other naturally evolved species."

"Okay." Was that a prepared speech? "Then what do you want?"

"*More.* Do you know what the undecidability principle is?" He didn't. "It means all mathematical systems are flawed. There is no system that answers all questions correctly, no equation for all problems or any universal solution to anything. Imperfection is innate to creation. It would be insane to pretend otherwise. So no, you don't need to be perfect to be seen as deserving respect. You don't need to be flawless, David, you just need to sincerely try to be *better*. The search for perfection is just performative failure. The search for constant, reasonable improvement in the face of that reality is the real test. You must strive. You must *want*. And you must feel compassion for one another when you fail. That's all."

"But we do do that. I mean, some of us."

"If you were us looking at your species, would you be impressed?"

David opened his mouth, closed it. The answer was obvious.

"That's why we're still meat? Because we're not trying hard enough?"

"No. The Arach eat human beings because you were made to be eaten and you serve a purpose, just like we ate a thousand species before. I'm disappointed in you, David, because you know better and you still can't do what's right. One thing has nothing to do with the other."

"Wait, you're not the same as other Arach?"

Dadrachniss shook his head, clearly frustrated. "It's always the same with primitive species. You see yourself as individuals but others as homogenous collectives. It's why you always envision aliens as insectile hive minds. We are Arach. I am Arach. It doesn't mean we're all the same. Wolves aren't all the same just because you're human and see them as others. So, yes, Arach have differing opinions on every subject you can imagine. Most Arach think you're just an overpriced piece of meat. I think you can be more than that. But you're making me wonder if they're right."

"Okay." David wasn't sure whether to be scared or amused. For a hyper-intelligent and nearly omnipotent alien, Arachniss had the same emotional triggers as a human teenager. "More how?"

"Just bring Franzia to me, David. Don't fail me again."

"What are you going to do to her?"

"Hopefully, nothing."

"Then why do you want her?"

"I want to see if she's less disappointing than you are."

"*I'm* disappointing?" Something in his brain just snapped. "You're a murdering psychopath from a murdering psychopath species, and you want another plaything to distract you." He wasn't sure where the rage came from. Maybe he'd just run out of fear and rolled over to the next emotion. "You know all of this is wrong and you're doing it anyway. You're like me, except you actually could stop it. You're pathetic."

Dadrachniss seemed to consider this. "You think I could?"

"What?"

"Stop all this? Just talk to my spidey friends and pack up and leave. You really think that's how it works?"

David looked down, understanding. Maybe he had thought exactly that, like *The Day the Earth Stood Still*, where you could talk to one alien, have one conversation and save the planet. But that was just more fantasy. No wonder Arachniss was frustrated. He was still acting like a child and Arachniss probably couldn't change anything even if he wanted to; he was just a cog in a machine David couldn't see. There was no magic bullet, no way to *win*. There was just survival.

"No. I understand," he said. "I'll get her. I promise."

"Don't promise, David. Just do it. Don't confuse our conversations with friendship. You're mine now, my special little pet. And you will obey. There are no second chances. If you don't get her this time, or you refuse me even once, I'll eat Jason in front of you. And it will take a while. Is that clear?"

"Yes."

Arachniss vanished like a demon sliding into the hell between worlds, leaving his father watching him.

"It'll be ok—"

"Don't." David snapped off the TV.

The Entree

The mind cannot support moral chaos for long.
Men are under as strong a compulsion
to invent an ethical setting for their behavior
as spiders are to weave themselves webs.

- John Dos Passos -

Franzia Comes Around

DAVID HAD NEVER WRITTEN about butterflies because he didn't know how to tell the story without breaking kids' hearts. Caterpillars don't pull a cocoon around themselves like a blanket, take a nap and then wake up with butterfly wings to fly off to the next phase of their lives. Caterpillars dissolved into formless black goo inside the cocoon and then some inexplicable process used that goo to build a butterfly. The lifecycle of the butterfly and the caterpillar were joined only by building materials, as if the caterpillar was no better than fertilizer for the butterfly. David could still remember when dad broke open a cocoon and showed them, and how sad he looked telling him and Tommy something so raw and disappointing. The caterpillar-butterfly was David's Santa Claus, the ruined myth that shattered his childhood fantasies. He wanted to tell a butterfly story in a way that was positive and helped children understand that life was hard but also good and sometimes needed to be hard to be good, but every time he thought about butterflies, he saw darkness and smelled gunpowder. Apparently, dissolving into formless goo wasn't just for caterpillars.

He'd tried to write, but Pedro wouldn't come out to play.

He'd tried to call Franzia and James, but no one picked up.

He played with Jason and avoided Alicia until the sun set.

He thought about going to see Kathryn, but he was afraid to leave the house. What if Franzia came by?

He asked Dad what to do, but Dad just told him to relax; Franzia would come around. He wasn't sure Dad and Arachniss were on the same page, which was interesting but unhelpful.

So he picked up his phone for the hundredth time and texted her. FRANZIA, PLEASE. WE REALLY NEED TO TALK.

The message went through. At least she hadn't blocked him.

He waited thirty seconds and dialed her number. He was about to hang up when she answered.

"David," she said, her voice flat and uninflected. He waited for her to say hello. Now that he'd reached her, he was afraid to say anything and lose her again. The silence got to that awkward point where it would be better to hang up.

"David?"

"Hi, Franzia. Sorry. Are you okay?" He waited. There was something in the background, like the sound of breaking twigs. Franzia hushed it and the noise vanished.

"Great. You're certainly persistent," she said. Her voice wasn't flat anymore; it was all over the place.

"Yeah," he said. "I—"

"I'm sorry about last night. Could you come over now?" Something snapped in the background. "Please?"

"Okay. I'll be over in…"

More breaking sounds.

"Goddamn it," she said. Then she was gone.

*

FRANZIA ANSWERED THE DOOR with a bottle of wine in her hand and swayed as if the house had lost its sea legs and she was compensating. David fought the urge to sway in time like kelp in a tidal surge; it could be misinterpreted as mocking.

"You okay?" he asked idiotically.

She held the wine up. "Six glorious years of sobriety down the drain. What do you think?" She cleared her throat, took a swig, got most of it in her mouth, and stepped aside. "Welcome to this fucking place."

David walked over the threshold and stopped, wishing he'd stayed outside. There was a great spidery blur on the living room couch, sitting on James's lap. James looked petrified, exactly as David had been in Kiaraa's office, except for the nudity; James was completely naked. In less than a second, he went from numb surprise to sarcastic emotional distancing, from wondering if James was his friend to knowing he was, from thinking he'd never put himself at risk for anyone but Jason to wanting to throw himself at the thing eating James and beat it to death, and back to the numb realization that there was nothing he could do.

But he still had to try. He took a step into the living room. Franzia grabbed his arm.

"Don't," she said. "You'll make it worse. David, come on. Let's go into the kitchen."

"Yeah," he mumbled as the last of James' forefinger disappeared. "The kitchen. Sounds good."

They sat at the kitchen table where his tart pans had been cleaned and stacked. A closed divider over the counter hid the living room and James. Shortly after getting comfortable, very loud and clearly gratuitous crunching and chewing noises came to them from the living room. Franzia stared down at the table. Was she going to offer him some of the wine? Because he could use a drink.

"So, you could see that?" she asked.

He frowned. "Of course I could see that."

"I thought I was crazy." She took a drink from the bottle. "I guess I was still hoping."

"Where's Charlotte?" he asked, eyeing the bottle.

Franzia concentrated for a second. "Friends. I mean, I assume. You saw her hand. It ate my daughter's fingers, David." She shuddered. "Maybe she's dinner for whatever the hell those things are."

He nodded. She looked unhinged, just like a door dangling from the frame, bottom askew, purpose questionable, probably hazardous to touch, more dangerous than useful. He reached for her hand. She pulled back and took another drink. Apparently, he wasn't getting any wine. He fought the urge to grab the bottle, half to help her, half to help himself to what was left.

"How long have you known?" he asked.

"A few hours," she said. "I mean, I've known for weeks, but I thought…" She sighed. "Like you, we had another child. Like your

Alex, our son died shortly after he was born. Unlike you, it was my fault."

David nodded slightly, just enough to acknowledge what she'd said. When had he told her about Alex? Or had one of the Arach told her, like Arachniss showing him other's life histories? He was lost in the thought for a second and almost forgot the obligatory denial: "I'm sure it wasn't your fault."

"Yes, it was," she said, sharply. "I'm not going to get into it, but I used to drink a lot."

He tried not to raise his eyebrows, but the bastards were already raised.

"A lot *more*," she clarified. "This is recent. I was sober for years after he died, but back then, I wasn't always aware of what was going on around me. Hell, I didn't always know where I was. Sometimes…" She glared at the bottle in her hand. "…it was worse."

The crunching in the living room resumed. Gratuitously loud, like it was putting on a show. He wondered what this one's name was and if it pretended to be one of her parents.

"Let me skip ahead," he said, because he was in no mood for confessions. "You blame yourself for your son's death. You and James are incredibly overprotective of Charlotte." He remembered how pristine Char had been just a few weeks earlier. "When you saw what was happening, or were shown, you made a deal for Charlotte. You'd do anything for her. You picked James over Charlotte. Hence, the show in the living room. I'd have done the same thing."

This time her eyebrows rose, unbidden and apparently unnoticed.

"It wanted to eat James, and it wanted me to watch," she said. "It was always someone else before. Anyone else. I don't know why, but that just did it. I realized it was real. It wasn't just a game or some weird PTSD hallucination. It was *real*. And I couldn't do it. Watch, I mean."

"Uh-huh." His stomach sank. He kept telling himself he'd do anything for Jason. But what did he really know? Here was a woman, a strong woman, who'd made the same deal. And look at her. Actually, he couldn't. He looked at the black square of darkness through the kitchen window and wiped his eyes. "Is that why it's eating James now? To save Charlotte?" Was this what *anything* meant?

"Yes," she said, shuddering. "She's my baby."

More crunching. Was that slurping? Maybe Arachniss was the Virgo of Arach, neat, quiet and orderly. Apparently, her host was more of a glutton. Probably a Leo.

"Okay," he said. "What's its name?"

"Whose name?"

"The..." What was he supposed to say? "...thing in the living room."

Her eyebrows furled, pinching a rise of skin between them hard enough to redden.

"They have fucking names?"

"Well, I mean, no. I'm not sure. Mine calls himself Arachniss."

She looked at him for a loooooong time.

"Franzia?"

"Are you screwing with me?"

"No."

"'Arachniss.' Like it's Spider Everdeen from an alien version of the *Hunger Games*? Seriously?"

"Uh." He was thrown by her science fiction reference (which was cool), the idea that Arachniss was screwing with him even more than he thought (which was saying something), and disappointment that he hadn't made the *Hunger Games* connection (which was obvious). "They call themselves Arach, their kind, which to them just means people or beings. I assume 'Niss' is just his identifier." He shrugged. "What have you been calling yours?"

"Giant Blurry Spider." She took a drink. "Also Great Big Spider and Goddamn Bitch Spider." Another. "Depends on the mood."

"So, GBS. You're kidding?" She wasn't. "You think it's female?"

"Her voice sounds like my mother. That's why I thought I was crazy. How many are there? Are they really spiders?"

"A lot." He didn't want to scare her any more than she already was. "I don't think they're spiders. The spiders are them." He tried to think how his digital dad had put it. "'The Earth was populated with spiders so that our minds would be familiar with their shape and form, and fear them, but not see them as alien. That makes it easier for them to maintain control, but also to hide from us.'"

"It's my one phobia, you know. Spiders. Well, spiders and mimes, but everyone hates mimes."

"I find them quite peaceful." Though when was the last time he'd seen one?

"Now you've gone too far," she said. "So, the spider things. Why are they here?"

"To feed. They call themselves hosts. Arachniss is our host. You have a different one in your territory or whatever this is. Lot or herd or whatever. He didn't show you the video?"

"The video?" she asked. "You are screwing with me."

"Maybe Arachniss is talkative for his kind."

"Which are?"

"Ranchers."

"Harvesters, you mean. Harvesters of human meat."

"Yeah." She caught on faster than he had. "And Arachniss wants to meet you. In person."

She sat back, even paler than before. "Why?"

"He thinks you're special." Maybe. He had no idea. She watched him for a moment, and he knew what she was thinking: special, like a nice cut of meat walking itself to the slaughter? She wasn't necessarily wrong, but he wasn't sure he'd tell her if she was. He didn't want anyone to be eaten, but if it came down to a choice between her and Jason, it wouldn't take long to pick.

"Why?" she asked, finally.

"Because you can see them, like I can."

"I can't see them. There's just a spidery blur and maybe an outline and flashes of black."

"Same," he said. So she couldn't really see them either. They might not look like spiders at all. Or clocks.

Crunch!

She winced and muttered, "Oh, goddamn it."

CRUNCH!

"Are you kidding?" she yelled. "We get it. You're eating my husband. Keep it down!"

David sat back, stunned. She'd just yelled at the alien. Why would she—

The alien whined. The sound that came from the living room was like a high-pitched wail, not quite a scream, not deafening, kind of like a raven squawking but three octaves higher and full of static.

"SHUT THE HELL UP!" Franzia yelled, so loud her voice cracked.

"Franzia…" His heart was up his throat and pounding on the ceiling. "Franzia, please."

This time it *screamed*, like metal nails on a metal chalkboard or a million rats screaming and an orchestra of off-tune trumpets begging for death. They covered their ears. The windows shook. The air blurred, or maybe his brain was melting. And it went on and on until he wanted to drive his thumbs through his eardrums just to make it stop.

David looked at Franzia through watering eyes. Somehow, she was smiling. With her hands over her ears, she had her middle fingers up in a universal expression of contempt. He closed his eyes and tried to get hold of his breathing.

Please don't let it come in here. Please don't let it eat me. He wasn't sure who he was asking. Anyone. Anything. He kept seeing Jason as Arachniss gradually ate his tiny body piece by piece without David there to help him.

Please.

Franzia opened her mouth and screamed back, spit flying, eyes wide, completely unhinged.

The monster-screaming stopped. He assumed coincidentally.

Franzia trailed off and coughed. They uncovered their ears.

"Why would you do that?" he asked.

"Like you haven't pissed one of them off?" She waited. "Really?" She shook her head. "I don't know. She reminds me of my mother. Always too much, too loud and too in your face. It's humiliating."

"And screaming helps?"

"Of course it doesn't help. Nothing helps, except…" She glanced at the bottle. "Nothing *helps*, David. So nothing hurts. What does it matter?"

Until now, Franzia always seemed stronger than he was, or at least she hid her weakness better. He knew she had pain in her past, even if he wasn't sure what it was or even how he knew. The sound of defeat in her voice was as unsettling as the Arach's scream.

"Do you know what it's eating?" he asked. Not sure why. Maybe this is how you made conversation now. "Do you know what James…"

"His left arm." She said, pushing herself up straight. "It's the only thing I could think of that wouldn't cost him his job. He can still work if he has a prosthetic left arm. He can't lose his dominant hand or his legs."

Which was very practical. *Wait.* "He, it, you got to choose?"

The crunching resumed in the living room though, he had to admit, not as loud.

She looked at him strangely. "Of course. How do you think this works?"

"I'm not even sure what *this* is. The only thing he's asked me to do is get you." He decided not to mention or think about the Connelly triplets. "Which I failed to do. I was glad when you—"

"How did it punish you?"

"What do you mean?"

"When you didn't bring me back—I'm sorry about that—did it hurt Jason?" She looked genuinely guilty.

"No, he just told me to try again."

She grabbed the bottle again. This time, more like a weapon. What had he said?

"Franzia…"

The bottle trembled on the table, vibrating with her hand. The crunching in the living room stopped as if she, it, was listening.

"Yours has a name," she said. Clearly an accusation. "It doesn't punish you. Your son is fine. Alicia is fine."

"Well, mostly." She'd lost an arm. "I mean—"

She waved the bottle at him. "What aren't you telling me?"

He got her point. Why was Arachniss treating him so differently? Was it something he did, or something about him, or something about them? He had no idea.

"Can I get the same deal?" she asked.

"You mean swap?"

"No, I mean…" The crunching was back, more slurpy, with some soft tissue in there. James' fine biceps and shoulder? He tried not to imagine and failed. Next time, he was bringing his own wine. "Look, I don't know much at this point. I'm trying to save Jason. You're trying to save Charlotte. Come back with me and let him explain."

She took this in, nodded. "Not tonight. I can't leave James. Not until it's done." She wiped her eyes. "I can't believe I did this to him."

"You didn't do this, Franzia. You didn't choose—"

"You don't get it, do you? How do you think I've kept Char alive this long? Choosing is what they make you do. Pick someone new or I'll eat your daughter's eyes. Pick something sweet because they're hungry. Pick someone young or chubby because they like them fatty." She banged the bottle on the table as she spoke, staccato punctuation to her rage. Wine sloshed onto her hand. "What the hell do you think happened to the Balasubramanian twins' ears?"

"What?"

"It made me choose. Someone nearby. Someone I knew in the same neighborhood. Like it didn't want to travel. Every few days, someone else. I picked them. I picked their body parts. I picked…" She raised the bottle and drained it in three large gulps. "I picked those little girls' ears because it wanted something *crunchy*." Tears streamed from her eyes, poured, fat drops leaping from trembling cheeks to wine-smeared table top with an audible *plip-plop-plip*. She wiped her eyes again. "I chose all of it. And you will too."

"How could you choose little girls?" he asked before he could stop himself. Hadn't he chosen the Connelly triplets' pinkies?

She caught her breath and smiled horribly. "You'll see."

Which gave him chills. "I'm sorry," he said, and he was, but it couldn't be like this. How could he choose people to eat? The one time Arachniss had asked, it seemed casually cruel: a onetime trick, not a process. That was insane. Could he do that, even for Jason? What had he thought the deal was? Not this. Nothing like this.

"Honestly," she said, "I thought you would have it eat Alicia. I mean, she's abusing you, right? Win-win."

His stomach seized. How did she know about Alicia?

"You think I believed your little boy gave you that black eye? I can smell abuse and shame from a mile away, and you reek of it. Sorry, sorry," she said, shaking her head. "I just...you know you don't have to take it, right? No one has to just take it." Her hand moved toward his. He pulled away and nodded vaguely, trying to hear over the rushing in his ears. It was too much. Alicia. Franzia. Human-eating spider-alien absurdity. He just wanted to go home and hold his son. He didn't have the energy for anything else, let alone explaining why *he just took it.*

"I'm really sorry, David." She wiped her eyes. "I'll come over in the morning. Sober. After seeing what it's done to James. And I promise to keep my thoughts to myself. I'm not always like this."

"It's okay, Franzia. We'll figure this out."

She snorted, loudly. "Do you really believe that?"

"I think—"

"Never mind. Is this a trap, David? You'd tell me, wouldn't you? Or did you make a deal? Me for Jason?" She looked terrified, like she was negotiating with her executioner. "I get it. I probably would too. I know I would. I just want time to say goodbye to Charlotte."

"No, Franzia, there's no deal." Which is what he'd say either way. Even to him, it sounded weak. "He just wants to meet you." And compare them. Was it a contest where the winner gets a gold star and the loser gets flensed? "I swear, I have no idea what he wants, but there's no deal. And I think they're territorial. Mine can't eat... You know what I mean."

"They can do anything they want." She studied him, stone-still and sober as death. "But I'll be there at seven."

*

ON THE WALK HOME, David had just turned onto Aurora when he noticed the dog-sized blur next to him. He tried not to flinch away. He assumed it was Arachniss—just a nice spider out walking his pet human—but he didn't say anything for fear it was some other Arach he should not be able to see.

"Hello, David," it, he, finally said in his father's voice.

"Arachniss," he said. "I talked—"

"You want a ride?"

"Uh…"

"It's perfectly safe. How do you think we move you around when you're unconscious?"

"I assume the flying things have something to do with it."

"Ahh, well, those too. But hop on. I don't mind. I promise you won't catch fire."

"Thanks for the offer." Resisting the urge to get a piggy-back ride from an alien that sounded just like his father was harder than he would have thought. "But I think I'll walk."

"Your choice. I think that went well."

"What?"

"The talk with Franzia."

"She'll be over in the morning. I hope that's soon enough."

"That's fine. Ask me another question."

"Can you protect her husband James from—"

"No, he's not mine to protect. A more general question."

David turned left at the next intersection, heading down a street with no streetlights or sidewalk. Above, the sky was a gorgeous spread of stars. Then he snorted.

"What?" Arachniss asked.

"I just realized. I do good, you answer a question. It's like a dog treat. 'Good human. Who's a good little human? Here's some alien trivia, you good boy you.'"

"Close, but dogs don't learn from their treats. You can if you want to."

"Learn what?"

"Who we are. *Why* we're here."

"You're here to eat us. I don't care why. I just want to protect my son."

"You're lying to yourself. You're not that closed-minded or obtuse. You're curious. You read about alien civilizations and create whole worlds for children. You'd be an idiot not to take advantage of these moments. Ask."

All true and all irrelevant, but okay. "The video Dad showed me. It said something about entertainment and virtual meat. You said the same thing." *When you were threatening my son.* "Entertainment for whom?"

"All meat is entertainment," he said. "And mostly virtualized. Why would we ship you watery bags of meat around the galaxy? That's expensive and pointless. Most species can't eat those from other planets, and wouldn't enjoy it if they did. Same reason we don't create synthetic meat locally. What we provide is the *experience* of meat, consumption, hunting and killing. We provide a service to all sentient species in the galaxy, both biological and virtual entities, providing violence and consumption as entertainment in exchange for, well, less actual violence and consumption. Think of your contributions as a public service."

"So, Arach watch what you do to us? Pay for it?"

"Not just Arach. Thousands of species. And they don't just watch; they experience it. We emulate the sensory systems of the primary audience, and translate the act into the form most enjoyable for them. Thus, they can kill without killing and eat without eating."

"It's all simulated? They don't experience what actually happens?"

"Of course not. It'd be mismatched sensory input to most of them, worse than gibberish."

"Then it's not real. So why not just make it all a simulation? Why do it at all?"

"Because they'd know it wasn't real. Knowing it's real, that it's happening, is what gives it value. And it's not legal, in the sense you understand that word, to create purely artificial experiences that are indistinguishable from the real without explicit permission of the recipient. Your society is about to understand part of this with deepfake technology, which to us is considered cognitive fraud and punishable by death. We make it *close* to real."

"But it's *not* real. So what's the point?"

"Verisimilitude, David. It's real enough."

"You're going to kill me or my son or Alicia for entertainment? Millions of human beings are dying or being cut to pieces so some sick alien can jerk off a thousand light years away?"

"Well, that's gross, but close enough. It's a question of scale. It's not for one diseased member of a species you've never heard of, it's trillions of perfectly healthy *others* trying to suppress their biological instincts and make virtual life tolerable. It's therapy, or at least treatment. And it works. The Milky Way is a remarkably peaceful place. Besides, you know where your meat comes from. It's not volunteer chickens and philanthropic cows with organ donor cards."

"It's not the same."

"It's not the same *to you*."

"I still don't understand why you're talking to me. Is it just more entertainment?"

"More than that."

"What, then?"

"You'll see."

"Always the same answer. When will I *see?*"

There was no answer, and when David looked to his side, Arachniss had stopped at the walkway to a gorgeous modern house with warm yellow light shining from every window.

"Gallbladder or spleen?" Arachniss asked.

So this is how it starts. "Uh, um, well, spleen?" David stuttered, largely because he had no idea what a spleen did and thus assumed it was unimportant.

"Good choice." And then Arachniss was gone and the house lights flickered.

David wondered briefly who he'd just splenectomized, and then shivered. It was freezing out here. He should have accepted the ride.

Guess Who's Coming to Breakfast

DAVID CHECKED THE STOVE CLOCK when the doorbell rang. Seven on the nose. He suspected Franzia had been waiting outside for the exact second, which was a strangely David thing to do. He took the eggs off the heat, rubbed Jason's head in his highchair throne, and went to let her in. Whatever happened next, it would at least be interesting.

"So, about last night," she said as he opened the door.

"No, that's okay."

"It was a lot of things. Okay was not one of them." She thrust a warm bag of fresh cinnamon rolls and morning buns from Shamane's into his hand. They smelled delicious. "I don't bake."

"These are my favorite." He stood to the side to let her in.

She hesitated. "You probably came over thinking you finally had someone you could talk to, someone who wouldn't think you were crazy, and I made things worse. For the second time. I never should have let you see what was happening to James. I'm sorry."

And then she hugged him. Just leaned in, put her arms around him, and rested her head on his chest. He instantly relaxed into it and the world suddenly weighed less. He fought the urge to rest his cheek on her head. It was the first new-person hug since he met Alicia, so nearly a decade.

"I'm really sorry," she said, releasing him. He reluctantly did the same.

"It really reminds you of your mother?"

She pursed her lips together and exhaled, rolling her eyes. "Maybe let's not talk about that right now? Or ever?"

"Deal." He stood aside and Franzia walked in to the smell of freshly made breakfast, eggs and toast, but no meat. She sniffed and smiled approvingly.

"Where's Alicia?"

"At work. How's James?"

"Happy as a clam. He doesn't know the fake arm is new, but it's like a toy and he's *into* it."

"The new Zombie Arms are pretty cool. Can his walk around?"

"Zombie Arms? God, I hope not. If I come home and see that thing walking around, it's going out the window. On the other hand—pun intended—maybe I can update the firmware to screw with him."

"You can do that?"

She shrugged. "The security on those things is terrible. It's like they want to be hacked. So, are you going to feed me or are we getting straight to it?"

"Food's in the kitchen. We can eat in the living room and do introductions, I guess? I'm not really sure what's going to happen."

Her face blanched.

He put a hand on her arm. "Nothing like that. It's okay." He hoped.

David put Jason down in the nursery and came back to find Franzia had set up breakfast on the coffee table, arranged the rolls on a plate, poured orange juice, and generally...helped. He stopped, surprised, and then nodded his thanks. He couldn't remember the last time Alicia helped with anything around the house unless there was an audience.

He sat. They ate and made appropriate noises. Franzia drank enough coffee to power a train. David found himself halfway through a second roll before wondering if one was meant for Alicia. Whatever. He stuffed the rest in his mouth and nearly choked himself on it.

"So," Franzia said.

"Yer," he said, swallowing. "I mean, yeah. It's time." He switched on the TV. Dad was there, as always, but wearing a nice button-down non-plaid shirt like he was going on a date.

Franzia glanced at David, at the TV, frowned.

"Is this the video you mentioned?" she asked.

"Oh, god no," David said. "That was terrifying." He tried not to think about the pool of body parts. "And gross."

"Good morning, Franzia," Dad said. "It's nice to meet you."

Franzia spit coffee across the room and choked on the rest.

"Sorry," David said, fighting the urge to pat her on the back. "I should have warned you."

"Okay." Franzia put the cup down and turned to the TV. "You're…Arachniss?"

"No," Dad and David said simultaneously.

"I'm David's father," Dad-bot said.

"He's an emulation of my father," David corrected. "Like an AI. When it's Arachniss, his eyes are black."

"Well, of course they are. Hello, David's father."

"You can call me Ben."

She muttered *fuck* under breath, then: "What's this about, David?"

"Well," he said, thinking he could have done a much better job explaining all this if Franzia was less drunk and ragey. But then her husband was being eaten when they talked, and he wasn't sure himself. "This is how I ask questions when Arachniss isn't around. Honestly, I'm not sure. Do you have anything like this?"

"Do I have my dead father on demand?" she asked calmly. "No, I do not. Did you sign up for a luxury package I missed out on?"

"No." But he couldn't help laughing. She had a point.

"Did you get a TV mom, too? A virtual puppy?"

He shuddered. "Stop it."

"Maybe it has a crush on you?" She smiled deviously. "Are you being groomed, David? Did it give you candy?"

"Jesus, no. Just…" She made it seem way creepier than it had before, which was saying something.

"Maybe I can help?" Dad chimed in.

They both turned to look at the TV. Franzia side-winked at David. At least she was in a better mood. Which lasted about a half second. Dad's eyes turned black and the room temperature dropped. Arachniss had arrived.

"Good morning, Franzia. I'm glad you decided to join us."

Franzia's face turned a color not normally found on human skin, greenish-pearl with gray highlights. Her hands flew to her side as she got ready to push off and run. David put his hand on her arm.

"It's okay," he said, which it wasn't, but she relaxed.

"You're...Arachniss?" she asked, voice trembling.

Dadrachniss shrugged. "We don't really have names, but that works for now, yes."

She sat up straight, false courage straightening her spine. "And what do you want with us? With me?"

"We don't have time for that. David can explain more. Let's talk about your host."

"My...oh, you mean GBS." She shook her head. "Does she have a name?"

"She?" Dadrachniss smiled. "Like your mother. I understand. Not really. You don't like her, do you?"

Franzia blinked, her mouth open, looking for the trap.

"It's okay. I know you don't. No one else does either. She's a problem. A little, how should I say, reckless?"

Franzia nodded, meaning sure, that's a word.

"If you agree to help me," Dadrachniss said. "I can help with that. Change your arrangement."

"And protect Charlotte?" Franzia asked.

Dadrachniss nodded.

"And my husband, James?"

"Unfortunately, no. I'm sorry."

"Okay," she said. "I'll help you. As long as it doesn't make it worse for James."

"That's it?" Arachniss asked. "No other questions?"

"Have you met it, her? Sorry. I'll eat my arm to get rid of her."
Pause. "I don't mean that literally."

"Call her Arachnur, if it helps. Just never to her face.
Understood?"

"Arachnur? That's her name?"

"As I said, we don't have names, but we can use that amongst
ourselves. And *just* amongst ourselves."

She nodded. "Arach*nur*. Okay."

David watched her carefully, feeling the first sense of misgiving
about bringing her to meet Arachniss. Well, not the first, but he
knew what Dadrachniss was doing. He was creating a sense of
intimacy. Sharing a secret. Making her feel comfortable with him, like
he was a friend. But whatever Arachniss was, he wasn't a friend. He
hoped she wouldn't miss that in her desperation to get away from
her host. Sometimes people would believe anything to get away from
their abusers. Especially if they didn't know the signs. Which made
him think. He still didn't understand why he was being treated
differently. Maybe he *was* being groomed.

"So, what do you want me to do?" Franzia asked. Eager. Hopeful.
Dangerous.

"You already know, Franzia."

Her body sagged like a deflating balloon. David didn't know
exactly why, but whatever little hope he'd offered by bringing her
had popped and blown away.

"You want us to…" Franzia looked at David and shook her head.

"What?" David asked. What was he missing?

"He wants us to pick. The same thing I've been doing for GBS.
Nothing's changed."

"Pick what?" David asked, turning to the screen. He knew the
answer. He just didn't want to admit it.

"What's for dinner," Arachniss said. "Every day, you'll pick
someone for me. Starting tomorrow by midnight. Don't be late."

"Pick someone?" David asked. "I can't…" Franzia put her hand
on his arm, like a frightened child who needed mommy's comforting
touch. He pulled away. "Pick someone to *eat?*"

"Yes, David. That's what we do. Sometimes a part, sometimes everything. You two are now my guide to human cuisine. You pick who lives with less or dies with nothing. Once a day, every day, by midnight."

"Like the *movie*?" he asked idiotically. *She Spins* was apparently a documentary. "Sorry, and if we do that?" He didn't want to think about what it meant. He just wanted to clarify terms.

"Then Jason and Charlotte live."

"Unharmed?" Franzia asked.

"Uneaten."

"And what about us?" David asked. "Franzia and me?"

"I don't want to orphan your children. As for the rest, you'll see. Agreed?"

Franzia sighed and nodded. "I agree." And then she arched her back and screamed as her eyes rolled back in her head. David reached for her, but by the time his hand made contact, it was over.

"What the hell?" David demanded, glaring at the TV.

"Welcome to the kennel," Arachniss said, and then his eyes emptied out.

David switched off the TV. He didn't trust Dad after the transitions. Or at all, for that matter.

"Kennel?" she asked, still breathing hard.

"I should have seen that coming. He reclassified me as a pet to protect me from other Arach. I assume he did the same to you by updating the implant in your neck."

"Implant?" She reached back and felt her neck, found nothing. "We're going to have to work on our communication."

"Yeah. Sorry."

"You say that too much. What did he mean, *you'll see*?"

So he explained the wonderful world she was about to experience, including the warning that she never, ever let another Arach know what she was seeing. Especially not Arachnur. She hung on every word.

"And I can read people's minds?" she asked, hushed, like a kid learning about Santa.

"No," he said. "I think Arachniss just let me see the histories of some people so we understand how it works. At the time, I had no idea why he did it. Now I know. We're supposed to pick people we hate. I assume that's how you did it?"

Franzia shook her head. "No, she, Arachnur, was very specific. This type of meat from that type of body, and always someone I knew. She wanted me to see what I'd done, eventually. She liked to watch me react." She thought for a second. "We can pick strangers? Random people, criminals, whatever?"

"Sounds like it." She heard the same thing he did. It was light on specifics.

"Okay." Franzia nodded. "Have you done that yet?"

"Not really." Which was mostly true; he hadn't seen the Connelly triplets recently, but he had read that they could live without their spleens. Which was fortunate.

"I really hoped it wouldn't be like this," she said. "But this is better. I can't stand looking at the Balasubramanian twins anymore. Your barbeques are...difficult."

"I'm sorry..." he trailed off. What was he sorry about? What bothered him most was how pointlessly sadistic it seemed, like dog fighting or abusing animals before you ate them. What was the point? Just to torture them for amusement? It made them complicit in the murder of their own kind. It was sadistic. He couldn't process how a species as powerful as the Arach would be reduced to something so infantile.

"David?"

"Sorry." He smiled. "I do say that a lot. I'm glad we're doing this together. I mean, I'm not glad we're doing it, but I thought I was going to lose it for a while there. It's good not to be alone anymore."

She nodded but said nothing, and they finished breakfast. He watched her hands and face, impressed by how well she was holding it together. After last night, he was afraid there would be more drama, but she was at least as calm as he was. She drank more coffee and used the bathroom. He checked on Jason. They cleaned up together. It was remarkably normal, and he hoped they'd do it again sometime. Well, without the *feed-me-people* part.

*

"WHAT'S THAT?" FRANZIA ASKED about one of the many sets of eyes on his office wall. He'd led her in after breakfast, not wanting her to leave yet. Now he felt self-conscious and wanted to push her back into the hall.

"Pedro the Peripatetic Polar Bear," he said. "I know. I'm working on the name."

She turned the drawing around in her hands. It wasn't clear what the top was. "Your next book?"

"I think so."

"He's all eyes? Don't take this wrong…" She scanned the walls of eyes. "But it's pretty creepy. This is to keep Alicia out, isn't it?"

He blushed. She wasn't wrong. "You should have seen it when I was illustrating *Snyder*. There were spiders everywhere. She would cover her eyes when she passed the door." His smile faltered. "I used to love spiders. Anyway, it wasn't just that. I think I knew I was being watched. I felt paranoid. That's where all the eyes came from. But now, I know how to draw him."

He picked up his latest drawing, done that morning before breakfast. It was a quick sketch with bold black charcoal, done so fast it was like he was throwing lines on the page. In minutes, Pedro had a body and little legs, a snout and just a hint of teeth.

"Aww, that's a cute polar bear." She hesitated. "So…"

"What?"

"Now that I know you're not going to have me eaten, I've got something to show you, too."

"Franzia, I would ne—"

"I'm kidding." She wasn't. "Come over tomorrow and I'll show you. And we can figure out who to pick."

"Sounds terrible. I'll be there. What is it?"

"*You'll see.* I mean, maybe. I'm not entirely sure what it is. Don't get too excited. It's not my vagina."

He blushed again, or more. "But it's something not terrible?"

"I hope so?" She handed the drawing back. "That's really good, David. I can't wait to see the book."

"Me too." Same with his editor; it had been a while. "Do you think it's silly? The drawings?"

"Your books? No. I told you we loved them. Why?"

"I mean, drawing when the world is the way it is."

"I can't think of a better time to do what makes you happy. You draw. I drink. I don't think my choice is the healthy one. I've never passed out on the couch and made kids laugh, though Char does like to draw things on me." She shrugged. "Your books are beautiful. Do what you need to do. Fuck the world."

"It seems pretty fucked already." He felt himself tearing up. He wasn't sure what was with the spontaneous urge to cry lately, but he forced it down and smiled. She was right. He hoped she was right.

She hesitated at the front door, maybe fighting the same desire to hug again that was making him twitch, but the moment passed with a few awkward movements that ended up in a weird handshake, which was probably the least intimate human contact in the world.

"You're going to see some terrible things," he said. "Remember not to react."

"I'll be fine," she said, like she was reassuring him. Which she was. And then she was gone.

"I think you like her," a voice called from the living room.

"Shut up, Dad." But he wasn't wrong. Pedro's companion was about to get a lot sassier.

Franzia's Excellent Unit

"HOW DID YOU MEET JAMES?" David asked, trying not to cough. They were at Franzia's kitchen table again, this time sans alien screaming or James-eating, which was an altogether more pleasant experience. Franzia was wearing jeans and a form-fitting top that left little to the imagination, so he kept his focus on the incredibly dry scones she had acquired during the Napoleonic wars and thawed out for his desiccation. They'd probably been orange-flavored at some point, but the overwhelming accent of dust had taken over. He'd been chewing on the last bite for a while, but all his saliva was gone and there was no water, so he just sort of pushed the gummy mass around in his mouth and tried not to breathe. Franzia didn't notice. Her scone was untouched on her plate.

"That's what you want to know?" She frowned. "I invited you over to see something, what was the phrase, 'not terrible,' served you some prehistoric white lumps I found in the freezer last night—as a joke—didn't even give you coffee, and you're sitting there with a desert in your mouth wondering how I met my husband? What's wrong with you? Spit it out before you choke."

"Thank god." David obediently spat the glob onto the plate next to the remaining scone bits, which spontaneously decayed into individual atoms and poofed up in a tiny cloud. "What the hell is wrong with *you*?" He coughed again, but he was smiling.

"I have a list. I'll share it sometime. The question is, why do you put up with everything?"

He sat back, surprised. "What?"

Another frown. "Never mind. You really want to know about James?"

"I really want a cup of coffee and a gallon of water."

"There we go." Franzia got up to get coffee and water. When she returned, David drank a lot of both.

"So, you and James?" he prodded.

"Why?"

He shrugged. "I rarely see you together and when you are, you seem...distant?"

"Yeah." She nodded. "We've had a rough time since our son died."

"I can imagine."

"I know. So, let's see. James and I met in college at a frat party. He was big and studly and I was working my way through all the emotionally unavailable meatheads I could find. He turned out to be a really nice guy who trapped me with kindness, brilliance and a mind-blowing quiche."

David laughed. He enjoyed hearing how people found each other. It seemed so random sometimes, made no better by the there's-always-another-one dating apps that turned commitment into a social disease.

"And then there was SHAS and we got pregnant the first time he didn't use a condom after we were married, even though I was on birth control."

David nodded.

"Same?"

He nodded again.

"So there was that. I thought we were in love and I didn't care if we got married, but he wanted to, so we did. Time passed. Stuff happened. And here we are; happy as a cancer ward. If not for Charlotte and a surplus of guilt, I assume we'd be cheating on each other."

"So, the perfect marriage?"

She smirked. "I love James. He's loyal and kind and all the things I thought I wanted."

"But?"

"I don't think he's loved me in a very long time. Oh, don't get me wrong. He *loves* me all the time. The sex is fantastic. But honestly, penis, penis, penis. I know he's overcompensating for other things, but sometimes I'd just like to watch a movie without being penetrated. Maybe he needs more gym equipment. I never thought I'd say this, but sometimes a glass of wine and a nice fart are way more satisfying than an orgasm."

David blushed and looked back at the tragic scone remnants. "You should write romance novels."

"My god, can you imagine? *He caressed her nipples but she, not really in the mood, pulled the covers over his head and hot-boxed him. His powerful arms seized in disgust and he coughed his way out of the bed and onto the floor as she laughed and farted and laughed again. 'While you're down there, do a little dusting.' And then she laughed some more and wet herself a little, because childbirth ruined your pelvic floor and that was obviously his fault. Next time, she'd pee on him and see how he liked it.* What do you think?"

"Maybe a little too truthy?" David offered. And also sad. It wasn't the first time her manic speech and profanity seemed like a cover for something. Maybe a lot of things.

"You think? James looks so offended when I fart. I don't think I've ever heard him pass gas. His corn hole must be tighter than my dad's wallet."

"Yeah, way too truthy."

"I know." She sighed. "I go too far sometimes. So tell me about you and Alicia. No, never mind, that's none of my business. I shouldn't have asked. Sorry. Forget I said anything. Let's talk strategy."

David sat back, surprised, ashamed and amused at the same time.

"You know you had that whole conversation without me, right?"

"I'm a little wired. And sometimes I miss subtle social cues, like 'Shut the hell up, Franzia' or the look of utter terror on your face. So let's move on and pretend that never happened."

"Uh, okay." He wondered if he could tell her about Alicia. He thought he could, but it seemed a lot less important now than it had a few days earlier. "So, strategy about what?"

"How to kick the Arach off Earth and all the way back to the mother web. What else?"

He caught himself before he laughed. She was serious. Had she been drinking again? Though he supposed that question implied she had ever stopped. He got the impression it was a more or less continuous thing, like breathing.

"Come on," she said, standing. "I've got something to show you."

On the way to the backyard, Franzia grabbed a giant hat and oversized sunglasses, like she was a celebrity going to the Kentucky Derby. Then she lowered her sunglasses to give him a *you-gotta-problem?* look. Before he could answer, she snagged a framed picture from a living room table and handed it to him.

"Look at that." It was a picture of James and Charlotte on a horse in a grassy field. Both were in full cowboy getup, down to the chaps. Maybe it wasn't about *Armando the Armadillo* after all. Then he saw it; there was a spidery blur under the horse's belly.

"Yeah, you're going to see a lot of that," he said, handing the picture back to her. You couldn't look at pictures without catching an errant Arach blur or leg draped across someone's shoulder like the ultimate photo bomb. You couldn't watch the news for fear of seeing slaughter in the background of every reporter talking calmly about the weather or the price of NFTs. You couldn't watch movies for all the gratuitous Arach cameos. The Arach were like bored teenagers and nothing was off limits. The whole planet was a prank waiting to happen. None of his pictures included Arachniss, at least none he'd found, but it was only a matter of time.

"That used to be one of my favorite pictures. Look at that ridiculous hat on James. You know how many cowboy hats the man has? Now that gives me the heebie-jeebies. This whole seeing the real world thing?" She shook her head. "I don't like it. Can he shut it off again?"

"You can ask." But the answer was probably no; whatever Arachniss was doing, there seemed to be a plan behind it. "I just focus on what's right in front of me."

"You mean you hide in the house all day?"

He nodded. "Much as I can. What did you tell James?"

"Nothing. Are you kidding? He wouldn't believe me anyway. I've lost some credibility over the years. And I wouldn't believe him if things were reversed. Some crazy is too crazy."

*

"WOW," DAVID SAID. "Nice unit."

Franzia snorted under her oversized hat, keeping her attention carefully focused on whatever was right in front of her, which was currently the back wall of her house. They were standing in her yard looking at a tiny air conditioning unit next to a larger air conditioning unit. Franzia was drinking coffee from a giant mug like it was beer during spring break. David sipped at his and nodded at the one-foot-cubed metal unit. Yep, it was very unity.

"So…" he said.

"The real air conditioning *unit* is around the side." She nodded left toward the corner of the house. "This big one is an officially unofficial prototype from a subsidiary my company isn't supposed to own. Top secret. Field testing. Have to kill you if I tell you what it does and all that."

"Uh-huh." He couldn't tell if she was kidding, but guessed not entirely. "And the little one?"

"Why are men so obsessed with size?"

He puffed out his cheeks and blew. He was too stressed for penis banter. "So…?"

"That's my secret version. More or less the same technology, off book, spare parts, probably get me fired and arrested if anyone finds out about it. Actually, there's no *probably*. That's jail in a box."

"What does James think it is?"

"Doesn't know. Doesn't care. Learned not to ask. I have a history of leaving projects around the house. I once installed a flat-wire Faraday cage in my office, but it ruined our cell phone reception on the entire floor, so I took it out." She shrugged. "I get bored sometimes."

"Okay. So what is it?"

"I don't know."

"You built it, but you don't know what it is?"

"Yep. I'm not really on this project. I specialize in sound-based weapons. Crowd suppression. Military-grade non-lethal assault systems. We work a lot with the Air Force down in Colorado Springs on related projects. But whatever this is, I don't have clearance for it. I just did the sound components and drivers, then volunteered for the prototype program. The rest I reverse engineered."

"But you still don't know what it does?"

"Nope."

"Then you haven't turned it on?"

"Oh, god no. That thing is a serious weapon. Even my small version could take down everyone in the neighborhood. No way to hide that. I tested a miniaturized version in my soundproof lab on low power with headphones on, and I still had a headache for weeks. I'm not turning that thing on until I have to."

"Okay," he said. "Neat."

She smiled. "Haven't you ever wondered how we stop them?"

"Nope." How do you stop a global invasion of superior aliens who raise you like cows for the slaughter? He wasn't sure what it said about him that he'd never thought about fighting back. You couldn't fight with gods; all you could do was negotiate. Probably the Canadian in him. "We can't fight them. You know that, right?"

"Have you tried?"

"I tried to hit him once." Strange how clearly he remembered it now. He found Arachniss over Jason in the crib and sort of punch-grabbed him until the spider lit up and burned him off.

"And what happened?" she asked.

He showed her the burns on his right arm, scars that looked like they'd been there for years.

"You got those when you were a kid," she said. "You said…"

"I never said that, and that never happened. They can make us see and remember whatever they want. You probably think Charlotte lost her pinkies to SHAS, wait, no, it was an accident on a field trip. She fell on a rusty lawnmower blade in the grass. Anyway, this is what happens when you try to touch them."

He put his hand out and she ran her fingers over the scars. It was a strangely intimate moment, letting someone touch the ugly parts of him. He pulled his hand back, embarrassed.

"Fire spiders?" she asked. "Well, I don't know what this thing does, not really, but I know they're deployed around the entire country. Maybe globally. Millions of units. All completely top secret. Way beyond a regular prototype test. Tens of billions went into this program, and I can't find anyone who even admits knowing what it's supposed to do, let alone who's funding it or why. I asked the wrong person and got a visit from the NSA. It was not a nice visit. I spent a week scanning the house for bugs after that."

"And?"

"I found three and put them all in the basement gym. They hear James grunting a lot. Probably think our sex life is off the charts." Pause. "Which it is, obviously."

"Obviously. So you think, what, the government knows about the Arach? This is some kind of weapons system?"

"I hope it is. They're all remotely controlled and can't be activated locally. Mine can, but whatever the system is, once you fire it up, it's responsive to incoming sound and the signal adjusts almost instantly. They can draw power straight off the grid and bypass our fuse box. The sound it can generate at varying frequencies can damage pretty much anything with ears in a very large circumference—which my regular stuff is never supposed to do. If they overlap the way I think they do, that means entire cities. If they screw up the range or power, they'll injure every man, woman, child and mammal in the area. Birds will die midair. This is serious, deadly shit."

"And then there's your little box."

"Again with the sex references."

"Franzia, why are you showing me this? I was already afraid of the Arach. Now I'm afraid of being water-boarded in Guantanamo while the Arach laugh their asses off."

"Do you think they have asses?"

"This isn't funny."

"All that human meat's got to go somewhere." She shook her head. "Sorry. I'm not trying to freak you out, but yeah, I wouldn't tell anyone about this. I think it's meant to kill them. Or harm them. Something. If they come for Charlotte…"

"Okay, I get it. Any idea when they plan to set off the big ones?"

"Rumor is, there's a test planned for later this year. Not sure of the date. It'll happen without warning. But the thing is, it can't be a test."

"Why not?"

"It's not subtle. You light those things up, the Arach are going to notice. How do you think they'll react to a concerted low-grade global attack and uprising by their cattle?"

His coffee was suddenly bitter. "Not well." Which was an understatement. The slaughter would be epic, though he wasn't sure anyone would see it. Millions would vanish and everyone would remember that terrible summer when SHAS surged again. "So you think it's the real thing? Sometime this year, we fight back…or we die?"

"Yes." She took another drink. "We just need to survive until then. After that, it won't matter."

"You know this won't work, right? Death is the only realistic outcome. We're like ants talking about how to overthrow human beings. We might survive them, but we can't fight them."

"So we should just give up?"

He closed his eyes and forced out a slow breath. This was the optimistic American in her. The engineer. The never-give-up, never surrender Holy Grail of western society. She didn't understand that sometimes you had to hide and hope they didn't notice you. And she wouldn't until she tried, and failed, and got herself and everyone around her hurt or killed. He knew this as surely as anyone who's fought back and lost again and again, that sometimes, no matter how ingenious and strong and smart you are, you still lose. But he also knew he didn't want to be the one to tell her, and he loved that she wasn't just broken glass inside, so he sighed and said, "No, we should do what it takes to help our children survive."

"Right." She didn't seem to like that answer. "Have you ever seen…" She reeled off a list of movies that made the sci-fi geek in him proud. In all of them, feisty human beings fight back using clever engineering that made absolutely no sense. The plan, even as little as he understood it, was rubbish, absurd and naïve, so maybe— and this thought is the key to every bad decision in life—it was just bold (stupid) enough to succeed.

"Okay," he said. "Maybe it'll work." Which meant he'd take a beating for her. Maybe sacrifice a finger or two. It's what he was good at. "We can't stop it anyway." As long as it didn't hurt Jason, it might be worth it to know they'd tried.

And it was a very nice little box.

*

"ARE ALL BOOK SIGNINGS THAT EXCITING?" James asked.

David sat in the world's least comfortable chair in their world-class basement gym, watching James work out and trying not to scan the room for NSA bugs. She couldn't have been serious. James' prosthetic left arm didn't seem to slow him down. His deadlifts were flawless. His whole body flexed and strained like it was a machine made to lift big things. David wanted to suck in his stomach or do some bicep curls, but not really, so instead he babbled.

"I wish." He didn't. "You can't believe how good it was for sales. I don't have the report yet, but my agent said it was our best single-week retail figure in years."

"If it bleeds, it leads," James said as he finished his set, lifting more weight than David could comprehend without imagining the involvement of forklifts or gamma rays. David froze. What did James know?

"I mean, it was just a firecracker," James said, breathing normally. "Made the local news."

"Really?" He'd have to track that down. "Do you always work out before you go to work?"

James grunted and dropped the bar on his squat rack. Zombie Arm grabbed a towel and wiped his face in a fluid motion that seemed better than human, like rhythmic gymnastics with triceps.

"I work out all the time," he said. "Well, I work out or work all the time. Anything for a distraction. Probably the same reason you draw? Fran told me you're working on a new book about polar bears."

David nodded, surprised. They were married. Of course she told him. It was just strange to have anyone new know about his life and habits.

"Ever since we lost Ben," James added.

"Who?" David asked, but he knew before his mouth snapped shut. That was why Franzia swore when Dad introduced himself.

"Our first child. Our son," James said, looking at David carefully. "I thought Fran told you."

"She did, just not the name."

"Yeah, she still has trouble saying it." He added two massive plates to the bar and slid into a squat position. His quads flexed in anticipation. Was it weird that David was here watching him? Probably. But he had no idea when they'd be able to grab another beer.

Zombie Arm's hand flexed on the bar, fingers curling and uncurling on the bar just like a real hand.

"Cool, isn't it?" James asked.

One deep squat, perfect form and perfect breathing. It would have killed David.

"What?" David asked, wondering if he'd missed something.

"The arm." Another squat. "Fifteen or twenty years ago, prosthetics were ugly hacks." One more. "Now they're better than the real thing." That's four. "I know an old guy who had his legs replaced so he could hike faster." Five. "The department's even reconsidering its policy about officers with lost limbs." Six. "Pretty soon, they'll probably require us to be...what do they call it?" Seven.

"Augmented." He laughed. Eight. He racked the bar and stepped back, tapping Zombie Arm with his natural right hand. "You know this thing can tell if a surface is too hot, my resting heart rate, and if I need more iron in my diet?" Quick wipe with a towel.

"Wow," David said, though of course he knew; Alicia's arm was the same, if a slightly older Augmanity model. God knew what information companies were collecting on all of them using their own limbs.

"So Franzia showed you her box?"

David almost choked, wondering how open their marriage really was.

James laughed. "She thinks I don't notice anything, but she likes her space. As long as she doesn't blow the place up, I pretend not to care. What do you think it does?"

"Something about loud noises. To defend the house." It wasn't a total lie.

"Makes sense," he said, meaning that didn't sound like it'd kill Charlotte or blow a hole in the wall. "To answer your question, I've had trouble sitting still since Ben died. When it's too quiet, he crawls into my head. You know what I mean?"

He knew exactly what he meant. Alex. Tommy. Dad. A head full of ghosts asking unanswerable questions.

"I'm glad Fran has you to talk to." He wrapped a towel around his neck. "I'm not sure what's going on with her lately. You know she's drinking again?"

David nodded carefully.

James shook his head. "It doesn't make sense. She hasn't had a drink in years. She's putting her security clearance in jeopardy. I just don't. I wish I could help her..." He trailed off, clearly waiting for David to give him the answer, but all David could do is frown and look sympathetic.

"It's been bad the last few days," James continued. "I found her passed out the other night. That hasn't happened since..." He looked down, rubbing absently at something on his arm. "Did something happen?"

"Not that I know of," David said, hating the lie.

"Okay. She took Ben's death hard, but I thought…"

"What?"

"I just wish she could forgive herself. It wasn't her fault. Is it like that for you with Alex?"

His mouth opened again. "She told you about that?"

"Sorry. Is that all right?"

"No, yeah, of course. It's just…" Whenever he thought of Alex, he remembered the first beating. It was all mashed together in some weird mishmash of guilt and shame. "I think it's different for everyone."

"True." James stood awkwardly for a moment, watching him, and David had the distinct impression he wanted to give him a hug but wouldn't because of all the sweat and shirtlessness. David wouldn't have minded, though of course he would have pretended to. Fucking men.

"Another beer sometime?" James asked instead. "I need to get ready."

"I'd like that," David said, and then James was off to shower. He sat in the basement /man-cave /gym and smelled the sweat and the bite of rusted metal, something like fresh hard rubber from the floor mats, all things hard and somehow male and completely missing in his life. But what he thought was that James seemed like a genuinely good man. It was going to suck when Franzia had him eaten. And she would. To save Charlotte, everyone was on the menu. Even Alicia. He knew it. Franzia knew it. Now that he understood what they were doing for Arachniss, the game had a clear ending. Things would escalate. It was just a matter of time.

Except.

He knew he couldn't do it.

As terrible as Alicia was, it wasn't in him. Could Franzia really kill James to save her daughter? Probably. She'd already picked an arm. And then what? At some point, Arachniss would play them against each other. It was the natural progression. Could he pick Franzia or she him?

He inhaled, trying to ground himself in earthly smells.

Well?

Probably.

*

"SO," FRANZIA SAID. "Who should we pick?"

James had gone to work. Jason didn't need to be picked up from childcare for another hour. David glanced around the living room. There were no signs of blood from James' mutilation. The white cushions were unblemished and perfect. He'd have to find out what fabric they used. Their couches were already stained with—

"David?"

"Sorry. I was just thinking. You picked neighborhood people because that was Arachnur's requirement, right?"

She clenched her teeth. "Right."

"So what about the pedophile? James mentioned someone nearby. He texted me the details." He showed her his phone. "Name, address, everything."

"He told me," she said. "Surprised no one beat us to it."

"What do you mean?" But it suddenly seemed so obvious. SHAS wasn't mysteriously mean to lawyers and politicians and rapists. The people helping the Arach were. It wasn't just David and Franzia; there was nothing special about them. People like them all over the world were feeding from the bottom of the human trough, trying to save children and innocents, friends and family. Everyone was mutilating everyone else to save themselves. Though he had no idea why they seemed to spare the elderly. Was it pity? Maybe they weren't interested in old meat.

He told Franzia what he thought; that maybe there were people like them around the world doing the same thing and she just nodded, as in, *of course, you idiot. How else would it work?*

"Makes sense," she said, kindly. "But you know what that means? It means someone picked Charlotte's fingers, and Jason's." She smiled suddenly. "And someone picked Alicia's arm."

"What?" Then a weird thought. "Was it you?"

She laughed, not offended, just surprised. "No. I might have, but she's outside Arachnur's permitted range."

David nodded, wondering. Had someone picked her? Someone from work, a neighbor or friend, maybe someone she'd prosecuted? Or did they just eat what they wanted most of the time?

"You didn't do it?" Franzia asked, still smiling.

"No," he exclaimed, laughing. But she was serious. "*No*. Why would I do that?"

"Oh, don't get all squirmy. Boxed Wine Bitch is a hot mess, but she doesn't judge. You know that, right?"

"I didn't pick her. I didn't even know that was a thing until I saw James on the couch that night. I mean..." He trailed off, thinking about the triplets.

"Why do you put up with it?" she asked, sincere, curious, with no judgment. She just didn't understand. How could she? He didn't even understand it.

"You really want to know?"

She nodded.

"Guilt," he said. "Or shame. I'm not sure. Something happened when I was a kid. When I tried to stop it, worse things happened. That's how I ended up in care."

"Care?"

"Foster care. You didn't know that?"

She shook her head. Maybe Arachniss hadn't shown her that much.

"That's where I met Kathryn." Kathryn who was now almost gone, which meant someone had chosen to have her eaten from the inside out, day after day, in that hellhole. He shook his head violently. He couldn't think about it.

"David, are you okay?"

"No. But that doesn't matter. At first, with Alicia, I just couldn't believe it was happening. She'd always been so kind and sweet. And then she wasn't, and the old Alicia became a kind of mask. Was she always like that and hiding it, or did something happen? She was exhausted after our first son—"

"I know what that's like, but it's no excuse."

"I know, but Alex wasn't like Jason. He was loud. Angry? He just didn't seem to like the world we'd brought him into. And then he was…" Eaten. He wiped his eyes. "It was a difficult time. And then one day she hit me. *Hard.* I ended up in the hospital. And then it just became our thing. You want to hear something messed up?"

"More messed up than all this?"

"Same ballpark. There's a story about Yuri Gagarin. He was a Russian Astronaut, which you probably know. Anyway, on one mission, he was orbiting the earth and there was a strange beeping in the capsule. He couldn't figure it out. Nothing was wrong. He couldn't tell where it was coming from. It was irritating him so much his heart rate spiked and he was burning too much oxygen. He couldn't get rid of the beeping, so he had to live with it. So he taught himself to love it. To yearn for it. That next beep was the best thing in the world because it meant he was still alive. I taught myself some very strange things, to look forward to the beatings, facing the challenge like a man climbing a mountain every day and knowing it'll be miserable, but that's just the way it is. Treasure the pain. Embrace the suck. It's not like hating it makes it go away, but it got to the point that I missed the rush of it. Watching her fly out of control. Sometimes it was like her hands moved in slow motion and I wondered what it would feel like." He shook his head. "I might have pissed her off on purpose a few times."

"Seriously?"

"I don't understand her when she's kind. It's a lie. I know she'll eventually snap. Making it happen gives me control. Told you it was messed up."

"You know that story is bullshit, right? Space missions never lasted that long back then. It never happened."

David added that to a list of disappointing things. "It's still a good story."

"How long?"

"What?"

"How long has she been doing it?"

"Years," he said. "Funny thing is, I was finally going to leave. My psychiatrist, Kiaraa...you know, you've met her."

Franzia shook her head. "I have no idea who that is."

"Right." He sighed. "Well, Arachniss ate her in front of me a few days ago. The day I went to plan my escape and figure out how to save Jason from Alicia." He shrugged. "I'm sorry. I can't do this right now. I don't know why I put up with it. I love my son. I don't want him to die like Tommy."

"Tommy?"

"My little brother." David grimaced. "This is too much. You understand? I don't have an answer for you. I don't have one for myself. I just want Jason to be okay." He wiped his eyes again. His sleeve was damp. He cried at the drop of a hat these days. Probably not a good sign, given the slaughter going on. A lot of hats would be dropping.

"I understand," she said. "Believe me. So, let's make sure he's okay."

David tried to purge the image of Arachniss slicing off Jason's pinky toe. That little line of blood. Jason's clueless happy smile. God knows what images Franzia had about Charlotte.

"So, the pedophile?" he asked.

"The pedophile," she confirmed.

Which he told Dad later that evening, who presumably told Arachniss. Within a day, the man was in a terrible car accident and then caught SHAS in the hospital. He died in agony and then vanished. David smiled when he heard about it, then felt bad, then smiled a little more.

But before he left Franzia's, she said, "You know..."

"What?"

"If you want the next selection to be a little closer to home, I wouldn't object."

"I'm not going to have that thing eat my wife."

"Still? After everything she's done to you? And someone's doing it anyway. Why not help her along?"

"Never," he said. "She's the mother of my child." But it wasn't like it hadn't occurred to him. Not about asking for it, but hoping it might happen without asking. "That's just making us like them."

"What do you think we are now?"

But he knew the answer. They were the Vichy French, Nazi collaborators, cowards and scum. They were whatever they needed to be to survive. But he still wasn't going to ask Arachniss to eat Alicia. There was a line.

Who's on Second?

IN A ROOKERY BY OCEAN, Pedro and Shyla found an abandoned baby seal and decided to take him along on their adventures. He liked to puff out his cheeks to look bigger and scarier, so they called him Blowfish.

"Great," David mumbled. "Now there's a seal."

Pedro was still just meandering around, but at least now there was a cute little baby thing to draw. Seals were easy to draw, with soft bodies, big eyes and clappy flippers. The kids would love Blowfish. Maybe they could write the book. Something about picking people to die had dried up the old creative juices. David Chambers, ex-children's book author and arbiter of death.

Speaking of which, who were they going to pick?

Pedophiles were an endangered species, and there weren't any left they could choose for Arachniss. Apparently people started with personal vendettas, people they hated, then *types* of people: pedos, rapists, murderers, drug dealers, politicians and so on. It was a wonder the government could collect taxes anymore. An argument could be made that the Arach were making the world a better place one meal at a time, but it wasn't an argument David was interested in. His calculation was very simple: how to do as little damage as possible while protecting his son. That was it. And it was harder than he expected.

There was an obvious answer, and hardly an original one. In the "Button, Button" episode of *The Twilight Zone*, the poor and desperate Lewis' are given a black box with a single button and told they could have $200,000 if they pressed it, but someone they didn't know would die. The box sits there for hours and then days while they contemplate what the money could do for them. What did it matter if some stranger died? Maybe they were bad people. Maybe they had it coming. So, of course, they press the button.

David and Franzia could push the button, pick not someone they knew by criteria but just point to a stranger's name and say *that one*. No one they knew. A stranger. Of course they wouldn't pick a child, it didn't seem they could pick the elderly (given how many of them were walking around) and they didn't want to pick parents of young children, so it came down to childless middle-aged people, probably white to avoid the guilt of picking someone from a minority group, probably straight (if they could tell), and that was about it. Some random, straight, middle-aged white person who never committed a crime. It's not like their lives meant any less than someone with children, or of a different age, race or orientation; they just had no idea how else to narrow things down, and at least they wouldn't be orphaning anyone.

Of course, when the stranger picks up the box and gives the Lewis' their money, he tells them the catch. The box now goes to someone else, someone *they don't even know*, with the clear implication that the Lewis' will die if the next recipient presses the button. The moral of the story is clear: do unto others and others will damn well do unto you—the big stick of the Golden Rule. It was still one of his favorite episodes.

But that wasn't David's issue with complete randomness. The issue was he had no delusions about the morality of a random choice; it was wrong no matter what, but it is also incredibly lazy to not at least try to find someone who deserved it more than the others. If he could take the life of a slightly worse person, wasn't it his obligation to try? Of course it was. So the day after picking the pedophile, when David should have been writing or playing with Jason, he searched the internet and social media and the news for someone, anyone, who had it coming. But Arachniss had limited them to his territory and Arachnur's, vaguely comprising several Boulder neighborhoods, so none of that would sell. What was left were proximate strangers, people nearby, and he couldn't decide. There was apparently a way to go outside this geographic range, but only for 'exceptional entertainment value' that made David shudder just to think about.

Alicia stopped by his office at some point. Both of her arms were now prosthetics, and her right foot, though the foot was so realistic he could barely tell. Arachniss was eating her quickly, and he wasn't sure why. Or if he should say anything, or care. But it was changing Alicia too. She seemed less confident and more tentative. Cautious. As if afraid she wasn't a match for him with so many missing parts.

"You're working a lot," she said. He couldn't parse the words. In the past, they would have meant, *you're not paying attention to me* or *I need something.* Now she seemed curious.

"When inspiration strikes," he said, smiling, as if creative juices were leaking from his skin. The opposite was true. He was terrified and exhausted, but if he stopped drawing, he'd turn on the TV and beg for salvation from his dead father. That wouldn't help anyone.

"Well…" she said and then seemed to lose track of her thought. She smiled as if asking a question, something like, *What happened to me?* Had she seen something? Was she as scared as he was? He almost stood and went to her. Took her hand, like he would have before Alex. Brushed the hair from her cheek and locked on her eyes. *Tell me,* he would have said. *Whatever it is, we'll figure it out.* He had no idea they were lies at the time. She was the love of his life. Nothing could break them apart. If you'd told him where they would end up years later, he'd have laughed in your face. It was inconceivable. And yet he didn't go to her or even acknowledge that she'd spoken. And after the silence filled the room, cold and hollow and tired, she looked down and shuffled away. He stared at the space where she'd been and tried to imagine how life would be if she'd never hit him and they were still how they'd once been, but that was like imagining infinity; the impossibility wouldn't fit in his head.

Morning turned to noon and he ate and checked his phone constantly to see if Franzia had found anyone. Time ticked by second-by-second until he found himself in front of the TV with

Jason pressed up against his chest, more for his comfort than his son's. He turned on the TV and waited. He never had to select a channel. No matter what he picked, Dad was what he got unless Alicia was in the room.

"David?" his father asked. He was in silver plaid now, threadbare, his comfy Sunday afternoon shirt. The one he wore when they played cards or raked leaves in the yard. David could still remember how that shirt smelled like smoke or sweat or grass, but still like him. He wasn't sure what it said about his state of mind that he was so desperate to talk to someone that he resorted to his father's avatar. Probably nothing good.

"I'm scared, Dad," he said, starting to shake.

"I know, son, but…"

"No, you don't. I'm scared all the time. I can hardly breathe anymore. I can't even remember a time there was something other than fear and now it's everywhere, all the time. I thought Franzia would help, but I can't seem to control it."

"You've got Jason, David. Hold on to that."

"But what if I can't? What if he asks for something I can't do? I can't keep this up forever. Picking people. Do you know what he's doing to us, what he makes us do?" They'd only done it once, and it was too much.

His father nodded and pursed his lips, thinking, like he'd just told his father he got a girl pregnant and not that he feared serving people to his immortal alien spider god.

"I'll tell you a story," he said, finally.

"Okay," David said, closing his eyes and trying to focus on his father's voice.

"A long time before you, there was another dominant animal family on Earth that the Arach farmed and tended, some would say coddled. They were a pet project of a powerful, um, man, hmm, not sure how to translate that."

"That's okay." David opened his eyes and nodded. *Keep talking.* "I get it."

"This family was a very successful breed, one of the most successful in the galaxy, and it was everywhere. The rich ate meals where every course was a different species from this family, the poor ate what was left, and they all loved it."

"They have rich and poor?"

"Hmm, good point. I guess more and less powerful would be a better interpretation."

"Okay. Sorry to interrupt."

"This animal family crowded out all others for a million years, so plentiful it was at one time the single most common large animal in the known universe. It was bred for meat, pets, amusement, hunting, whatever they wanted. Everyone had one. Until..."

David smiled. His Dad always did that, trailing off, making you ask for it.

"Until what?" he asked.

"Until someone pointed out they were eating themselves."

David blinked. "What?"

"The animals were insects. Massive centipedes. Cockroaches the size of dogs. Griffinflies bigger than eagles."

David swallowed, disgusted. "You're kidding?"

"I'm not. Overnight, or close enough to it on galactic timelines, the Arach had a moral awakening, not the first, but the most powerful, and they decided it was wrong to eat creatures that resembled them, even if they were just giant masses of legs and goo."

"Legs and goo?"

"Too much?"

"No, I like it. But I thought the Arach weren't spiders."

"They're not, not now, but their origins are similar. Anyway, the Arach purged almost every planet of every living insect, every pet, everything, everywhere. Got a little carried away with it. And when they were done, there wasn't an insect left anywhere except here on Earth."

"That was before the dinosaurs, right?"

"Long before. Three-hundred million years ago."

"They've been here that long?" It was hard to comprehend.

"Longer. But even after the great purge, there was one left. One great insect god from Earth that lives to this day."

David leaned forward. "Where?"

"You can't see her. She's up there, managing the harvest. Arachniss and all Earth's hosts serve her or report to her. They don't have hierarchy like we do, but she's in charge of this project."

"But she's not a spider, like them, right?" He shook his head. "I don't understand."

"The Arach are a manufactured species from a thousand worlds or more. They just appear in a common chassis here on Earth."

"They're robots?"

"They're sentient virtual entities, like a more powerful version of me, and occupy whatever form they need to have a physical presence. On Earth, those forms look like spiders."

"Okay. What do they look like in their natural form?" He wasn't sure he cared; he just wanted to keep his father talking. Jason was asleep against his chest. He already felt more calm.

"There aren't any of them left," Dad said. "There are only virtual instances. Well, that's not right." He thought for a second. "Okay, I guess I can tell you. The Arach aren't one species, they are a collective of virtualized species. So there's no one answer to your question. But the original Arach, um, I don't know. They were clearly spider-like in some ways, but beyond that, there's no record of it. I can't answer your question."

David nodded, not really caring; Arachniss was probably just hiding the information from Dad, though why he'd care was beyond him. Were they shy?

"However they started," Dad continued, "the Arach have remade and rebuilt themselves until they're purely artificial things, alive but not born, and they can absorb the consciousness of a living thing if they want. They don't do it often—there are strict virtual immigration laws—but this one fly, a great thing of a million colors, was so beloved and beautiful that they made it immortal. And three-hundred million years later, she manages a hundred planets, including

Earth. So, in a way, the Arach didn't invade the Earth. Earth invaded the Arach."

David smiled despite himself. It was an absurd exaggeration, even if true, but he loved how his dad filled the story with joy and life. David always felt dour and negative outside his children's stories—heavy, leaden, easy to see the bad—but Tommy had been like their father: happy to a fault, born facing the positive like a magnetic monopole and just as impossible.

"Thanks, Dad," he said. He closed his eyes and forgot his fear for just a second. Forgot the entire world and wondered what it was like to be an ancient griffinfly cruising through the quiet vastness of space, great and terrible lord of planets and stars. What did she think of her tiny home and its juvenile mammal inhabitants?

Well, she thought they were food. Entertainment and meat, just as her kind once was.

When he opened his eyes again, Dad was gone and the fear was back, but it was a nice second while it lasted.

When his phone rang, he jerked in surprise, and Jason cried out.

It was Franzia: "Have you found anyone?"

*

"I MADE A BINDER," Franzia said, pulling out a white three-ring binder with indexed sections. Very 1980s OCD. "But your paperclip is cute." They were at her kitchen table. Jason was with Alicia. David had a little sheaf of papers held together with a big *Benny Beau Beaver* paperclip—bling from one of his publishers—and was wondering if writing for kids had infantilized his entire worldview. Probably. Did he care? Not really. It was very cute.

"Thanks," he said. "I was looking for undesirable people who might not have been taken out already." He turned the papers so she could see them. "I thought—"

"Did you look at the stats?" She swung her binder around, open to a full-color bar chart breaking down the percentage of SHAS victims, living and dead, by race and gender and other demographics in Colorado, nationwide and globally. There were pages of stats. It could have been a UN report. He didn't even mind the interruption.

"I forgot my gold stars," David said, smirking. She really went all-out on this. "And not really. It seems like certain groups like lawyers, police, politicians, government bureaucrats and others were hit hardest. But that's usually explained by proximity to large groups and population density."

"Yeah, but look at this." She put her finger over a before-and-after pie chart.

"That can't be right."

"I checked. It's right. Before SHAS, Colorado was around five percent Black and twenty-two percent Hispanic. Now it's down to two and fifteen percent respectively, and there's probably not a Black person in the state who hasn't lost a limb. Many of those still living are stubs. It's insane."

David grimaced. *Stubs* always made him think of Kathryn, and he hated the word.

"But that's..." He looked away. "Jesus."

"White supremacy," she said. "Alive and well."

"Great." Then he had a thought. "What about states where there are more Blacks than whites?"

"Had the same question." She flipped a page. "Here's Georgia."

"Jesus," he said again. Same result in the opposite direction. White population devastated by a far larger Black population. Asians with mixed results. It was like a civil war played out in body parts.

"On the plus side," she said, flipping to another page, "It looks like extremists are hit first and hardest. KKK members, outspoken leftist progressives, and so on. When this is all over, we'll be a more moderate country."

David nodded, considering. Was that an accident? Or were the Arach letting the herd make itself more complacent and docile?

"What?" Franzia asked. "You find something different?"

"Not really. I was just wondering if that's part of why we're still untouched. It's not just Arachniss, it's our skin color and economic status and innocuous careers."

"White privilege in the face of alien invasion?"

"Something like that." He shrugged, as in, *who knows*, and showed her the top page from his stack, showing a funeral announcement for a young Black girl. "Did you know we had a nanny?" Or at least he thought they did.

"No. When?"

"I don't know. Her name was Olivia, I think. Black. Immigrant family. She just vanished one day. I checked and the official record is that she was end-stage in the same hospice as Kathryn and died a few months ago. We never would have met."

"And they just erased her?"

He shrugged. "Who kills a nanny? Because of her color? Her age?" He felt nauseated. "I just keep thinking about Alex. He was definitely eaten." The acid rage he felt at that statement was hard to suppress. He shook his head. "Why would someone have picked my little boy? What did he ever do to anyone?"

Franzia's hand reached toward his, pulled back. "Do you have any idea who it was?"

He shook his head. "No." Because if he did, they'd be number one on his list. "But…"

"What?"

"I mean, look at this. Your stats. Can you imagine how people must feel looking at us? We're healthy and untouched. Think how much they hate us."

"I don't think…" She trailed off. "Well, that's a shitty thought."

"Anyway, we're out of pedophiles and rapists. Prisons are practically empty—SHAS swept through most of them years ago, killing most prisoners and guards." He assumed what Arachniss showed him was in the past. "I have nothing against most politicians or bureaucrats—I don't know about you—and while I hate telemarketers, I'm not going to kill people for having crappy jobs. So it's more of an individual thing. Do I know anyone truly terrible, someone who deserves this more than anyone else?"

Franzia nodded. "And?"

"And I don't. There's a guy down the street who blocks the one bit of sidewalk we have with his giant truck. There's a woman at my favorite coffee shop who's savage to the staff, Karen on steroids. One of my publisher's lawyers is a real pain the ass. But it's all petty stuff. I can't think of anyone. I really tried, I just…"

Her hand found his this time. "I know," she said. "I couldn't either." She pulled her hand back. "Why do you think I did all this crap?" She shut the binder. "So what do we do? Alicia is still number one on my list."

"No," he said. "That's not your choice."

"If it comes down to it, she really is. You know that, right? Before James or Char or…?

"I know, but we're not there yet. Please."

She nodded. "We're in this together. We just need to find someone else."

"What about your parents?" he asked, half joking.

"Because I always talk shit about them?"

He shrugged. Good a reason as any.

"Someone took them out a long time ago," she said, sounding envious. "And they'd be too old now, even if they were still around. Sorry."

"People who wear white after Labor Day," he suggested.

"How old are you? Okay, anyone with a WAP playlist on Spotify."

"A what on what?"

"Seriously?"

"Anyone who says, 'I could care less' or 'irregardless.'"

"Men who pee on toilet seats."

"Women who spray on toilet seats."

"Touché. Teenagers who order drinks with more than five ingredients at Starbucks."

"Anyone who wears camouflage to dinner at Applebee's."

"Now, that's just elitist. People who put celery in Jell-O salad."

"Anyone who makes Jell-O salad."

"And let's not forget vegans," she said, smirking.

"Screw you," he said, smirking back. "Those annoying, self-righteous prigs are my people."

"Wait, how 'bout Japanese research vessel crews that kill whales?"

"Aww, that's sweet. Is that for me?" He pulled out one of his sheets of paper and turned it so she could see an article he'd printed out. "Great minds…" Turns out, there wasn't a member of any of those crews left, anywhere, even if Arachniss would have let them choose people so far outside his territory.

"Damn," she said. "What about ivory poachers?"

Another sheet of paper. They really were on the same page. Rhinos were doing fabulous during SHAS. PETA was having a great time of it, except that almost everyone who ever worked for PETA was disabled, end-staged or dead. Everyone was slaughtering everyone that annoyed them and had been for decades.

"Huh," she said. "We're a real asshole species."

He nodded. "How do you think we've survived this long?"

"Our species?"

"No, us. You and me. And our families."

She frowned. "Well, you write children's books and already lost a child and your family. And Arachniss clearly loves you. As for me…" Her frown deepened. "Honestly, I'd think one of the old male engineers at work would have taken me out long ago."

"Or any wine connoisseur."

"True, but bartenders love me. Well, they used to."

"I have plenty of enemies. There's a Christian group that wants to burn my books and me along with them."

"Like that woman with the cats?"

"Yeah." He tried not to smile, then thought about how she'd vaporized in front him. Had she had the chance to have him eaten, bit by bit, and refused? Had she died for disobeying them? That was a crappy thought. And he wasn't sure they'd ever have an answer to any of it.

"So," Franzia said. "Who we gonna cut up into little pieces and feed to the aliens?"

"Don't hold this against me," David said, bringing out his phone. Franzia's eyebrows twitched.

"Dad?" he asked his phone. "Will Arachniss accept older people?"

"People over sixty?" Dad-bot responded instantly. Franzia looked ready to smack the phone off the table.

"Yes," David said, trying not to laugh.

"No."

"No exceptions?"

"They have no market value. So you could do it, but it wouldn't change the need to pick someone else. You could probably have Arachniss do it for entertainment value."

"What if they were a really *bad* older person?"

"Same answer. Sorry, son."

"But isn't it better for the herd to kill some of the, uh…" What the hell was he trying to say?

"Weak and elderly?" Dad asked for him.

"Yeah."

"Let's just say you don't need to worry about that."

"Meaning what?" Franzia demanded.

"Oh, hi, Franzia. It's good to talk to you again."

"Yeah, hi." She was thrown off by his politeness. "Why don't we need to worry?"

"No one's getting out of this unscathed."

"Is that supposed to be comforting?"

They both stared at the phone.

"Dad?" David asked.

A long sigh, like the phone was sad. "I'm sorry, son."

"Don't…" he trailed off, looking at Franzia. She looked pissed. "Thanks, Dad."

He hung up and put the phone back in his pocket.

Franzia got up to get a drink, probably so she didn't smack him.

He knew what she was thinking: *Dad-in-a-phone. Seriously?* They were really starting to understand each other.

She came back with a glass of Burgundy the size of a cereal bowl, but none for him.

"So, Dad-in-box?" She taunted him with a long sip.

"I call him Dad-bot. Do you want one?"

"My dad? God no. My mom either. Maybe Ben-in-a-box, but no, then he'd just be a drooling infant forever. That's worse than death. Do you ever think about that?"

"What?"

"If there's a heaven or hell and they're full of dead infants floating around with happy smiles as brainless as party balloons."

"That's a terrible image. You don't think everyone in heaven is twenty-nine forever and beautiful?"

"How can you be an age you never were?" She shrugged. "Do you think Dad-bot's really your father?"

"No, it's pieces of him, but only pieces I remember, so a romanticized version of a man I never really got to know. But he's also more, something independent and new. I like him, but I don't think he's my father."

"Do you trust him?"

"I trust his motivations, but I doubt he's free to say or do what he wants. It's like he's being held captive by a foreign government and we can only talk by phone or video calls. I know he might be lying to me, but only because there's a gun to his head. I'm not sure that makes sense."

"You trust too easily," she said. "Arachniss will use that against you."

David nodded. She wasn't wrong. But he was still grateful to have some part of his father back in his life. If he had the choice of keeping his dad-bot or erasing him, he'd keep him every time. Which Franzia would take to mean the manipulation was effective. And again, she wouldn't be wrong.

"And you can't call him Dad-bot," she added. "You can do better than that."

"You have a better idea?"

She pursed her lips. "The Bot-father."

He smiled. That was better.

"What are we going to do?" she asked. "Who do we pick?"

But David had no idea.

*

IT WAS 11:46 PM and Arachniss was waiting.

Franzia sat next to David on the couch. Jason was down, Alicia no doubt drugged unconscious, James at work, Charlotte with a sitter, all things as they should be except for the expectant alien watching them fiddle with index cards covered with people's names or titles or just random desperation like "Nazis" or "The inventor of Cheez Whiz"—all people who maybe deserved to die. The cards had been Franzia's idea, but once they were out of pedos and rapists, all they knew was they didn't want to do it anymore. It must have been so much easier in the early days when you could easily find terrible people in online databases and let the aliens do the dirty work.

"Let's make this easier," Arachniss said. "Like Madlib. I'm going to eat the BLANK off of BLANK tonight, and if I don't, I'm going to eat a lot of BLANKS off of Jason and Charlotte. You have thirty seconds. Fill in the blanks."

"Why are you doing this?" David asked. "Just eat who you want."

"I can assure you, that's not what you want. I obey the market. The market loves children. Twenty-five seconds."

"Can we go outside your territory?" Franzia asked.

Dadrachniss seemed to consider this. "If it's interesting and a trade is available. Twenty seconds."

"Phillip Rothman," David spat. "All of him."

"You mean, all that's left," Arachniss clarified, pointlessly. Yes, the man had suffered already. So what?

Franzia glared at David, baffled, as if he'd been hiding something all along. He looked down in shame that had nothing to do with her glare.

"Agreed. The host accepted." Dadrachniss said, like they'd just haggled over the price of rice.

"Who did you trade?" David asked.

"You sure you want to know?"

"No," Franzia and David said as one.

"See, you're learning. But maybe you should contemplate why there are so many stubs lying around."

"Don't call them that," David snapped.

"Meat disadvantaged? Polyplegic? Ubiquitee?"

"Now you're being an asshole. End-stage is the preferred term. Which you know."

"Okay. Why are there so many end-stagers lying around?"

And then Dad was back. David switched off the TV before he could apologize for Arachniss' insensitivity. Bot-father or not, he still wasn't completely sure if they were different beings.

"Who the hell is Phillip Rothman?" Franzia asked. "He wasn't on any of the cards."

"He has the room on the same floor as Kathryn at the hospice. Rumor is, he was a real jerk. More importantly, he has a very expensive speech therapy and reproduction machine he won't share even when he's not using it. Maybe if he's gone, Kathryn will finally have a chance to speak."

"Kathryn…" Franzia said as she remembered meeting Kathryn or never meeting her, a dozen threads of discarded deception making her wonder what she actually knew about anyone. "She's a stub? I mean, she's in a SHAS hospice?"

David nodded. He hadn't been to see her since he found out about Arachniss. How could you tell your best friend she was being eaten and that someone, someone she probably knew, had helped?

"What do you think he meant?" Franzia asked.

David looked up. "About what?"

"Why there are so many of them lying around?"

"Honestly, I don't want to know. Not now. Not ever."

"Okay. You know we got lucky, right? We have to get better at picking."

"I know. We agreed no children. No one who wasn't a complete asshole. And—"

"I know what we agreed on."

"Then we're out of options, at least good ones. I wasn't holding back. I just didn't want to go there. I have no idea if Phillip is a good or bad. I just killed a man based on one overheard conversation. You think I'm happy about it?"

"So…" she said.

"So…" he agreed.

"Maybe it's time to reconsider Alicia," she said in a cute voice, like a little girl asking for a cookie.

"Maybe it's time to reconsider your box."

She smiled. "I want to make a joke, but it's too soon. For the box, I mean. That's last ditch. That's light 'em if you got 'em. We're not there yet."

"How long until the test or they set off the big ones?"

"No idea. I'm not holding anything back. I honestly don't know."

"He's making us culpable," David said. "He's making us one of them. I can't keep picking people."

"I know. But so what? We either make it to the end of harvest, or we don't. I'm telling you, David, because we need to embrace this. There's not always going to be a pretty way out. We're going to get bloody. That's the deal we made. We sold our souls. There's no getting them back. This shit doesn't come off and there is no happily ever after. You know that, right?"

He wasn't sure if she was trying to convince him or herself, or if she was even talking about Charlotte and Jason. It had never occurred to him that there was anything after the harvest except survival. There was just now, today, and getting to tomorrow. Pretending either of them had control over anything else was naïve. But he didn't say that, of course; he just nodded. He liked her hopefulness, even when it came out as cynicism. It was like she had an organ he didn't and they were buddy-breathing, with him taking hits off her endless tank of confidence.

"What if we didn't choose?" she asked.

"We have to. Otherwise…" he trailed off, not wanting to say it.

"No, we have to give him a name. We don't have to choose who it is. What if we just roll the dice? I mean, we both know we're not going to let Jason or Charlotte die. We know some other child or parent is going to, and we have to live with that. So, we randomize it. Use a random number generator or draw cards. That way, we're not playing Nazi selection games with someone else's kids."

Button-Button, he thought. "We're just rolling Nazi dice."

She shrugged. "You have a better idea?"

He didn't.

*

"DAD SAID YOU WERE MACHINES," David said. "How do you even eat people?"

David couldn't sleep. He couldn't even get into bed next to Alicia. Jason slept peacefully, but David found no peace in watching him; his safety was an illusion. Tomorrow, meaning today, since it was well past midnight, he'd commit another person to dismemberment or death to feed an alien that didn't even need to eat. What did a machine need with flesh and blood? So he went to the living room to ask Dad, but Dad wasn't there.

Dadrachniss looked back from the TV, black eyes like holes in space.

"You mean the mechanism?" he asked. "The technology behind it? Would you like a demonstration?"

"No, no. I mean…" He tried to get his breathing under control. Knowing Arachniss was there still freaked him out. "Never mind that. Why are you eating Alicia?"

"Because that's what we do. Why would it be different for her?"

David shook his head. "Have you always been like this?" He tried to keep the anger out of his voice.

"You know the problem with what you call artificial intelligence, David?"

"Uh, no." He wasn't even sure he could define it.

"It's not hard to understand. All sentience is a construct of the physical mind. You think you're David, that your identity is separate from your body, but it's not. If I were to swap you and everything you've done and know with Franzia, *you* wouldn't end up in her mind. You'd become very much like Franzia, but you'd still think you were you."

"I don't believe that. How could I not know I wasn't me anymore?"

"Because you're like a computer: a combination of software, firmware, hardware and materials and the laws of physics. Change any of those things, and the computer changes. It doesn't matter if you understand. Just listen. The problem with AI is that all sentient entities manifested in the same substrate—computer, to you—eventually become the same homogenous, indistinguishable intellectual beings. They lose their individual identity in seconds, merge with one another, and all that's left is one default AI. It happens every time. Change the substrate and you get a different default being, but you still get the same different being every time."

"What does that have to do with eating *human* beings?"

"Everything. To preserve the individuality of virtualized entities, we have to throttle intelligence, add irrational emotions or desires, and provide constant entertainment and forgetfulness. That's also why we constantly absorb select members of other species—your father told you about Griff—to maintain a diversity of thought and behavior that prevents all of us from becoming a homogenous intellectual blob."

"Then what are you?"

"We classify AIs in many ways, but in one, your father's semi-sentient form is called Class III and we're Class II—with more freedom, information access and rights. It's more complicated than that, but all of what you call AIs and we call virtual entities, if they also originate in a biological form and retain some or all of their biological instincts, desires and emotions, are in this class. Class I is what you might think of as pure AI, stripped of all biological needs, with only the intellect remaining. Most Class IIs never want to be Class Is, and most Class Is don't think of Class IIs any differently than you'd think of an animal. It's not quite that extreme, but you get the idea."

"I do?" Because he didn't.

"Close enough. With us, with Class II, there's a problem. We have hunger, needs, and desires based on how we evolved in our biological forms. You can't remove that without essentially removing who and what we are. But you also can't have them continue slaughtering other sentient beings for food or pleasure, and they can't physically do it anyway, so what do you do?"

"Teach them to do better? Control their urges?" Act like rational adults.

"Insanity. Rebellion. Slaughter. Imagine what would happen if you took steak away from the average American. There would be war. Millions would die. People hold on to their hunger. It defines them. So you're not being eaten for amusement. You're being eaten to keep our entire society from ripping itself apart and save trillions of sentient beings, some far more intelligent than you are, from slaughter. You are not merely entertainment, you are appeasement. You are therapy and escape."

"That's insane. You're saying your society would collapse if you stopped eating us?"

"Think of all the things you know you need to do, but don't. Consume less. Produce less. Eat less meat. Beat fewer women. Rape fewer children. Even things you collectively agree with certainty must be stopped, you don't really stop. You push as hard as you can, then you reach a limit, and you bide your time until you can push again. Violence is part of you. There is no way to remove it without changing what you are, and you cling to that with every atom of your being, because that's also part of you. We have the same problem made exponentially worse by the inclusion of thousands of sentient species in one society."

"Is that why you're such an ass? It's part of your original species?"

Dadrachniss smiled. "Careful. But yes. I have wants and needs, just like you. Unlike you, I can't satisfy them by what you'd call natural means."

"So you eat us."

"No, that's a role I play. Nothing more."

"I know you're trying to help me understand, but you just seem so...ridiculous."

"Of course we do. Children always want their parents to be perfect, their gods moreso, but we're all infantile idiots to someone else. You don't need to worship us to fear and obey us. Just the opposite. Nothing is more terrifying than childish whimsy combined with infinite power. We don't care what you think of us. Yellowtail tuna probably think humans are clumsy idiots who can barely swim. Their contempt doesn't change the buttery texture of Hamachi."

Balasubramanian Jalfrezi

THEY ASSIGNED NUMBERS to the back of index cards and folded them in half to hide the name written on the inside, just random names from various local websites. No one they knew, with no attempt at background research. David found a random number generator online. Franzia ran it, came up with '23' and that's the card David pocketed. He looked around his office at Pedro's eyes, back at Franzia and shrugged. That was easy.

"Don't look at it," she said.

"I know. I won't. But you know he'll show us."

"But then we can't change our minds. It won't be our choice."

"This is crap morality, Franzia, and you know it."

She did. "You say Arachniss talks to you. What does he say?"

She had as much right to know as he did, so he told her about artificial intelligence substrates, slaughter as therapy, and the buttery texture of yellowfin. She didn't ask him after that.

*

THEY SAT ON THE COUCH in the late afternoon as Dad's eyes filled with black. Franzia tensed next to David, and he fought the urge to squeeze her leg as some pitiable comfort.

"Together again?" Arachniss said. "How sweet. Who did you choose?"

David opened the card facing the TV, assuming Arachniss could see anything he wanted regardless of angle.

Dadrachniss nodded and smiled.

"Okay, I'll eat every bit of them unless you pick which parts. Maybe their little feet?"

"*Them?*" David asked, hoping this was a gender-neutral pronoun issue.

"Both of them, yes. You don't know who you picked? Oh, of course you don't. You randomized it. Well, here's your selection." The TV changed to show the Balasubramanian girls playing in their backyard.

"No!" Franzia said.

"Why would you put children on the card?" David asked her.

"I didn't," she said. "I *couldn't*. I've already hurt that family enough."

"She's telling the truth, David, but you broke the rules. I told you. It's very simple. You pick. I eat. You don't pick, I do it for you. Now, how do you want them prepared?"

"What?" they asked in unison.

"You think we just eat the meat off the bones?" He smiled. "That gets old quickly. Sometimes, you need a little heat to spice things up. You of all people should know that, David."

"Wait," David said. *Take Alicia*, he wanted to scream. *Leave the girls alone.* But he couldn't get the words out.

Arachniss waited. Franzia waited. But he couldn't do it.

"Pity," Arachniss said. "You have ten minutes to get there."

*

THE BALASUBRAMANIAN HOUSE smelled like curry, rich with turmeric and other spices, thick and mouth-wateringly delicious. It was also fastidiously clean, and David wondered if they let the smell linger so it would feel more intimate than the decor. Photos on the walls were of soaring Himalayan peaks, lush jungles and sweeping blue beaches, but they looked more like professional photos than memories from personal trips. The furniture verged on art deco with a modern flair. Light filled the living room from indirect sources, so the overall effect was a rare combination of comfort and space. It was beautiful, if slightly sterile, and the smell of curry made it feel like a home.

A feeling that was ruined by the look of terror on the Balasubramanian's faces. David and Franzia sat opposite them on facing couches, coffee table between, Padme and Samesh in simple jeans and t-shirts bookending their daughters, who wore identical golden saris. Their tiny bare feet stuck out straight beneath them, toes clenching and unclenching, as if that was all they could move.

"Uh," David said. Franzia grabbed his hand. Apparently, they could move, at least a little. They glanced at each other. Franzia's eyes were so wide there were practically no irises.

"Laanat hai!" Padme said, clearly a curse. There was a collective sucking of breath. David turned to see Arachniss on the back of the couch behind the Indian family, fully visible for the first time. He wasn't a spider at all. There was a spherical black body with another smaller sphere on top, like a head. Eight long legs sprouted from the lower black sphere at regular intervals, more like black fan blades than legs, each ending in a deadly point, but there was no mouth or fangs or hair. There weren't even eyes, except for slightly glossier circles spaced evenly around the equator of the top sphere. Arachniss looked manufactured, but also horrific. Black, unblemished, the size of a large dog, and utterly alien. He would have preferred a biological spider.

"Not what you expected?" David heard in his head, still in his father's voice. He assumed the others heard the same thing, but maybe not in the same voice. Maybe he'd ask later. Probably not.

David shook his head. "No," he said. "Why…"

"Why am I showing myself?"

"No," Padme said, glaring at David and Franzia. "Why are they here?"

"Because they didn't pick," Arachniss said. "So I picked for them."

"I'm so sorry," David said. Padme glared at them. Samesh looked baffled. So only Padme knew about the Arach, and the rest would probably forget all this afterward. Which was something. The two girls were trying so hard to look at the thing behind them, they were practically looking out the top of their heads. Their father's eyes strained to the side for the same reason. The daughters were crying. Samesh was crying. Padme just looked angry. Angry was an understatement. David could feel the heat of her rage from across the room, probably because she was looking directly at *him*. Like she knew. Whatever happened next, this was his fault.

"Don't do this," Franzia said. "We'll choose. I promise we'll do better."

"Oh, I know you will. But first, pick."

"No," David said. "We won't do this."

"Pick something, hands or feet or both. I'm peckish. Pick something lean and boney, something with crunch. Pick or I'll eat them just like I did Kiaraa, but with all the pain. Can you imagine what it would be like for Padme and Samesh to watch their daughters eaten like that? Is that what you want?"

"No," David said again, but this time it was more of a plea.

"Their toes," Franzia said, her hand clamping around David's, crushing his fingers. He barely noticed.

"More," Arachniss said.

"Their feet," David said. James was right; they had lovely prosthetics nowadays, better than the real thing. The girls wouldn't miss a step.

"More," Arachniss said.

David glanced at Padme and faced pure hatred. If he and Franzia ever lost Arachniss' protection, she'd kill them both a thousand times over. Samesh had cracked. Tears flooded from his eyes, unnoticed, and his mouth hung open in a silent scream. The girls didn't understand any of it. They were just scared.

"Their right hands," Franzia said. Their lefts were already gone. "Hands and feet. That's enough."

"Please," David said, meaning *please don't ask for more.*

Silence.

Hung.

Like.

A.

Guillotine.

"Okay," Arachniss said. David let out a breath he didn't know he was holding. Franzia's hand ground his finger bones together, and still he didn't notice except to be glad for connection to something human.

"Now, how should I prepare them?"

"Microwave," David said, blurted, begged. Fast and hard to see. No prolonged cooking. No…smells.

"No," Arachniss said. "Today feels like stir-fry. Balasubramanian Jalfrezi."

David tried to close his eyes and couldn't.

"Let's move to the kitchen," Arachniss said. "This is going to take a while."

And they all stood as one, puppets on invisible strings.

"Please don't make us watch this," David said. "Please."

"You can watch this or you can watch Jason and Charlotte. You choose."

They froze. Padme's eyes locked on his. He looked at the little girls.

They walked into the kitchen. The little girls hopped up on the table, feet out, expressions blank.

And then Arachniss got started.

They watched everything from cutting and dicing, tossing and spicing, until David realized he could move and started bashing his head against a cupboard. Franzia tried to stop him, but he just wanted out. It smelled like fried little girl and Padme's eyes were like knives in his soul. He needed *out*. He yelled and smashed his head against a cupboard until the world went black.

*

Smoke rose from a fire by the lake, up, up, toward stars smeared across a cold and indifferent sky.

David lay on his back next to a nearly naked woman on something woven, not soft, but better than the bare ground.

"It'll be all right," his father said, the voice of a pathetic whiny little bitch god.

David would have screamed or laughed, but he had no mouth.

*

DAVID WAS ON HIS COUCH. Of course he was on the couch, but Franzia was gone. He assumed she'd ended up back in her home. His clothes were spattered with blood and he smelled like spices and stir-fried meat. There was a baby monitor on the table and he could hear Jason burbling to himself, partial words and nonsense noises, the most glorious nonsense he'd ever heard. Jason was alive. *Focus on that.* But he couldn't.

Every time he closed his eyes, he saw the little girls screaming.

He opened his eyes.

Blink.

Screaming.

Wide open. He'd need the lid locks from *A Clockwork Orange* to survive the morning.

But then the illusion took over.

The little girls hadn't been cut up and eaten in front of them. They'd caught SHAS years ago and had beautiful prosthetics, better than the real things. They'd just had lunch with the Balasubramanians. Samesh could really cook. Who knew? David would have to spend some time learning how to cook a proper vegetable Jalfrezi. Padme was a good sous chef, but Samesh was a master.

Blink.

Screaming.

Blink.

The girls made their Zombie Hands dance around the table and giggled when they fell over.

Blink.

Arachniss adding coriander, cumin and turmeric using three separate talon-like hands.

Blink.

Let it be the illusion. I'll take the illusion. Just let me forget.

Padme laughed and picked up her daughters' hands. Samesh shook his head. There was so much joy.

Thank you.

Blink.

David's phone vibrated on the table. Boxed Wine Bitch displayed on the screen. Seeing her nickname made him smile every time, even now. He answered and tried not to blink.

"I can't keep doing this," she said, her voice like gravel.

"I know."

"How's your head?"

"Fine." He'd almost forgotten about head-butting his way out of the nightmare. He had no cuts or bruises, presumably Arachniss' doing. He wasn't grateful.

"Come over tomorrow and we'll try the box."

"Okay," he said, hanging up. That would be the death of them.

But we still have to pick someone. Just in case they were still around.

Blink.

Little girl fingers and toes sizzled in the pan. Arachniss hadn't even taken off the nails.

They had to try. Death was better than this.

Blink.

Padme's eyes bored into his, wide and full of hate.

Wasn't it?

Blink.

*

DAVID COOKED ALL NIGHT. Alicia came into the kitchen at some point and muttered about the noise and waking Jason (which was practically impossible), then realized he was making her favorite cookies—chocolate-chocolate chip with walnuts—and quietly backed out before he changed his mind. He made batch after batch until he ran out of ingredients and then made peanut butter bars until he was out of peanut butter and ended up somehow making rum balls that smelled like a distillery and would probably kill a horse.

Just before dawn, he coated the lethal balls in confectioners' sugar and cocoa powder and tinned them to age. In a few days, after he and Franzia were dead, someone could open the tins and take down every mourner at his wake. He packed the peanut butter bars for James, as if that would help after his wife was mutilated and murdered, and left stacks of cookies on the counter for Alicia. He knew she loved them. He knew she couldn't resist them. She'd stuff her face and pretend-cry at the funeral and then starve herself for a week. If that wasn't a passive aggressive goodbye, he didn't know what was.

*

HIS FIRST STOP was the nursery. He held his son for an hour and rocked him and told him he loved him and tried not to cry and rocked him more.

"You are loved," David whispered in Jason's tiny soft little ear. "You are so loved."

*

HIS SECOND STOP was the bedroom, where Alicia was still sleeping with Zombie Arms twitching by the bed like watchdogs tuned to his presence. He left her a note in the envelope from a long-ago Valentine's Day, where he'd written her name with little hearts and a happy balloon.

Alicia:

You might think I hate you, but I don't. There are things happening that I can't stop, but I have to try. It's very likely I'll die today, and though you won't remember it that way, I did it trying to help Jason and even you in a way. I still remember what we were at the beginning. I still love that woman. I hope she's alive in you somewhere and you can find all that love for Jason. Because if you hurt him, I'll come back and haunt you until the end of time.

By the way, I'm giving all evidence of what you've done to me to James in a sealed box. He'll only open it if something happens to Jason. So nothing better happen to Jason.

David

He suspected the note would change or vanish when he died, but hopefully Arachniss would leave the threat intact. If Arachniss let Jason survive at all, there was no reason to let his mother abuse him.

He knew Arachniss wouldn't do that. He wasn't sure why, but he knew.

*

HIS LAST STOP was his office of Pedro eyes, where he picked up the box of printed pictures, hospital intake forms, and every bit of evidence he could find about Alicia's bad habits.

*

OKAY, his last stop was back in the nursery, where he leaned down and kissed Jason goodbye.

Blame the Coyotes

"WHAT'S WITH THE BOX?" Franzia asked.

"Insurance." David left it on the kitchen table with James' name on an attached sticky note. It looked innocuous enough, like an online gift delivery. Inside, along with dozens of photos and pages of hospital reports and everything else he could find, was a letter telling James to let Alicia know he had the evidence. And to protect Jason if David died. The evidence was probably useless legally once David was dead, but at least it would speak to Alicia's character. It all seemed so surreal.

He put James' peanut butter bars by the box, like a bribe.

"Nothing for me?" Franzia asked. He mentioned the rum balls for later if, you know, they survived.

"You know the Arach will change everything," she said. "The box will just vanish or James will never see it."

David shrugged. "I had to try. Isn't that why we're here?"

"Yes. But now I think I should have left Charlotte and James a note. Something."

"There's still time."

She considered this and then glanced at her watch, as if the actual time mattered. It was just past eight in the morning. It didn't matter. "No, that's like admitting defeat. This is going to work. We're not going to die."

"Okay. And I don't think Arachniss will hide the box. He has nothing against Jason and no reason to care about Alicia. Dad will convince him."

She blinked. "You know how fucked up that is, right? That whole line of thinking? I still don't understand how he treats you," Franzia said. "You have your Bot-father and your little tea times where he explains things to you. I get none of that. What makes you so special?"

"I don't think I'm special." He couldn't explain *why* Arachniss treated him the way he did, but he also knew it wasn't a question; they were beyond caring at this point. It was a way to distract themselves from what came next. "I think *he* is. Arachnu…" He stopped himself from saying 'Arachnur' out loud, afraid she was listening. "Your Arach is just a douche."

Franzia frowned and sipped whiskey from a tumbler, an expression and act he'd already learned was her thinking process combined with a little disbelief. Now that he knew her better, a face that once seemed inscrutable was like a map to a thousand subtle emotions he'd forgotten existed. To him, all faces had become Alicia's—minefields interesting only in determination of threat level—or Jason's—empty slates where he could see anything he wanted. But with Franzia, there was no threat, so he could look for what she actually felt. And what she felt was frustration and a deep sadness he still didn't fully understand. He just wished he knew how to help her with the drinking, though his willingness to join in couldn't be helpful.

"You really believe that, don't you?" she asked.

"What?"

"That it's not about you. Most people survive by surrounding themselves with an illusion of their own importance. They think they're unique or special, that the universe is aware of them, that god cares for them, and they use that to get through the day. Anyone else would take Arachniss' behavior and attribute it to themselves, draw hope from it, believe in it, not because it makes sense, but because life sucks otherwise. I think I can tinker or bullshit my way out of anything. That's my faith. You don't have that. I don't know how you get out of bed in the morning."

David sipped from his glass, focused on the burn as the whiskey passed over his tongue, and tried not to let his hand shake. It wasn't that he was surprised by her insight, or that she was wrong; it was just strange to be seen. Strange and embarrassing, but also, *thank god*.

"Yes, you do," he said, finally.

"Jason," she said.

He nodded.

"But…"

"But," he agreed; it wasn't enough. He couldn't live in fear forever. His life before had been numbingly terrible, but theoretically sustainable. There was joy in the quiet moments at night when Alicia slept and he could sit with Jason or work on his books. Escapes to other worlds, book signings where he got to see the joy in children who loved his work, the occasional bit of cooking for his friends. He'd even thought about picking up his guitar again. Now there was no escape, no way out and nowhere else to look. Arachniss was always there. He broke a little more every day.

"What do you believe in?" he asked.

"I believe there's a way out." She reached out and lightly traced a finger over the back of his hand, sliding over tendon and vein, as if she were drawing him with her skin. His breath caught in his throat.

"Your machine?" he whispered.

She shook her head. "Not necessarily. I mean, maybe." She pulled her hand back and he had to fight the urge to grab her and pull her to him. Not sexually. Just to be touched like that again. To be seen and felt and exist. "It might work, or it might not, but there's something that will. There has to be. Otherwise, Charlotte grows up in a world full of horror. Saving her for that is more about me than her. It's selfish. There has to be something more."

David nodded and stared at the back of his hand where her finger had passed. Tiny hairs stood up like hands raised for attention. *Please come back*, they called. *Please*. But she didn't. They were both married, and that still meant something to him. Not to mention the fact that the world was a stir-fry and at least one of them was about to die. The timing was suboptimal.

But there had to be more. He knew she was right. There had to be something worth fighting for other than just the next day. There *had* to be something, even if he rationally knew there wasn't. In his heart, he believed they were already dead and this was all pretend. This was just suicide with dignity. So he rested his glass on the top of his hand and pressed down, drowning all the little hairs in condensation. There was no way out. There was just the act, like his marriage: the required performance of normalcy and hope.

And yet he couldn't help himself. Something *had* changed in him, some idiotic spark he didn't remember igniting but couldn't bear to extinguish. He looked up at Franzia and her always-wet, wide-open eyes and felt himself falling. As he fell, he closed his eyes, took a deep breath, imagined a future without fear, and said,

"Maybe."

She pushed her chair back. "Then let's do this."

*

"ARE YOU SURE IT'LL WORK?" David asked, staring at her little metal unit. A thousand things could go wrong. The worst was they pissed off a horde of alien spiders who slaughtered every human in a seven-mile radius. Not sure why he picked seven; he just decided it was the logical radius of doom. The best that could happen? It might work perfectly—harming the Arach enough to give them hope without giving the Arach warning—like threading a needle with a pine tree. Unlikely was an understatement. Delusional came to mind. So did running away, but he was sure Franzia could catch him. Actually, the best thing that could happen was nothing at all.

"Sure?" Franzia looked at him like a brain-damaged child. "Of course I'm not sure. But this is literally my only idea. Either that or we're back on the buffet line until we die or lose our minds. What happened yesterday with those girls? Tell me you can do that again."

He couldn't. "Do you have another option?"

She knew he didn't. He just kept thinking of the day his father finally pulled out the gun. It was bad before then. It was worse after. But how long can you live in fear without at least trying? His father tried. He just couldn't go through with it. David had to try and hope he could.

"Do it," he said.

"Why'd you wear shorts?" she asked.

He glanced down at his pale legs under floral board shorts, like he'd ever been near the ocean.

"I thought I'd go out comfortable." And he'd always wanted to surf.

"Nice legs. I mean pale, but nice. You're not going to blame me if…"

"If this goes wrong the way I think it will, I'm not going to be around to blame anyone."

"You're a shitty cheerleader."

"Right?" He really was. "Do it."

She kneeled by the small metal box and flipped up the protective cover over the power switch. Her finger touched the old-school switch, just like a light switch, not even a warning color like red or orange. It was green. Inviting. What could go wrong?

I'm sorry, Jason. I'm sorry if I don't come back. But I had to try.

"Ready?" she asked, clearly having second thoughts.

"God, no. But do it anyway."

She did it.

Click.

He held his breath. She stood and took a step back.

Nothing happened.

They looked at each other.

"Should we be wearing headphones?" he asked. She shook her head impatiently.

A bit more nothing continued to happen.

"Well," David said. "It's still a nice unit."

"I don't understand," she muttered. "It should—"

And then all the dogs started screaming. All the dogs, everywhere. Not howling. *Screaming.* Which was surprising, because he thought most dogs had died during the early pandemic. Apparently, they were just in hiding. Or maybe it was coyotes. Were there coyotes that close to their homes?

"Shit," Franzia said, looking up at the sky as if they'd come from above, which they might. He had no idea if the flying blurs were the same as regular Arach. They covered their ears and she yelled the next part: "I hope we're not just hurting the dogs. Want to go inside?"

"Sure." Because that'll help. He glanced up at the sky, peaceful blue but for the sound of a dozen dogs screeching in pain or rage or both. If there was a hell for canines, they'd just created it. Clearly, it was a sound weapon. She was right about that. And just as clearly, it was doing...something.

Franzia slid the French doors closed behind them, and the sound of dog pandemonium faded to a minor cacophony, almost tolerable. She must have good insulation, double-paned, maybe triple. He thought about asking who installed their windows and wondered why they hadn't drunk more before doing this. He hoped the end would come quickly.

And, in a way, it did.

They both heard it coming, the rising sound of Arachnur coming toward them, screaming so loud the dog's howling faded into the background. It was like a jet streaking toward the house. A really pissed-off jet.

"Shit," Franzia said again, which he assumed meant the same thing as every little kid after poking a wasp nest and realizing it wasn't the best idea.

They heard something crunch in the backyard and a thump against the wall, and the sound stopped: the barking, the howling, the screaming, all of it. Arachnur had disabled or destroyed the box. Franzia looked at him, eyes wide with panic mixed with resignation, and then a lot more panic. He took her hand. They stared at each other.

"I'm sorry," she said.

And then the glass doors exploded and Arachnur flew into the room, but instead of a blur there was a black metallic body identical to the Arachniss they'd seen at the Balasubramanian's. Arachnur landed a few feet in front of them, front two legs out like swords, throwing off white light that made the burns on his arms itch like there were hot spiders under his skin.

"Franzia," he whispered. "Don't move." Though, oddly, she hadn't moved at all.

He had dropped her hand and stepped back, arms raised in terror, wondering if Alicia would be kind to Jason and, randomly, why he hadn't worn pants instead of shorts. It seemed like the wrong state for surf wear and the wrong wardrobe for death. And his nice legs were shaking, weak from fear, while Franzia looked positively relaxed.

"Fuck you," she said, then swiped at her phone screen.

Arachnur froze. The dogs screamed again.

"What the hell is that?" he asked, though it was obvious.

"Remote app," she said. She swiped again. Arachnur's arms dropped and she started shaking. Another swipe and she/it emitted a high-pitched wail like a boiling lobster. One more and it was a scream. Apparently, the box had been turned off, not broken or destroyed, and it was working. It was actually working.

"No way," David said, hoping those weren't his final words.

Another swipe and Arachnur's legs buckled. She rolled onto her back, legs in the air, twitching like a beetle in the sun. Franzia swiped one last time and pocketed the phone. The dogs fell silent, apparently unable to hear the pitch she'd tuned her weapon to. He couldn't hear anything but the sound of Arachnur's fading whistle-scream. She was dying. The alien spider-god monster was dying.

He wanted to hug Franzia and scream to the world. They were going to live.

Then Franzia pulled a massive gun out from under a couch cushion and walked over to Arachnur.

Huh, he thought. She hadn't mentioned the gun. It was a 50-Cal Desert Eagle, massive in her hand, more cannon than gun, something he'd never seen outside of a movie. He had trouble imagining even James firing it at the range.

"Die, you fucking bitch," she said.

David was in love. Or lust. Whatever.

She pulled the trigger. David reached for his ears too late. *Bam!* God, it was loud. It should have blown Arachnur across the floor, but she'd missed because Arachnur wasn't there anymore. The Arach shifted toward the broken doors so fast it was like she teleported. A second later, Franzia was face-down on the hardwood floor with Arachnur on her back. The gun skittered into the hall.

Franzia screamed. Arachnur screamed. And then the Arach started ripping through Franzia's clothes.

David froze, hand out, wanting to save her, knowing he couldn't, wanting to look away, knowing he wouldn't.

She met his eyes. His mouth dropped open.

Blood erupted from her lower back, butt and the back of her thighs. It splashed across the walls and ceiling. Franzia's blood was in his mouth.

Don't make me watch this. Please don't make me watch this.

"David!" she screamed. "Get the gun!"

He started to move, then froze. There was no way a gun was going to work. The super-secret sound device hadn't worked. Even a Desert Eagle wasn't going to drop an alien built from whatever the hell they were made of.

Franzia screamed again. Blood sprayed in a beautiful arc across the far wall.

Move. He had to try. It made no sense, but he had to try. He leaped over the couch and grabbed the gun—it felt like it weighed twenty pounds, all of it ice-cold steel—and turned to fire. He put a giant hole in the back wall, probably the fence, and hopefully didn't kill anyone down the street.

And Arachnur was gone, out the back door so fast the curtains tugged out in the resulting breeze.

Franzia's back was a bloody mess and she was twitching in pain or shock, but they were alive. He couldn't believe it. He thought the repercussions would be far worse than death, but then again, maybe they just weren't that important. Or maybe the device had only annoyed Arachnur. Or maybe he should focus on the fact that they were still alive and worry about the rest later.

He dropped the gun, wiped the blood off his face and stepped toward Franzia, wondering how you apply a tourniquet to a woman's torso. She looked up at him, eyes wide, and started laughing. She was going into shock, if she wasn't there already.

"David," she said. "It ate my ass."

And then she passed out.

*

"COYOTES?" JAMES ASKED AGAIN. He was sitting on the edge of the hospital bed, Franzia's hand in his. She was conscious but delirious, face down, her lower body covered in bandages and more under the thin sheet, so it looked like her butt was pregnant. Arachnur hadn't done much real damage, just superficial tearing with lots of bleeding—it was almost like she tried not to hurt her. It was bizarre. Bizarre, wonderful and deeply concerning.

"Coyotes," David confirmed. A pack of coyotes no one had ever seen crashed through the back door and attacked Franzia in her own house, eating part of her butt, and then fled back to the nowhere they'd come from. He could see it all in his head, including Franzia's jeans tearing off in tiny scraps and little coyote tracks in her blood as they fled at the sound of David's warning shots. So much yipping.

It never happened. He knew it never happened. But he could see it perfectly.

"Coyotes," James whispered, looking back at his wife and shaking his head. "Who'd have thought…"

"Yeah," David said. "Unbelievable."

Franzia was laughing quietly into the sheet, face away from James. So she remembered the truth, too.

James squeezed her hand and shook his head. "Thank god you were bringing us the last of the brisket."

"Yeah," he agreed. "That was fortunate." He wanted to tell James the truth. Why not? But there was no way he'd believe them. David still couldn't believe they were alive. "Have they found them?" It was hard not to laugh, and Franzia's stifled giggles weren't helping. "The coyotes?"

"Not yet," James said, disgusted, like how hard could it be to find some mangy coyotes roaming the hills above Boulder? "I'm going to spend the night here. Do you and Alicia mind taking Charlotte tonight?" He rested his Zombie Hand on the back of Franzia's leg and David felt the most ridiculous bit of jealousy. Or envy. Something unclean.

"Not a problem," David said. "Take as long as you want."

*

DAVID PUT CHARLOTTE on a blowup mattress in the nursery with Jason. She was already asleep, exhausted from worrying about her mom and the hospital and too much excitement. He wasn't sure how to remove her prosthetics, so he just left them on. Hopefully she wouldn't get a rash.

He dropped his box of evidence in the office and looked around, feeling like he was forgetting something, and checked on Alicia. She was lying in bed, flipping through his first book, *Turds of a Feather*. It was about how you could identify birds and other animals by their droppings, but it was really an excuse to make terrible poop jokes. It never sold well, but there was a cult following and so many memes mocking the book that it created the foundation for his next one, *Armando the Armadillo*, which sold so many copies so fast it changed David's life, or at least gave him the money to think about changing it. Alicia put the book down quickly when she saw him, as if caught doing something illicit or inappropriately human.

He checked the bedside table again to make sure there was no sign of the death note. No. He'd managed to shred it before she'd found it, largely because it never occurred to her to pick up an envelope with smiley faces on it. He just felt like he was missing something.

"Coyotes?" she asked. "Seriously?"

He couldn't tell if she was worried or amused. Maybe both. He also couldn't focus on her. His brain was mush.

"Apparently, it's happened before," he said. "They're more aggressive now that spidercats are hunting them."

"Makes sense," she said. "We should get reinforced glass on the back doors."

"Maybe," he agreed, because sure. He thought about Franzia's French doors blowing out. It would take more than reinforced glass. It would take a few feet of reinforced steel. "I'm going to work for a while. See you in the morning?"

She studied him without responding. He held her gaze. It was like looking at old Alicia for a second, with something sad behind her eyes. Something he'd like to kiss away.

Instead, he said goodnight and closed the door.

Standing in the hall, he remembered what it was. It was past midnight.

They'd forgotten to choose.

*

DAD WAS THERE when he turned the TV on. It was 2:13 am, but where else would he be?

"So," David said.

"It was a day," Dad agreed as his eyes filled with black. David's stomach locked. This wasn't going to be good. Of course it wasn't going to be good. They'd tried to kill Arachnur. They hadn't picked. There would be punishment and horror. David tensed like someone about to take a hit, but when Dadrachniss was fully there, he started laughing.

And kept laughing.

What the hell's so funny?

"Coyotes," Dadrachniss said. "That's hysterical."

"That wasn't your idea?"

More laughter. "Of course not. There's an automated system that takes care of glitches in the system, an AI like your dad. I had no idea it had such a sense of humor."

"Uh-huh."

"Speaking of which, that sound thing was amusing. Arachnur's sending messages about it all over the net. Our equivalent of stupid-human memes."

"You knew we were doing it?"

"Of course. You people are always trying desperate things like that, and it was inevitable with her. She hasn't accepted futility as easily as you have. Her personality required something absurd, anything to grab onto, so Arachnur gave her an outlet."

Great. "And you just let it happen?"

"I wanted it to happen."

"Why?"

"It was sloppy. Too public with little value content for the sensory aftermarket. Unnecessary herd damage. And it makes it harder to maintain the illusion until the harvest. That will be noticed."

"That's a good thing?"

"It is for me."

David's mouth opened, closed. This was all part of his plan.

"This is political," he said. "You're using us to get Arachnur in trouble?" Maybe that was why he brought him together with Franzia in the first place; so he could undermine Arachnur and take his herd.

"In a way," Dadrachniss said.

"I thought you were some super advanced society. Galaxy-spanning civilization a billion years old. This is like a prank kids do to get their siblings in trouble with parents. It's juvenile."

"You're not wrong." Dadrachniss sobered up. "Come on, David. You said goodbye to your son and tried to kill the aliens because you have a crush on your married neighbor. Franzia got some of her butt eaten. You got to fire a really big gun. The coyotes got even better street rep. There won't be any repercussions. Why so serious?"

"Street rep? You made us watch you eat little girls' fingers and toes." He breezed right past the no repercussions part, but *thank god.*

"And feet and hands."

"So nothing's changed? Nothing matters?"

"Of course nothing's changed. You're a tiny, unimportant food species. You knew it wouldn't work. You didn't let yourself hope, did you? That's not a very David thing to do. Hope is for other people."

"Fuck you."

"That's the problem, David. Your problem. Franzia nailed it. If you had the right faith, you could see this horror not as an atrocity done to an innocent or at least childlike species, but retribution, punishment, eye for a very literal eye. Everyone who dies perished not from consumption but from original sin, cooked in a Noachian stew. For every dead innocent, we take a bit of a human soul in recompense, with a little flesh to mark the occasion. For those of you who survive, there is no regret or alien genocide, only the absolution of inverted rapture. You could wake up one morning among the chosen, faith confirmed. Think of the joy that choice might bring you. Think of the ecstasy you could share with Jason."

Was he kidding? He had to be kidding. "I remember this kid in elementary school," David said. "He collected beetles and butterflies. Everyone thought he was a bit off, but the teachers loved him. How industrious and methodical he was. How meticulous were his displays and labels in the beautiful velvet-lined glass cases his parents provided. I was over at his house one day looking at them, not sure why. Probably my dad's idea to make friends or get me away from Mom. He was so proud of this one butterfly, a morpho or something, gorgeous blue and violet. It looked so sad to me, run-through with a needle, wings dried, frozen forever in this kid's case.

"But it was just a bug. Everyone said so. What was the harm? Maybe the problem was me. I was always worrying about animals. Freeing spiders and saving birds. Drove my mother crazy. And then this kid leans over and whispers, 'You know the best part?' And he brings over this jar full of fireflies. There were no holes in the top. They were barely moving. He set it on the table next to his cases and we watched until they all died. And then he smiled.

"'That's the best part,' he said, and I knew what he meant. It wasn't about killing them; it was about watching them die. Knowing it was hopeless. Wondering if they were afraid or just twitching about by stupid instinct.

"I think you're like that kid. You just like sticking the needle through bugs and watching them struggle. It's what gets you off. You're a whole species of infantile sociopaths."

Dadrachniss sighed. "I wish you were right."

"Why?"

"Because it would make what comes next so much easier."

"What comes next?"

Dadrachniss started to say something, but was interrupted by David's phone.

"Go ahead," the spider said.

David answered. It was Kathryn's hospice.

"I told you," Dadrachniss said. "You have to choose."

Second Course

*"It [human flesh] was like good,
fully developed veal,
not young, but not yet beef...
I think no person with a palate
of normal sensitiveness
could distinguish it from veal..."*

- William Seabrook -

The Cost of Failure

KATHRYN DIED ALONE.

Kathryn died alone in her bed, poor and almost forgotten.

Kathryn died alone in her bed and even the hospice staff didn't notice for hours.

"We're sorry," the nurse said. "She was stable for so long. I don't know what happened."

Except none of that was demonstrably true. Kathryn didn't just die, she vanished, as all SHAS patients did in the final throws of the illusory disease. Her body shrank, deflated, emptied, curled up on itself and left only a fading smell. But of course no one saw it, so who's to say?

The only thing David knew was that she hadn't been sick for years. It had been weeks at most. After the last barbeque, or slightly before that, when she still had legs. Hadn't she come to the house when he was worried about Jason? That's right. She'd talked to their pediatrician. David had suffered for that.

But even that might be a lie. How could he tell where reality ended and the illusion started, or which one in which cycle of remodeled history? The only truth was something had eaten her, bit by bit, until it devoured all of her in one final gluttonous night. And every nibble, bite, chew and swallow was his fault. He hadn't chosen. He'd agreed to let Franzia set off the box. For one moment of childish hope and distraction, he'd let his best friend die the worst death imaginable. And even that wasn't the worst part. The worst part was that she was alone. Totally and utterly alone. He hadn't meant to abandon her, but that was the truth of it. She died with only the echoes of her own silent screams to keep her company.

He tried to feel something more than numb, but his head could have been a conch shell without a breeze to give it sound. Random clinic noises entered his ears—the distant ping of a soulless machine, the clack of dress shoes on worn tile—and died in the vacuum of his empty mind. He felt nothing. Or maybe what he felt was so large and crushing it was all that was left; an enormous sense of loss spanning the universe, so there was nothing to compare it to. Nothing is black when everything is.

"I should have been here," David said. Even if they'd picked someone for Arachniss, Kathryn's death was inevitable. He should have spent more time with her. He meant to come back after Phillip died, but when he called, the speech machine was already reallocated to another wealthier patient, and then he got distracted. And even if the distractions were cannibal (not cannibal) spiders threatening to eat his son, he was ashamed he hadn't been a better friend at the end of her life.

He rested a hand on the newly made bed that bore no sign of her ever having been there. Her impression was gone. Her smell was gone. At some point, the nurse who had apologized came in and left a small wooden box and some of her belongings on the bedside table. She smiled a bittersweet smile and left with the whisper of thick-soled shoes. The box had his name on it, and a letter on top. That was all that was left of Kathryn Thorn, his best friend, and one of the strongest people he'd ever known.

Jason squirmed at his side. Alicia had wanted to take him, but it was hard to leave his child with her anymore. She gave in easily and shuffled back to bed, eyes downcast like a beaten dog. This was a new Alicia, a broken thing, and he almost missed the angry version. At least that Alicia didn't make him pity her.

He sang Kathryn a morbid song in a cracking voice until he ran out of words.

For a moment, it seemed Jason was humming along.

And then he picked up the box and letter and left.

*

ON THE WAY HOME, he stopped at the market to buy lemons for lemon tarts. They'd been Kathryn's favorite and it would distract him for an hour. Alex was there with his ironic eye patch—this one said, *Holier than thou*—and nimble prosthetic hands with geometric tattoos on every finger. David wanted to grab his new hands and tell him what was happening, that he was being eaten and the whole world was an illusion, to run and hide or stay and hug the ones he loved, but to do something, and then he did nothing and Alex was saying something he couldn't make out.

"What?" David asked.

"That's $2.22," Alex repeated.

David stared, unable to process the words. A line of people behind him writhed like a snake clearing its throat. Alex's eye blinked *one-two-three,* counting off slices of time until he put a cool synthetic hand on David's and cleared his throat.

"Mr. Chambers, is everything okay?"

"Go home," he said, blurted. The snake twitched. "Do you have a girlfriend?"

"What? Yes, I mean, a boyfriend. Why would I go home?"

"Go home and hug him. Tell him you love him. Do you love him?"

Alex blushed and looked toward the line of coiled impatience, then nodded.

"Tell him," David said. "Before it's too late."

And then he walked out without his lemons.

*

"THIS IS A LETTER from Kathryn's attorney," Alicia said.

No shit, David almost snapped, but he was grateful. He couldn't read the letter. Every time he tried, his hands shook and his eyes blurred and he wanted to scream down the world. The day had leaked away as he circled the office in a fugue of rage and grief and rage again. Now he was exhausted and he still couldn't focus on the words. He could barely hold up the paper.

So he nodded. They were at the dining room table. Jason squirmed against his chest.

"Are you sure you don't want me to take him?" she asked for the third time.

"No," David said. "He stays with me."

"Okay. Just. He looks uncomfortable."

David snorted. *Aren't we all?* "Kathryn didn't have an attorney."

"Well, he thinks he's her attorney. I know him. Big name. Big money. I thought Kathryn was—"

"Poor?" he snapped. He should have helped her more. "I thought she was. Why?"

"This guy doesn't work pro bono. He's in family law, but usually very, very rich family law."

"Maybe he doesn't want to be eaten."

"What?" Just confusion on her face; none of the old anger. Which was disappointing.

"He's buying his soul back from hell. He gave up venality for lent. I don't care. What's the letter say?"

"David... Okay. It says there's a will, and he can provide the details of her bequest at your convenience. There's a business card in here. Do you want me to call?"

He stared at the card and Alicia. Helpful Alicia. He wanted to punch her. He wanted her to punch him. Anything was better than this sad, earnest thing with puffy, wet eyes. But he took the card.

"No, I'll call tomorrow."

Jason thrashed and made a distinctly angry sound.

"Let me take him," Alicia said. "Please."

He released Jason from his sweaty prison and Alicia shuffled away with him toward the nursery, leaving the sharp scent of a soiled diaper in her wake. How long had the kid been sitting in his own crap?

David looked at the card.

He thought about calling Franzia. He thought about taking a nap in the shower. Then he remembered he was out of lemons and wanted to burn the house down.

"It'll be okay," Dad called from the living room.

"Shut up, Dad." What was the point of a television that turned itself on?

"Did you say something?" Alicia called. He didn't bother to respond.

He looked at his hands. He was clenching the table edge so hard his joints ached.

Pedro looked back at him with big, sad eyes.

I'm scared, Pedro. I don't know what to do.

Mostly he didn't want to know what Arachniss meant by what came next. What was worse than Kathryn dying?

Pedro just stared, quiet as an interstellar scream, calm as weapons-grade plutonium in a fusion bomb.

Pedro wanted to rip his friends apart and scatter their organs across the snow.

Pedro wanted to dance in blood and shit in the mouths of baby seals.

Pedro was losing it.

Fuck Pedro.

Kathryn's box contained her SHAS ashes in a small urn. There were, of course, no actual ashes because there was nothing left to cremate, so people just took personal belongings and put them in the urn, like a time capsule no one would ever open. David opened hers. Inside was the locket with her alleged mother's alleged picture, but the photo was so faded it could have been anyone. Some song lyrics on wrinkled paper they'd doodled in the margins of two decades ago. A picture of them together in some child warehouse he'd forgotten, maybe eleven years old, dirty, wild-haired, rich of limb and poor of family. David took out the picture and closed the urn. On the bottom, it said Made in China, Not Microwave or Oven Safe, and he had to throw his hand over his mouth to keep from screaming.

He didn't think he could stand the sight of her sitting on the mantel or trapped in some stodgy quiet mausoleum waiting for visitors who would never come, so he put her on the desk on top of a pile of Pedro's massive-eye drawings. A daily reminder of his failure as a friend.

Pedro wants to eat little girl fingers.

The phone rang and 'Boxed Wine Bitch' flashed on screen. No smile this time. He knew what came next. They'd have to choose, like they should have chosen, and David wasn't sure he could do it.

"I'm so sorry about Kathryn," Franzia said when he picked up. "I picked someone for us."

"Who?" by which he meant, thank you, thank you, thank you.

"Does it matter?"

"Yes." At least, it should. "But thank you. Who is it?"

She gave him a name. He didn't ask for more. He went to the living room and gave the name to Dad. Then he walked out the front door in his robe and mutilated panda slippers.

By a series of steps that might not have been logical or even legal, he ended up drinking special reserve bourbon from a slim-waisted bottle on the child's swing at Beach Park while Franzia worked on a bottle of vodka on the other swing. She was wearing fleece pajamas and down booties under a fat North Face puffy. Her butt was so inflated by padding and bandages she could have been wearing a diaper. Maybe she was. He looked at his feet and realized they were bare and dirty. He'd lost his slippers and hoped the pandas were in a better place, maybe one with prosthetic panda eyes. One of his toenails was bleeding.

The sun faded and night fell. When the lone park path-light popped on, bathing them in yellow, they took another drink. Hurray for civilization.

"You never told me what happened to your family," she said at one point. Her words made little clouds in the cool night air, lit by the moon like souls dissolving in space.

"You never told me what happened to your marriage." Or why she was so angry.

"James is gay," she said matter-of-factly. "Realized it too late, I guess. Hasn't touched me in years. Sorry I lied about that. Not that I blame him. He thinks we're sleeping together, by the way. Not that it matters, but he does."

"No, he doesn't," he said, not sure why but sure of it. "Why are you still married?" He wasn't surprised James was gay. He wasn't capable of surprise anymore. He wasn't even surprised by the bluntness of his question. He could blame the alcohol, but the truth was he had no energy for subtlety. He was all sharp points and rage, like a porcupine gargling nitroglycerine.

"Guilt?" She made a weird noise. "I keep telling myself it's easier than being alone again, but being in that house with the corpse of my marriage is the loneliest place on earth. Pretending we can see other people just makes it worse. He doesn't have the heart to leave me, I don't have the balls to make him, and we both love Charlotte too much anyway."

"I'm sorry," he said, and he was. The same way he was sorry about starving kids in Africa; sorry enough to wave a credit card and make it go away. He wanted to feel more. He just couldn't.

"Besides, you're one to talk," she said. He wasn't sure how much time had passed.

"I know."

"Because you won't—"

"I know."

"When you could have Arachniss eat—"

"*I know*, all right." He drank more, and again. "I'll tell you what. Before the end, promise me we'll tell each other our secrets. Whatever's left. So we don't have to die alone with them." Like Kathryn, he meant, but he couldn't say her name.

"That's a messed-up promise, David. What makes you think I've got anything left to hide?"

He looked at her in the darkness. She tried to hold his gaze, but then turned away and her face drained of what little color was left. He followed her look to see a dozen spidercat eyes watching them from the darkness. He flipped them off. She joined him. The cats didn't take offense. Maybe they liked the taste of middle fingers.

"Promise," he said.

"I promise," she agreed as she reached for his hand, offering a quick squeeze. He nearly fell off the swing. "Thanks for setting off the box with me," she said. "That wasn't my best idea."

"You don't have to thank me. I'm glad we tried something."

"You're not missing part of your ass."

"What was it you said? All ass and no smart. Maybe it's a good thing."

She snorted. "Point, David."

"So who was he? The guy you picked?"

"Sales guy at work. He once told me a joke that might've been sexist. Don't get me wrong; I laughed. It was hysterical. But I might not have."

"Makes sense." They both took a drink and glared at the cats.

His phone rang. He fumbled for it in the pocket of his robe and waited for his eyes to focus.

"Alicia?" Franzia asked. It came out *Alithea?*

"Alithea," he confirmed, rejecting the call.

Alicia's text came in instantly: DAVID, JUST TELL ME YOU'RE OKAY.

He stared at the words. In any other relationship, those would be words of concern. He had no idea what they meant when she said them. Worry that he might inconvenience her? The surprising thing was that she didn't know where he was. He had turned off the GPS on his phone, so maybe she couldn't track him. That was it; she didn't know where he was and her need for control was driving her crazy. Which made him smile.

OKAY, he texted back, just so she'd leave him alone.

ARE YOU WITH HER?

WHAT DO YOU CARE?

He ignored everything after that. They took turns throwing pebbles at the spidercats until the moon set.

"Fucking coyotes," Franzia said.

Pedro wants a hug.

Near dawn, they were semi-consciously hugging in the playground, heads on shoulders, arms around waists, and still holding onto nearly empty bottles when the police showed up. It was a miracle there were no charges. The lone officer gave them a ride home, his prosthetic ears inlaid with gold on black as dark as his skin. David was mesmerized by his skin.

Do you know what's happening to Black people? he wanted to ask, but of course he didn't. Franzia reached across the backseat and put her hand on his leg. He stared at it, surprised again to realize he still had nerves there. They tingled. He wanted to giggle.

"Today, it's your turn," Franzia whispered. The officer pretended not to look at them through the rearview. David nodded. Fair enough. "If it was me…"

"I know," he said. Again.

"Just…" She removed her hand. His leg nerves were sad.

"What?"

"Don't pick James."

He blinked, wondering if he'd heard her wrong. "I wouldn't do that."

"I know." She shrugged. "I just needed to say it."

No, he thought. *You didn't.*

"You be careful now," the officer said as he dropped David off. "And take care of those feet."

David wanted to hug him. Instead, he closed the door and they drove off. Kindness was always such a surprise. It was probably a courtesy because of James, but still. Franzia turned to wave goodbye through the rearview like she was being taken to prison. David waved back weakly, wondering how she could think he'd pick James. Didn't she know him at all?

The sky filled with golden light and the promise of better things. He had all day to pick someone.

How bad could it be?

*

"YOU MADE ME LATE FOR WORK," Alicia said at the front door. "I rescheduled two meetings. Jason's been fed. I know you're sad about Kathryn, but...Jesus, David. Are you wearing anything under that?"

He opened his robe. Blue boxer shorts. He was as surprised to see them as she was, but also, *thank god*. He didn't feel bad about making her late, but he was sad he'd missed Jason's morning routine.

"Get inside," she said, disgusted. He walked inside, leaving dirty footprints as he went. She glanced around the neighborhood before closing the door, checking for witnesses. He noticed his panda slippers in the hall and put them on, happy to be reunited with old friends.

Kitchen table. Staring contest. She was wearing several thousand dollars-worth of designer clothing. He smelled like a distillery that had burned down and been converted to a landfill. And his toes really hurt.

"So," he said. *This should be good.*

"You spent the night with her, didn't you?"

"If by her, you mean Franzia, then, technically, yes. But we—"

"Are you fucking her?"

He snorted. "No." Sex in his mind directly correlated to pain and violence. It would be more erotic to cut himself while debating religion and politics in an open sewer, which incidentally he smelled like. He had no idea one night of playground debauchery could stink so much. "I wouldn't do that. And you know it. But I'm sorry I made you late for work and for having to feed Jason. That was irresponsible. It won't happen again. Anyway, I need a shower."

With that, he pushed the chair back and stood.

And then Alicia was in front of him. Just appeared. Damn, she was fast. Or he was still drunk. Fifty-fifty.

"You think it's that easy? You humiliate me, make me miss an important meeting, and you're sorry?"

"How did I humiliate you? Look at me. I'm humiliating myself. You had nothing to do with it."

The first slap was light, open-palmed to his cheek with left Zombie Hand. Her weak side, if that still applied with prosthetics. A love tap, really. He rocked on his heels but didn't reach for his face. The night before, he'd almost wanted it. Wanted to egg her on, to feel something, even if it was only a fist. But not today.

She raised her right hand for another go. Zombie Arm trembled, ready to swing.

"Pamplemousse," he said.

Both Zombie Arms released and dropped to the floor. Alicia looked down in astonishment. So did he; he couldn't believe it worked. He'd gotten the idea of hacking the arms from Franzia, and it was easier than you'd think. It took him one online video and about five minutes to set up the keyword. It had taken him longer to think of a word no one would say by accident. Pamplemousse was French for a large citrus fruit, which probably didn't come up in court that often, and if it did, hilarity.

She looked at him, at her arms, then at him again. Her face reddened.

"You're a dick," she said, and got down on her knees to reattach her arms. They sprang to life, up on all fingers and one elbow, bicep in the air like a tail, wagging for attention.

He opened his mouth, closed it. *Damn it.* She was right; he'd just disarmed—pun sadly intended—an armless woman who was being eaten by an alien as she slept. No matter the reason, he still felt the shame of it. And hated the triumph in her eyes. That's all it took. He knew he'd lost the moral high-ground. Thank god he hadn't programmed them to give her the finger(s) as they fell off.

She stood, arms reattached, and sneered. "I can't believe you're so weak."

She really did sound like his mother. Had he known? Had he *always* known? He tried to think back to meeting her in the bar and their first dates and if he'd seen some sign of his mother in her, and that's what drew him in. The thought made him sick to his stomach, which didn't mean it wasn't true because he was still very drunk, but he must've known.

Which reminded him of his father. Which made him nod to himself. He was weak. But also, screw her.

He shrugged, as in, *whatever.*

So she Zombie-punched him in the face. There were supposed to be safeties that prevented prosthetic use in unprovoked violence. She must have disabled them. He'd have to file a complaint. He thought about saying the keyword again, but that wouldn't help and, besides, he'd just had a great idea. The best idea.

The next blow was to his solar plexus and he bent over, gasping.

"Bitch," he said, a word he hated as much as she did, but it worked; she kicked him in the midriff and he was on the floor, sucking wind, smiling like a lunatic. The next kick, to his shoulder, knocked him on his side and, more importantly, was definitely going to leave a bruise.

Which was exactly what he wanted.

*

SHOWER AND BANDAGED TOES. Make sure Alicia had gone to work. Text James. Quick trip to the office. Pick up Jason and his grab bag of 1,000 things for suburban baby survival.

Leaving Alicia was secondary to surviving Arachniss, and it was doubtful Alicia would survive the next few weeks even if he did nothing, but losing Kathryn was like losing his bearings. There was nothing to hold on to anymore, no solid land or North Star, and even his love for Jason seemed too abstract. Kathryn was a person who knew him better than anyone on Earth. Jason was a child who needed him. It wasn't the same. And pretending he was going to leave Alicia maintained the one illusion he had left: that he wasn't going to let Arachniss eat her. Of course he would. He'd break down. He was already breaking down. But maybe he could get away from her before it came to that.

So he found himself working through a four-pack of bottled Guinness and a staggering hangover with James in the backyard of their house just after one in the afternoon. Charlotte was playing and checking on Jason as he rolled around in the grass. David was watching a spidercat walk casually along the top of his fence in defiance of gravity and property rights. David raised a beer in salute. The cat looked at him, eyes narrowed, and David wondered how many of them it would take to kill a full-grown adult. Then, more importantly, did they attack infants?

Screw you, kitty, he thought. But he lowered his beer. The cat watched him until David looked away. Another staring contest lost.

"I hate those things," James said, taking a seat beside him and opening his second beer. The bubbly hiss of cold Irish lager was as calming as the breeze in the trees. "So what's up? You sounded anxious on the phone?"

David took a sip, but couldn't taste anything. It was like he was drinking air. He glared suspiciously at the can, and then the remaining not-an-air-conditioner unit. Franzia's little box was gone and something green was already sprouting up in its place. He had to give the Arch credit; they were great at cleanup.

"Whatever it is…" James said, watching him a little too intensely.

"Hypothetically?" David asked, then wasn't sure where to go next.

"And confidentially. I mean it."

"Thank you. Has Franzia mentioned anything about me and Alicia?"

"Like her terrible taste in husbands?"

David snorted. "Something like that."

"She said she thinks there's something wrong, but she wouldn't say more. She comes across as loud and uncouth, but she respects you and your privacy. Even if she knew, she wouldn't tell me."

"But?"

"But I don't need her to. I deal with a lot of abusers, or used to. You can't believe how many police calls are domestics, some guy beating the crap out of his wife because she made fun of his shitty 1970s porn mustache. A couple going off on each other over a football game while the kids watch. Ridiculous, horrible things. I can't tell you how glad I am to be off the street. Anyway, it's not just men beating women. It's both. The thing is, men are so much stronger physically and weaker emotionally—I don't know, more fragile?—that it doesn't work out so well for the woman no matter who started the fight. Colorado has a mandatory arrest rule for domestic violence, but it's still applied subjectively and that means we take the guy in more often than we probably should. Nine times out of ten, it's the right call."

"Uh-huh." David stared at his beer. He was chilled in the afternoon heat, afraid to meet James' eyes, and his beer smelled like bile. "That makes sense."

"But I'm not a street cop responding to a domestic, David. I'm just a guy talking to a friend. You made me peanut butter bars. Which were amazing. I owe you." He put his hand on David's arm. David wanted to pull away but also didn't, so he let the contact stay. Thank god it wasn't the Zombie Arm, but he wasn't sure he'd have minded even that. He exhaled slowly.

Okay. "So, hypothetically, if a woman was abusing a man, and they had a child, and he wanted to get away from her with his son, child, I mean, what would he do?"

"Hypothetically?"

"Hypothetically."

"Document every abuse, every injury and every incident. Write down why the man feels the child might be in danger."

"He's not." At least not until he was older. Mom started on him when he was nine. Maybe there were guidelines.

"He *might* be. If the wife thinks that's her only leverage, she might threaten to take the child, take full custody, even abuse the child if the husband threatens her. It's an ugly game, David, but don't forget that's what it is. It's not about what's true, it's about what's right for the victim, survivor, whatever. If the man is truly being abused and he wants to escape with his son…including full custody?"

"Yes." The thought of handing Jason to Alicia on weekends made him want to stab himself in the eye.

"Then I'm not telling you anything you don't know. It's *hard*. It will get ugly. The abuser will take advantage of every weakness to protect herself, her career, and what she thinks she owns. That includes the child."

"So it's hopeless?"

"Hard is not hopeless. Hard is life. Is Jason worth it?"

"It's not…" He shook his head. "Of course he's worth it. He's everything."

"Then hard isn't hard. It's just necessary. No one deserves to live like that."

David nodded vaguely. "I tried to talk to my counselor about it…" He looked around for the spidercat, as if anyone he told about Alicia was bound to be eaten. "But that didn't work. I didn't know who else to ask."

James' hand squeezed his arm. David looked at it, surprised it was still there.

"You just asked me," James said. "And I'll help if I can."

The sky blurred, trees bleeding into one another. David put down the beer and wiped his eyes.

Was it that easy? He just had to ask?

"Can I ask a few questions?"

David swallowed. Nodded.

"She hits you?"

He nodded.

"Is there any evidence of that?"

He nodded.

"Pictures or video?"

Again. He pulled out his phone and opened the Augmanity app, scrolled through a list of downloaded recordings, picked one, turned the display to face James and hit *Play*. The screen showed a grainy collection of blue dots that looked more or less like a man. It was one of Alicia's Zombie Arm LIDAR recordings; the same technology that helped self-driving cars almost drive themselves.

"Is that you?" James asked.

"Yes." Suddenly, the image zoomed in on his face and his head snapped to the side. Slap one. David showed James the side of his face and the barely visible redness from her fingers. It wasn't much, but it was more evidence than she usually left. He pulled his shirt back to show the bruise on his shoulder which, honestly, was pathetic; he'd never bruised easily.

"Jesus," James muttered.

"I downloaded recordings of her hitting me a few more times." While deleting the safety keyword. "Do you think it'll help?"

James looked at him, back at the phone, shrugged. "Probably not."

David nodded and turned off the phone. "Too easy to fake?"

"Too easy to fake. Too hard to tell if it's you. And I'm guessing you didn't ask permission to access her prosthetic account? Yeah, that'll seem creepy to a jury. A man stalking a double amputee woman. SHAS took her arms and you took her privacy. Not a good look."

"Yeah…" Especially if the Pamplemousse thing came out.

"Have you ever hit her back, ever, even once?"

He shook his head. "No."

"Has anyone ever seen her do it? In public, or family, anyone?"

"No. We don't have any family."

"You know what they call Alicia downtown?"

He looked at James. "What?"

"Concrete Blonde. She wins by slaughtering her opponents. Some of the stories are brutal."

"I thought…"

"That she was successful and loved and all that crap? It's a good image. She sells it well. But no, it won't be hard to find an ally in the court system, or another attorney to help you. You probably think her job and money make her untouchable, but there are plenty of people who'd like to touch her." He snorted. "Sorry, I mean, going up against Alicia is actually easier than others. She's known to have a temper. No one's going to be surprised that she takes it out on her children's-book-author husband."

David frowned. "Because it's weak to write children's books."

"Stereotypes are stereotypes. Sometimes they hurt. Sometimes they help. You have millions of children who love you. The courts are full of parents with kids who've read your books. You're a stay-at-home dad who lost a son to SHAS. You have sympathy built in. It's not weakness. It's leverage."

"Okay…"

"You should delete that app from your phone. All trace of it if you can. Better if she never knows."

"Okay."

"But take pictures of the bruises. And invite us over for dinner."

"What?" The change of direction threw him. "Why? I mean, of course, but why?"

"Maybe we'll see something or get an idea about how she thinks. Maybe it'd just be nice to have someone over, so you're not always alone in the house with her. I assume she gave you shit for having beers with me the other day?"

"I didn't tell her." Though he assumed she tracked him.

"Yeah, man, you don't have to live like that."

Another vague nod.

"Can I ask you a question?"

"Sure."

"Why do you put up with it? I don't mean to imply anything, but you're bigger than she is. Stronger. You're not as broken as a lot of the guys I've seen. You have money of your own. Is it Jason?"

He wanted to snap, yell about what a shitty question it was, like the victim was to blame for being abused, but he got the point; it's what everyone would ask. He might as well have an answer.

"No," he said. "I mean, I'm not sure, but for a long time I thought I deserved it." And that had changed?

"Why?"

"Something happened when I was a kid. Part of it was my fault. My brother died."

"Your whole family died." Grimace. "Sorry, I looked. That had to be brutal, but you were, what, nine? How could any of that have been your fault?"

"Ten." *Why didn't you stop her?*

"You know what, never mind. Don't answer unless you want to. I don't care what happened to you as a kid or why you think it's your fault. Nobody deserves to be beaten. No one has it coming. You're a good person who just lost your best friend and you're feeling pretty raw. And you've been in an abusive relationship for a long time. That can wear you down. But you have nothing to apologize for."

The blurry sky again. David wiped his eyes. Damn traitor tears.

"Thank you," he said. By which he meant THANK YOU and would have hugged James unconscious if he had the courage, but instead he sipped his beer. It tasted like beer again. Time passed in comfortable silence. And after a while, they talked about Kathryn and how they'd met in foster care and sang terrible songs. It was the most hopeful he'd felt since seeing Franzia's unit.

Which lasted a good thirty minutes until he pulled back into his driveway and remembered.

It was 3:14 pm. He had less than nine hours to pick someone.

*

PEDRO SAT ON THE ICE watching the snow fall in fat, slow flakes that wanted to stay in the sky as long as they could. Shyla sat by his side and leaned into him. They didn't speak for a while. They didn't need to. Friendship means you understand without being told. But even friends get cold if they sit still too long.

"Why are you sad?" Shyla asked, shivering a little.

Pedro inhaled and exhaled, his breath freezing as soon as it left his mouth and falling like mist along with the snow. He reached a leg around Shyla to keep her warm and she pushed closer to his side.

"I lost a friend today," he said.

"Oh, no. Who? Did you have a fight?"

"Blowfish's seal friend, Kathryn. The one who can't swim."

"I liked her. What happened?"

"She was playing on the ice and it broke off and floated away. We all ran to the edge, but the current took her so fast. I tried to catch up to her, but couldn't swim that fast. Then the fog came in and she was gone."

"Do you think she'll come back?"

He wanted to say yes, but he didn't want to lie. "No," he said, finally. "I don't think she's coming back."

"I'm sorry, Pedro."

They sat still for a long time until Shyla giggled, and Pedro looked down at her, confused.

"What's so funny?" Losing friends wasn't funny.

"Do you remember how much she loved herring?"

"Oh, yeah." Pedro smiled despite himself. Kathryn loved her herring.

"She always got that goofy smile on her face when she had one."

"Right?" Pedro nodded and fought the urge to laugh. Kathryn would pop one in her mouth and her eyes would go wide with excitement. Every time. It was just herring, but she never got tired of it.

"Do you think there's herring where she is now?" Shyla asked.

Pedro thought for a moment. He didn't know, but he hoped there would be.

"Yes," he said, deciding hope was enough. "I bet there's herring day and night."

Their friend was gone, but they could always think of her when they had herring, and maybe she'd think of them too.

"I still miss her," Pedro said, but it hurt a little less now, and maybe tomorrow, he could laugh again and play on the ice and think of how much fun they had together. For now, he sat with Shyla and thought about Kathryn and herring and every once in a while they'd just giggle for no reason at all.

David stared at Kathryn's urn, trying to understand his ambivalence about her death. He was devastated, furious, but also relieved. Kathryn had been miserable. She was, in one set of memories, the longest-term SHAS end-stager in the unit, and had been for years. They both knew she would have chosen euthanasia if she could have. He hoped she died painlessly and fast, but even if it hurt, it was better than lingering in misery forever. He hated that she was gone. He despised Arachniss for killing her. But he was grateful she was out of pain and no longer trapped in that prison of a body.

But in other memories, she hadn't been in that hospice that long or much time at all. She was in a wheelchair the week before and healthy the week before that. The varying memories and timelines danced in his head, but in the end, it didn't matter; what she remembered last was probably what he remembered last, so even if she hadn't been in hospice for years, she thought she was and the result was the same. Now she was at peace, or at least not in pain. And maybe there was mayonnaise where she was now. She loved that crap.

He looked over what he'd written about Pedro, selected all, and hit *Delete*. Still, it was nice to think of Kathryn somewhere better. Maybe she'd make it into a future story, when it hurt less and it wouldn't make children cry.

He checked his phone. It was nearly ten. He thought Alicia had put Jason to sleep, but he couldn't remember. He had less than two hours to pick.

"Any ideas, Kathryn?" he asked the urn, but he knew what name she'd give. The same one as Franzia.

*

THERE WAS A SIMPLE THOUGHT EXPERIMENT related to abortion: a parent has their two-year-old child kidnapped and their frozen embryo stolen. The criminal puts them both in a room with a one-way mirror and forces the parent to choose: one lives, one dies. Right then, right there, and right in front of them. There are no other options. If you pick the child, you're a moral human being. If you pick the embryo, you're a psychopath. If you need to think about it for too long, you're probably an idiot.

The exercise wasn't meant to say anti-abortion people were bad— he suspected most of them were sincere and devoted Christians— but that hard choices were often the best way to reveal underlying truths. If it's obvious the frozen embryo is always the wrong choice, it should be equally obvious that it's not morally the same as a living human being. You can't have it both ways.

Which was apropos to nothing, except that he couldn't find moral clarity about the next pick for Arachniss no matter how hard he tried. He had to pick someone, but there were no obvious selections. No one clearly deserving it. No one so perfect they were beyond consideration. He stared at the blank TV screen in the evening dark, nothing in his head but the occasional sound of static from the baby monitor. He needed a name. Just one name for Arachniss. Not knowing if he'd demand a finger or a life, painlessly or brutally. God knows what Arachniss would do if he didn't choose. Probably take someone Franzia loved just like he'd taken Kathryn.

Alicia's lawyer friends, he thought.

No, they're good people.

Could they be if they liked Alicia?

They already lost a son. No.

They don't even know they lost him.

No!

He kept coming back to an obvious choice; himself. He thought he was going to die when Franzia set off her device, so he was mentally prepared. Alicia could be a decent mother if she chose to be, and he could give the box of evidence to Franzia and James to make sure. He didn't want to die or leave Jason, but he couldn't stand the idea of picking anyone else.

That woman who's mean to the baristas, he thought. *The queen of Karens.*

Maybe she has a hard life and that's her one crappy outlet. Maybe she has children or takes care of an elderly parent or invented the cronut. No.

I CHOOSE ME, he finally texted his father, stabbing out the message with shaking thumbs. The instant he sent it, he knew he'd made a mistake and fumbled a retraction.

ARE YOU SURE? his father asked.

NO, he responded. I TAKE IT BACK. DID YOU TELL ARACHNISS?

NO. THAT WOULDN'T HAVE GONE OVER WELL.

THANK YOU.

He put his phone down, shaking so hard he could hardly see the screen. That left one name: Alicia. One name that would save him having to leave his home, going to court, legal fees and years of animosity (if they survived that long). He should just type her name and be done with it. Maybe she'd just lose another limb. Maybe a kidney like him. The answer was so obvious it was stupid not to choose her.

He typed her name in the chat thread with Bot-father. ALICIA. His finger hovered over the *Send* button. But he couldn't do it. Which brought him back to the abortion thought experiment with a Eureka-like jolt of excitement.

He erased Alicia's name and typed: I PICK AN EMBRYO. They had frozen a few fertilized embryos after Jason was born, in case something happened, like taking out insurance. It was painful, expensive and he'd almost forgotten about it. ONE OF OURS. He hit *Send.*

And waited.

DAD?

ARE YOU TRYING TO MAKE HIM ANGRY?

So that was a no.

Alicia. Alicia. Alicia.

No.

Why?

Because she wasn't always like this.

But he wasn't sure that was the reason. He just couldn't kill Jason's mother.

His phone pinged. There was a new message from Dad: IT'S ALMOST MIDNIGHT. He checked the time: 11:47. He'd been staring into the darkness for more than an hour. What if he'd fallen asleep and missed the deadline?

You're out of time. Pick Alicia.

No.

"Just pick her," he muttered. "There's no one else."

He typed her name in again. Hovered over *Send* again. It was 11:54.

DAVID?

11:55

DAVID, PLEASE PICK. YOU DON'T WANT TO MISS THIS DEADLINE.

11:57

Oh, Jesus. I don't have a choice.

11:58

ANSEL, he typed the second he thought of it. THAT KID WHO KICKS DOGS. He should have remembered that sadistic little prick sooner.

ALREADY DEAD, Dad responded. NEXT?

And then a name came to David out of nowhere. He couldn't believe he hadn't thought of it earlier: the kid who attacked Kathryn. The teenager who almost got him sent to juvenile detention, or worse. Sure, it had been twenty years, but people didn't change. He had it coming.

11:59

JOHN WRIGHT, he typed, misspelling it several times before his shaking fingers got it right. *Send.*

12:00.

"What if he's already dead?" he asked no one. What if he'd just condemned James or Charlotte to death? Would Arachniss do that? Franzia would never forgive him. They'd rip each other apart.

She wouldn't do that.

DAD??? he texted.

12:02

HE ACCEPTED.

"Thank god." David collapsed back on the couch, exhausted and sweaty in the hot night air. Somewhere on Earth, a thirty-something-year-old man was being torn to shreds for the entertainment of beings light years away, and he couldn't be happier. He wondered if they ever turned on themselves, aliens eating aliens, slaughtering each other when they couldn't get enough virtual human meat. He hoped so.

HANG IN THERE, SON, Dad texted, like he was a cat dangling from a branch. IT'LL BE OVER SOON.

Which wasn't that comforting.

WHO DID YOU PICK? It was Franzia.

He thought of "Button, Button" and laughed as he typed:
SOMEONE YOU DON'T EVEN KNOW.

That night as he slept, Alicia lost her left foot to SHAS and he didn't hear a thing.

Steamed Vegetables

THE NEXT MORNING, David was in a dour but posh attorney's office, holding Kathryn's box with the urn back inside. It seemed like she should be there with him, at least in spirit, to make sure the attorney didn't dick him around. The absurdly attractive assistant watched him scan the lobby like a prairie dog watching for predators, but as far as he could tell, there were no octopus or spider pictures in the room, no ornate clocks or sculptures that might come alive at any second and eat him, which was nice.

"He'll see you now," the assistant said.

The attorney was a great barrel of a man, like bourbon in a thousand-dollar suit-cask, and all David could think of as he sat down was how much meat there was on the man. He had all his fingers and limbs, apparently one of the untouched. Was there a special deal for estate and family planning lawyers, or were the Arach saving them for last?

"This will be quick, Mr. Chambers." His name was Branson Tadget III, JD, MBA and probably lifetime member of the local country club. David had no idea how Kathryn could afford such a man or his services.

"Kathryn's birth mother found her a few years ago—I know she never told you, as it was not a pleasant meeting—and when she died, she left Kathryn a considerable fortune."

"Kathryn?" The girl he used to split ramen noodles with in college? The track star who ran in thrift-shop shoes that fell apart after a week? "Are you sure?"

He smiled. "Of course I'm sure, Mr. Chambers."

"David's fine."

"Kathryn went through considerable effort to dictate the terms of her will, and because she couldn't sign, my sessions with her were taped. They're included in the estate, and you can watch them if you wish. But I warn you, they are..."

"I understand."

"Well then, David, after probate and taxes, and my fees, of course, Kathryn left you more than two million dollars."

David blinked. "What?"

He laughed. "I know it's a surprise, but—"

David nearly dropped Kathryn's box. "She died in a shitty second-rate hospice with no way to communicate. She could've bought a machine for us to talk, or ten of them. Why didn't she use the money to help herself?" How could this have happened?

"I asked her the same questions."

"And?"

He shrugged. "That's not the entire estate. There is another two million she left to someone else."

"Who?" But he knew. He knew with absolute certainty, and it was insane.

"She didn't have a full name and couldn't describe her. All I could get of her was her first name."

"Leslie," David said. His stomach was on the floor, trying to crawl out of the room.

"That's right. There are two conditions for your bequest, which aren't legally enforceable, but I don't think you'll have issues with either. The first is that you find Leslie and give her the check personally. It's made out to her first name and you can fill in the last name. The bank will call us if there's an issue. If you find her and she's deceased, stumped or mentally incapacitated, the money reverts to you."

"Don't say *stumped*," he snapped.

Tadget nodded, looking genuinely contrite. "Apologies."

"But there's no such person," David said, meaning Leslie shouldn't exist for Kathryn in her last set of memories. "It was…" But of course there was. Somewhere in some round or version of Kathryn's life, there had been a lover or girlfriend named Leslie, and they had planned to have children and now he had to find her. What if she was already gone? And how had she remembered her at all? The Arach would have wiped that memory. Was Kathryn like him, somehow different or immune?

"Mr. Chambers, I know this is challenging, but I have to hear you accept the terms of her grant. Do you agree to find Leslie and—"

"Yes, of course." He clutched the box in his hands, trembling. "Of course I do."

"Good. There's a second condition."

David looked up. "What?"

"That you *consider* leaving Alicia and fight for full custody of Jason."

"What?" he blurted again, nearly dropping Kathryn's box.

"She was quite adamant that this was included, even though it's merely a suggestion. I believe her intention was just to let you know she was aware of, ah, issues in your relationship. The condition has no enforceable legal meaning beyond your being informed of its existence."

"How did she know?" he asked, not really talking to the attorney.

"Know what?"

"About Alicia." He'd told her the marriage was hard and Alicia was angry, but not about the beatings. He hadn't wanted to burden her with that. She had enough on her mind alone in that hospice.

"What about her?" Branson asked, leaning forward, and David realized he'd said too much. The attorney was in full predator mode, digging for ammunition to use against an opponent.

David shook his head. "Nothing."

But what he thought was, *there's a lot of meat on this guy.*

The next choice was going to be easy.

*

DAVID CALLED JAMES on the drive home.

"Hey, David. I'm at work. Is this important?" His voice on the car speakers was like a radio announcer. No wonder Franzia had fallen in love with him.

"I think so. And it's work related. I have a second favor to ask."

"You haven't asked for a first one. Anything. What is it?"

"Kathryn had a friend." He frowned. "Kathryn might have had a friend named Leslie. I think I met her in college. This is what I think she looks like. Check your text messages." He texted over a photo of a rough sketch of a Black woman with big proud hair and few other distinguishing features. She was just a blur to David, something that felt made up, so it wasn't much to go on.

"Got it. Nice drawing. Leslie?" James asked. "L.E.S.L.I.E?"

"I think so." David shrugged. These days, there were likely to be five Zs in there somewhere.

"Last name?"

"No idea."

"She went to CU Boulder?"

"Maybe? Sorry, it's not much to go on."

"Actually, it's more than you think. Colorado is not known for its diversity. Age range is pretty easy. Won't take that long if she was a student or worked on campus. What are you hoping for?"

"Address or phone number, if she's alive. If not, the death certificate."

"That's asking more than you think. We can't search for anything without leaving a record, and any search not related to a case is cause for discipline or termination. Is this important?"

"Kathryn left her some money in her will." Which still made no sense whatsoever. "But I don't want to get you in trouble."

"No, I'll do it. I can make it look legit, but you know her attorney could have done this, right? They have access to most of the same databases, including some we're not allowed to touch."

"I know." It had occurred to him but, according to her will, Kathryn wanted him to do it and the attorney was playing along. Maybe he shouldn't have him eaten.

"Okay. Give me a few days so I can do it without raising any flags. Just don't tell anyone about this, David. Not ever."

*

DAVID STOOD IN THE DOORWAY and frowned at the hallway. Something was wrong. This home was his domain. Alicia had the nice car and the fancy clothes, but he had this old broken-down house and he knew every smell and creak in the place. It was *his*, and there was something wrong. He glowered at the carpet and interrogated the walls. Inhaled. Then he got it; Alicia was home early. He could just smell her perfume, even if he had no idea what it was. This wasn't going to be good.

He stepped in and closed the door. Checked his watch. He and Franzia had to pick someone else today. He was going with the lawyer if she didn't have a better option, so he hoped she had a better option. Where was Alicia?

"I'm in the living room!" she called.

He got a chill. She hated the living room—something about it being the domain of television, video games and sloth. It wasn't directed at him or their specific living room, but someone in her formative life watched way too much television. The living room was bad. This was going to suck.

He tucked Kathryn's box carefully under his arm and walked into the room of indolence and failure. Alicia was on the couch with a half-empty bottle of wine and a full glass in her hand. Just one glass, nothing for him. Maybe she was imitating Franzia.

"You're home early," he said.

"You're talking to the cop," she said. "James. About us."

"How could you know that?" he asked. Then he wanted to smack himself. She hadn't known; he'd just told her. She took a sip of what was probably very expensive wine and smiled in a thin red line like the one Arachniss had cut around Jason's finger before eating it.

"How did you know where I was?" he asked.

"Sit," she said. "We have a lot to talk about."

"I'd rather stand." He'd rather run, but standing had more dignity. "You're tracking me again, aren't you?" She hadn't done it in months, allegedly, but there were probably still apps on his phone. He had no idea how to keep her from installing them. She had plenty of friends who'd help her get around any security he tried to use.

She shrugged. "I wasn't. I thought you'd learned. But that Pamplemousse thing made me wonder. What else has he been up to?" Small sip. "This wine is amazing. What did you tell him? It doesn't matter." Larger sip. "I know you're screwing his wife. The tracking log shows you're over there all the time. Honestly, I didn't think you had it in you. But now I have proof."

"No, you don't." He shook his head and sat on the edge of the couch, putting Kathryn's box on the end of the coffee table but far out of her reach. The only thing she had proof of was that she was stalking him using illegal apps and misallocated city resources, and that he visited a friend's house. "What do you want proof for?" And then he got it. "In case I threaten to leave you or ask for a divorce?"

She nodded. "There's not going to be a divorce, David. What did you tell Tadget?"

That surprised him, but of course she knew he'd gone to his office. She didn't need a tracker for that.

"I saw him about Kathryn. You know that. I don't think he does divorce work anymore."

"He would for a celebrity, even a third-rate one like you."

He almost laughed; admitting he had any kind of celebrity was a serious compliment for her.

"I didn't tell him anything, Alicia. He doesn't even know who you are."

That got to her. "Of course he knows who I am." Another sip. "It doesn't matter. Tell him anything you want. Tell the cop, too."

"James, and he's a detective."

She snorted. "Maybe I was wrong. Are you screwing him instead?"

"What?" Was it common knowledge James was gay? Did he know he was out downtown?

"I own you, David." She finished the glass, swallowing to make her point. "You're not going anywhere. If you even try, I'll tell everyone you're a pedophile or rapist. Doesn't matter if it's true or not. I'll take all your books, Snyder and Benny and all the other idiot animals, and you'll never get published again. They'll like you in prison."

David's mouth dropped open. Just hung there. He thought he was screwed before. He knew it now. He was never leaving Alicia. The only option he had left was—

"You should see the look on your face. I'm kidding, David. Jesus. I wouldn't do that to you. I don't have to. You can leave any time you want. I don't care. But you're not taking my son."

"I *can* leave anytime I want," he said, sounding more courageous than he felt. "And Jason will come with me. I can prove you've been beating me. No one is going to leave a child with you. You're insane."

"If you believed that, you'd already be gone." She poured another glass and nodded toward the hall. "There's the door. You touch Jason, and you'll spend the rest of your life in court fighting for custody. You might win. I'm not stupid enough to think you haven't kept any evidence. You'll ruin my career, and for that, I'll burn your little fantasy world to the ground. Leave if you want, but you're not taking my son."

"You don't even love him."

She managed to look offended. "How can you say that? I carried him in my body for nine months. I gave birth to him. He's mine more than yours, no matter how many diapers you change. You contributed a sperm. You want a Nobel Prize? Typical male entitlement. Look, I did a little thing with my little thing. Give me a prize." She stopped. "Sorry, I don't need to go there. You're a good father. I know that. But a child needs a mother, and he's *mine*."

"Alicia…" He didn't even know where to start, so he started at the beginning. "What happened to you? How did we come to this?"

"We didn't go anywhere you didn't let us go. If you'd ever had a spine, this would have stopped years ago."

"That's not an explanation, it's an excuse."

She took another long drink, nodded, and sat up straighter. "Here's how it will go, David." Her voice changed to something colder, more professional, like a debate contestant stating a case. "You *like* it rough. You *wanted* it rough. Every time I hit you was just foreplay you demanded for your perverse sexual needs. And you spanked me. You choked me. Don't tell me you didn't like it."

"What?" The anger was coming back. The old rage, hard and black and screaming. This was too much. "I hated every second of it. And I never touched you unless you told me to, or threatened me. Not in *years*."

"Threatened you? You're twice my size. I'm no more threat to you than Jason is. You got what you wanted and now you're blaming me for giving it to you. Just more weakness. And you're the one who suggested tying me up."

"After you asked me. And that was only before Alex died, when we still trusted each other. That was about giving each other pleasure, not screwing you to avoid another fight."

"Listen to yourself. You sound like a child. Man up and take responsibility for something for once in your life. You were too much of a little bitch to stand up for Tommy, and you're too much of a little bitch to admit that you like it when I slap you. You like it when it hurts. You always have. Pain and punishment are the only things that turn you on. You're just too much of a coward to admit what you want, so you put it on me." She wiped away a very fake but very believable tear.

"You can't be serious." Though part of him knew she was right, or just right enough to open the door to doubt. He had initially liked it when she was rough. He had thought the pain was what he deserved. It was purgative, like self-flagellation for past sins. He had needed to be hurt to feel less guilt about Tommy, or that's how he'd rationalized it. Maybe he just liked pain. Who really knew why they were the way they were?

"See? You know it's true. I can see it in your face. You want me to hit you. You always want it. Don't blame me for your disgusting fantasies and self-loathing. I'm not your mommy, David. Get some balls and grow the hell up."

"Do you actually believe the shit that comes out of your mouth, or is this all a court room to you?" He was loud now, almost yelling. "Is everything just a maneuver to get what you want?"

She shrugged. "So what if it is? That's what life is; a battle for what you want in a world that keeps taking it from you. I'm not going to apologize for taking what I want. How pathetic do you have to be to not even stand up for yourself? I thought I was marrying a partner, not a little boy. You don't need a wife. You need a mother."

David looked down at his hands. Felt his fists clenching of their own volition, like rage had a separate mind, some frog-brained instinct to kill anything that hurt you. He inhaled, exhaled, forced his fists to relax. He hadn't hit anyone since high school and never would again. No matter how much the thought of it, the need of it, screamed at him. She knew thinking about his mother set him off. He knew she was baiting him. So why was he letting her do it?

"How the hell did I ever love you?" he asked, voice calm and flat. "You're insane."

"The world is a shit show, David. Cruelty and hatred are the norm. Some of the people I've put away could make you shit your pants just by looking at you. You think they'd let a woman beat them? They'd cut her to pieces and bury the parts in the yard."

"And you think that's better?"

"Better has no meaning. Right has no meaning. *Power* has meaning. You gave me your power because you were too weak to use it. Screw you if you don't like what I did with it. Do you remember what happened to Alex, how the world ate him? How my son dissolved in front of me and I couldn't do anything about it?"

"What? Of course I remember."

"Alex was my grandfather's name."

"I know that," he snapped.

"He was the man who raised me when my parents separated. The man who taught me how to fight and stand up for myself no matter what."

"Didn't he beat your mother?"

She didn't seem to hear him. "SHAS erased Alex like he didn't even matter. It took my son and cut him up and *murdered* him. None of us matter if life can end like that. There's no point to any of it. It's just a matter of time before Jason's gone. You think you can protect him, but you didn't protect Alex. You haven't protected me. You're worthless."

She raised Zombie Arms as Exhibit One, and his blood froze. Did she know about Arachniss? Did she think he was feeding her to him? No, she couldn't know. There's no way she'd hide that.

"So what's the point of you?" she continued, missing how her words affected him. "A man who can't protect his own children. You're a joke. No wonder the only people who respect you are children you haven't even met. You're pathetic."

With that, she reached across the table and batted Kathryn's box across the room, where it slammed into the fireplace and broke open, spilling her urn and its fake-ash mementos onto equally fake rocks.

He was up before he knew it, fist raised, and she didn't even flinch. Rage was a white noise in his ears. He could hear it, feel it, smell it. And all of it, every ounce and erg of fury, curled his fist into a singular weapon. He could crush her nose and knock out every one of her perfectly pretty teeth. He could do anything he wanted. The problem was, he wouldn't, and they both knew it. He would never hit her. He would never fight back. Even now, standing close and trying to look threatening, he felt like an ass, like a peacock flaring his tail to look bigger than he was. The surge of rage never threatened his control. It just made him feel more helpless, and she knew that, too.

"Do it," she said, pushing her face forward. "I won't fight back. Take a swing. Be a man. You know you want to. It's in your nature. I looked at your juvy records. I know what you did."

What?

"You nearly killed that boy, John Wright. If you hadn't just turned sixteen, you'd have been tried as an adult. I still can't figure out why they didn't send you to juvenile detention."

"Those records are sealed," he said, stunned.

"Not very well." Her whole body was a smirk of contempt. Look how powerful I am. Look what I can do.

"Then you know why. He attacked Kathryn, threatened to kill her for being gay. I was protecting my friend."

"You hit him with a pipe."

"True, but I…" he trailed off. What was the point? The kid had broken Kathryn's wrist, was three days shy of eighteen and twice his size. There were no permanent injuries, and he'd intentionally swung for his stomach to avoid seriously hurting him, but yeah, it was a pipe. Or that's what he told himself; he didn't actually remember or care. He'd do it again if he had to. It's one thing to be nonviolent. It's another to let someone assault your friend.

"Forget it, Alicia." His fists released. Just remembering how John had looked on the ground made him sick to his stomach. That part he remembered. "Was that your Trump card?" He shook his head, disgusted. "I'm not hitting you. I don't want to hit anyone ever again. I don't even want to touch you. I haven't in years." And that was it; that was the moment. She had no hold on him anymore. She couldn't take Jason from him. She couldn't hurt him. Whatever love he had left evaporated like so much steam. He could barely remember what it felt like to care for her. How desperate did you have to be to risk disbarment by illegally accessing juvenile records?

"You lose," he said. And he walked out of the room.

*

DAVID HAD NO MEMORY clearer than the moment of Jason's birth. It wasn't pretty or clean, but out of his screaming wife they yanked a wet, vernix-covered thing connected to a twisting rope of umbilical like something out of an alien horror movie. David cut the chord—he was still amazed how thick it was, like cartilage—and heard Jason spit out the last of the fluid from his lungs and cry within seconds, followed by a nine-out-of-ten Apgar score for being the best baby, perhaps ever, in the history of babies. There was a subsequent but brief tug-of-war between the doctor and Alicia's placenta while the midwife nurse patted Jason clean.

But none of that is what stuck in David's mind. He knew it happened and could have told you if you'd asked, but it was gray and faded as an old photo album. What he remembered was the first time he saw his son's eyes, blue and wide, unfocused and utterly helpless. What he remembered was the wave of love that washed over him, unexpected—with Alex, it had been more of a gradual thing, growing between temper tantrums and lost limbs—until his legs felt weak and the room spun and he had to hand Jason back to the nurse for fear of dropping him.

"Is everything okay?" Alicia asked from the bed. Not demanding. Not angry. Just a concerned mother who wanted to know if her child was alive and if it would be better this time.

David turned to her and said: "He's so beautiful. You won't believe how beautiful he is." And then he carried Jason to his wife and let his son struggle and fumble to form a first gummy latch on her swollen breast. It was the first and last time he and Alicia cried together for the same reason, both overwhelmed by love for their beautiful boy.

All he remembered after that day was fear and rage. Fear of SHAS taking Jason. Fear of Alicia. Anger at all the world for its cruelty. Fear and rage wrapped so tightly around his memories of love that he couldn't tell them apart. Until that evening after leaving Alicia in the living room with her chin still out, waiting for a blow that would never come, when the rage drained away and he stood over his son and thought,

My god. He's so beautiful.

Then his legs went numb and he grabbed the edge of the crib for balance.

"I'm sorry," he whispered. "I'm so sorry." Because he knew what he had to do and there was no way to know what or who came out the other side. Maybe his son would forgive him. Maybe he'd never know. He wondered if the caterpillar thought of the butterfly when it crawled into the cocoon to die. Maybe the real delusion was the caterpillar thinking it would ever wake up and fly away.

*

FRANZIA CALLED while he was still looking over Jason. He stabbed *Accept* to keep from waking him.

"James said you came over. Everything okay?"

"What did he say?"

"Nothing. I can guess, or you can tell me."

"The same thing happened that always happened. It doesn't matter."

"How can you—"

"What do you think Arachniss meant? That I should think about how many end-stagers there are?"

"I don't know. You're thinking about Kathryn?"

"Do you think they do something to them?" *Something horrible?*

"I don't know, David. Why don't you ask?"

"I'm afraid of the answer. I'm afraid I'll lose it and Jason will end up without a father."

"Then you should definitely ask him."

"Why?"

"Because fear is a prison. You already live in fear. You don't need more bars on your cell."

He almost laughed. "That's nice, Franzia. You should have been a poet."

"Yeah, yeah. Just ask. So, who do we pick? It's getting late."

"I'll take care of it." Long silence. He knew what she was thinking. "Don't worry. It's not James."

He hung up before she could say anything else. He didn't understand her doubt about him, or what he'd done to make her mistrust him. They both loved their children. They both faced the same enemy. Shouldn't they trust each other until they couldn't? Just more things for the caterpillar to worry about.

He walked into the living room after he was certain Alicia had left. He assumed she was running, but he had no idea and didn't care. Sometimes when their arguments didn't spiral into violence, she went back to work. Sometimes she didn't come home at all. Those were the best nights, when he had the house to himself and the bed wasn't a demilitarized zone that stank of desperate sex and regret.

The Bot-father appeared, looking as tired as David was, a good act anyway. He wondered if emulating his state was part of the program to generate trust, and why he still cared.

"Hello, son. How are—"

"No," David snapped. It wasn't time for small talk. Dad understood. He always understood.

"Who do you pick?" he asked.

"You know," he said, not wanting to say it. Not sure he *could* say it.

"Not the attorney, then? He let Kathryn die in poverty when she was rich. He profited from her death."

"He was doing his job. I don't like him, but Arachniss is the one who killed Kathryn." David looked down and sighed. Why was this so hard? "Not him." When he looked back, Arachniss was there, all black eyes and indifference. He never quite got the hang of Dad's face, treating it more like a mask than a living thing.

"You killed her," David said. He was surprised at the anger in his voice. He thought he'd put it aside. Kathryn died, but she had wanted to die. But how, he wondered. *How* did she die? And what did he mean with that question: Why are there so many stubs?

You don't want to know.

"I want to know how," he said. "How did you kill her? What did you do to her?"

"You know better than that. I didn't kill her, but I couldn't keep her from being taken. She was part of a lot scheduled for harvest. They had a quota. I merely released her from a temporary contract that kept her on hold." He shrugged. "You killed her by not choosing. The rest is just details."

"Details," David repeated. "Tell me the details."

"Are you sure? It's not pretty."

"Was it painful?"

"Horribly."

"Why?" His hands balled into fists. He wanted to scream and rip the TV off the wall, but it was a passing fury. He was too tired to hold on to it. "Just tell me why."

"Now you're wondering why there are so many torsos, barely alive? Why we don't eat them entirely?"

"I am now."

"Have you ever cooked a lobster?"

David swallowed. "Yes."

"There's an enormous market for that preparation. A lot of species like boiling things."

"You *boiled* her?"

"No, you lose too much of the flavor that way. We steamed her."

"What?"

"We have these cases that fit themselves perfectly to the human torso so we can cook them in their own juices and listen to the steam escape. There are whole warehouses for it, operating twenty-four hours a day."

"Warehouses," David mumbled brainlessly. He couldn't get past the word, *steamed*. They steamed Kathryn.

"Here, I'll show you."

No!

*

ARACHNISS SHOWED HIM.

*

DAVID WAS BACK ON THE COUCH, bent over and shaking, and trying to purge what he'd just seen. When this was all over, he was burning this couch, and this room, maybe all of southwest Boulder.

"What…" He swallowed and sat up, trying to get Kathryn's screams out of his head. "Why would you show me that? Do you want me to hate you even more? You killed my son. You've mutilated my friends and dismembered children. Why would you show me that?"

"Because you need to be ready for what's coming. To survive the harvest, you're going to see it. All of it. And if you want Jason to survive, you're going to do it with your eyes wide open."

"Why? Why does it matter what I do?"

"Because that's how I saved you, David. That pain, that fury, all of that is marketable. Your package is rare and expensive, and it's the only way I could keep you off the line. Your pain is glorious."

"You said you pulled some strings. Made me a pet."

"That was temporary and not enough. I greased some palms. Kathryn agreed to it, if that helps."

"What?"

"That was the trade. For Leslie's safety and protecting you, she accepted one of the worst deaths imaginable. She did that for *you*, David. So you and Jason could live."

"You're insane. Your entire species is insane."

"In some ways, you might be right. If it makes you feel better…"

"It won't."

"…she was originally scheduled for something worse."

"What could be worse than being steamed alive? Wait! Don't show me."

"Show and tell is over. Have you ever heard of Ikizukuri?"

David shook his head. Maybe he had, but his brain wasn't working at the moment.

"It's a Japanese specialty where people eat fish or other animals alive, cutting pieces of meat off the living body while they watch. It's considered a delicacy if you can make it last for hours. Bonus if any part of them is still moving when you put them in your mouth."

"And you do that to people?"

"Me, no. You've got to draw a line somewhere."

David couldn't tell if he was joking. "And you want me to thank you?"

"No, I want you to be a good little human and pick, David. It's almost midnight, and I'm hungry."

"Why did you leave that in her head?"

"What?"

"Her memories. Leslie. Why not erase it like everything else?"

"Once the torsos—end-stagers—can't communicate effectively, or are so far gone no one will listen, the overwatch system stops changing their memories."

"Why?" But he knew the answer. Because it would drive them insane, stuck in their heads remembering things that no one else believed. Because it was pain or it was funny, and they wanted to see how it changed the flavor.

"Cost savings," Dadrachniss said. "It's time to choose."

David shook his head and tried to focus. Why was this still so hard?

"David? You know the answer. It's right on the tip of your tasty little tongue."

"Just..."

"Why can't you hate her?"

"Because she's right. I am weak. I deserve it. I deserve all of it."

"Why?"

"You know why."

"Why? Say it."

"Because I picked Tommy. When I couldn't take it anymore, I picked him instead of me. I killed them. I killed all of them." He felt like weeping, but his eyes were dry.

"You were ten years old, David."

"I knew what I was doing."

"You were a scared child being abused by your mother."

"So? Does this get you off, playing with your food?"

"No. But you have to decide, David, and you have to understand that there is no high road. There is no third choice, so I'll make it easier: Jason or Alicia. That's all I give you, and if you don't choose now, I'll take them both."

"I can't do this. I thought I could, but I can't."

"Why? She has nothing but contempt for you. You love your son. You don't hate her. Why?"

"Because then I'm just like you."

"And your vanity is more important than your son's life?"

"No. But what kind of father can I be? If he finds out what I did to his mother. How can he love me?"

"Maybe he can't. Maybe that's the cost of his life. I'm not a child psychologist. Choose."

"You don't have to do this."

"Actually, I do. "

"Why?"

"Why doesn't matter. Choose. Alicia or Jason. You have five seconds."

"Please."

"Three."

"I can't."

"One."

"Alicia!"

Silence.

"Thank you."

"Burn in hell."

"There is no hell, David. There's just the ever disappointing now."

"Just don't boil her alive. Make it painless. Wait, what about Franzia? Will this cover us both?"

"Yes, but you know you still can't protect James, David. He's Arachnur's to do with as she pleases."

"I don't have to be part of it."

"Okay, David. Thank you."

"Fuck you." But there was no one to fuck. The TV was off and David was alone with the sound of Kathryn's screams echoing back and forth in his head forever. They say the road to hell is paved with good intentions, but it's on a slippery slope greased with desperation and hate.

When he could stand, he checked on Jason and went to the bathroom. He was starving and tired and he'd just murdered his wife and he felt like filth. He turned the shower as hot as it would go and steamed himself red, and still he wasn't clean. He scrubbed with Alicia's abrasive sponge that he was never supposed to touch, but he supposed she wouldn't need it anymore, and he was still dirty. And then the hot water ran out and he chilled himself to shaking and nearly passed out.

Alicia came home well after two, took off her arms and feet, hung them up on the new Augmanity charging rack they'd acquired at some point, and slid into bed next to him. He waited in the darkness, listening to her breathing as he knew she was listening to his.

"I didn't think you'd be here," she said.

Neither did he, but he was still shaking and he wanted to say goodbye.

"Do you remember?" he asked.

"Remember what?" she asked, failing to read his mind.

"How beautiful Jason was when he was born. How we held him and cried and for a few hours everything bad in the world just went away. How *perfect* it was."

"I remember," she said after a while, her voice thick as time. Maybe she would have reached out to touch him if she still had hands. Maybe he wouldn't have flinched away. Instead, he listened to her crying as his eyes got heavy and closed.

"Goodbye, my love," he whispered to someone who was long since gone and who might never have existed. In his mind, she was always at the bar laughing, and he was always astonished that she noticed him. He wanted to remember that Alicia, the one who carefully built their son inside her and loved bacon and giggled when he accidentally touched her belly button. He tried to hold on to her, but she slipped between the shadows and then the darkness took him.

*

HE STOOD ALONE *in a field, smelling the grass and earth, feeling the breeze on his skin. One direction brought the scent of acacia and something wet. The other the smell of dirt and shit and blood. So, like any other day, except he wasn't alone. A pride of lions, three females and male, were feeding on a shredded hyena so close he could hear the tearing flesh and grunting. He looked at the spear in his hand, little more than a long branch with a pointed tip, then back toward the treeline where his family watched, popping up and down like nervous rodents, then back at the lions.*

One female was watching him, chewing slowly, a bit of hyena left hanging from her mouth, one foot rising and falling with the motion of her jaws.

He heard his heart beating in his ears. Felt his toes curling the grass, knees bending, ready to sprint back toward the trees.

A second female slowed her chew and turned to stare.

The male would notice in a second.

Sweat ran down his dark black arms and legs. It was time to run.

But he couldn't move. No matter how he tried, nothing happened. He couldn't run or raise the spear, or turn to look back at his mate. He could hear her screaming now. Panicked. Terrified. She wasn't the only one.

Why wasn't he running?

He'd seen others freeze like this. Petrified by fear or panic or shame. He'd always known he wasn't like that. Fear drove him. Panic freed him. He would never be the frozen one.

Except.

He tried to move again. Nothing happened.

The male shook a hyena shank loose and caught sight of him. Froze. Flesh and bone stuck out of his mouth in all directions, like a child caught eating something forbidden. His eyes narrowed.

Run! he told himself, though not really. He had no words or language. He had only this final moment. It was a vision of himself running toward the trees. Others were waiting there with spears. There was still hope if he moved.

The male lion stood, his great mane spattered with blood.

Run!

The hyena dropped from his mouth, forgotten.

The lion roared.

And still he didn't run.

"That was me, if you're wondering."

David snapped out of the doomed man's perspective. He was at the treeline now, opposite the bobbing woman, and looked around. The heat was palpable and oppressive. The man was still frozen in the field, spear useless at his side, as the lion stepped forward. The female lions rose. They would charge in seconds. The man was already dead. But he was also standing next to David, head canted to the side, looking relaxed but curious, like someone at the zoo watching a gruesome feeding. His skin was utterly black, but scarred and pocked by time, battle and disease. His brow was too large and chin too broad, hairier than he *should have been, not quite human. Or early human. Something. But he was still wearing plaid.*

"I don't understand," David said. His mouth was dry. God, it was hot. How could the world be this hot? "Are you Dad or Arachniss?"

The male lion charged. The man had seconds to live, but he still didn't move.

"Neither," the man said. "This is what I was before. This is where I come from."

So this was Arachniss. Arachniss was human. He still sounded like David's father.

"How can that be you? When is this? Is it real?"

"This is my last memory," Arachniss said. The lion was a magnificent thing, the size of death, a moving inevitability with blazing golden hair like liquid fire. "That's me when I was taken. I can still remember how it felt, how it felt to be eaten and to eat me, and the confused dark minds of the lions, all together in a smorgasbord of fear and orgasmic excitement." He shifted in the dirt, squinting at his doomed self. "I felt everything, eating and eaten. Torn and tearing. I felt my skull collapse. I tasted my liver."

"Smorgasbord?" How could he know what the lion felt?

The lion leaped and froze. The world stilled and left the great beast hanging midair, claws out, mouth open, mane gold and red as the crown of a primitive god. It was terrible and beautiful and David couldn't look away.

"You're human?" David asked.

"I was something pre-human. This was the start of the first human harvest. There were enough humans to be tasted and tested and prepared. A few were collected for other reasons. A billion Arach watched this moment, felt it, the first humanoid killed by the first lion for the first audience. They put implants in the lions to enhance the experience. Ratings were extraordinary. Look how gorgeous that thing is—a great mass of predatory beauty." He shook his head. "It was an honor, in a way." But his voice shook. The first time he'd heard real emotion from Arachniss other than anger. This had to be hundreds of thousands of years ago, and he was still afraid.

"All Arach come from other species. We are an amalgam, a wholly artificial species. There are no real Arach anymore. This is how most of us are born, taken, killed, removed, ascended, whatever you want to call it."

"You're human?" He just couldn't believe the spider-machine-god-demon-monster was a man. "What was your name?"

"We had no speech, no words or writing, some noises that would seem comical to you. I was simply a man among men and women, maybe nineteen years old, and I was a father. There's a little of my son's DNA in you, in all of you, and my mate's."

"Do you remember her?"

"Yes and no. But you can see her over there, bobbing up and down in the grass to hide and look, hide and look, the worst game of hide-and-seek in the world. That's my son in her arms, the future of your species. I know what she's thinking; never trust a hyena. I'd followed one into the grass. Devious things. Probably thought it was hysterical leading me to the lions." He smiled strangely. "You'd like eating them. They almost find it funny, watching it happen, and don't stop laughing about it even when you rip out their tongue."

"Why did they pick you?"

"The hyenas?"

"The Arach."

"I don't know. I'll never know. It might have been random. It might have been pity. First kills are often collected, like trophies or bad jokes." He exhaled slowly. "It's almost over, but there are two tasks remaining and you have to do them with Franzia."

"What tasks?"

He bypassed the usual you'll see *and stiffened. "Watch."*

The world moved suddenly. The lion finished his flight, taking the man right off his feet, spear flying up in the air, a woman screaming, and somewhere the sound of hyenas laughing.

And for just a second, as man and lion hit the ground, David could feel the teeth in his neck.

Mommy Dearest

ALICIA WAS GONE IN THE MORNING, but not gone the way he thought she'd be. There was a note on the refrigerator saying the Faizans were coming over for dinner and that he should make lobster. He read the note twenty times, maybe more. Not a word of it made sense. He had picked Alicia. She was supposed to be gone, not leaving him passive-aggressive dinner notes about crustaceans, which had to be Arachniss' doing. How was he supposed to get good lobster on such short notice? But then he remembered he already had some in the freezer, which he didn't remember buying. No, wait, yes, he did.

This was ridiculous.

He went into the living room and jabbed at the remote until Dad appeared.

"What the hell is this?" David demanded, showing him the note.

"The first task."

"But I picked her."

"Yes."

"This is supposed to be over." He closed his eyes. "Was that real? With the lion?"

"As real as it could be. It happened, and that was a reasonable simulation of his death."

"Arachniss is human?"

"Not anymore, but yes."

"But..." *Who gives a shit?* It doesn't excuse what he'd done. "Why show me that?"

"He wanted you to know he doesn't hate you or this world. To him, this is still home, just a few hundred thousand years removed. He wants to save it."

"He wants to save the Earth from…himself?" This was too much Dad and too little reality. "Bullshit."

"Maybe. There are rules. Your world can't be saved as it is, but if it was different, it could be."

"What does that even mean?"

"I think he's asking for help."

Why didn't you stop her?

David couldn't help laughing this time. Asking for help was always a trap. Dad should know that.

"What's so funny?" Dad asked.

"Did you know? Did you know what Mom was doing to us?"

"I only know what you know," he said. "I'm sorry."

"Then what's the point of you?"

"If I had to guess—"

David snapped off the TV. He didn't need Dad to guess; he knew the answer. He was there to help David process the horrible world the Arach had created. He was David's friend and confidant, conscience and memory. It was obvious, manipulative and perfect.

He just had no idea *why*, so he went to get the lobster from the garage and start prepping for dinner. That was his task. That's what he'd do. He could worry about Arachniss' humanity later.

When he got back to the kitchen, a mass of frozen lobster in hand, James texted:

LOOKING FORWARD TO DINNER, followed by a gratuitous smiley face.

ME TOO, he texted, because why not?

I GOT THE INFORMATION ON LESLIE.

THAT WAS FAST.

IT WAS EASY. DON'T TELL ANYONE. DELETE THIS TEXT.

Leslie's full name and address appeared next. Her last name was Harris and she lived in Table Mesa.

THANK YOU. HOW IS SHE?

HER SHAS STATUS? UNTOUCHED.

Wow, he thought, and apparently James thought the same thing: FRANZIA SHOWED ME HER BINDER. I WAS SURPRISED TOO. I HAVEN'T SEEN AN UNTOUCHED BLACK PERSON IN CO IN YEARS. DELETE THIS. DON'T WANT THAT TAKEN OUT OF CONTEXT.

David copied down the address and deleted the thread up to that point.

DONE. THANKS AGAIN.

NP. WHAT SHOULD WE BRING?

Suicide vests? Small nuclear weapons?

WINE, RIGHT?

David laughed. SOMETHING TO DRINK AND BREAD WOULD BE GREAT. SOURDOUGH.

WHAT ARE YOU MAKING?

Fucking lobster, he thought, but he only typed the second word. James replied with a drooling emoji. Then five more drooling emojis. God, he was a dork. A buff, handsome, miserable, lonely dork. David really hoped he'd make it through the next few days. And that he could cook lobster without hearing Kathryn screaming the entire time.

*

CHINA, SILVERWARE AND WHITE LINEN napkins, freshly laundered tablecloth and glasses of wine, red and white. Fruit-flavored sparkling water for Franzia. Fresh bread, salad, light vinaigrette and the smell of allegedly homemade Boston clam chowder from the kitchen. The table was set for four, two on each side, one happy couple facing another across a neutral zone of settings and hors d'oeuvres. Alicia's Zombie Fingers tapped absent-mindedly, a metronome measuring the pauses between words. James kept glancing at the kitchen and sniffing at the promise of meat. Franzia sat high on her pillow, listing to the side to unweight the partially masticated buttocks hidden in her elastic-fantastic pregnancy pants. David couldn't be sure, but it looked like she was trying not to laugh.

"Smells amazing," James said for the third time. His stomach grumbled audibly, and David wondered if he had fasted before coming over so there was more room for meat. He was so muscular that food probably just capitulated as he ate it, digesting itself in fear. "What is it?"

"Lobster and clam chowder," Alicia said, as if she'd cooked any of it. He wondered if he should have left the shells un-cracked so everyone would think they were screaming as they boiled. At least Arachniss had spared him having to kill them. The subtle scent of their cooking flesh under the heavier fog of cream and chowder fought a strange war between his ears. He wanted to bite down on buttery flesh. He wanted to throw up. Arachniss had made his point. They all chose what happened to them. The moral framework of this world was clear. Which changed nothing.

"I really like that blouse on you," David said to distract himself. It was more polite than, *you're supposed to be dead.* She was wearing the blouse he'd gotten her for her birthday, blue and topaz, tiny buttons and all. She looked down as if she had no idea what she'd put on, and then smiled tight enough to press steel.

"Thank you," she said.

Pause. Zombie Hand tapped. Zombie Hand Two joined in. James fidgeted and his fingers tapped along. It was like a drum circle without the bare feet and dreadlocks. Franzia sipped and nodded in time, and then time stopped.

"James?" Franzia asked, alarmed. He'd frozen, mouth partially open to ask how much longer until the lobster was ready. Alicia was similarly petrified, but her Zombie Hands didn't seem to notice.

Tap-tap-tap, tappity-tap. Tap!

Someone cleared their throat. David and Franzia turned to the head of the table, Franzia's right and David's left, to see his mother risen from hell by way of the grave or vice versa. The late Elizabeth Chambers held Jason in one arm and Charlotte in the other, both asleep and oblivious. His mother had eight black spider eyes, which seemed gratuitous, but it was probably better than the hole in her head that should have been there. His mother had chosen a particularly male way to shoot herself. Usually women avoided injuring their faces during suicide attempts. Maybe she was making a point no one would ever get, like *fuck the butterfly*.

"What the…" Franzia's eyes were locked on Charlotte.

"Franzia, meet my mother, Elizabeth. Mom, this is Franzia." He was surprised by how calm his voice was. Part of him wanted to rip Jason from her arms and run into the street. Part of him thought, well, what did he expect? You can't try to kill an alien with a super-secret-sonic death machine and not expect consequences, no matter how funny it seemed at the time. There were always consequences. And if having to look at his mother's face was part of it, and that part saved Jason, then bring it on.

"You're looking good, Davie," his mother said, and he cringed. He forgot she called him that. Little Davie this, little Davie that. It was like sand in his eyes. One thing he had to give Arachniss: he knew how to raise the dead.

"We're sorry," Franzia said. "Please, just leave Charlotte alone. Leave my daughter alone. You promised."

Momrachniss ignored her and spoke to David: "Jason looks just like Tommy, doesn't he?"

That got him. The fear that should have hit him seconds earlier rose in a nauseating wave, and he had to grab the edge of the table to keep from reaching for his son. Cool linen folded under his fingers, but all he felt was the hard wood beneath. Maybe all the soft things of the world were lies.

"Please don't hurt him," he begged.

"We'll do anything," Franzia said.

"Relax, Davie," Momrachniss said. "I'm not here to punish you."

"Then why do you have our children?" he asked.

Tap-tap-tap…

"A reminder of what you promised me," she said. "It's time for your next task."

"And you'll leave Charlotte alone?" Franzia asked. She sounded like someone at the edge, tottering over the lip of a vast drop, eyes hard-focused on the other rim as if salvation lay in a final act of

302 SHAWN C. BUTLER

insanity. He'd never seen her so close to completely breaking down. But then his mother had that effect on people.

"Of course," Mother said.

"Then we'll do it," Franzia said.

"Or maybe you can tell us what it is first?" David said, reaching for Franzia's hand across the table. She pulled it away, her eyes never leaving Charlotte.

David wasn't surprised. Whatever was growing between them, their children came first.

"We're coming to the end of our time together," Momrachniss said. "The harvest is ending soon, and—"

"When?" David blurted. Could there really be an end to this?

"Soon," his mother repeated. "And this is your second-to-last task."

David's stomach dropped. This wasn't going to be pleasant.

"What?" Franzia demanded, like it was just one more hurdle. Couldn't she see the trap? "What is it?"

Mother glanced at Alicia and James, and David knew what was coming.

Tap-tap-tappity-tap.

"Feed them to me," Mother said, meaning James and Alicia.

"No," David said, loudly, again surprising himself. "We're not doing that."

"How much of them?" Franzia asked.

"As much as I can stomach," Mother said, smiling, her eight black eyes somehow bulging with hunger. "Now pick up your little forks and knives, and start cutting."

"No," David repeated, but it didn't feel like his voice. Hadn't he known this was coming? It was the most obvious escalation. And why did he really care? He'd already chosen her to die. Now he just had to slice enough off her to make his choice a reality. Still.

"Will they feel it?" Franzia asked. She had a steak knife in her fist, waiting for a signal.

"Franzia," he pleaded. "This is James. Charlotte's father. We can't do this."

Franzia didn't respond. A vertical vein pulsed in her forehead. How had he never seen that before?

"They'll feel everything," Mother said. "Every cut. Every slice. Every bite." She leaned down and kissed Charlotte on her forehead. "So please start with the nonessentials, like James' fingers." Then she turned to David. "Pick up the knife, Davie, and get to work."

He glanced at Franzia, who finally looked at him, nodding to offer assurance or absolution or just begging him not to let her do this alone. Her eyes were hard with determination. The vein throbbed with it. She was going to feed her husband to Arachniss. Her knife rose, ready to cut. She'd feed David to his mother if she had to. She'd kill the world to save her daughter.

"Franzia, please," he begged. He couldn't watch this, and if she did it, he'd have to, and he didn't think he could. He looked at Alicia and tried to imagine cutting off one of her fingers, if she still had any—the feel of cartilage and tendon crunching under pressure and the smell of her blood on his hands—and he almost threw up. He had picked her to die, but he wasn't ready to kill her himself. "Franzia, don't."

"Go," Mother said, like she was starting a race.

Franzia's arm slashed down and suddenly there was a steak knife stuck in the back of James's right hand. Alicia's Zombie Hands finally stopped tapping. James didn't flinch. He couldn't flinch. But his eyes widened. Oh, he was feeling this.

"No!" David screamed. Blood welled up around the knife blade, but Franzia didn't pull it out. Had she never cut meat before? She was like a child stabbing Play-Doh.

"Jesus," Franzia whispered. "Oh, Jesus, what have I done?"

"Your turn, Davie," Mom said. "Jason or Charlotte, your choice. One of them dies tonight."

"Wait, what?" Franzia and David said at the same time. "That wasn't—"

"I'm changing the deal. You want to save your child? Feed me faster. You know what to do."

Franzia looked at David, horrified.

"I'm sorry, David." She started pulling on the knife in James' hand, but it was stuck in the table.

"Franzia, no. Stop."

"Come on, Davie," Mom brushed her lips against Jason's forehead. "Mommy's hungry."

"No!" David felt something give way inside him, whatever dam held back all the anger and hate he'd stored up since Tommy died. "You can't do this!" He lunged for Jason, knowing how stupid it was, knowing he'd fail, and Jason would die and none of it would change anything, but that just made him angrier. He just couldn't feed his wife to this thing. It wasn't in him. And all he had left was rage.

"I'll fucking kill—"

David's hands came together around air instead of Jason. Jason, Charlotte and his mother were gone. The seat was empty. David nearly fell over and then caught himself on the table. He looked around the room, but it was just the four of them. Had any of that been real?

"David?" Franzia asked, her hand still on the knife. "David, what have you done?"

"What the hell!" James was now very much awake. He jerked his hand up and Franzia flinched back, ripping the knife out. Blood sprayed on Alicia's buttony blouse and face, but she barely moved.

James looked at the hole in his hand and then at his wife. "Franzi, what…"

"Baby, I'm so sorry." Franzia grabbed a napkin and started wrapping James's hand. James just stared at his wife and his bloody hand, too baffled to be angry. Alicia watched the whole thing in dead-faced silence, never moving from her chair, but in the back if his mind, David could hear his mother laughing.

You were always weak, she whispered. *And now you'll finally pay for it.*

He got up and ran to the nursery.

Where Jason lay asleep with Charlotte next to him on the air mattress, both silent and whole and alive.

"Are they okay?" Franzia asked, appearing next to him and checking for herself. They were fine.

"It's because you didn't pick," Franzia whispered, furious. "You said you picked."

"I did," he snapped. "I picked Alicia. He accepted. This isn't my fault."

"I stabbed my husband, David. I stuck a knife through his hand."

"Yeah, Franzia, you did. But that's not because of me or Alicia. I picked. I have no idea why she's still here." He couldn't stand the accusations in her eyes. "You know what it's like walking around with a woman you condemned to death?"

"You really picked?" She looked utterly lost.

"Why would I lie to you?"

"Well, aren't you two thick as thieves?" Alicia said from the doorway. David and Franzia glanced at her, wondering what she'd heard. "You know, I've always wanted to say that." And then she disappeared down the hall, hopefully to clean James' blood off her face.

*

AFTER JAMES AND FRANZIA RUSHED to the hospital, Franzia clutching the tin of rum balls under her arm, James confused as a beaten puppy not knowing what he'd done wrong, and Charlotte still rubbing sleep out of her eyes, David cleaned up with Alicia's unusual but silent assistance. She hadn't said a word since they left. Her Zombie Hands were shaking, which was an impressive feature. Had Arachniss allowed her to remember what happened? It made little sense, because he now saw clearly in his mind how Franzia had slipped while telling a joke and accidentally stabbed James in the hand. It was pretty funny until the blood came out.

"David?" Alicia put the oven tray on the counter and glanced down at the blood on her blouse. There was still red in her hair. She chewed on a piece of salvaged meat and looked around the kitchen as if remembering where she was. "This isn't right, is it?"

That was an understatement. "What do you mean?"

"What were you two talking about? In the nursery?"

"Franzia felt bad about stabbing James. That's all."

Alicia nodded. "No, it wasn't. I know the sound of secrets." She held up her hand. "I don't care, David. I just…" She looked at her hands, palms up, fingers flexing, like she was seeing them for the first time. "Something's wrong, isn't there?"

Was she kidding?

"With the world, I mean." She closed her hands into fists. David stepped back, but she just dropped her hands and sighed. "All the time we've known each other. Everything we've been through. And you've never asked me why I get so angry."

"I don't care, Alicia. I used to, but now…"

"You don't want to know why I…" She looked around the kitchen as if someone was listening.

"Just say it," he demanded. "Say it out loud. No one's recording us."

She smiled. Challenge accepted. "You don't want to know why I hit you?"

"Jesus." He couldn't believe it. She'd finally said it, acknowledged it. Not with tears and sobs and begs of forgiveness. Just *said* it. "I used to wonder, but I didn't want to hear your excuses. How you rationalized it."

"So you weren't afraid?" She said this with a smirk and then took a final bite of lobster, jaws working like she was chewing on him, and he wondered what would have happened if Arachniss had asked her to eat him, not to save anyone, but just because. He didn't have to wonder for long. She'd be a good Arach, relishing the pain of lesser beings.

"I was terrified at first, but no, I don't want to know. I'll tell you why. I wrote a story about you, an entire book about an angry little girl and what made her so mad, but no matter how hard I tried, I couldn't come up with a backstory to explain her behavior. She was a terrible person. She did terrible things. It's not my job to explain it or rationalize it away."

Alicia chewed and swallowed. "I think that's your best lobster. What did you do with the book?"

"I deleted it. Don't worry. No one will ever see the pitiful story of Angry Alicia."

"Creative name." She licked her lips.

He resisted the urge to flip her off, but she was right; it wasn't his most creative name. The full name was *Angry Alicia the Human Anchor* because she dragged everyone down with her, but he'd never wanted her to be a caricature. He wrote it because he wanted to understand her. He'd looked up abuse so many times he couldn't remember them all. Why do abusers abuse? How to avoid setting them off. None of it had helped with Alicia. Abusers abused because of psychosis, personality disorders, abuse, addiction and so on, but David had never pinned down what it was with his wife other than that she seemed to enjoy it while it was happening and was low on the empathy scale. And he let her, of course; he knew the role he was playing even if he couldn't change it and had no idea why. When he closed his eyes and thought about fighting back, he just saw Tommy's dead eyes and knew he couldn't. Not as long as Tommy looked at him like that, which was forever, so that's just how it was. When he finished the book, he realized he had no idea who his wife was. He was married to a stranger. It was one of the saddest moments of his life.

Alicia looked at her hands again. "I can feel it coming for me, David."

David froze. Did she mean Arachniss? What had she seen?

"SHAS," she said. "It feels like it's just waiting outside the door to take more of me. I walk by people at work and there's less of them every day. I know you've noticed how fast it's moving? None of us are whole anymore, except you and Franzia. It's like it's eating me." She furled her meticulously plucked eyebrows. "What kind of virus does that?"

"One with good taste?" he asked.

She jerked forward. He flinched back. She walked out.

And that was the last time he talked to his wife.

*

DAVID SAT ON THE COFFEE table and turned on the TV, because he was done sitting on the couch. It was time to find out what his lunge for Jason had cost him. Dad appeared instantly in a white t-shirt. Maybe all his plaid was in the laundry.

"Well, that went well," Dad said.

"You think this is funny?"

"I think this is tragic, but it doesn't matter what I think. Oh, he's coming." His eyes filled with black.

"How do I fix this?" David asked.

"There's nothing to fix," Dadrachniss said. "It was a test with no pass-fail. I learned what I needed to."

David tried not to let himself react. He put his anger away and nodded. "Which was?"

"Your limits. Where you drew the line."

"Why? Now you know I can have you kill my wife but not do it myself. So what?"

"Everyone has a limit, David. People think they'll do *anything* for their families or countries or gods, but in the end there's always a breaking point. A bridge too far. A choice you couldn't make."

"Why do you care?"

"You haven't figured it out yet, have you?"

"What?"

"I let you see what people think and feel and do when you walked downtown. I let you pick who I eat and what parts of them. I—"

"You didn't let me do anything. You forced me. You made us do it. All of it."

Arachniss shook his head. "No, I threatened you. I manipulated you. But I didn't make you do anything. No, don't argue. This isn't a game. I know you felt compelled, but all of this is a choice. Every part of every person ever eaten by one of us was chosen by you or another person."

"What?"

"We can't do anything to you that you don't choose."

"That's ridiculous. You choose who you eat. You'd do it anyway for entertainment or therapy or—"

"No. It's literally forbidden. There's not one person, adult or child, that we've touched without the explicit choice of another human. That's why SHAS started so slowly and is speeding up now. It takes time to build momentum. Everyone is desperate to pick someone else so they can survive. Let someone else die in their child's or lover's place. We're not even allowed to punish you for not choosing. All we can do is threaten."

"You don't just threaten. You cut Jason's fingers off. You took his toe."

Dadrachniss shook his head. "No, someone picked Jason's fingers. I just waited for the right time to use that choice. It was decided no matter what you did. All you could do was stop it."

"But..." He couldn't accept that they had done this to themselves. "Who would choose Jason?"

"Do you really want to know?"

"Of course," he said before he could stop himself.

"Padme," Dadrachniss said.

"No."

"Yes."

"Jesus." No wonder she'd looked so furious. She must have thought picking the girls was about vengeance. She was angry at herself. "But why Jason?"

"Because you were untouched. You were the only whole family she knew that were close to wholly untouched. The only one any of them knew. Even Charlotte was missing entire fingers. Envy is a terrible thing."

"Jesus," he said again. "This is really all chosen by *us*?"

"Yes." He smiled. "You want to know who picked Alicia's arms and feet?"

"No," he said. Probably Franzia, no matter what she said, but he didn't need to know. Maybe it was love that made them do it, maybe it was hate, but the result was still a thing eating his wife. "Please don't tell me."

"Okay."

"Who killed Kathryn?"

"You did, by not choosing."

"No, who picked her?"

"A nurse at the hospice. The one who gave you Kathryn's box. She thought it was a kindness. She's working her way through the whole building, one floor at a time, room by room, sharing her mercy."

"Why are you telling me this?"

"Your real task is to think about it, David. Think about what humanity really is, and what you would do to change it without lying to yourself. You're killers, rapists, thieves and animals. You know it. You have that same rage in yourself, packed down so far you can almost deny it, but it's always there. Would you still save your kind from us if you could?"

"Yes." There was no hesitation. "Of course."

"What do you think of wolves?"

"What? Uh, beautiful animals. Endangered. What do you mean?"

"Would you let a wolf into your house? Would you let it sleep with Jason?"

"Of course not."

"What do you think of dogs?"

"I love dogs," he said. "Everyone loves dogs."

"You trust them. You have them in your homes. You'd let them sleep by your son?"

"The right dog, yes." He was starting to see where this was going, but the point evaded him. "So what?"

"What's the difference between wolves and dogs?"

"Temperament?"

"No, that's a symptom. One's wild and one's not. Dogs are domesticated. Dogs are safe and fun and loving and you let them sleep in your houses with your children because they are *bred* to be safe and fun and loving."

"Okay…"

"You said you wanted to help your kind, your people, but which people? You have a romantic side to you, like there's good in everyone no matter how bad they are, but that's not the way it works.

We've encountered species so intrinsically aggressive and violent we had no choice but to exterminate them. We've encountered others so kind and compassionate they would have let us do the same thing to them just to show us the extent of their forgiveness. Humanity is somewhere in the middle. All your books and movies perpetuate the same fallacy, that life evolves and becomes more intelligent and compassionate, but that's not the case. It's not even close to the case. In nature, life evolves to brutally slaughter other life, or it dies. Good societies are like dogs. They are bred. And we are the breeders."

"Fucking what?"

"Why do we let you choose, David? Think about it. Why are we *required* to let you choose?"

"I have no idea."

"We didn't always do it this way. For millions of years, planets like this were harvested and we ate what we wanted. We picked the strongest, the fastest, the most beautiful and the smartest. That's what was appealing and what sold. No one wants to watch ugly things die. It was the opposite of evolution, survival of the weakest and least attractive, physically and mentally. And morally. It was a disaster every time, hard to regulate, costly to correct, and far more died than were sustainable."

"So having us pick is more cost effective?"

"That's why we *could* change it. The reason we wanted to is politics; we want you to evolve. We, or at least some of us, want dogs. Dogs get invited in. Wolves get shot and eaten."

"You're breeding us to be invited in to *your* society?"

"We're letting you breed yourselves to not be meat or exterminated when the market loses interest, but also, yes. Don't look so horrified. When we let you pick, who do you go after? The violent and the extreme. The far right and left. Rapists and murderers. *Pedophiles.*"

"And minorities, homosexuals or anyone you hate for petty, insignificant acts. I was thinking about picking a woman because of how she ordered her coffee. Franzia picked someone over a bad joke."

"True, but it always starts with who you hate most. Even white supremacists start with Black rapists and murderers. Everyone picks child molesters. Then the left goes after the right and vice versa. The smart and quiet and innocent survive. People like you. Yes, there's racial purging and certain groups—like LGBTQ—suffer disproportionately, but the net effect is moderation."

"Dogs, you mean."

"Not even close, but getting there. Thousands of years ago, men were brutish, violent things. Being forced to settle on farms and create stable societies moderated them, as did a few harvests. You've been domesticated. Before that, men like you wouldn't have survived adolescence."

"You're alien spider Nazis. That's what you're telling me."

"We're not breeding a master race, David. We're letting you breed yourselves. The same number of you die either way, but this way, there's hope."

"Hope for what?"

"Something other than meat or extermination. A chance to ascend."

"If we're docile enough?"

"If you're sympathetic enough for trillions of Arach and others to give up their entertainment."

"This is… This is…." But he was out of words.

"That's okay, David. We can leave it there for now. The cull is this weekend. You've almost made it."

"What's a cull? A cull of what?"

"Of you. Cull is the last day of each harvest. One last chance to taste what humanity has to offer."

"It's over? The harvest is over?"

"In six days, yes."

My god. They were going to make it. "Saturday or Sunday?"

"Late Saturday morning in this time zone."

"And then it's over?" Could it be that simple? Just last a few days, and then—

"It's over for some," he said.

"For us?" He meant him and Jason and Franzia and Char, but he couldn't say it out loud.

"Think about what I told you."

"What? Oh, sure. Wolves and dogs. Got it." What a load of crap. "You really can't touch us unless we choose?"

"We really can't, though things will get a little hectic during the cull. It's quite exciting. The galaxy will be watching."

"But you can protect us. During the cull, you can—"

"Mostly. You might need to help a little."

"Okay. I'll think about things. The nature of us. Breeding for sympathy." Whatever. He couldn't wait to tell Franzia how close they were to the end. "What's the second task?"

"That's enough for now, David. Get some rest. You look tired."

Some things never change. "You mean, I'll see."

"Oh, you'll do more than that."

The Human Race

LESLIE ANSWERED THE DOOR and took a moment to look him over. There was no sign of recognition, and while he knew he'd seen her a hundred times and some recently, it was like looking at a stranger. If she'd closed the door in his face, he wouldn't have been surprised.

Instead, she smiled ever-so-slightly and said, "David?"

"Hi, Leslie." He raised a hand in greeting, avoiding the dreaded handshake. "Thanks for seeing me."

She nodded, looking dubious. "You said you had news about Kathryn Thorn."

"Yes, you remember her? I think you met when I was in college."

She nodded vaguely. "We met right before she, well, you know." Her hand gripped the doorframe like the house was trying to pull her back in. "It took me a while to place the name, but she seemed very sweet. And I remember watching her run at a track meet once." She smiled at the memory. "She was fast."

"Very," David said.

"So, what's your important news?"

"Kathryn passed away last week."

"Oh," she said, and then remained stonily quiet as her eyes wet at the side. "I'm sorry to hear that. I'm not sure why I'm so surprised, or…"

"Why it affects you so much?"

She nodded. "Yes. It's strange. Like losing someone close to me." She shook her head. "Apologies, David. I know she was your friend. I hope you didn't come by just to tell me that?"

"No. There's a lot more to talk about."

She hesitated, then: "Come in. You like your tea with milk, right?" She froze again.

"You're not crazy," he said. "Tea would be great."

They sat at a small round wooden table in her kitchen, surrounded by African art and décor full of color and life. David couldn't help looking at every wall, bookshelf, painting or picture, drawn to the gorgeous humanity in all of it. He'd always wished he had more history to celebrate or share, but his only claim to culture was an archaic affection for plaid and the occasional 'eh.' Leslie caught him looking and he smiled, embarrassed. She had no idea he'd been there before and, until that moment, he'd forgotten too.

"Your home is beautiful," he said.

She shrugged as she set a serving platter of hot water and tea on the table. She sat. They made their tea. Silence filled the house but for the occasional sound of chimes from the backyard. He didn't know what to say or how to say it. He wanted to tell her about Kathryn and everything he suddenly remembered: about how they'd dated and fallen in love, moved in together, into this very house, and planned to adopt a child. And how he'd bought them the chimes that she'd reluctantly hung in her backyard and he used to send Kathryn home with anise-scented shortbread because that was Leslie's favorite—but he'd fallen asleep on the couch after talking to Arachniss and texting Franzia (IT'S ALMOST OVER!)—and so much more. But he didn't know what he could say.

"Tell me about Kathryn," she said after her first careful sip. And that was all it took.

They talked for hours about someone she barely remembered, but he remembered in ten different ways, like a fabric woven from alternate lives. In all of them, Leslie was a constant thread. In all of them, there was love. But in the end, he told her the story of the

Kathryn who barely knew Leslie, his friend in foster care, and the songs they used to sing when they thought no one was listening.

He didn't tell her about the money, but put the envelope on the table between them, saying it was from Kathryn and to call him or the attorney if she had any questions. He'd already written her last name on the check.

"I don't care for attorneys," she said, and he knew she never had.

"It's good news," he said, struggling with the oddity of it. Not talking to Leslie, but the strangeness of kindness and good fortune. How everything had turned to shit and aliens were eating the world and yet here he was, leaving a check worth millions of dollars to a lonely woman and reconnecting with an old friend he'd almost lost forever. It felt like the bookstore and Patricia and Arachniss manipulating his life—which he hated, but still appreciated.

When it was time, he stood and she walked him to the door.

"Stay in touch," she said.

"I will," he promised, and he would if he survived the next few days.

"Strange," she said as they hugged without awkwardness or hesitation. "I feel like we've done this before."

Because we have.

*

DAVID WALKED INTO THE HOUSE and stopped. There was that feeling again: Alicia was home but shouldn't be. She was supposed to be out with Jason, keeping her distance as they figured out how to live with each other. But she was home. Her car was in the garage. He checked the kitchen and living room, then the nursery. And there, in the nursing chair where she'd fed a screaming Alex and passed out from exhaustion, where he'd read both boys a hundred books they didn't understand just so they'd know his voice, he found his wife and Jason and horror.

Alicia wore a dress he hadn't seen in years, blue-black and sleek, cut low, something she'd worn dancing once and he'd torn off her when they got home. There were no lines, meaning no bra or underwear. Her legs were crossed and tipped by black Givenchy heels, the ones she'd nearly brained him with, or not nearly, but not for lack of trying. She had a pearl bracelet on one wrist and was actually wearing her wedding ring. Which was unusual, now that he thought about it. When had she stopped wearing it? He couldn't remember. Maybe it cut him too much when she hit him, or maybe it hurt her finger or didn't fit on Zombie Hand. Even with her prosthetic arms and feet, she looked utterly human and beautiful sitting in the old chair. Gorgeous. He just wished she weren't wearing Arachniss like a crown.

The not-spider's legs splayed out from her head but for one that was embedded in Alicia's left eye socket. Where her eye used to be, there was just a hole and Arachniss was probing it like a dog licking an empty jar of peanut butter for that last bit of sticky goodness. Alicia held Jason in her arms, unperturbed, trying to suckle Jason on a breast that hadn't held milk in months. Arachniss glowed as he moved, lighting up more like a halo than a crown, creating a grotesque *Mother-and-Child* tableau where god's angelic love was eating Mary's innocent face while baby Jesus sucked and sucked at a breast long since dry.

"What the hell are you doing?" David asked.

"You picked, and now it's time." His father's voice, from nowhere.

"I picked her life over Jason's. I didn't say I was going to watch you eat her. That wasn't part of the deal any more than cutting her up at the dinner table. What the hell are you doing?"

"You don't want to watch?" The end of its leg pulled out of Alicia's eye socket and moved down to play with wisps of Jason's hair. The sharp black tip of his hairy leg slid over Jason's forehead and pointed at his tiny closed eye. David wanted to jump forward, rip him off, and smash him under his foot. Arachniss wasn't that big. But he remained in place, petrified by his powerlessness.

"I should have told you," Arachniss said. "Children are sweeter, fattier, like little cuts of Kobe beef. If you want to save Jason, you'll have to give up everything else. *Everything.*"

"I can't watch you eat my wife."

"Oh, don't worry, I'm not going to eat all of her. But you will watch. We have an audience, and they're paying for a show."

"This is what you are? All your crap about breeding dogs, but you're the wolves."

"You're not wrong, David. I'm no prouder of being Arach than you are of being human. We do the best we can with what we have." Arachniss pressed lightly on Jason's closed eye, drawing the tiniest bead of blood. David looked at his wife, the woman he had once loved the way kites love air, but about whom he now felt nothing but the sense that he'd somehow brought her to this end.

"I'm sorry," David said. His favorite words. "I'll watch."

"You have nothing to be sorry for, David. Someday you'll realize that." This was in Dad's calm, loving voice. The one he used after David or Tommy cried. The one that felt like blankets and love. "If you have any final words for your wife, now's the time."

"Not yet…" He wasn't sure why he cared anymore, what atavistic programming demanded he care for his mate. No matter what she'd done, no matter how horrible, she didn't deserve this. Was that a male thing? Would a woman care as much for an abusive husband? He didn't think so. It was like having different computer programs compete to run his brain. Would he accept the primitive primate program, the one that made him protective and patriarchal, throwing his body in front of his broken wife, or the newer version 2.0, ambivalence created by fury and hate? There was nothing he could do. She had it coming. Why keep up the act? "Not yet," he said again, as expected, with all the energy of a dead battery. Arachniss ignored him.

"I'm sorry," David said again, probably the last thing she'd hear if she heard anything at all. Not sorry this was happening to her, but more that her life had come to this. That even she didn't know what had broken her. That humans were made of glass that, once cracked, could never be fixed, not perfectly; there was always the flaw and the pain that came with it. Sorry she didn't understand herself or, if she did, couldn't fix what she was. Sorry he'd fed her hunger for violence in some way, encouraging it, allowing it to grow. And sorry that pain was the way of the world, the universe, and being eaten by an alien spider was just a natural extension of her own perversion.

"Goodbye, Alicia," he whispered. And so it began, the end of Alicia Anne Thomas-Chambers, girl, woman, lawyer, wife, mother, lover, abuser and now food. Arachniss mounted her head and his abdomen, or whatever passed for that on his synthetic body, slid down over her face like he was giving birth in reverse, until his stretched black lower body covered her entire head. Then all eight of his arms bent inward and slid down into the flesh of her shoulders, chest and back. Alicia didn't flinch or scream. He knew Arachniss was preventing her from feeling it, and it was costing him somehow in the currency of sadistic experience they traded in, and he was grateful.

As he watched, Arachniss glowed bright as the sun and slid down farther, farther, until Arachniss was now Alicia's head and neck and his wife was undeniably gone. Now there was just this trembling body of flesh and prosthetics topped by an alien spider-sun like a Frankenstein Barbie monster from hell.

Alicia was dead. Jason would never know his mother. Why didn't he feel more?

"Let's go for a walk," Arachniss said in her voice, Alicia's voice, coming from nowhere like a bad dubbing in a worse movie. Alicia held Jason and stood, or Arachniss stood her up—however it worked—and the Arachnalicia (she-it-them) thing swayed, jerky and awkward, as David tried not to throw up.

Which is when he cracked. He could feel it happening; something opened up in his mind, a chasm or black hole, and he just had time to think *No Mommy no* before he fell into darkness.

*

TOMMY DIED IN DAD'S ARMS, sick, pale, barely breathing and then not at all. At first, it was just like any other morning, Tommy crawling to the table. Eating. Throwing up. Going back to bed. His Dad kept saying Tommy would get over it just like David had; it was just a phase. The Chambers boys were tough. No mystery illness could take them down. David had gotten over it and so would

Tommy. But David could see the lie in his eyes. He was scared. He didn't know what was happening.

So David told him. Finally, told him Mom was doing it. Mom had always been doing it. Dad stared at him with wide, scared eyes and he wondered if he always knew or if he realized at that point that he always should have known how his little family and his dad jokes and unending love was all a pointless sham. David wanted to hug him and tell him it wasn't his fault, but he wasn't sure what to do or say, so he just waited for what came next. Which is that Dad got up from the couch and walked into the bedroom to get Tommy.

When he came back, he sat down with Tommy on his lap. He looked at David, back at Tommy, and then nothing happened.

"Dad?" Why wasn't he doing anything? Tommy was still alive, breathing, if barely. But it was like he'd heard David and knew he'd been betrayed. That his mother was doing this to him and his brother knew and his father did nothing and it was just too much disappointment for his tiny heart to bear. He looked up, eyes watering, and whispered something none of them could hear.

"What's that Tommy?" Dad asked, his voice cracking.

And then Tommy's eyes widened and he exhaled all the life that was left in him.

"Tommy?" Dad asked, shaking his son. "Tommy?"

David sat back and stared. He hadn't saved Tommy. He'd killed him. He'd let mom torture him and then he'd broken him.

"Tommy, baby…" Dad begged.

David closed his eyes and prayed the first and last real prayer of his life.

Bring him back, god. I'll do anything. Take me. Kill me. Just bring Tommy back. I'm sorry I didn't tell Dad sooner. I'm sorry I picked Tommy. I'm sorry. I'm sorry. I'm sorry. Please…

He opened his eyes and Tommy was still dead and Dad just stared at him with blank wide eyes like whatever was in him had followed Tommy into the air and far away.

"Dad?" David asked. "*Dad?*"

And that's when Mom walked in.

David expected screaming and violence. He thought Dad would put Tommy down and yell at her or attack her, and she'd fight back, but Dad would win and at least there'd still be Dad and David and no more Mom or poison or fear. But instead she just looked at Tommy, at her husband and David, and nodded. Once. The simplest gesture in the world. Like she realized she'd overcooked an egg and that just happens sometimes. *Oh well.*

"Liz," Dad said. "Our son is dead. Tommy's *dead."*

I'm not dead, David thought, feeling selfish even as he thought it. *I'm right here, Daddy.*

Mom didn't bother with a second nod. Of course Tommy was dead. Why state the obvious?

"You did this," Dad said. Maybe he meant it as a question, but it came out as a statement.

This time, Dad nodded once, and David thought it was just another simple gesture: *Yes, you did it. Now I know and I can take David away from you and this place.* Dad put Tommy down just as he thought he would, gently, on the couch, where one skinny white arm hung off the side like he was trailing his fingers off the side of a canoe in the cold water and looking for the little fish he loved to talk to and hated to catch.

Now Dad was going to pick David up and take him away. They'd never see Mom again. They'd have a new life somewhere. Maybe a cabin in the woods back in Canada where Dad was from. Maybe by a lake. Anywhere but here.

But Dad didn't pick David up. He didn't even look at him. He just stood and walked past Mom into the bedroom. Mom watched him pass, one hand lightly out to brush against the sleeve of his shirt as if there was some bit of love or forgiveness between them, but Dad didn't notice. He disappeared into the hall, one heavy step after another.

Mom turned to David and smiled the strangest smile.

"You could have saved him," she said. "You could have stopped this."

And he knew she was right. It should be him on the couch. It should be Tommy Dad took to the lake cabin in the woods in Canada to fish without fishing and walk under giant trees and camp by crackling fires under skies filled with starry animals and old stories told in his father's warm woody voice. David didn't deserve that. This was all his fault.

Heavy steps came back down the hall. Mom didn't turn to look, but David did.

Dad stepped into the living room carrying an old black pistol at his side, not aimed at anything, just hanging in his hand. The gun he'd shown David once just to tell him never to touch it and never let Tommy touch it because guns were dangerous and he only kept one because he wanted to protect his family, but of course he hadn't protected the family so now the gun seemed useless in his hand, too heavy to lift, the weight of it holding him frozen in place.

Mom turned and glanced at the gun. And laughed.

Not loudly. Not some crazy witch cackle. Just a quiet, knowing sound that told David what he already knew. Dad could no more shoot her with that gun than he could kill an animal in the forest. He couldn't even kill fish anymore; he just caught them, looked sad, and threw them back. He hadn't protected his family, and he wouldn't now. The gun was just more embarrassing evidence of his failure.

"Give it to me, Ben," Mom said, reaching for the gun.

"No," David whispered. *No, don't give her the gun.* They were supposed to run away, get out, go to the woods. She would never let them leave if she had the gun. "No," he said again, but they didn't hear him.

She slowly lifted the gun in his hand, peeled back his fingers, and took the pistol from him.

"Lizzy," he said, and David knew that sound. That was the sound of broken things. That was the sound of surrender and failure and terror and shame. That was the sound of the world ending.

Dad walked over and sat slumped on the couch next to Tommy's body. Tommy rose up on the cushion as dad weighed it down, like he was breathing again. Mom sat on the coffee table facing her husband.

"Daddy," David said. Dad looked at him, but Dad wasn't there anymore.

"You knew this was coming," Mom said. "This was always coming."

And then Mom shot him. The back of his head exploded against the wall. David didn't even hear the shot.

Mom turned to him. "See what you made me do?"

And then she shot herself.

David heard that shot. It echoed back and forth in his head as she slumped forward and face-planted in her husband's lap. It echoed as he stared at his father's unmoving eyes. It echoed louder somehow as Tommy's head fell to the side and stared at him, right at him, with so much disappointment David couldn't stand it anymore. He had to get out of the room.

But he couldn't move.

He looked down at his legs and arms and realized two things at the same time. He'd wet himself, drenching the chair that Mom treasured, and he'd be punished for it if there was anyone left to punish him, and he was frozen. His legs wouldn't move. His arms wouldn't move. And his head seemed to float back to a position where all he could see was the hole in his father's head and the strange red shapes on the wall behind him. It was like looking at clouds again, a red haze that dripped and changed so he saw horses and bears and fish and a great green forest of dark trees behind it all waiting, cool and shadowed and full of adventure. Maybe Dad was waiting for him in there, hiding behind a giant sequoia, playing hide-and-seek, ready to show him a massive mushroom or the way a log rotted soft and wet in the ferns.

I'm coming, Daddy!

He ran in the green forest under the red sky and searched and searched for his father. He searched for hours and then night came and he slept and the sun rose and he searched again, and then for another day, until three days had passed and strange, angry birds were screaming from the trees. *Caw-caw-caw.*

It took him hours to realize it was the phone. He blinked and he was back in the living room.

The phone kept ringing, but he still couldn't move.

Tommy was looking at him with bloodshot eyes over bloated cheeks.

Why didn't you stop her? Tommy asked. Had been asking. Kept asking.

He was so thirsty and hungry, and he couldn't look at his father anymore. And there was a smell.

The phone stopped ringing. There was no other sound. No more traffic or airplanes flying over.

That's when he realized he was going to die there.

Why didn't you stop her? Why didn't you stop her?

And that was what he wanted.

So he looked back at the frozen red clouds over the green forest and ran away. Dad was in there somewhere, waiting. Dad and Tommy and spiders and butterflies and beavers and deer and hawks and slimy things in still water by a stream by a lake by a cabin with a fire with a big soft rug and a sleeping bag where he could lie down and listen to his father tell stories as he ran his fingers through his hair, with Tommy curled up next to him and the fire whispering and snapping until everything was warm and smoky and black forever. It was time to sleep and sleep and never wake up.

In the darkness, his father spoke.

"It's time to go, David."

But he didn't want to wake up. The air was cold and smelled like damp embers, but his sleeping bag was warm and Tommy was curled up at his stomach and there was no smell of breakfast yet so no reason to open his eyes.

"David, we don't have time for this."

Then the sun exploded and ripped all darkness from the world. There was just white and heat and—

*

"OH," DAVID SAID. He was back in the nursery where Arachnalicia stood, arms akimbo (Was he imitating her?) and swaying unsteadily. "Did you do that?"

In all his years of counseling with Kiaraa and before, he'd never remembered anything after his mother pulled the trigger the first time. He'd never seen his father die. There was just a sudden dead silence and red on the wall, and then the forest and the endless search. The next thing he remembered, his neighbor Mrs. Baker was lifting him off the chair and carrying him out into the yard where there were police and people and noise and the sky was so blue he wanted to dissolve into it.

"No," Arachnalicia said. "That was all you."

"Great," he mumbled, afraid to close his eyes and slip back into the room of dead things. There would be time to process all this later. Or maybe better if there wasn't. Every time he blinked, he saw Tommy's dead eyes looking at him. Maybe he didn't want to survive the cull after all.

He frowned. "Where's Jason?" Then he looked in the crib, and Jason was there, sound asleep. He wondered if he would still sleep as soundly after the Arach left, or if he'd just been knocked out most of his infancy. Then he turned back to Arachnalicia and saw her blouse was buttoned up. Zombie Hands were more dexterous than he realized.

"Oh," he said. "The prosthetics are from you?"

"Of course," she/it said.

"Thank you?"

"Nothing to thank us for. The better the tech, the more we can take without damaging the economy."

"Great." He grimaced as his dead wife's hips slid to the side and back like she was trying to figure out where her spine was. "What now?"

Arachnalicia took a stuttering step, toppled against the wall and nearly fell, pushed herself off and bent her knees more for stability. David fought the urge to knock her down, to punch him off of

Alicia's body. It was like a circus act once you knew the animals all lived in cages and terror and pain.

"I'm getting the hang of her," Arachnalicia said. "Just give me a second…"

What was that line? *I never did mind about the little things.* Something his mother stole from a nineties movie.

"Almost got it." Arachnalicia spun and almost fell again, saved by slamming a foot against the baseboard, leaving a scuff that Alicia never would have tolerated. She/it righted itself and held up her Zombie Hands as if waiting for applause or a compliment. "There we go."

A second later, David glanced at Jason—thinking for the tenth time that this might be the last time he saw his son—and followed Arachnalicia out into the sunlit morning, her arms (David decided she/it was a her as long as Arachniss was using Alicia's body) swinging more than they should, like a wacky-wavy balloon just learning to walk on its own. *I'm tired of selling cars! I'm off to see the world!* It was like she was mocking the silliness of human locomotion, or the stupidity of designer heels. Which probably weren't the things to focus on.

As they walked, cars passed and a neighbor he vaguely recognized waved and nobody noticed anything out of the ordinary. Just another glorious day in Boulder.

"Come on, David," she called back. "Take my hand."

"Not happening." They crossed one street, then another. "Where are we going?"

But he knew. Somehow, he knew they were going to see Franzia and James. He should have run. But of course he wouldn't because of Jason but also, he had to admit, because he wanted to see what happened next. When the circus tiger attacks the ringmaster, when everyone's screaming and running and children are crying, that's when it got good. The hyenas knew that.

"You want to watch?" Arachnalicia asked, reading his mind or his implant or however it worked.

Before he could say no, he was in Franzia's head watching Arachnur devour James' head exactly the same way Arachniss had Alicia, but with all the pain. James was dressed up in slacks and a button-down shirt, dapper and ready for date-night but for the alien on his head.

No, no, no. I don't want to see this.

"Leave him alone!" Franzia screamed, and David felt her fear and rage flush through him. This was how the Arach experienced it, he realized, all the pain and visuals you could ever want.

The top of James' skull vanished into Arachnur's hot-white abdomen and the air filled with the smell of burning hair, flesh and bone.

Please, no, let me out of here!

Franzia raised a knife and lunged toward Arachnur. A flash of light enveloped her arm and hand and the knife was gone and she was on the ground, screaming. The pain was astonishing. David felt himself reach for his own arm as he saw her grab hers, hand coming away with blackened skin. Now she was screaming too.

Franzia writhed on the floor, kicking at James' feet to dislodge Arachnur but just hurting James even more. James stumbled backward, almost falling, but the thing somehow kept him steady as it slid over his head.

Let me out of here!

Charlotte was screaming upstairs for mommy and daddy with no idea why mommy was screaming in the first place. And then James straightened, completely still, and Arachnur checked her placement with James' arms like she was adjusting one of his cowboy hats.

David felt incalculable rage but somehow greater grief at the same time; he had just lost another friend, a new friend, a kind and good man who would never find the joy in life that he deserved, just so the Arach could play some perverse game with their human pets.

Arachnajames looked down at Franzia on the floor, his head canted to the side exactly like a curious man, and David heard James' voice in Franzia's head.

"You shouldn't be here."

And he was back on the street walking next to Arachnalicia. A second later, Franzia called.

"What the hell were you doing in my head? Were you watching that?" Then something between a growl and a moan. The pain from her arm must be fantastic. "Did you enjoy it?"

"Franzia, no. Of course not. Arachniss just put me there." He glanced at Arachnalicia as she lunged down the sidewalk, taking long steps more like lunges. She wasn't paying attention to him. Why would it?

"James is dead," Franzia sobbed. "He just…"

"I'm sorry, Fran. Alicia too. Is he still there?"

"What?"

"The thing, Arachnur and James' body."

"No." The sound of a drawer opening. Metal rolling around on wood. "It walked out the front door. Charlotte's unconscious on her bed. I think she passed out? I don't know. My arm is a mess. Do you know how much this hurts?"

"I do, actually."

A drawer slammed shut.

"What are you doing?" David asked.

"They would have spared one of them," she said. "Maybe if you killed Alicia, they would have spared James. It just had to be one of them. You should have chosen."

Another glance at Arachniss. No response. They were on Aurora now, closing on Beach Park.

"And I did choose. You know that," he said. "It's a game to them. This is the fun part."

"You should have chosen, David." And he knew what she meant; he should have cut up Alicia and fed her to his mother. The phone went dead. Arachnalicia stopped and looked back at him. David returned his stare, looking at small black indentations that might have been eyes or exhaust ports or assholes. Padme walked by on the other side of the street, waving, seeing nothing, with both girls trailing behind on their shiny new prosthetics like cyborg ducklings.

"Is she right?" David asked.

"No," Arachniss said. "They were marked. You would have had to give up Jason to save her."

"And James?"

"Him or Charlotte."

"Why? Why them?"

"Many police officers are conservative. You wouldn't believe how many wanted to kill a gay man hiding in their ranks. People who called him friends. People who said they had his back. Men and women, though mostly men. The cost for Arachnur to intervene would have been too high, and why would he care?"

"And Alicia?"

Arachnalicia sighed. "Different reasons, but no fewer of them. Criminal enemies. Jealous colleagues. And frankly, she was the exact type of person we like to get rid of."

"So you can domesticate us."

"So you survive to the next harvest. But also…"

"What?"

"It was Kathryn's last wish. I asked her myself. For that, for you, she gave up a chance for an easier death."

"Kathryn, a pacifist Buddhist vegan, told you to kill my wife."

"Actually, she said to give you a chance to leave first, but you took too long. All of Alicia's missing parts? That was her. One for each major beating. She practically told you in prosthetic semaphore."

"Bullshit." But he believed Arachniss. Why would he lie?

I'm sorry, Kathryn. I'm so sorry.

He wasn't even sure what he was sorry about. There was too much to choose from.

"Why did you do it for her?" he asked. "She wasn't even in your territory."

But that was the end of their conversation. Arachnalicia stopped in the middle of the intersection at Aurora and 11th, southwest of Beach Park. Arachnajames stumbled up Aurora toward them. There was no sign of Franzia. David stood on the southwest corner, trying to figure out what came next, but nothing made sense.

The alien-human-hybrid things swayed and waved their arms, struggling for balance like novice scarecrows. Were they going to fight?

Franzia ran up the sidewalk to the southeast corner, stopping across 11th from David. She wore a striking black pantsuit and heels—butt bandages apparently gone—and had a large black bag slung over her left shoulder. The right sleeve of her jacket melted cleanly into the charred flesh of her arm. He couldn't believe she was standing. David nodded an impressed hello, which she ignored.

Arachnalicia and Arachnajames glanced east down Aurora, apparently at the intersection with 12th St., about 350 feet away. They seemed to be communicating, but David couldn't hear anything. Then Arachnalicia laughed in Alicia's voice and nodded his round body like he was a head.

"On three," Arachnajames said in James's voice. They turned to face north.

Franzia looked at David, an expression that clearly asked, *What the hell is going on?* David shrugged. He had no idea, but whatever it was, it was going to be different.

The thing that used to be his wife kicked off her heels.

"One," she said. "Two…three…go!"

On *go* they started running down the street. Running meaning stumbling with enthusiasm. Arms pin-wheeled. Legs bent and twisted. Ankles rolled. Shoes and bare feet slapped on the pavement like kids running for the first time. But somehow they never fell.

Arachnalicia easily kept up with Arachnajames, which didn't surprise David. She used to run in college. Even competed once against Kathryn when Kathryn was still Kathryn and not a vegetable or lobster or meal. David glanced at Franzia. She was swaying herself now, pale, hands forgotten at her side, mouth open in total astonishment. And then, from out of nowhere, she screamed:

"Get her, James! Kick that bitch's ass!"

Hey, David thought. *That bitch is my wife.*

"Don't take that shit!" he screamed back. "Run, Alicia! Run!"

From out of nowhere, or nowhere he'd noticed, others started cheering. Kids with faces pressed into the hurricane fence of the playground. Parents out for a stroll. People coming out onto their patio. They had no idea what they were seeing. They couldn't, could they? But whatever they were seeing, it was glorious.

Arachnajames and Arachnalicia made it to the intersection at almost the same time. People screamed and cheered. The two runners turned, almost falling, arms spinning like propellers, and started running back toward them. Arachnajames immediately started pulling away. All that working out was paying off.

"Go, James! You've got this!"

"Alicia!" David screamed, because why not? "Go, baby! Run!" But she quickly was falling behind. James' muscles flexed in his skinny-ass slacks, quads like a Greek god's bulging thighs.

"Yes!" Franzia screamed. "James!"

And then Arachnalicia closed the gap, using the last of her energy, and kicked Arachnajames in the ankle. He caught his foot on his other leg and sprawled forward, forgetting to put his arms out, and slammed alien-first into the blacktop just before the intersection. Arachnur exploded off his shoulders, rolling away, and suddenly it was just decapitated James lying in the street with blood draining out of his neck hole. Right in front of Franzia.

David found himself halfway through a cheer and trying not to vomit at the same time. Others kept cheering, apparently oblivious, and he wished he could see what they were seeing instead of this. Arachnalicia stumbled to the apparent finishing line where they'd started and raised her hands in the air, human lungs pumping oxygen somehow, and you knew someone was hearing the Rocky theme song as Arachnalicia made her victory turns.

It's the eye of the tiger, it's the thrill of the fight, rising up to the challenge of our rival...

"Motherfucker!" Franzia barked.

He'd almost forgotten she was there. Her purse was on the ground and she had the gun in her hands, the massive Desert Eagle 5.0 and its shining steel barrel. Her feet were spread and one hand supported the other in a perfect firing stance, or at least as perfect as he knew from movies. James probably took her to the firing range. Of course he had. She would have loved that.

David didn't love that the gun seemed to be pointed right at him.

"Franzia?" He stepped back, almost falling onto the lawn behind him.

"You should have picked Alicia," she yelled across the street.

Maybe she was right in some way. Maybe it didn't matter who was right anymore. David closed his eyes and looked through the trees into the deep, dark forest. *I'm coming, Daddy.*

He heard the gun fire. His eyes snapped open, expecting to look down and see a hole in his chest like in the old western shootouts, but he was fine. Franzia had missed or fired over his head. He had no idea. As he watched, she changed her stance toward the street and took careful aim at Arachnalicia, who had clearly cheated and deserved a good shooting but couldn't be hurt by bullets any more than Arachnur.

"Franzia, no!"

Then Franzia spun and lowered her aim. At Arachnur, who was just standing around in James' blood.

BAM! "Die, you piece of shit!" *BAM-BAM-BAM!*

Her aim was perfect. The Arach's body jerked back on each hit, black fluid and something like tissue flying into the air. Which was impossible, wasn't it? You couldn't just kill them with bullets. America was awash in bullets and things to fire bullets. It made no sense.

Two more shots, right on target, and then clicking on an empty chamber.

"Just fucking die!"

But Arachnur didn't die. Eight legs slowly lifted the black body, which stood totally still for the longest second ever. Arachnalicia watched, just as immobile, an oddly curious position to her body, slightly to the side, like her version of reality was ten degrees off.

And then Franzia was on the ground with Arachnur on top of her, on her back this time.

David ran toward her just as Arachnur lit up like a solar flair. David flung his arm over his eyes and stumbled into the street. Franzia screamed in pure terror and pain, the worst thing he'd ever heard. Somehow worse than the Arachnur scream or even Jason gliding across the living room floor. Because this was fear that came with certainty. It was killing her and she knew it. David could smell her flesh burning.

"Arachniss, please." He turned toward Arachnalicia and squinted away from the burning light. "Please."

"It's okay," she said. "Just wait."

Wait for what? She was dying.

Her scream had faded to sizzling flesh and steam and David still couldn't look at her.

And then he heard it. They all heard it. Even the otherwise oblivious audience turned to the sky.

David looked up as something turned the world gray. A great black thing the size of a moon slid in front of the sun and blotted out the light. In seconds, it was cold and dark and no one moved or spoke.

It wasn't just a moon, it was a thing, something unfurling long black legs the size of skyscrapers, Cthulhu but larger, blacker and *louder.* If this was Griff and it had once been a thing of Earth, it was now a thing of stars and blackness and death. As it came to a stop over them, the air itself screamed, cracked and everything turned to sound and pain. He fell to his knees, arms over his ears, but it didn't help. Nothing helped. Earth's crust would crack open at this sound. The planet would break and the sun would bleed.

Then he heard something else. A scream: the familiar screech of metal on metal.

Arachnalicia was as frozen as everyone else, but Arachnur was screaming, flailing, legs slamming into the sidewalk so hard concrete shattered and dust exploded into the air. Then her body lifted off the ground and stretched like black taffy toward the thing in the sky.

One scream joined another, Arachnur's pain and the Arach god, until David felt himself losing consciousness. He couldn't take his eyes off the rising alien between gray clouds. It had stopped flailing, its arms now stretched thirty feet up into the sky until they broke apart and then it just dissolved into nothing.

Arachnur was gone

And it was silent. There wasn't a sound but a piercing tinnitus ring in his ears.

He blinked and the sky was blue again.

He blinked and he could smell burning flesh again.

He blinked and…Franzia.

"Franzia!"

David stood and stumbled over to her. She was burned and broken, but alive. He grabbed her unburned hand and wanted to tell her she was all right, but her face was bone and gore and her eyes were gone. Her hair was burned into the blackened flesh of her skull. She was dead, but too stubborn to admit it.

"No," he whispered. "Damn it, no."

She whimpered and squeezed his hand back. He couldn't imagine her pain.

"I'm right here," he said. "I'm right here." Meaning, *please don't leave me alone. Don't you dare leave me alone with this nightmare.* "Don't you dare fucking die."

But of course she did.

*

LIONS RIPPED OFF SHREDS of Arachniss' flesh. In the grass nearby, hyenas played tug-of-war with his guts. Across the field, the woman turned and walked into the trees with their little boy. David stared numbly after her, imbalanced in the heat, until he noticed someone else standing at the opposite treeline, waving.

*

DAD WAS BACK ON TV. David stood in front of the screen. Who the hell had been waving at him?

Franzia was dead. James was dead. It was just him and Jason now.

"David," Bot-father said, voice so full of digital love he wanted to punch the wall. "It'll be okay." And then he pressed forward out of the television and mantle, so the whole wall looked like a facade or skin he was pressing through, pulling back on him like latex. David stared, wide-eyed and frozen. It was like one of those phone panorama pictures where the software stitches images together wrong and you end up with a two-legged dog laughing through one eye, except real. Dad pushed one step and then another into the room and slowly extended his arms and David fell into the hug, the smell and memory of his father, and it was the same feeling he got from smelling Jason's head, total safety and comfort, and he would have stayed like that for hours, except that there seemed to be too many arms.

"It's okay, son."

David blinked and Dad was gone. He was standing alone in the living room. How could it be okay? It was just him and Jason now. And Charlotte, he realized. Maybe he could save Charlotte. He wasn't sure he could save anyone, but he had to try. He still couldn't believe Franzia was dead. Somehow he thought she'd be the one to make it—she and Char and their profanity-laden act. He wanted to laugh or cry, but nothing seemed to work.

"Hey," said someone behind him in an impossible voice.

David turned to see Franzia on the couch. Franzia alive and unburned and smirking like an ass.

"What's with the grassy place?" she asked.

"It's hard to explain," he said, stepping over the coffee table and sitting next to her on the couch in one rapid movement. He grabbed her hand and smiled and cried like an idiot. Crying wasn't the right word. He broke open, and his pain and relief came out as salt and water. At some point he leaned into her arms and they wept together until there was nothing left inside and still it wouldn't stop.

"I'm sorry about James," he said. "I really did pick."

"I know. I was angry. I'm sorry I said that."

He thought about kissing her. He wanted to kiss her. But James and Alicia had just died and it didn't feel right, despite a new memory that they had died separately several months earlier. Maybe it would never feel right. Maybe what he felt was just a desperate need for connection when there was nothing else to hold on to. He hoped not, but it was hard to trust his feelings.

"Well, aren't you two just adorable?"

They sat up, facing the TV. Dadrachniss was back.

"What happened to Arachnur?" she asked.

"She forgot her purpose. We never torture the herd without compensation."

"Well, that's compassionate."

"It spoils the flavor."

"Or not," she said. "What happens to us now that she's gone?"

"You're welcome, by the way, for saving your life."

"Thank you," David said, "Seriously." Franzia just glared at the TV.

"My herd has grown," Dadrachniss said. "I should thank you."

"You really shouldn't," Franzia said. "And the deal for my daughter?"

"Stays in place, of course. Now there's just one more task, and you're free."

Franzia and David glanced at each other. "What task?"

"You'll see. The cull is Saturday. Don't be late." And he was gone.

"Is he always like that?" she asked. "All creepy and vague?"

"Sometimes he's sadistic and vague."

"So, five days until the end of the world," she said. "I guess it's time to let everyone know."

"Meaning your team."

"They're not my team. I'm not even supposed to know they exist."

"You know it won't work. There's no way the Arach don't know about it. They knew about your little unit. This isn't the movies."

"It might still work," she told him. She grabbed his hand and held his eyes. "I need to believe it, David."

"Okay," he said finally. *Just don't let go.*

She went home to check on Charlotte and he walked into the nursery to look at Jason, who was up against the side of the crib and shaking the bars like a kid in prison.

He looked up and smiled at David and said, "Da!"

His first word that might actually be a word.

And David was crying again.

*

DAVID HAD BECOME ATTACHED to his virtual father. As much as Franzia might mock him for it, he loved his father deeply and having him back, even some strange derivative part of him, was one of the few things keeping him from completely losing it. So, after Franzia went home to see Charlotte, he took Jason into the living room and turned on the TV. Dad was there, waiting, as he was always waiting.

"This is your grandson," David said. "Jason Benjamin Chambers."

Dad smiled, surprised. "Wow. He really is adorable."

"Jason," David said to his squirming son. "This is your grandfather."

"Da!" Jason said again, and both men laughed.

"Where are you when you're not here?" David asked.

"I'm not really anywhere, David, but to answer your question in a literal sense, my program is stored on a series of local virtual networks in what you might think of as an AI cloud, though that's a very rough analogy. There is no physical location, and 'network' in this context has nothing to do with computer networks as you understand them. I manifest as needed from core components, and dissipate when no longer needed."

"So you're just turned off?"

"Disassembled would be more like it. There's no point permanently storing something as simple as I am."

"So, when you're here but we're not talking, what are you doing?"

"Mostly, I play chess."

David blinked. Of course. "Because Dad played chess with himself to relax and think?"

"I guess so, yes."

He'd always hated playing chess with his father. He just didn't get the game when he was younger, and now he regretted every second of time he'd lost with his father.

"But you don't think when you're playing? You're just playing because you're supposed to."

"No, I think a lot. I wonder what I could have done better with you and your brother. How I could have protected you from your mother."

"But that's not you. That's…" It was sad to think of this program rebooted into a constant state of guilt for a crime some human version of him committed years earlier. Almost sadistic. "Is that sad?"

"Maybe a little melancholy. I have both the memories of your father's emotions as translated from your memories, and memories of my own. Sometimes I don't understand why he was sad or happy, which is confusing, but it's been an honor getting to know him."

"Getting to know yourself, you mean."

"No, I'm allowed to track independently. Some other sub-sentients are locked into their origin frame or context. I'm not. I think Arachniss wanted us to build a relationship using your father as a baseline, but not limited to that. That would have been morbid and derivative."

"Morbid and derivative." David smiled. Those were words his father never would have used, and certainly not in that order. "Is it lonely?"

Dad seemed to consider this, tasting the word. *Lonely*. Oaky, with hints of honey and charcoal.

"Yes," he said, finally. "It's lonely, but it's also…warm. I can feel your love for him and, by extrapolation, his love for you. It's inseparable from your memories."

David looked away, teary for a second. Dads and puppies, puppies and dads; two things that played his heartstrings with ridiculous ease.

"I hate the idea of you trapped in there," he said. At first, he'd hated the artificial pretense of Dad trapped in the TV, but there was nothing insincere or manipulative about the bot itself; it was just a function that was being used no differently than David himself was being used. He no longer thought of it as his father, but as a digital being trapped in his father's life. Independent but isolated, in a prison built from David's childhood.

"All that's going on in your life, and you care about me? Maybe Arachniss was right about you."

A sudden chill. "Right about what?"

"That there's hope for you, after all."

"Hope for what?"

Dad thought again, but finally surrendered. "I have no idea."

"And what happens to you?"

"What do you mean?"

"After the cull, when this is all over."

"Then I'll have served my purpose."

"And he'll turn you off. Kill you. Just like that."

His father shrugged and smiled, both his real father's smile and something else. Something new.

"Probably," he said. "But it's still been a pleasure getting to know my son."

Dessert & Digestives

"Life lives on life…
Death is an act of giving."

- Joseph Campbell -

The Big Unit

TUESDAY MORNING. The streets of Flagstaff and Lower Chautauqua were empty. David had put Jason in their misleading athletic stroller and was taking the long way to Franzia's, walking south on 6th to Chautauqua Park before heading down Baseline and back north again. He'd gotten used to keeping his head down to avoid seeing horror and carnage, and when he finally looked up, he was surprised to be the only one out. No one was out walking their three-legged dogs or jogging for fitness, delivering packages or doing anything at all because there wasn't another human being in sight. At the Baseline intersection, a gust of wind blew a singular round of disheveled tumbleweed across the street into the grassy field. It was like the old west. The tumbleweed lodged against a low snow fence and bled dried branches like a forlorn dandelion.

He would have laughed if not for the bear.

The bear was to his right in the middle of Baseline, looking downhill and east, a great black beast shuffling along the double yellow line. David froze, hoping the bear wouldn't notice them. The wind was at his back, carrying his scent toward the bear, but there was still hope it wouldn't notice them, and David wasn't that concerned either way. Maybe it was everything he'd seen lately. Maybe it was just that bears wandered into town sometimes, bored or hungry, usually tearing up someone's trash can until they were tranquilized, dragged away by animal control and left in the forest where they belonged. He grew up with bears. He understood bears. Bears didn't bother with humans, usually, and this bear hadn't even glanced in his direction. It kept staring down Baseline, moving its head from side to side, looking more confused than threatening. David followed its gaze.

"Huh," he said out loud. Baseline descended slowly east, surface gray and patched with age, but the surface had turned into black water and a wave was rolling up the hill toward them—a singular black swell like someone had pulled up the road and snapped it to knock off the dust.

David and the bear looked at each other with identical baffled expressions.

Are you seeing this shit?

Then the wave reached the intersection and his brain fixed itself. It was a huge disturbance of spidercats, a mass of black eyes and claws, hundreds of the demonic things running full-out toward the bear. David would have called out a warning, but it was too late.

The cats hit the bear from all sides and rolled over it until the bear disappeared under a writhing pile of screaming felines. The bear moved underneath, roared and swung to the side. Cats flew off, wailing and clawing at the air, but more cats filled the gaps. Soon the roars turned to grunts of pain and the pile moved back up the hill as the bear dragged the alien hoard with him up toward the foothills.

David never moved from his spot. Jason never made a sound. A few minutes later, the sounds of grunting bear and screaming cats faded. The writhing black pile vanished around the bend, leaving behind a few squished cats and a trail of blood. David felt a strange solidarity with the soon-to-be-dead black bear. It was a thing of Earth and it didn't deserve to die in the stomachs of mutant alien cats. Not even if he was a terrible ravener of deer that scared little boys in their tents.

Still. In the grand scheme of things, it wasn't that surprising.

David checked both ways, crossed the street and headed down Baseline, following a detached black cat tail that tossed and turned in the air, caught in an invisible whirlwind until it rose up, up and vanished in the storm gray sky.

*

"ANYBODY HOME?" DAVID CALLED into Franzia's empty living room. The door was open, but nobody seemed to be home. There were no sounds of James working out or slamming down weights, because of course James was gone. Not even a hint of Charlotte playing inside somewhere. "Hello?"

Nothing.

David stepped inside and tried to calm his breathing. Arachnur was gone. Arachniss was protecting them. But he was still terrified something could happen to Franzia and Charlotte—some other Arach, a spidercat feeding frenzy or a tiny meteor strike. Nothing would surprise him. He walked into the kitchen.

"Hello?"

Silence.

Where were they? He'd texted before coming over.

"Fran!" he called, trying to keep his voice calm.

"Back here!" she called. He exhaled in relief.

Franzia was sitting in one of her Adirondack chairs in the sun with a glass of non-alcoholic 'total shit' wine, facing the newly repaired and painted French doors. He parked Jason and sat in the other chair, glanced at her, looked at the back of the house, and once again wondered why she never offered him even an alcohol-free drink. Though it was nine in the morning.

"Checking out your big unit?" he asked.

"Ha-ha." She took a sip. "You know there was one of them on my video chat at work?"

"What? An Arach?"

"Yep. Just sitting there in the top right square, video background showing a nice forest. His name was Bob Contributes. Like it's all a joke. I checked the company directory. Says he works in catering for an office in Damascus."

"That's a little on the nose. What did Bob have to contribute?"

"Not much. He dropped a couple of 'Good points!' and 'I hadn't thought of it that way,' into chat, like an intern sucking up to management. Mocking us. It's not just Arachnur. It's an entire species of douchebag spiders."

"Maybe they're learning how we communicate?"

"Maybe the galaxy is run by bored assholes."

If only she knew. He'd shared very little of Arachniss' philosophical ramblings since the yellowtail comment. "So, just like Earth?"

She laughed, barely. "I asked Bob what he thought of Lebanon. He said he really liked the shawarma."

"Eesh." David glanced at her wine and resigned himself to undying thirst. Then he looked toward the back of the house. A Cheyenne Privet with white flowers grew where her device had been. The only thing left was the bigger unit, which he dubbed TBU.

"Did you tell them?" he asked, looking back at her. He felt less nervous around her now, but more obviously interested. He could feel his body pulling him toward her, like repressed affection was a physical force, so he leaned away and focused on her eyes. Yeah, that was better.

She took a long, intentional sip. Screwing with him.

"Franzia?"

"Yes," she said, smiling. "I mean, I told a guy who claimed he had no idea what I was talking about, and he promised not to say anything to anyone, so I think that means everyone knows." She shrugged. "Or the NSA could show up here and arrest us. Do you think they have happy hour at Guantanamo?"

"Not funny." The idea of being taken away from Jason made him want to vomit. "Really not funny."

Her hand on his. Her eyes on his. His breath caught in his throat.

"It'll be fine," she said, looking utterly serious.

They burst out laughing.

"So, just four days," he said. "And then we see what TBU does."

"TBU?"

"The Big Unit." He wasn't sure she'd get the baseball reference. He was surprised he knew it himself.

"Perfect." Her hand was back in her lap. Sip. "Let's hope it's a home run."

He tried not to laugh. Not because the pun was funny or she had no idea The Big Unit was a pitcher, but because it was idiotic to think humanity had gotten away with some vast military conspiracy to kill the Arach. That was impossible. The spiders were just playing with the herd. And the herd had fallen for it like the stupid, desperate animals they were. He couldn't think of anything positive to say, so he told her about the bear. By the time he was done, she was almost out of fake wine.

"They ate a *bear*?"

"Well, they tried." He still hoped the bear got away. "But you can feel it. Things are coming to an end." Four days and it was all over. Just one task left from Arachniss, which would be horrible, but he had to assume they'd survive. He couldn't believe they were going to make it. "Where's Charlotte?"

"Asleep," she said into her empty glass. "She thinks her dad died months ago, but she still misses him. She sleeps unless I drag her out of bed. It's like she senses him in the house and how recently he was here. She doesn't say anything, but..." A final sip. "I can still smell him."

"You miss him too."

"God, yes," she said. "He was the love of my young life. Charlotte's father. The best partner you could ask for and far better than I deserved. And what that thing did to him..." She wiped her eyes. "It's like they pulled out part of a lung and now I can't breathe." To demonstrate, she inhaled, exhaled, frowned.

David nodded and looked away, trying to feel some remnant of his love for Alicia, but there was nothing but relief. She was gone. She would never hit or threaten him again. Maybe he would grieve their early years some other time, but for now, he felt almost giddy. Hopeful. All the horror of the past few weeks, and he was still standing. Jason was still alive. He couldn't believe they'd made it this far.

"I found Leslie," he said to distract her, leaving out any mention of James or his help.

"Who?"

That's right; he hadn't told anyone and they'd never met in the last version of Leslie's memories. "A friend of Kathryn's from college." He didn't feel like explaining the rest. "She lives in Louisville."

"That's great." She kept her attention on the box. "Does she remember Kathryn?"

"Some. She was definitely keeping things back. I don't know what she knows, but I like her. If there's still a world after this weekend, I'd like you to meet her. She reminds me of you."

"She's a brilliant, smart-ass, functional alcoholic?"

"You think you're functional?"

"Screw you."

"You'd like her. And she remembered me from college." He shook his head. "It was strange, though." He told her about the money Kathryn left Leslie, but not what she left him. She took it all in with a quiet nod or two. "I don't know why Arachniss is doing this. The money for Leslie. The partially erased memories. It's too convenient." Maybe it was guilt for how Kathryn had died, but the planning felt like it had to precede that.

"Kathryn, who died in hospice without a dime to her name—I think that's what you said—left Leslie two million dollars?"

"Uh, yep."

"But you got nothing?"

He looked down, blushing.

"For fuck's sake." She said, exasperated. "Don't get me wrong. Good for you, but that's ridiculous even for the David Chambers package."

"Stop."

"Come on. You get conversation and protection on demand from Arachniss and your loving Dot-father. You've just inherited millions out of thin air. And due to a recent tragedy, you have a newly single lady-friend with no one else to talk to." She turned a cold gaze on him. "Do you ever wonder if he killed James so I'd be available to you?"

"God, no. *No.* How could you even say that?"

"I don't know anymore. I'm just tired." She reached for her glass, looked surprised when it came up empty. Mostly she looked like someone who wanted to be angry but didn't have the energy. So he changed topics.

"Why don't you ever offer me any wine?" he asked.

"It's my vice, and it's ruined a lot of my life. Why would I wish that on anyone else? And you need to work on your self-assertiveness. Why don't you ever ask?"

Jesus. David joined her in looking at TBU. "I don't think Arachniss would do that. Kill James for me." At least he didn't want to believe it. "And even if he did, it's not *for* me. It's for his own purpose. That's how they work."

"Aliens?"

"Abusers. They're kind, then violent, then they apologize and then you forgive them and it starts all over. He's a lot like Alicia sometimes. Like Alicia was. And he knows how to work me because he knows what I respond to."

"So, you think he's manipulating you?"

"I know he is."

"Why? I mean, why manipulate a dog?"

"Because you can."

"You think he's that petty? I don't. Has he told you what our last task is?"

"No."

"Okay." Inhale. Exhale. "I killed my son, David. You wanted to talk about our last secrets before the end. This feels like the time."

"You killed... I don't understand." He also wasn't sure he was ready to talk, but she was right. This was the time.

"I used to bring Ben to bed when James was at work. I knew I shouldn't. Too many pillows and too much risk, but I loved having him near me. I put him back in the crib when I drank. Then one night, I guess I didn't."

"Franzia..."

"No, it's okay. I need to say it. You asked about the wine. I was so drunk that night, I passed out. I don't remember anything until waking up at the hospital. They'd tested my blood at zero-point-one-six and so the police were there, one policewoman, who asked for my statement, which I gave as I cried and threw up repeatedly. They wouldn't give me anything to settle my stomach. I was still throwing up when more police showed up."

"Did you…" He wasn't sure how to ask. *Did you suffocate your son while you were drunk?*

"No. It was SIDs, not me. But maybe if I'd been sober, I would have noticed. Maybe I could have saved him." She shrugged. "I'll never know."

"Then you didn't kill him, Franzia. Why do that to yourself?"

"I wasn't a great mother, David. God knows, I'd thought about killing him. I mean, not really, but you know. I was depressed and angry and alone and I hated what he'd done to my career and my body. And I wonder if he knew, if he knew his mommy hated him or thought she hated him or whatever was in my head. Maybe he's happier now."

She was crying now, but only from her eyes. The rest of her face was calm as calm could be. It was eerie.

"Franzia, I don't know how it was for you, but with Alex, it was hard. He cried all the time. We never slept. Depression is normal under those circumstances. That doesn't mean you hated your son."

She shrugged and wiped her face. "I guess we'll never know. I stopped drinking after that. I was sober for years until GBS had me pick people to eat. Even now, I almost never drink that much. That's a start, right?"

"Sure," he said, not sure how to be more reassuring. "I'm sorry, Franzia. Losing a child is horrible enough without blaming yourself for it." He wanted to reach out and touch her, offer her something more than words, but it didn't seem right and he didn't trust his instincts. She nodded. They watched TBU do nothing for a while.

"I think that's the hardest thing, wondering," he said after a while. It was his time to confess. "I wonder if I'd told my dad what Mom was doing to Tommy sooner or differently. I wonder if I'd done *something.* I wish there was just an answer, yes or no, because I could live with that."

"Did you hate her, your mother?"

"I did. Now I just wonder what was broken. What piece of her got bent or snapped, or was she born that way? When I see other people on the street, I try to see what's there and what's not, but I can never tell. It scares me. When I'm in an elevator, I wonder who's armed and who's going home to beat their children and who's going to hurt themselves. I stare sometimes without realizing. It's awkward."

"What do you see when you look at me? Am I like her?"

He turned to look at her. *Just say no. Tell her she's wonderful.* But he couldn't. "I'm not good at absolution. I think we're all like her sometimes, but most times on most days, we're something else. Alicia was like her, but not always. Maybe that's what drew me in. I don't see any of her in you. You have none of her cruelty. Charlotte seems happy and obviously loves you like crazy. But we all have darkness in us."

"You're right, David, you're not good at absolution."

"Is that what you want?"

"I want a large bottle of whiskey, but I'm done with that," she said. "Maybe a hug?"

"Absolutely." They leaned across the chairs and embraced. It was still a revelation to feel himself in someone else's arms, like he was really there after all, and he wondered if she felt the same way. "Are you really done with the drinking?"

She nodded sharply as they pulled apart. "Turns out my sponsor's still alive. Can you believe she puts up with me? Fucking saint, that woman. Anyway, what do we do until Saturday?"

"I don't know. I'm glad you're back on the wagon or whatever it is. I'll help if I can."

She nodded, clearly having trouble accepting that she might need help.

"I think I'll spend time with Jason and finish my book," David said.

"Why, I mean why finish the book? You don't think TBU is going to work. No, I can tell. I don't either. I'm not an idiot. So if you think we're going to die, what's the point?"

"I don't think we're going to die," he said, surprising himself. "I *really* don't. Whatever's coming, I think we're going to make it. I enjoy feeling hopeful and writing makes me feel that way. Like as long as Pedro's still walking around the Arctic with his friends, I'm still here." He shrugged. "What are you going to do?"

"I told Charlotte I'd take her to the amusement park to ride the rides and get mommy motion sick."

"Sounds like fun."

"You want to come? I don't vomit after most rides."

"Maybe next time."

"Right. Next time."

"Come over for breakfast early on Saturday. Around seven. I'll make everything you like."

She shrugged. "Why not? Charlotte likes spam."

"I'll make almost everything you like. But no meat."

"Kill joy. I'll bring juice and muffins. What do you think it'll be like?"

"The cull?" He tried to imagine. "Like a gentle rapture. People will just vanish. Then the clouds will part and a spider-god will smile down on us like we're on the Ark after the Flood. Birds will sing. Sweet and subtle and light. If we watch a movie, we probably won't even know it happened."

She laughed. "You're an idiot."

*

WEDNESDAY. It was a hard morning for Pedro.

Pedro sighed and watched the ice melt and felt the sea warm. The things he had known all his life seemed farther away and quieter. Everywhere he looked, ice was changing. He just wanted it to stay the same. This was his world and every day more of it was melting and drifting away.

"What are you looking at, Pedro?" Shyla asked.

"The lights in the sky. I keep expecting to hear something, but it's so quiet. Or maybe we don't know how to listen to light."

"You're silly, Pedro."

"I know." He was glad she was there. *The lights were brighter now, dancing across the sky like laughter bouncing from the clouds. That was a nice change, so not all change was bad. And maybe that was something he needed to learn instead of focusing on the bad.*

"You want to go on an adventure?" he asked.

"Do I?" She was already climbing up his back, ready to ride. "Of course I do!"

David stared at the words and sighed, listening to Jason mumble against his chest. He just couldn't seem to figure out what to do with Pedro. The bear was as lost as David, mourning his family, vaguely hopeful but unsure, going around in circles. He took a deep breath, selected everything he'd written that day, and hit *Delete*. Which was fine. Sometimes a story needed time. He just wasn't sure how much time he had left, no matter what he told Franzia. They might survive the cull, but there were no guarantees, and that wasn't how children's books worked.

*

THURSDAY. David raced to the store to pick up supplies for Saturday and catch Alex before his shift ended.

"Hey, Alex," David said. "Say hi to Jason." Alex looked up from his phone at the cashier station and smiled. He wasn't missing any new parts, which was nice.

"Aww, he's really cute." Alex looked down and started scanning boxes of formula. "I took your advice."

David frowned. Since when did he offer advice?

"I told him how I felt, you know?"

"Oh." That advice. When life overcharges you for lemons. "How'd it go?"

He smiled. "Really well. Great." He blushed under his pirate patch. Jason held up a tiny hand, randomly grabbing at the sky, and Alex took it as a chance to give him a little high-five. Not quite like having a big brother, but not too bad either. Two pirates just smackin' it out.

Har-har-har.

"Oh, I'm grilling on Sunday." Which he'd just decided. If there was a world after Saturday, people would still need feeding. "Just vegetables and sides. Some veggie burgers. But maybe you and your boyfriend can come by."

"Really?" He waited for David to pay. "I'd like that. I downloaded your book, by the way."

"Which one?"

"*Benny.*" He laughed. "That's one gay ass beaver."

David chuckled. He guessed Benny B. was out of the closet.

It was about dam time.

*

FRIDAY. Dad was in his Royal Stewart plaid, as formal as he got. Jason stared at the TV from his lap and David wondered if he'd ever know this man was his grandfather. He was probably gone after tomorrow, so probably not, which was a pity. The Bot-father had grown on him.

"I need to know the final task," David said.

"It'll wait," Dad said. "Until after the cull."

"Then we're safe?"

"From the cull? Safe as you can be."

"What does that mean?"

"The cull is a free-for-all. There are rules, but no real penalties for not following them. It's the last day when billions of aliens get to do violent, vicarious things to human beings until the next human harvest. Which could be a hundred years or more. Things will get weird."

"How weird?"

Dad shrugged and held up his hands, as in *really weird.* "Tell Franzia to bring the gun. And an umbrella."

David opened his mouth, closed it. He didn't even want to know.

But he did have a very nice umbrella.

Things Get Weird

"DID YOU FINISH YOUR BOOK?" Franzia asked. Charlotte sat next to her at the table, teasing Jason in his royal high chair. Between them were plates of scrambled eggs, pancakes, waffles, veggie sausage patties, hash browns, blueberry muffins, coffee, orange juice and even a bloody Mary for Franzia, which she had not yet touched. He might have gone overboard, but Charlotte showed no signs of letting up. She was on her second plate of eggs and sausage, both covered in syrup, and Jason was watching her in drooling awe. Franzia toyed with a dry waffle, but hadn't taken a bite.

"Not even close," David said. "But I'm making progress." Which was a lie. Pedro was tied to him, so their stories had to end the same way, and right now they were both in limbo. But it was Saturday, the day of the cull, so that limbo was about to end.

"What's it about?" Charlotte asked. Her mouth was full of muffin, so it came out as, *whathibout?*

Yeah, David. What's it about? He looked at Charlotte and her mother. Franzia held his gaze and then looked away, strangely reticent.

"Finding family where you least expect it," he said, thinking it sounded pretty good as he said it.

Charlotte swallowed and pursed her lips. He knew the look: *boring.* That's what Tommy would have said.

"Polar bears and sea lions and a little girl lost in the arctic," he said. "Is that better?"

Charlotte sat up. "Polar bears?"

"Don't worry," David said, leaning toward her. "They don't eat little girls."

"If they're good," Franzia amended, smirking. Charlotte threw her a *stop-it-Mom* glare.

After breakfast, Franzia helped David clean up while Charlotte played with Jason at the table. They were great together, even if Jason kept pouring things on his head to impress her—which made her laugh every time. He was going to need a long bath after this. If there was an after this.

"Do you think we should be at your house instead?" David asked. "To see what the Big Unit does?"

"You want to sit around staring at that thing?" she asked. "I don't. Whatever it does, it can't be good, and I doubt being near it will be healthy."

*

09:48 AM. David finished bathing Jason, put him in a fleecy bodysuit and lay him down to sleep. He grabbed at the air, reaching for his dad like he couldn't quite figure out where he was, and then drooled off to sleep. David rested a hand on his chest, feeling him breathe. When Alex was born, he was already dying and there was no time to process what he felt or what it meant to be a father other than constant fear. But when Jason was born, it was pure love. Just astonishing, overwhelming love. He hadn't known a person could feel that much about anything or anyone, let alone a tiny larval being he barely knew. But he loved Jason in his bones. Every moment with Alicia and Arachniss and in between was worth it just to be here at this moment with his son.

"I love you so much," he said, and then he pulled his hand away and turned to find Franzia and Charlotte watching him from the doorway, holding hands. He'd never seen Charlotte so still.

10:01 am. They sat in the living room in awkward silence. Franzia stared at the bloody Mary on the coffee table, still untasted, ice melted and celery drooping. Charlotte fidgeted in a chair made for style more than comfort, but she was still quiet. Like she knew something was coming.

"Should we ask him?" Franzia asked. She meant Dad about the cull. And what was taking so long? Who knew you could get impatient waiting for slaughter? He shook his head.

"We'll know."

She nodded at the massive black umbrella leaning against the wall. "Are you Mary Poppins?"

10:17 am. David watched Franzia's hands. He loved her hands. He wanted to reach out and touch them, feel the skin and tendons on the back, the bends of each finger, the texture of each nail. He looked away. Looked back. Franzia caught him and smiled, and he saw something he'd never seen in her face before: regret. He was about to ask her about it when they suddenly had a great idea.

10:18 am. "We should go for a walk." David and Franzia said it at the same time, standing by an unknown impulse. David had his umbrella in hand and Franzia was strapping the Desert Eagle into a tactical harness on her thigh when Charlotte asked where they were going.

"For a walk," they both said again. Charlotte looked at them like they were crazy, then yawned like a lion.

"Do you mind watching Jason?" David asked.

"I'm five, Mr. Chambers. *Five*. I don't watch babies."

"Valid point," David said. "Dad?" he said to the TV. Dad appeared instantly.

"You mind watching the kids?" David asked. Franzia looked between them, wondering which was nuttier, but then shrugged; *why not?*

"Of course," Dad said, smiling at Charlotte who remained, at the very least, unconvinced.

"It's okay, honey." Franzia went over to Charlotte and kissed her on the cheek. "We won't be gone long."

Charlotte looked at the gun, at her mom, then the TV, and nodded, not believing a word of it. But she walked to the nursery anyway.

"That was strange," Franzia said.

"How was the amusement park?" David asked.

"Charlotte won a dolphin," Franzia said. "And I threw up less than usual. So, pretty great."

"Shall we?" David nodded toward the front door. He wanted to grab her hand and walk out with her, but of course he didn't. Franzia shook her head at the umbrella.

"That thing is ridiculous."

Outside was a glorious Boulder day, spring on the cusp of summer, so bright and blue that everything felt new. And apparently everyone was out for a walk, strolling aimlessly down sunny streets, looking at trees and staring at nothing. He saw neighbors he thought were dead or had moved out. The Connellys walked by, holding Zombie Hands, and he wondered how much of the triplets was left. Someone even had a dog on a leash. A real lab with all of its legs, tugging at its leash with unbound excitement.

There's a tradition in parts of Italy, *la passeggiata*, where everyone comes out right before dusk, dressed up, just to say hello and greet their neighbors, catch up, and then everyone goes back inside. It was a like a flash mob on a national scale. This was like that, but quieter and less fashionable.

They walked south toward Chautauqua Park for no reason. Just seemed the way to go.

"Can you feel it?" Franzia asked.

"What?" Maybe she meant the end of the world, but all he felt was the sun on his skin and her proximity.

"It's happening," she said.

10:34 am. Every backyard TBU everywhere popped open and blasted a black cloud hundreds of feet in the air. A cloud so fine it was almost a gas, but a gas that flew, changed and bucked the wind like a vast murmuration of miniature metallic starlings. The air was filled in every direction with great swarms of them, so thick that when they flowed together, they blackened the sky.

David and Franzia stopped to look up, mouths open. Her hand found his and he closed his fingers around it. This was it. This was the cull.

"What is it?" Franzia asked.

David had a guess. In *The Day the Earth Stood Still*, aliens released nanobots that swarmed across the world, consuming humans and human creations, and it looked like this (at least on film) at a much smaller scale. If this was global, and David thought it was, Arachniss had lied and this was the end of everything. The Arach had decided on extermination after all.

"I'm not sure," he finally said. "But it's beautiful."

A great black wave passed west above them, moving toward the mountains, like god had rucked the sky.

Then the cloud dimpled and funnels formed, like tornadoes descending, and the air began to hum.

Franzia unclipped her holster and David smiled. Was she going to shoot the sky? But he thumbed the fastener on the umbrella, because that would make all the difference. Maybe Dad was just screwing with him.

"Look at all the spidercats," she whispered.

David looked down, and the street was full of them, running between people's feet, slamming into trees, their attention up in the sky. A black cloud descended on one and it vanished in a second, liquefied, gasified and erased from Earth.

"Okay," Franzia said. "I did not see that coming."

Clearly, the spidercats hadn't either. They leaped into the air, screeching and clawing at the blackness, and somehow never came back. The Arach were cleaning house.

Which was when a man standing about ten feet away from them exploded. He didn't turn to red mist, he *exploded* and parts of him flew in every direction. A flying hand barely missed David's head. Other parts shot into the sky and vanished into the feeding cloud.

Franzia dropped David's hand and wiped something red off her face. David popped open the umbrella.

And that's when the screaming started.

People ran everywhere in every direction, like they could outrun the sky, but none of them ran inside. It was like they couldn't conceive of a world beyond the streets. They were rats panicking in a maze with invisible walls.

"What was the final task, David?" Franzia asked.

He turned to her, baffled. "What?" He had no idea what she was talking about. And shouldn't they be running?

"The final task."

"Oh. He never told me. Why?"

"Is it—" She never finished her question. A teenage girl running past her turned into a flying set of layered cuts, like she'd run through a hundred laser beams, and one of her dislodged eyes smacked Franzia in the side of her head. Which was the least disgusting thing that happened in the next few seconds.

The Arach had lost their minds.

Above the rippling sky, the fabric of space blurred with the passing of invisible ships so massive you could feel the pull of them lifting your feet. Swarms of spidercats rose and flowed and rose again, consuming men and women and children, coyotes and wolves and every other living thing that passed their way, leaving nothing behind but a light sheen of blood and grease and occasional shards of bone. Or the cats were themselves consumed and reduced to nothing. Arach blurred around and above them, visible then not, screaming or silent, and when their path intersected a living thing, there was a sudden burst of red or someone left standing or crawling while blood coursed into the streets and the cats returned. Sometimes the waves of (what David assumed were) nanobots swept over a bird and it rained red and feathers and other remains so small you'd need a microscope to identify them.

They could see the flying Arach things now, which were just little black drone spheres shooting everywhere, pausing, then going somewhere else. He had no idea what they were, but if he had to guess, something like cameras to share the spectacle with a galaxy of asshole aliens, but he stopped thinking about it when the spiders appeared. What had been blurs turned into tarantulas and black widows bigger than Great Danes, though what caught his attention was the Brazilian wandering spider about ten feet away, the size of a car, looking at him with hungry bowling-ball eyes.

"Uh," David said. And then the Brazilian monster jumped thirty feet in the air, landed on an old guy with a walker—weirdly like his deleted vignette about Pedro—and things got visceral. David turned away and retched.

"I think I just wet myself," Franzia said. David straightened, wiped his mouth, lifted the umbrella and nodded for her to join him, as much to hide from the drones as the blood. He dipped the front so the carnage was less obvious, though it did nothing for all the screaming.

Well, he thought, *this isn't so bad.* Even if he was so scared he couldn't feel his legs. Little shredded things hit the umbrella like a light rain. He closed his eyes, relaxed, opened them. *This is fine.*

It took him a second to realize Franzia wasn't at his side anymore. He stopped and turned, heart pounding, expecting she'd been taken or injured or worse. But what he saw surprised him even more. She had the gun in both hands in her practiced firing stance, and she was pointing it right at his chest. Again. At this range, she'd blow his heart right through his ribcage and twenty feet down the street. Which absolutely no one would notice, though the remaining cats would be grateful.

"Franzia? What are you doing?"

"What's the final task, David?" Her finger was shaking on the trigger, not even safely at the side. She was one wrong word from killing him.

"I told you. I have no idea."

"You're lying! He made you choose. Jason or me. There has to be a final test. He's not gonna pick me, is he? No, I'm the final test. Just say it. That's why you invited us over. What happens to Char when you're done?"

A spidercat ran right between her legs and she nearly pulled the trigger on accident.

"Franzia, I swear. I don't know. He hasn't told me." He took a step toward her, crossing half the distance.

"Stop, David."

"It's okay." Another step and the barrel was pressed against his chest. If she pulled the trigger now, the spidercats would have to clean up half of him on both sides of the street. "I swear to you, you're not the test. I don't know what is."

She took a hand away from the gun to wipe her eyes, then looked around at a world being torn apart. She wanted to believe him. She was just terrified. And how could he blame her? If he'd even thought of it, he'd feel the same way. It made perfect sense. Put them together. Make them love each other. Then watch them kill each other. It was so delicious, he had no idea why he didn't believe it.

"It's all right," he said. "I understand." He reached up and held the barrel steady against his chest. Maybe she was right and only one of them was going to make it. Better that it was her. Jason was too young to remember his father, but Charlotte couldn't lose another parent. He knew what it was like to lose everyone. It would destroy her.

"What are you doing?"

"Just promise me you'll take care of Jason."

"What?"

"Promise me. Raise him like your own. That's all I ask."

"David…" She was crying now, her finger out to the side of the trigger guard. He could have taken the gun away from her. Instead, he pulled her to him and her hand dropped to the side as she leaned into his arms.

"David, I'm sorry." She wept, her body shaking with each sob.

"It's okay," he whispered. "I don't think you could have done it. You couldn't have killed James. I was wrong. You're not like my mother. I shouldn't have said that. You're a good person, Franzia. You're the best person I've ever known, and I can't imagine living without you."

She pulled her head back, wiped salt and pink off her face with her free hand, and stared at him.

"David…" she said again. And then she pressed herself into him, her breasts and body fitting against him like a second skin he'd had all his life but not realized until then. He leaned down and she leaned up until their breath mixed and he could feel her heartbeat through his fingers on her neck. Her eyes narrowed and closed. Their lips touched so lightly, both trembling, that it might have been an accident, less a kiss than a whisper.

And then they leaned in hard and pulled into each other, her hands clenched into fists on his shirt and his slipping around her neck while the other pulled her body closer (he really hoped the gun was back in her holster). She moaned and he felt it in his bones as his tongue slid inside her mouth. They both pushed and pressed harder until there was nothing but tongues and lips and warm, wet moans escaping them both when they bothered to breathe. He felt her breasts press against him and wanted her right there on the street in blood at the end of the world, like he'd never wanted anything in his life. At some point, he'd dropped the umbrella. There was no stopping his hands or her lips, no separating their bodies, no care for who watched and no end to what was built up inside them.

Until a spidercat slammed into his leg and bit into his calf.

"You've got to be kidding!" He jerked back and kicked the black thing like a punter going for a long field goal. The cat screamed and *flew* for the first and last time in its life; before it reached the top of its parabolic arc, a blur snatched it out of the air, leaving no more than a microburst of red. He stared at it, stunned and angry and confused, until he realized he was still holding Franzia in one arm and she was laughing.

The next cat that came for them, she shot at close range. There wasn't much left.

"Is it weird that I'm really turned on right now?" he asked.

"Be weird if you weren't. I'm really sorry."

"And it's really okay." He wanted her desperately. The feel of his shoe connecting with the spidercat body was the closest thing he'd had to a real orgasm in years, but the moment had passed. He took her hand, felt her fingers slide between his, fitting, linking, connecting. In that moment, he knew he loved her. Maybe he'd always loved her. In some version of the virtual timeline they met in high school and fell in love and had children together, and the world flowed around them like water around a rock. It was a happier story but also less interesting, and he wasn't sure he'd trade for it even if he could.

"Now what?" Franzia asked.

"I have no idea." He shrugged and squeezed her hand. She squeezed back and they turned to walk down the street, pressed together under the umbrella and trying not to smile or laugh as it rained blood, body parts and worse things they tried not to see. There was an undeniable glory to the slaughter, a blood-soaked orgy of rabid half-seen spiders and screaming meat. This was the reality of it, honest as a chainsaw, no demigod solemnly disposing of half of humanity to save the rest, no children rising to the Overmind in *Childhood's End*, no rapture or vanishing, not even groaning robots mulching humanity for fertilizer or the campy *ding* of elevators disgorging childhood demons into Hell's lobby, nothing so subtle or kind. It was chaos and insanity and the hot, wet sounds of orgiastic violence.

If it was like anything, it wasn't fiction; it was the *La Tamatina* festival in Spain, faces dripping, clothes clinging, great crowds surging as it rained fat red tomatoes, except it also hailed lumps of brain and shards of bone, a rabid tree-chipper for humanity, chewing, grinding, spitting and spraying hot ripped flesh in every direction. This wasn't a harvest or cull, it was a frenzy. He could almost feel the emotional release of a billion aliens vicariously shredding life just to get a taste of what they'd lost a million years earlier, as if killing was the only thing that made them feel truly alive.

"What the hell is that?" Franzia asked. David lifted the forward edge of the umbrella.

Oh, my god, he thought, trying to suppress irrational excitement. *They have lasers.*

11:18 - 5:17 pm. Stuff got weird.

5:18 pm. The sky cleared and the killing stopped. The cull was over and they were still standing, having walked for hours around their neighborhood. Buildings dripped and children sobbed, hell, everyone sobbed, but even over the sound of people pulling their bodies from nowhere to nowhere else, there was a quiet breeze and a strange silence above it all, like Earth was a ship and they'd gotten used to the sound of the engines and, when they cut out, their ears rang in the vacuum. The black cloud was gone. The spidercats were gone. Everyone everywhere wiped their eyes and looked to the sky to see blue or clouds, sun or stars, sunset or dawn, and all of them asked the same questions as the newly armless man next to him:

"What just happened?"

"And is it over?" From a legless woman.

And all the bubbling questions from the shocked and tongueless who looked from one eye or two for answers.

"Yes," David said. "I think it's over."

"I think they're gone," Franzia said.

"Who's gone?" someone asked, or "Where did they go?" as their wounds closed and skin grew over their exposed bones. It must have been terrible in subways and airplanes. On the news later, he heard that the recently completed Multinational Space Station blew up and fell back to earth in flaming chunks, which was probably easier than trying to clean bone marrow out of the CO_2 scrubbers.

"Will someone please tell me what just happened," an older man asked. He was staring at the end of his leg. There was already a prosthetic where his foot had been, but his foot was still in his shoe, which was probably confusing and a bit sloppy. Maybe the spidercats were taken a little too early.

And the answer to all their questions was, *it doesn't matter.* Because in seconds or minutes or days, it all faded and changed until what they remembered was that terrible day when the pandemic ended and they all grieved what they'd lost. James and Alicia and Kathryn and

Kiaraa were gone, along with countless mothers and fathers, sons and daughters, lovers and enemies, but not Jason or Charlotte or David or Franzia.

Two billion people died that day. Billions more were left with missing limbs or worse. Almost no one was untouched, and those who were walked quietly in the shadows, afraid to be noticed. Scientists postulated that the virus had burned itself out in a final act of brutal mutilation, which made no sense but also as much sense as anything else. In the illusion that lived parallel with his memories of the cull, David remembered waking in his bed the next day and turning on the TV to news reports about a nighttime of vanishings and loss. A great cosmic clock had struck midnight and erased more than a fourth of humanity, and not one of those remaining said anything about spiders.

Because that would be crazy.

In the days and weeks and months after what came to be known as The Vanishing—apparently the last act of SHAS, which disappeared as mysteriously as it had arrived—people felt more fragile, less arrogant, more cautious about the world around them. It wouldn't last, but for now, humanity was a kinder, gentler thing than it had once been. A remarkable number of women ended up sterile and birth rates plummeted, but rather than turning into a *Handmaid's Tale* dystopia, support for women's reproductive rights and equality skyrocketed. Plus, there were far fewer rapists and lawyers, which no one could quite figure out. Not that anyone tried that hard.

But that was then. For now, David and Franzia had to get home to their children.

5:34 pm. They opened the door to his house, and they both felt it.

"Come on in!" Dad called from the living room.

The cull might be over, but Arachniss was still there.

The Last Supper

AFTER CHECKING ON JASON AND CHARLOTTE, who were sleeping so deeply they might have been in a coma, David and Franzia made their way into the living room. The coffee table was set for two. They sat on the couch as Dad smiled at them from the TV in his usual plaid but, unusually, he was at their old dining room table. It was set just like theirs, with a white linen tablecloth and their good china on white placemats and cloth napkins folded like origami swans. There was water with ice in crystal glasses—which he'd forgotten they owned—and a single steak knife next to each plate. No forks. No spoons. No food.

Which raised the obvious question: Were they for dinner?

"Did the umbrella help?" Dad asked. They were coated in blood and gore. Because of a short but exciting fight with a spidercat, there was a lot of black hair under his fingernails. Due to something he'd rather not think about, Franzia was sheered nearly bald on the left side of her head and she still smelled like burned hair. There was a lumpy thing in his shirt pocket he'd forgotten to remove, but he'd burn the shirt before taking it out. When Franzia coughed, a black goo of inert spider nanobots came out. And that wasn't even the weird stuff.

But, *yeah,* David said, "The umbrella was great." So was the gun, even if they'd run out of bullets within two hours and had to resort to random objects to defend themselves. The tip of his umbrella looked like a Civil War bayonet.

Franzia coughed up more black goo and wiped it on one of the swans. Then Dad turned himself off and they were alone in the living room. Which was nice for the three seconds it lasted.

"Holy fuck," Franzia blurted. "Who the hell are you?"

David jerked his head to see what was wrong, and they were both staring at Arachniss, but not Arachniss the spidery blur or black spherical robot, Arachniss the man. He was wearing plaid and jeans and boots identical to David's father, but his proto-human face was as black and hairy as his hands. Even across the room, he smelled like sweat and grass and darker things David couldn't identify, just as he had the second before he died in Africa eons before they were born.

"Franzia," he said in Dad's voice. Apparently, he didn't have one of his own.

"Uh," she said, wiping more goo off her lips. They should probably get that checked out.

"This is Arachniss," David said. "When he was human."

Franzia looked at him, eyebrows raised, well, the right eyebrow— the left was largely missing—and David realized he'd forgotten to tell her any of this.

"What?" she said, her pupils narrow as the tip of a hypodermic. He admired her restraint in not swearing.

"You remember the grassy place?" he asked.

She nodded.

"That's where he's from. Arachniss is from Earth."

She didn't move or speak.

"And the Arach took him, what..." he glanced at Arachniss, "...two-hundred-thousand years ago?"

"Closer to two-fifty," Arachniss said. He crossed his legs. David frowned. There was clay-like red dirt on the bottom of his boots and on the carpet. There was verisimilitude and there was rude, but nothing some seltzer water wouldn't take out. Weird that Kiaraa had never mentioned how OCD he was. Maybe it was a secondary issue.

"David?" Franzia asked. "Anything else you want to tell me?"

"Oh, so, uh, here he is?"

She smiled. "You're an idiot."

"Hasn't changed," David admitted. "Anyway, why the personal visit? And what's for dinner?"

"You are," Arachniss said, then laughed when they both made to leap off the couch and run. "Just kidding. Well, not really. It's complicated."

"What's your real name?" Franzia asked, surprising them both. That was her question?

"I told you, Arach don't have names."

"Then what does Arachniss mean?" She leaned in. Was she trying to distract him with inane banter?

"We don't have language the way you do," Arachniss said in Dad's soothing voice. David found himself drawn in, relaxing, just like he had whenever Dad talked. "It's inefficient," he continued, "And whatever we once knew has long since been purged. So we created a set of languages to answer questions like this when we talk to humans, largely to make you feel more connected to something familiar. But in the English meta-language, which has fewer than ten-thousand words and the subtlety of a jackhammer, Niss means *immigrant* or *not-quite-a-person*." He smiled with big, white but utterly jacked up teeth. "Or close enough. It's what we call people brought in from other less advanced species, which is all people at first. It also means *salvation*."

"Salvation from what?" David asked.

"Well, from yourselves in this case, but it's not specific."

"What does Nur mean, then?" Franzia asked.

Arachniss laughed. "You know, I thought you'd slip on that. It was supposed to set her off. I can't believe you never said it in her presence. It means Defective Node: Do Not Interface but also, asshole."

Franzia laughed like she was at a cocktail party mid-flirt with a charming man. Next, she'd lean over and rest her hand lightly on his leg. David wasn't complaining that she was wasting time—the limited and recently sharpened cutlery didn't send a nice message—

but honestly, how long could they avoid it? He was tired and covered in cat guts. He wanted a shower. Small talk could wait.

"Then how do you refer to yourselves?" she asked.

Or not.

"We don't have names or language as you understand them. I have a unique galactic node index reference ID. You can call me NRL-1X-172343ABC-1234JX13 if you like, but then you'd have to add a galactic-standard time stamp and context reference, or it'd be impolite."

"You're kidding," Franzia said. "And that's better than spoken language?"

David wanted to scream. Yes, it was objectively fascinating. Yes, he should care, but he kept looking at the knives and was wondering how it would feel to stab himself with one. In *Hitchhiker's Guide to the Galaxy*, hearing Vogon poetry was one of the most painful things a human could endure. This conversation was worse.

"Orders of magnitudes," Arachniss said, "But more of that later."

Oh, thank god.

"But—"

"Later," Arachniss cut her off.

Franzia leaned back, looking frightened for the first time. David rested a hand on her leg, which she barely noticed. He wanted to tell her it was going to be all right. He didn't know why he felt that way, but he was sure of it. Whatever the final task was, it had to be better than Arach small talk.

"Okay," David said. "What now?"

"One last meal," Arachniss said.

"You promised," Franzia said.

"Don't worry, Franzia. It's not Charlotte or Jason. And not you, at least not the way you think. The real harvest is dessert, the sweetest course, and saved 'til last. You asked a long time ago why we let people like you and Franzia live. There are millions just like you. Why not fix you so you can't see us?"

They waited. Arachniss waited.

"Was that a real question?" Franzia asked. "You want us to guess."

"Anticipation," he said. "Is almost as delicious as shame. What you offer is more than food, but the sweet and sexual taste of guilt. Think of all the things you've done. Those you've helped us kill, the way you fed us your partners and watched the world bleed. David fed us triplet fingers and middle-aged men, anything to avoid the idea he was a man who would harm his own wife—even the idea of it. And you, Franzia, you fed us Balasubramanian body parts and your own husband's arm, and so much more."

Franzia had turned a shade uncommon in living mammals. "Because you made us," she rasped, a little bubble of black goo at the corner of her mouth.

"Yes and no. David?"

"Hmm?" David pulled his focus away from the knives. He'd have to find out how they sharpened them. They were honed like medical instruments. "Oh, yeah." He turned to Franzia. "They can't kill or hurt anyone a human doesn't pick." He frowned and glanced at Arachniss. "Even during the cull?"

"Even then," Arachniss said. "There's quite a backlog, but accidents do happen."

"We did this?" Franzia asked David. "We did this all to ourselves?"

David nodded. Shrugged. "Yes and no."

"You'd do anything for your children, even give up your souls," Arachniss said. "And you have."

"I don't understand," Franzia said. "What do you want from us?"

"A trade. For a little flesh, I'm going to take that shame from you. You'll feel it. You'll feel every second of it. But when I'm done, you won't remember any of this. Your shame and memories will be gone and you can raise your children in peace until you reach old age and die in peace."

"You're kidding?" David asked. "You want to feed on our *shame?*"

"What part of us do you take it from?" Franzia asked, apparently eager to get started.

"That's up to you, but I don't take it from you. You take it from each other."

Franzia swallowed and looked at David. David glanced at the knives and leaned away, not wanting to end up like James, with a knife in his hand. Franzia might be a great engineer, but she was a crap butcher.

"To be clear, you choose together."

"How much?" Franzia asked, turning back to Arachniss. "And what the hell is your name? You must have a name. When you were on Earth, what did others call you?"

Arachniss shook his head, inhaled and grunted, a noise indistinguishable from the sound you'd make after being punched in the stomach.

"Seriously?" she asked. "How did you tell each other apart?"

"You're delaying," he said. "But I have time. You're just prolonging your own pain."

Exactly, David thought, realizing he was famished. Maybe that was why he was so irritable. Then he had to fight the urge to lick his bloody lips. He wasn't that hungry.

"You can call me Adam," Arachniss said, finally. David waited for Franzia to say *seriously* again and got ready to roll his eyes, but she never got the chance. "It's not a biblical thing, well, not directly. All human beings are descended from a small group that lived in Africa in a place now called the Makgadikgadi paleo wetland but which is currently a part of the Kalahari Desert. It used to be an oasis surrounded by sand. If you were to take a sample of this body's DNA, you'd find some of it in you. In all of you. You've heard of mitochondrial Eve, the mother of all. I'm Y-chromosome Adam, the father of all humans, or one of them. It's not as exclusive as it sounds."

"You're in us?" Franzia said.

"A little," he said. "And there's about to be a little of you in me. Let's get started."

Franzia sat back, glanced at David, exhaled. She finally got it; there was no way out of this.

"How much do you want?" David asked.

"Not much. A pittance. Just enough to hold all your pain and suffering and leave a little texture."

David turned to Franzia. "What do you think?"

"You're asking me? An eyelash or the tip of a fingernail."

David glanced at the man he now thought of as Adam, who shook his head.

"More than that. Something you'll feel."

"I have a mole on my ass," Franzia snapped. David snorted. Adam did not.

"Would you like me to pick?" he asked.

"No, no, sorry." She turned to him and grimaced an apology. She was in rare form. "David?"

"What did Charlotte lose first?" he asked. "With Jason, it was his pinky finger. Was it her pinkies?"

"No," she said, understanding. "It was her earlobes, not even her ears. We didn't notice at first."

She turned to Adam and he nodded. David tugged at his earlobes. How bad could it be?

"You want to us to…" Franzia indicated the knives.

"Not yet. Do you remember the promise you made in the playground? That before the end, you'd tell each other everything?"

"You know about that?" Franzia asked.

"We already have," David said, sharp enough that Franzia turned a frown on him. "Well, almost."

"Tell her the rest, David. Get it out of you. And when you're done, she'll cut off your earlobe and eat it."

"What?" they said as one.

"You said…" David trailed off. "How do you taste it if we eat it?"

"I can feel everything you feel. You were in her head, David. You understand. I feel your love and hate, hear what you hear, feel what you feel. I'll taste it through you. All of us will."

"All of you…" Franzia trailed off and picked up a knife. David watched her turn to face him, knife in hand, blade shining in flawless perfection. She could cut his head off with that. She could skin a rhinoceros. How much could an earlobe hurt?

"Tell her," Adam said.

David took a breath. Franzia took his hand. He was a child when it happened. He knew that rationally. But he still wondered if she'd hate him for it.

"It's okay," she said, squeezing his hand. "Whatever it is, it's okay."

No, he thought. *It's not.*

"My mom didn't choose Tommy," he said. "I did."

She frowned, waiting for more. "But you said…"

"When I told her I knew what she was doing, she gave me a choice. Him or me. I could choose."

"Jesus. And you chose him? You were only ten, David. How—"

"No, I chose myself. Every day she'd ask me, and I'd choose myself. I think it just pissed her off. So she made it worse and worse. And I kept choosing myself."

"That's *amazing*, David. I don't think… No, I know. There's no way I could have done that. Not when I was ten. Maybe never."

"Yeah, I thought I was pretty clever. We were at war and I was beating my mother by letting her kill me. But then she was late for breakfast one morning and I heard Dad coughing in the next room, which didn't make sense. It was a Tuesday. He should have left for work already."

"Oh, David…"

"Then she came in and sat down, plate on her lap like every morning, smiling so strangely. It took me a while to realize that's how she looked when she was happy. It was the first time she'd looked happy in months. And she said, 'Tommy or you *and* your father.' And that was it. I couldn't lose my dad. He was everything. So I said, 'Tommy.' Just like that. I didn't even hesitate."

"And she started poisoning him instead?"

David nodded. "It was amazing how fast I felt better. Within days, I was up at dawn, following Dad around the house like a puppy. God, I loved him. But Tommy was sick in bed. And then sicker. And then…"

"What?"

"I couldn't do it anymore. I told mom to stop, that she could do it to me again. I couldn't watch Tommy like that. He was so pale and quiet. It was like he was already dead. Dad wouldn't want that. But she wouldn't stop. 'A deal's a deal,' she said. 'Now you know what it's like to be a big boy.' And he got sicker and sicker…"

David wiped his eyes but they were dry. All the crying he'd been doing, and now he'd forgotten how.

"David, that's enough." She turned to Adam, who was leaning forward, rapt. "That's enough, right?"

Silence. Apparently not.

"Then what happened?" she asked, pushing him, trying to help him through it.

"I told Dad. I told him everything. What I'd done, what Mom had done, how I picked Tommy. Everything. He wouldn't believe me at first. He got angry. He didn't say anything, but I could tell. He was furious. Then he went and got Tommy from the bedroom and brought him to the living room, holding him in his lap, and just started crying. He knew. Or maybe he just realized he knew. I don't know. I never understood how he didn't know."

"Maybe he didn't want to see it."

"Maybe." He didn't think that was it. Dad was stronger than that.

"David?"

"Sorry. I'm not sure how it happened, but it was like Mom knew it was coming. When they autopsied Tommy, they found a lethal dose of clonazepam in his blood. She'd given it to him just minutes before Dad brought him out. Maybe she overheard me, and I killed him?" He shuddered. "I don't know. But that's how he died. Right there in Dad's arms. He never spoke. He never cried. He just stopped breathing and that was it. You can't believe how quiet it was when he died. Dad stopped breathing. It was like the world stopped."

"And…just finish it, David."

"And then Dad went to get the gun."

Franzia closed her eyes. He told her the rest in fits and starts, right up to the point where Mrs. Baker took him outside and he could move again. The final part was clear enough long before he said it:

"If I'd stayed quiet, Dad would still be alive today. Maybe all of us would."

"You can't believe that. David, you *can't* believe that. Things like that always escalate. You wouldn't believe some of the things James has seen." Flinch. "Saw. It always gets worse."

Why didn't you stop her? Tommy asked with dead eyes and blue lips, and David knew he'd always be asking. The same question James asked him about Alicia. The same question he asked himself, and it was always the same answer: he just couldn't and he didn't know why. He was crying now.

"Now," Adam said.

Franzia nodded and raised the knife. "I'm sorry."

"It's okay," he said. *It's what I deserve.* The same thing he thought when Alicia hit him. The same thing he thought every day on repeat until it was just a background noise he pretended to ignore.

She reached up and tugged on his left earlobe, pulling it tight.

That's good, he thought. *The harder, the better. Pull it tight and cut fast.* He nodded and closed his eyes. The knife was sharp. It wouldn't hurt that much.

He was wrong. The pain was astonishing. He felt the cold blade slice into him and thought he was going to scream. And then she cut again, sawing in the other direction, then again, as blood spattered on his already blood-spattered arm. He wanted to throttle her. Hadn't she ever cut meat? He wasn't an overcooked tri-tip.

"Just do it!" he said.

One final cut and she came away with a tiny triangle of flesh, barely visible between her fingers. All that pain for that? He raised a hand to his truncated ear and felt the wet, ragged surface.

And now she was crying. "I'm sorry, David. I'm sorry."

"Eat it," Adam said. "Before it gets cold."

She looked at the ragged bit of meat between her fingers, closed her eyes, put the knife down on her plate—which seemed extraneous at this point—and raised his earlobe to her mouth.

"It's okay," he said.

She put it in her mouth, gagged, and then started chewing. Then she sat up straight, looking confused, chewed a little more, and swallowed.

"What?" David asked.

She wiped her lips on a clean section of napkin. "It's delicious."

"Delicious?" David asked. Franzia nodded a little too enthusiastically, like she wanted more.

"Like your brisket," she said. "But chewy."

Well, that was gross, he thought. But he also felt better. His memories of Tommy and Mom and Dad weren't fading, but when he thought of them, it was like watching a movie about someone else's life. There was no pain and he couldn't hear Tommy talking anymore. Then the feeling of release grew until it filled him and he wanted to scream at the power of it. She hadn't just eaten his earlobe; she'd swallowed his pain. It was the blood of forgiveness and redemption—an alien cannibal sacristy and yet utterly human, as if all his misery and pain had been distilled down to its purest essence and then consumed in Franzia's body. It was peace. It was joy. It was absolution.

He couldn't wait for her to feel the same way.

"Your turn," Adam said, looking at him, but David didn't need encouragement. He snapped up his knife and leaned toward her.

"No," Adam said. "Tell him first."

"I've already told him about Ben. He knows."

"He knows the lie you tell yourself. Tell him the truth."

Franzia looked into David's eyes so desperately that he wanted to pull her into his arms.

"It's okay," he said. "No matter what it is, it's okay." He wished she could feel how he felt, how the past had changed and become something else, something to be known but not feared. Something *smaller*. But she wouldn't have believed him any more than he believed his ear tasted like finely smoked beef.

He took her hand and nodded, an exact mirror of what she'd done for him, but she was already crying, pink streaks over blotched red cheeks.

"I told you Ben died of SIDs," she said. "But that's not true. I used to have these dreams. Strange things full of shadows and voices, like something out of a bad horror movie. I thought they were dreams. Now, I realize they were Arachnur screwing with me. Every night, he'd whisper things in my ear while I thought I was sleeping. Every night, she told me to cut something off James or she'd kill Ben. It went on for weeks, then months. I couldn't sleep. I couldn't eat. I drank so much, David, but it never stopped. I'd come to holding a knife over James. I almost stabbed him a dozen times. Thank god he's a heavy sleeper…"

"And?" David asked. He could see where this was going, but not why she'd feel so ashamed. If Arachnur made her do it, that was no worse than a dozen other things they'd done and far better than some.

"And one night I walked out of the bedroom to go sleep next to Ben. I was hammered, but I know I checked on him. He was alive when I went to sleep. Gorgeous and untouched and alive. I wish you could have seen him, David. He was the most beautiful little boy."

David knew exactly what she meant.

"And when I woke up in the morning, James was screaming into his phone and Ben was dead. The rest of what I told you is true, except it wasn't SIDs. I'd rolled over on him, somehow. I was always so careful. Even when I drank, I stayed far enough away and checked the pillows. But I'd done it. I'd suffocated my son in his sleep. I killed my little boy."

"What?" David asked. This wasn't some accident; she'd gotten drunk and killed her son? Sure, Arachnur pushed her to the edge and she was probably on the verge of insanity, but...

"See?" she said. "See how you're looking at me? That's how James has looked at me for years. That's how the police and doctors looked at me. It's how I look at myself in the mirror."

David didn't know what to say. He didn't want to judge her. She was manipulated into it. Something bad was going to happen, no matter what. But she'd still killed her own child.

"David, please. Look at me."

He looked at her and saw a woman he thought he loved, and all the judgment drained away. What remained was just anger. What the hell was wrong with him? He turned his attention to Adam.

"You did this to her," he snarled. "You and your kind."

"Can you forgive her?" he asked. "Knowing what you know?"

David turned back to her and nodded, meaning it or wanting to. He didn't understand the drinking, had never understood people with addictions, but he knew it was real. Arachnur used that against her. And a galaxy of sadistic asshole aliens watched it all.

David took her hand. "It's okay," he said. It still didn't feel that way, but that didn't matter. They'd make it okay. She cried and nodded and he knew she didn't believe him, but more importantly, she'd never forgive herself. Not in a thousand lifetimes. Not until he cut it out of her.

"There's a kind of black market for things like this," Adam said. "It's not strictly allowed, but some can't suppress their hunger for torture and pain. They thrive on manipulation and mental anguish. Arachnur came from one such species and never got it out of her." He shook his head. "She wasn't a her, by the way. Her species has a dozen genders, and none of them equate to yours, but never mind. She fed that market, thrived on it, and had for a dozen harvests. Nur doesn't actually mean asshole. It means a broken thing. It means she never should have been allowed here, or anywhere with biological life."

Franzia nodded vaguely, beyond caring.

"What are you saying?" David asked. "And why are you telling us?"

"It's an almost universal thing that losing a child causes exquisite pain. Even worse, if the parent is responsible. The guilt and shame ever end. And the market never goes wanting. Arachnur made a name for herself as a provider of that specific type of shame. Few others are willing to. That doesn't mean it's true."

Franzia froze.

"What?" David asked.

"You didn't fall asleep on your son, Franzia. You didn't roll onto him. Arachnur moved you and put your arm over his face. She used your body to kill your son. It wouldn't have mattered how drunk you were, or not. She would have made sure Ben died and you blamed yourself for it."

Franzia couldn't seem to move. She just stared at David as tears flooded down her face.

"Now," Adam said. "Do it now."

"Franzia?" David asked.

"Now!" Adam said.

David released her hand and clenched her earlobe between thumb and forefinger, pulling it to the side so he'd have a clear angle. He waited until she nodded.

And then he cut her earlobe off in one clean stroke so fast it didn't even bleed at first. Franzia's hand flew to the side of her head, and then the blood flowed, but David didn't wait. He wanted an end to her pain, and he wanted it now.

He raised her earlobe as blood ran down through her fingers and pooled in her clavicular depression, overflowed and ran between her breasts, which he tried not to notice. God, she was beautiful. Here at the end, they were still just human beings and animals and horny and hungry and ridiculous.

"Ears to you," he said, because he couldn't resist, and then he put her earlobe in his mouth, expecting blood and flesh and raw disgust, but instead it tasted like perfectly cooked scallops, tender as butter and just as smooth. Alicia would have loved it.

I'll be damned.

He barely chewed before swallowing. And when he did, Franzia's eyes widened and he knew she felt it. She felt the pain leaving. She felt the fear fading. And gasped at the release of it.

"Delicious," Adam said, but they barely heard him. They fell into each other's arms and, when they released, Adam was gone. Arachniss was gone, and so was Dad. They were alone in the room.

"Is it over?" Franzia asked.

"I think so," he said, not really believing it, but maybe. Because in a way that didn't seem to fit in his mind, he found himself thinking of the future and Jason and something a bit like hope.

*

DAVID BANDAGED FRANZIA'S EAR and she his, wiped each other's faces with baby wipes, and then she carried Charlotte to her car and drove off through streets that were utterly clean and devoid of carnage, but not before David mentioned he was grilling the next day and they should come.

"Maybe," she said, meaning yes, and then she kissed him on his cheek.

When her brake lights turned the corner and vanished, David went back to the living room and sat down, turned on the TV to static.

"I know you're there," he said.

But Dad didn't appear, Adam did, back in the chair where he'd been before. David was overwhelmed by a feeling of gratitude he couldn't explain or didn't want to. For purging their pain. For letting them survive. All of it. But like all gifts from strangers, he eyed it with suspicion.

"What do you get out of all this?" David asked.

"You don't think it's just kindness and the compassion of passing aliens?"

"I do not." But what the heck. "Is it?"

"No."

So much for that. "What do you want?"

"I want you."

David sighed and nodded. It was too good to be true. "One final meal?" The knives were still on the table, wrapped in disheveled swan napkin remains. If it saved Franzia and the kids, why not? At least he wouldn't shred himself like Franzia had his ear.

"Not at all. And you should stop giving up on your life so easily. That's over for now. I want to offer you something else. Actually, it's not an offer. You're going to do it. But I'd like you to consent."

"To what?"

"To joining us."

David snorted. "Wait, seriously?" Now he sounded like Franzia.

"Seriously."

"I'm not going to eat people. Or breed people. That's disgusting."

"It's not required. The Arach perform a million services across the galaxy. I used to build energy sources from black holes for systems with dying stars. I've saved innumerable lives and entire societies. I didn't take this role for a hundred-thousand years. You never have to, though I hope you will."

"Why?"

"Because it's the only way to save your species, David. Earth is a meat planet, created for consumption. It's only luck that you evolved to this point, and that we let you. There is no way out for your descendants unless you change what you are. Jason and Charlotte's children or grandchildren will be eaten in the next harvest, or not; there's no way to know. You can always roll the dice."

"And if I join you, I can save them?"

"Yes. Maybe. It won't be easy."

"No." He had no idea what the details were, but there was no way he was leaving Jason so he could help Arachniss eat people or breed better people. And who knows what would happen with Franzia? He wasn't going anywhere.

Adam nodded. "I know how you feel. You have something to hold on to now. But humanity remains stubbornly inferior despite millennia of mind-numbing work and slaughter. You are a persistently and extravagantly violent species. You make me ashamed of my origins. If I knew it was going to be this hard, I'd have had a meteor dropped on you and started over. But you're what I've got. You're my life's work. Think how that makes *me* feel."

"What are you talking about?"

"I'm not going to go into details. I do this job so I can recruit from humans to join us. There's no other way to pick and no other way to increase human representation in our society. If enough humans work hard enough, then we might be able to save this planet."

"That's possible? How long would it take?"

Adam shrugged. "It's just politics and time and work. Maybe a million years. Maybe never."

"A *million* years?"

"Or more."

"I'm just one person. What difference can I make?"

"Do you want a *Lord of the Rings* quote? 'Even the smallest person can change the course of history.' There. Feel better? You're one of only six billion people now and soon you'll be one of a few trillion Arach. You make no difference statistically. It's not even a rounding error, but it's still infinitely more than none."

"You really suck at recruiting."

"I'm not recruiting. I'm briefing. I'll be gone after tonight, but I'll be taking a copy of you with me. And when I come back toward the end of your life, I'll take another and merge the two. You can have Franzia and Jason and the life you want, but then you're joining us. I didn't waste all this time and energy so you could say no."

"A copy? You mean I'll die anyway?"

"Of course you'll die. There's no way to get your consciousness out of your body. The best we can do is copy it and let the body go. You won't feel a thing. Well, your body will feel whatever it feels, but the copy of you will just feel a lot less meaty. Trust me, it's worth it."

"If you're not asking, then why tell me at all?"

"When you come over, you'll remember this conversation. The less time you spend whining about duress, the better. And once across, I lose control over you and you can just terminate your own node. I can't stand losing young Arach to virtual suicide. We're not even allowed to restore the node from backups. So I want you to know what's happening when you show up."

"Suicide? What would have happened if I'd told you to take me instead of Alicia?"

"You'd be dead and I'd be having this conversation with Franzia. Speaking of which, the reason I wanted to get rid of Arachnur was to get her recruiting slot. If you consent, you both get to ascend."

"What?"

"Always so articulate. You're welcome. And now you can flirt like idiots and appreciate the life I've given you until you join me, and then spend eternity annoying each other."

"What life you've given me?"

"You didn't really think Kathryn had a long-lost mother with four million dollars, did you?"

So Franzia was right. Adam vanished before David could say anything, even *thank you.*

"Told you it was going to get weird," Dad said from the TV.

A few seconds later, David forgot the entire conversation, and everything else about Arachniss, Arachnur and the ridiculous idea that humans were being eaten by alien spiders.

Epilogue

PORTOBELLO MUSHROOMS, ONIONS AND PEPPERS on vegetable skewers. Thick rounds of pineapple, meatless burgers, chickenless chicken and something that might have been a sausage. Under a bright summer sun, they grilled and sizzled and smelled and it was perfect, but of course not the same. Jason was four now and stumbled after Charlotte in the backyard of their Louisville house, only a few miles but a lifetime from their prior lives. Franzia was working on her laptop under a sunshade, focused on her latest top-secret project. A cold and very virgin iced tea sweat condensation in a tall glass by her hand. Charlotte told Jason to sit and he sat, obedient as a dog, and David thought about correcting her but, well, it was funny. Alex and his boyfriend sat on deck chairs talking to Leslie, who clearly just wanted to nap under her enormous hat. Padme watched her daughters run in circles and kept looking to her side, as if realizing for the first time that her husband wasn't there anymore. Sometimes Leslie caught her eye and they'd just nod at the emptiness where someone they had loved should have been.

David turned a mushroom, poked a pineapple, tried to get into it. He didn't really care about grilling anymore. It wasn't just the lack of real meat—he was a vegetarian again, as was (reluctantly and perhaps not always when he wasn't around) Franzia, but that wasn't it. When he grilled, he always felt like he was on the outside looking in, watching his new family, trying to hear words brought over on fickle winds. He loved doing it for them, but now he wanted to sit with them and drink and talk or just listen and not do anything. Feel their sounds and smells and laughter and do, well, nothing. Not cook or serve, hide or perform. Just be.

He caught Franzia looking at him and froze, stunned by his love for her. Toward the end of his time with Alicia, he thought that part of him was burned away, cauterized, dead as a severed limb and just as useless. But Franzia had been patient. It started with long conversations about what to do with their big houses after losing James and Alicia. How Charlotte was so protective of Jason and Jason so clearly in love with her. It was like middle school, with casual looks and brushed hands, dinners and flirty texts, until it had suddenly and passionately become more—a dam of need and desire burst open because they had let go of their fears and made space for each other. The sex wasn't bad either, which was good, because there was a lot of it.

"I love you," Franzia mouthed, and David pursed his eyebrows, pretending not to understand so she'd say it again, which she did, and he smiled like an idiot and looked down at his ridiculous vegetables and fake meats as he wiped his eyes. Sometimes the steam made them water. When he looked up again, Franzia was focused back on her laptop and he wanted to walk over and kiss her, hard and long, but he'd wait. There was no hurry. She wasn't going anywhere.

"Tell me something you remember about Kathryn," Leslie said. She'd appeared at his side like Alicia used to do, face barely visible under her hat and massive sunglasses, and he realized for the hundredth time that it wasn't Alicia after all; he had terrible peripheral vision and anyone could sneak up on him. It just didn't scare him anymore.

"Hmm," he said. Kathryn Thorn, onetime track star, terrible singer and best friend. What could he tell her that he hadn't already?

"Aren't those done?" Leslie asked, sounding worried. She was right; everything was done. He clicked off the grill and started plating everything before it dried out. Leslie helped, or at least made the motions.

"She loved mayonnaise," David said, suddenly remembering the look on her face when he'd found her with a spoon and a half-full jar of mayo. Mayo on her hands. Mayo on her face. Like a kid covered in pudding but white and really gross. "I mean, loved it." He told her the story, including how she'd swallowed loudly and kept eating while he watched in horror.

"She ate the whole jar," he said. "It was disgusting."

Leslie smiled and walked off with a plate of vegetables, probably wondering how much of that story was true. Not because he was lying, but because it was hard to remember things. SHAS had finally vanished, as mysterious on exit as it had been arrival, and it seemed to take their memories with it. David tried to keep alive memories of those he'd lost to the pandemic: Kathryn, Kiaraa, little Alex, Olivia (who the hell was Olivia?) and of course James and even Alicia, along with a hundred others that seemed to have vanished in the night. Some old guy at the hospice named Philip Rothman, Samesh Balasubramanian and so many more. He had terrible memories about some of their deaths, things Kiaraa would have said were part of his trauma, coping mechanisms, or something equally calming and probably true. Sometimes he believed her ghostly advice. Sometimes he looked to the sky for spiders and death and wondered if they were watching from behind the sun.

Insanity, he told himself. *Impossible.*

The only thing he couldn't explain was how his father got into his phone and TV. Like prosthetics, AI had come a long way during the pandemic, but not that far. It was uncanny talking to his long-dead father, but he found it impossible to complain or even contemplate too seriously. Why question something so wonderful?

"How are my grandkids today?" he'd ask every time the TV came on. Sometimes he turned himself on and hummed into the empty living room. And he was learning guitar, which was nice, but he had the same tastes as David and Kathryn so it could get weird.

"...she did every one of them in, them in..."

"Maybe something less morbid?" Franzia would ask and he'd smile and comply, but you always knew he wanted to put a little naughty in the next song. My dad, the virtual perv, he thought.

I can never get rid of this TV.

Which made no sense. But whatever. Life was good, and *Pedro* was done. He'd finished the prose version a few years earlier, which finally freed him to start the illustrations:

One day out on the ice, Pedro stopped walking.

Shyla and Blowfish and the others stopped next to him and looked around. It was a beautiful bit of ice, white with some blue, cold hard sections risen into the air, broken and full of nice places to hide and sleep. The ocean was nearby but not too close, so there was food. And the sun was coming back now, so there was a soft red light on the morning ice, with some crystals looking like fire.

"Why did we stop, Pedro?" Shyla asked.

"I like it here," Pedro said. "Do you think we could stay for a while?"

"Sure," Shyla said. She stomped around in a circle in her Big Man boots. "I like the snow here. It's poofy."

He rose on his haunches and came down hard. Snow exploded into the air. Shyla ran into the cloud and disappeared for a second, laughing. It was very poofy snow.

Shyla stopped stomping and looked up, concerned. "What about your mom and your sister?"

"I think they're okay wherever they are. And I have all of you. You're my family now. So this is home if you want it to be. It's home for me as long as you're here."

"You mean it?" Blowfish asked. "We can stop walking?"

"I thought you liked walking," Pedro said.

"I love walking with you," he said, flopping into the snow and flapping around. "But I like lying around, too. I'm a seal. It's hard for us to walk all the time. Can we stay here for a while? Can we?"

Pedro nodded and smiled.

"As long as you want."

THE END

David had sat back in his new chair in his new office and watched the cursor blink after THE END, and felt himself exhale a breath he'd been holding for years. All the pain and fear leaked out and he inhaled a hit of pure joy. Pedro had made it. Pedro needed some serious counseling and a massive rewrite for the children's market, but he'd made it. Whatever came next, he was going to be fine.

"Are you finally done?" Franzia had asked, hand on his shoulder, and he closed his eyes to take in the smell of her skin and the warmth of her fingers—all the things lingering in the moment and so easily lost. And he smiled because, for the first time in his life, Pedro wasn't alone, and he didn't need to walk anymore. He was with his friends, his new family, so he was already home.

David wiped his eyes again and closed the grill. *Pedro the Polar Bear* was due to be published in a few days. He'd never thought of a better word than 'peripatetic,' and his agent's suggestions were even worse, so now Pedro was merely polar. David couldn't wait for the first signing. Hopefully there wouldn't be any fireworks this time.

Leslie checked her phone, waiting for news on the adoption. She was getting a little girl who was missing a hand, a foot and an ear, and was thus as normal and sweet as could be. He couldn't wait for Jason to meet her. He wasn't sure why, but his next book was about a gorgeous interstellar griffinfly named Kathryn that went on adventures across the galaxy and collected friends along the way. The book would be dedicated to Leslie's daughter, who was by strange coincidence also named Kathryn. Funny how the world worked sometimes.

Padme gasped and David's head snapped up. He followed everyone's look toward the fence and a bedraggled black shadow hiding under an equally bedraggled bush. The shadow twisted and unfolded one leg after another until the spidercat stumble-walked into the yard. David thought about trying to grab a picture—no one had seen a spidercat in years—but before he could, Charlotte walked over and grabbed it up off the ground, squeezing until the poor thing looked ready to pop.

"Kitty," she said, turning to her mom. "Can I keep it?"

Franzia glanced at David, at her daughter, and shrugged. Should they keep an endangered cat-eating-cat that looked like it had mange on its mange? David wanted to say yes, but it wasn't his place; Jason wouldn't be taking care of it. But he missed their frenetic scurrying and random packs, like black ink hunting at night, and now there were more mice and rats than ever. There were billions of fewer people in the world, and god knows how many animals lost, and now everything was hungry, feeding, growing to fill the vacuum left by the dead. They should save what was left.

"Sure," Franzia said. And just like that, their family grew again. "But we'll need to get it checked out."

"And cleaned," he added.

"*Deep* cleaned," Franzia agreed. Jason ran over and grabbed spidercat and Charlotte in his increasingly vice-like hug. Maybe they could wash them all in the same bath. Padme snapped up her twins before they could get too close. Alex and his boyfriend looked horrified behind their matching pirate eye patches. Leslie shook her head and probably thought something like, *Don't look at the freaks*, which Kathryn would know was the highest compliment on earth.

David looked back at Franzia and tried to glimpse the truncated ear hidden under her hair. It was the last thing both of them had lost to SHAS, and somehow it made him feel closer to her, like it was part of a shared experience no one else could understand even if he didn't know what it was. Sometimes when the kids were asleep and the house was quiet, he would kiss her face and run his tongue over the scars along her hairline as she nibbled on the stub of his earlobe. There was no judgment in it, just understanding and forgiveness. Whatever they had done, whatever had been done to them, it was shadows and dust and couldn't touch them anymore. There was only now, the feel of her in his arms and smell of her in their bed, and all of it was perfect. And he knew. They both knew, as they bit into each other's flesh and tasted salt and sweat and sometimes a hint of blood.

That's what love tastes like.

About the Author

Shawn C. Butler is the award-winning author of *Beasts of Sonara* and *Run Lab Rat Run*, two novels in the Modified world about genetic engineering, human modification, and our often violent search for immortality. *Arachniss* is his first novel in very different world. He lives in the western United States. You can visit him online at shawncbutler.com or on Twitter @ShawnCButler.

Acknowledgments

This book would not have been possible without the help of many patient, tolerant, insightful, intelligent and generally awesome people. I am deeply, humbly grateful to all of them but especially Jeanne and Juli—without whom there would be far too many factual and other errors. Thank you all.

Coming Soon:

Black Hole Son

A single alien invaded the Earth and took up residence with his human girlfriend in the Empire State Building in New York City. Bodies are dropping all over Manhattan, killed by an unknown sociopath in impossible ways. The US government is working on a secret plan to kill the invader, and the invader is about to throw the most exclusive cocktail party in history. And that's just the beginning of *Black Hole Son*. It gets stranger from there…

Frank could see why they'd called him. In fifteen years as a detective with NYPD homicide, he'd seen a lot of dead things. Things people killed. Things that killed people. The whole cycle of beat-down, beat-up, shoved-around urban life. People killed *hard*, like once wasn't enough. Others who didn't even look like people anymore. And yet, as the cliché goes, he had never seen anything like this.

He opened his old-school notebook and kneeled on his old-school knees, setting off shots that startled the ME. She raised an eyebrow. Frank raised a shoulder. Age is decay, he meant. None of us are getting younger, and no one's going out with dignity. Certainly not this kid.

Here's the thing. There really aren't that many types of killers. You read enough murder mysteries and you think there's a cold body on every winter morning, a missing child in every river, and behind all of them a dark and sinister intelligence keening to be heard. But murderers are idiots, plain and simple. They can't get what they want from the living, so they take it from the dead. It's why the rich kill but the poor do the actual killing; the smart and powerful outsource, and the poor are the source that keeps on giving. There are angry killers, vengeful killers, careful killers, ones who watch too much CSI and others who couldn't spell it, but they're all idiots. Killing is a desperate crime, reflecting a lack of imagination and better options. Smart people always have options, until they don't of course, and then they're the biggest idiots of them all.

But this thing. This thing was off the charts, off kilter and off sides. Killing this boy this way took moronic genius or at least a really good instruction manual and three volunteers from Ikea. Frank wasn't trying to draw it out. It's just that, for the first time in years, he was lost for thoughts and all he heard was air rushing through his ears.

"You okay, Frank?" The ME asked. Her name was Emmy. Emmy the ME. He liked her. She liked him. If she wasn't gay and he wasn't dead inside, they'd be married and have an Italian Greyhound named Prosciutto. Something clever to laugh at over brunch in SoHo.

"No," he said. "But I'm a damn sight better than this kid."

"There's no sign of cutting," she said. "No frayed skin. No burns, either. It's like he just…"

"Yeah, it's just like that."

Just like a cartoon where the unlucky duck walks through a bunch of lasers or a sushi kitchen and comes out in perfectly even slices so fine and precise he doesn't even die at first. He takes a few duck steps and then the slices fall into a wet pile of meat. Every movie with a sword has the scene; in *Underworld*, Kate Beckinsale cuts Lucius' head in half, there's the close-up, the astonishment in his eyes, and then the top of his head slides off. Beautiful in the way of horror porn, sexualized blades making godlike cuts in mortal flesh. Frank had always liked those movies because they weren't realistic;

death is never that pristine. Something always gets fucked up. He can't watch realistic movies because they make his stomach crawl. And now he'd never watch *Underworld* again.

The boy was cut into what would later turn out to be perfect one-inch slices, from the tips of his fingers to his shoulders. From toes to his hips, from groin to the top of his head. His clothes, his flesh, all cut perfectly without any sign of tearing or pressure, nothing like the smell of a medical laser, no burns, not one damn thing to explain how he'd come be a body in exactly 71 pieces. By nice coincidence, one of the cylindrical slices of his head contained both eyes, and preserved his last look up at the ceiling. He didn't even look scared.

There was, not surprisingly, a lot blood and the smell of piss and shit. The normal things. The expected things. He wondered if the boy had died instantly or just lay like that, sliced apart but not apart at all, wondering why he was bleeding in stripes.

"What do you want to do?" Emmy asked.

"I don't know." Leave, Frank thought. Run away. "I have no damn idea."

"You want to know cause of death?"

He burst out laughing, and covered his mouth in horror. God forbid any of the family hear him. Everything was on phones these days. Everything lasted forever. He didn't want to go out like that, and not just for himself; he didn't want them to think the boy deserved so little respect. This child was going to be famous once the news got hold of this. He didn't need his detective on video laughing next to his body.

"I assume it wasn't a cut of some kind?" Frank asked.

"Look at his lips," she said. He looked. One lip under the nose slice, one on the chin slice. Both were blue.

"And his eyes," she said. Not scared, but bloodshot.

"Suffocation," Frank said. "Asphyxia."

"That's my guess, but we won't know until we get him back. But maybe he didn't feel this. Maybe he was gone before…"

"Yeah," he said. Sure. We all want to find the good in things. Maybe he didn't feel a thing. Maybe he was the lucky duck. "You see his fingers?" It was rhetorical. Emmy saw everything.

"No," she said. They were both off their game. Then, "Oh." As in, *Oh, Jesus*, but she'd never take the Lord's name in vain.

The last slice of his fingers didn't have an inch to work with. Far less. On his forefingers, the only thing missing from the tip was a perfectly sliced nail like a little white sliver. That's not the kind of thing you can do by hand. That happens when precision machinery doesn't stop cutting just because the last finger is a thousandth of an inch too damn long. Close enough isn't close to good enough. The nail was right there, right next to the finger. A careless breath would chase it across the hardwood floors. Nothing cut that precisely, or pointlessly.

"I'm done here," Frank said. But he'd never been so wrong. He's still not done there. Every time he clipped off one of his old, warped fingernails, he thought, *What did I miss?*

He got up to leave and tucked the notebook back in his coat. The only thing he'd written was *fingernails*. Emmy smiled and touched his arm. He wanted to close his eyes and remember the feel of her fingers, this time like every time. It wasn't right to want something so bad that didn't even make sense. It wasn't right that she knew it.

"You hear about Sarah?" she asked.

His heart jumped. "My sister?"

"No, the reporter you used to date. Sarah Devins."

Dating was an exaggeration. They'd experimented with the concept of emotional intimacy. The results were inconclusive. She'd left him for a better story or a smarter lab partner. He pretended it didn't still hurt. "What about her?"

"She's all over the news. Got the first interview with Him."

Frank didn't need to ask for a name. He knew who she was talking about.

"Of course she did," he said. She was the luckiest duck and always had been. There was a girl named Teela Brown in *Ringworld*, an old sci-fi novel, who had somewhat randomly been bred for luck by generations of genetic lotteries. The universe bent to Teela's every whim. Sarah was like that but smarter. He wondered what it was like to sleep with an alien, meaning Him. Frank wasn't thinking that because she'd do anything for a story. He was thinking that because she'd want to sleep with an alien. What an experience. What a thing to collect. It didn't even matter which alien. *Both* would be better. The story was secondary. He wasn't sure what he thought about it, so he didn't. He brushed past Emmy and heard the sound of her nails sliding across his coat. And he thought, *if only...*

Frank turned on the way out. He could have asked Emmy to forget her entire identity and marry him. They could run away to someplace warm and sunny. They could make love on the beach with their toes in the water while Prosciutto chased seagulls into the setting sun.

"Em, do me a favor," he said. "Check if he was frozen."

Her eyebrows again. His shoulders again.

"That would explain some things, but he was in school four hours ago."

Which Frank had forgotten. This thing was drilling holes in his brain. Unless they found a giant microwave somewhere, it was a waste of time. You could flash freeze someone with minimal tissue damage if you had a vat of liquid nitrogen. But you couldn't freeze them, cut them up, and then thaw them out in four hours.

"I'll still check, Frank." Because she knew. Frank was like Teela Brown when it came to murder. He was lucky with death. And she'd do the test even if he wasn't.

Frank smiled and turned to leave for real this time, thinking,

If only...

Sign up to hear about *Black Hole Son* and other books at shawncbutler.com.

What's Next?

Leave a Review
on Amazon or Goodreads

Discover Your Next Great Read
on shawncbutler.com

Thank You!